Jon
Jones, Pauline Baird.
Missing you

$

MISSING YOU

MISSING YOU

Lonesome Lawman Series
3

PAULINE BAIRD JONES

Five Star • Waterville, Maine

Five Star First Edition Romance Series.

Published in 2002 in conjunction with Pauline Baird Jones.

Set in 11 pt. Plantin by Al Chase.

Printed in the United States on permanent paper.

Library of Congress Cataloging-in-Publication Data

Jones, Pauline Baird
    Missing you / Pauline Baird Jones.
        p. cm. — (Five Star first edition romance series)
    ISBN 0-7862-3748-1 (hc : alk. paper)
        1. Police—Colorado—Fiction. 2. Missing persons—
Fiction. 3. Rocky Mountains—Fiction. 4. Ecoterrorism
—Fiction. I. Title. II. Series.
PS3560.O52415 M57 2002
813'.54—dc21   2001055573

I'd like to dedicate this book to Jamie and Ann—who held my hand through the writing of it, and who read it and told me what sucked dead toads—and what didn't. To Sharon, who listened to me whine about it. And to my daughter, Jessica, who helped me find the warts and remove them. My deepest thanks!

Chapter One

Snow flakes fell thick and fast as Luke Kirby stopped his 4x4 in front of the family cabin, just south of Estes Park. On a clear day, Long's Peak was visible from the cabin, but now his headlights had trouble penetrating more than a few yards ahead. The wind kicked up the falling snow, erasing not just the tracks his truck had made on the dirt road, but the place where sky and earth met, turning the world into a disorienting, white tunnel.

The storm hadn't been bad when he left Denver but had turned nasty with the rise in altitude. If the storm hadn't quickly moved to cut off his retreat, he might have turned back and faced a family determined to distract him from the significance of tomorrow—the anniversary of the death of his wife, Rosemary.

He rested his arms on the steering wheel, remembering a time when he couldn't think the word "dead," not about Rosemary, who had been so very much alive. He knew all the euphemisms and all the synonyms for death. None of them had changed the reality of being left alive, left alone in a world without her. How he'd hated it. He'd spent a lot of time dodging being alone, trying to stay too busy, too surrounded by people, to face it. He'd loved the "ball and chain," had relished being one half of a whole that included her.

A platitude, but true—time did heal. So gradually had time done its work that he'd hardly noticed at first. One day he'd realized he was above the shadows. Not happy, but no longer sad, and possibly, finally able to feel whole—and be whole—all by himself.

If someone asked him why he was here on this bitter night, instead of with his family, he could tell them it *wasn't* because he was living in the past or because he begrudged his brothers their happiness. They'd earned their time with their women the hard way. Matt and Dani had saved each other from the jaws of death up on Long's Peak just over two years ago.

Jake had saved his Phoebe's butt, and now she regularly kicked his up over his ears. Luke could see that Jake didn't mind; in fact, he seemed happy to bend over and present his backside for her boot. He had a tiger by the tail with that girl.

Luke grinned. Even Matt had given in to the Phoebe juggernaut, after strong initial resistance, allowing her to stand as godmother to the first Kirby grandson. Young Mark had them all wrapped around his tiny, pink finger. Even Phoebe was smitten. He expected her to enter the motherhood stakes any day now.

The only two people more amusing than his brothers were Bryn Bailey, Jake's FBI partner-in-crime solving, and Dewey Hyatt, Phoebe's former partner-in-crime committing. He just hoped he was there when Bryn realized she was in love with her pet criminal, though Jake had hinted she also had softer feelings for the elusive Phagan, who Dewey was supposed to be helping her hunt down. Luke had his own ideas about Phagan and Dewey, but it wasn't his job to point out the obvious, not when it was so entertaining to let events play out on their own.

No, he wasn't here because he couldn't handle their happiness. In a way, their happiness had lifted him with them and had brought him here tonight. In the headlights, the cabin was dark. Empty of everything but years of memories, not just of Rosemary, but his dad, killed in the line of duty not long before Luke graduated from the police academy. This was the first time he'd been here alone since Rosemary's death.

She'd loved the mountains, loved the cabin, even in a storm—if they were safe inside with a good fire.

With a start, he realized the cabin had almost disappeared into the storm. Already the warmth from the truck's heater had faded. As he exhaled, his breath turned into a white fog in the icy air. Snowflakes, lit by the headlights, swirled in a wind-driven frenzy. He'd better get moving before he couldn't find his way from here to there. He had no intention of spending the night in his truck. Good thing he'd brought plenty of supplies with him. If the weather report was right, he could be stuck up here for a couple of days. Looked like there'd be enough snow for some cross-country skiing when it cleared. Nothing like a brisk battle with nature to remind you that you were alive.

He left the headlights on while he unlocked the door, though their benefit was limited, and unloaded his supplies. Inside the cabin, he tested the silence and found it bearable—though uncomfortably cold. He turned on the refrigerator, wondering how long the power would stay on, while he stowed the perishables. Well, he'd used a snow bank for a fridge before, no reason he couldn't do so again.

A gust of wind caught the window over the sink, lifting it, then dropping it with a bang. He caught it before it could lift again, making a mental note to tweak Jake about it when he got home. He and Phoebe had been the last ones to use the cabin. He noticed a bit of snow and some dried stuff on the counter under the window and brushed it into the sink.

The air was chill, damp, and tainted with the smell of old fire and older food, but a new fire would soon burn it away. He didn't turn on any lights besides the kitchen. He knew his way around and besides, there was enough light spilling out from the kitchen until he got the fire going. Rosemary had liked the room lit by fire. Many a snowy night they'd huddled together under a pile of quilts and watched snow pile up in drifts against the windows.

He stopped for a moment as the memories caught up with him. Rosemary laughing as she pelted him with snowballs. Rosemary smiling up at him from the blanket as the mountain sun bathed her in its crystal light. Rosemary looking at the mountains and not at him when she told him she was dying and there was nothing either of them could do about it.

Seven years. Like Jacob in the Bible, he'd served his time, done his duty and now it was time to move on. Not to forget, but to move out of the shadows and live again.

"Don't mourn too long, Luke," she'd said to him that last day, her voice the only part of her he still recognized. She'd never said what too long was, but he could almost see her standing in the light from the kitchen, tapping her watch the way she had when he'd been out on the mountain too long.

"I know, Rose," he murmured. "I know. As always, my timing is great. Just great."

He checked the wood box and found it filled. Jake had also laid out logs in the fireplace. Only needed a match. That made up for the open window, Luke decided. In a short time, he had the fire started, putting out cheerful heat against the winter chill. When the power went, he'd be warm and have hot coffee. He could live without a lot of things, but hot coffee in the morning wasn't one of them.

He'd sleep in front of the fire. It would be warmer and he could feed the hungry fire. He and Rosemary had slept downstairs the last time they were here. They'd made a bed for two on the floor. He'd use the couch. Wouldn't be the first time he'd done time on one. Life with Rosemary hadn't been all smooth and easy. The Kirby men had a weakness for spirited women.

He did a quick run upstairs for a couple more quilts. There

was a sturdy mega-sized lap quilt kept folded over the back of the couch, but it wasn't enough on a night like this. He also grabbed some pillows to soften the hard arms on each end. Back downstairs, he noticed that the quilt wasn't folded over the back, but spread across the seat. In the flickering light from the fire, it almost looked like there was someone under it. For a minute chills snaked down his back, until common sense reasserted itself.

If someone was here, it was a squatter who'd likely used the unlatched window to get in. Damn, he couldn't kick a dog out on a night like this. So much for being alone. He dumped his blanket load on a chair. Odd that whoever it was hadn't heard his noisy arrival and made their presence known. It was enough to make him uneasy, so he pulled his gun. As a cop, he'd learned to err on the side of caution. He knew which boards creaked and took care to avoid them as he approached the couch. Keeping the figure covered, he reached out and flipped the edge of the blanket back and saw . . .

Feet.

Or more precisely, a pair of hiking boots and blue-jean covered legs below the knees. Good boots. Not a squatter then. Maybe a hiker?

Luke felt a bit ridiculous and a little anxious about the lack of movement as he moved to the other end. Being alone with a body wasn't what he had in mind either. This time when he flipped the blanket back, he saw hair. Lots of it. Tangled and blonde enough to make Marilyn Monroe jealous. The ends of most of it were hidden under the part of the blanket that still covered her middle, except for a bunch that hung over her face and off the edge of the couch, forming a question mark on the wood floor.

It seemed Goldilocks had come calling but found only one bear.

He stowed his gun and knelt down beside her. Bits of dried brush, brown grass and twigs were caught in the tousled strands of her hair. She had a thick, fleece jacket on, with bits of dried brush stuck to it, too and it had been torn in several places. One of her arms hung off the edge of the couch; the hand at the end of the arm was bare and badly scratched. A couple of her nails were broken, the edges ragged and torn.

"Who's sleeping on my couch?" he muttered, as he gathered up the trailing strands of hair, icy cold and soft as silk, to expose her face. It was scratched, too, and there was a nasty looking bump just above her temple. A thin trail of dried blood disappeared into her hairline. The bones under the scratches were good, the kind that wear well over time. Her jaw was strong and determined. Laugh lines at the corners of her mouth and eyes seemed at odds with a mouth that was full and rather sad. Her thick lashes lay in dark fans against her pale, bruised skin, hiding her eyes. Equally dark brows arched over them.

It was hard to be sure because memory was so unreliable, and his memories of Rosemary as a young woman were buried under her last months of wasting away from ovarian cancer, but she kind of reminded him of a young Rosemary, or her sister, if Rosemary had had one. It was a bit eerie on a dark and stormy night. If her eyes were blue when she opened them, he might just have to join the X-Files fan club.

Luke felt along her neck. Her skin was cold, but he found a pulse—rapid and a bit shallow—but there. She wasn't dead. Yet.

Luke knew a bit of first aid—most of it about hypothermia, since he and his brothers spent so much time in the mountains. She needed to be warmed up fast. He grabbed the quilts he'd collected and piled them on top of her. When he knelt down to ease a pillow under her head, he realized she was looking at him, her eyes wide and puzzled.

Violet. He hadn't expected that. Deep, pure violet. They brought the pale mask of her face to instant, vivid life and put a good bit of his unease to rest. Not Rosemary. He hadn't really believed she was. It was just weird. Weird enough for his imagination to activate. Thank goodness neither of his brothers was here. Wouldn't they get some mileage out of this situation if they ever found out?

He'd put her in her late twenties, but now, looking into her eyes, he upped that by a few years. Her eyes were wise, more aware than the average twenty-something, despite the confusion clouding their depths.

"Do I—know you?" she asked. Her voice was a thin thread of sound, but clear and crisp. It suited their mountainous surroundings, reminding him of a stream running over rocks on its way to the low lands.

"I don't think so. Name's Luke Kirby. My family owns this cabin."

Her lashes closed for a moment. Her brows drew together in a frown. "Cabin?"

He reached past her, turned on a rustic styled lamp and gestured to their surroundings. "Cabin."

Her lashes lifted, her gaze making a limited survey of her surroundings. "Oh."

Despite this, he could tell the lights were still out inside her head. He waited for her to orient herself. Something had happened. A fall of some kind, he guessed, based on what he's seen of her injuries. It sometimes took time to put the pieces of memory together in the right order after a shock.

"Would you like some soup and coffee?" he asked. "We need to get you warmed up, if you're up to it."

"I am hungry." She sounded surprised. "Thank you."

He left her for the kitchen, glad for the time away from

her. He still felt a bit off balance by her resemblance to Rosemary, and, if he were honest with himself, her unexpected beauty. His body had taken in more input than his brain could process, but the main gist of it was basically, *wow*.

He put water in the coffeepot, started heat under it. Found a can of soup and dumped it in a pan. Maybe he should start dating again, just to let off some steam in his "wow" reflex.

He turned and found her standing in the doorway studying him with a seriousness that did nothing to relieve the pressure. She was taller than he'd expected from someone with so slight a build. She stood carefully, but with a grace and elegance that her discomfort couldn't erase.

"Is there—" She stopped, color flooding her cheeks.

Luke found he could grin and felt better, more balanced and in control again. "Bathroom's through there. Light's on the right."

It was odd, but kind of cute. Usually only old ladies were embarrassed to ask for the john these days. There was something a bit old-fashioned about her, despite her very modern clothes. He could see her behind a tea pot in a room full of antiques. In a dress that matched her eyes and had a bunch of white at the neck. Something like Katharine Hepburn would wear.

"Thank you." She turned, wobbling a bit.

He fought back the urge to leap to her assistance. Partly because he didn't want to scare her and mostly because he wasn't sure he could leap. His body had surprised him a few times lately by not responding to his mental commands. A reminder that he wasn't as young as he felt. Instead he asked, "Do you need help?"

She smiled. "Thank you, but no. I can manage. Stiffened up a bit while I was asleep."

Her back straightened, her chin lifting as she made a determined beeline for the bathroom door.

Guts and beauty. Interesting. It wasn't until Luke heard the door creak closed that he realized he still didn't know her name. While he kept a watchful eye on the soup, he dug out the first aid kit and a flashlight. If she had a concussion, her eyes would show it. And if she was? Well, he'd deal with it then. He had his phone. He could call for advice.

The soup started to bubble. He lifted it off the heat, gave it a stir, and then poured it in a bowl. Grabbed some crackers and a cup of coffee and put it all on a tray. He heard the door creak open and found his thoughts bubbling like the soup. It was, he decided, like something out of a Raymond Chandler book. Snowed in the mountains with a mysterious woman— who had probably missed her step, taken a tumble and then lost her way, he reminded himself. No mystery, just Mother Nature's pointed reminder not to take her for granted.

She hadn't just used the toilet, he saw. She'd also washed the blood off her face and tidied her hair. Most of the bits of brush were gone and her hair was now pulled back into a sort of knotted ponytail that hung down to her butt. She was also white and shaking from the effort. Luke jumped forward, surprised and pleased his body did as requested, and helped her back to the couch. He got her settled with a pillow behind her and blankets tucked around, then brought her the tray.

"Can you manage for yourself?" he asked.

She nodded, a grateful smile flickering across her face. She picked up the spoon using, Luke noted, her left hand. When it became apparent she wasn't a southpaw, he folded back the blankets and found her right wrist swollen to twice its normal size. He probed it gently and heard her gasp.

"Sorry. Can you move your fingers?" She flexed them. "How about your wrist?"

She managed to bend at the wrist, but the effort drained

more color out of her face.

"I don't think it's broken, but it should probably be strapped until it can be X-rayed. A hairline fracture and a sprain can both cause swelling." He should know. He'd had both. He opened the first aid kit and rummaged through it until he'd found everything he needed.

"Are you a doctor?" A few bites of the soup put a slight flush in her cheeks.

"Actually, I'm a cop. And an all-too-frequent patient." He grinned at her. "My mom claims most of her gray hairs are my fault, but my brothers did their share, believe me. Most of it from rock climbing." While he talked, he helped her out of her jacket, a painful exercise, then applied a wrist splint and wrapped it with elastic bandage. When he was done, he touched the tips of her fingers. "Can you feel this?"

She nodded, relaxing back against the couch with a sigh of relief. "It feels a lot better."

"Let me know if the tips of your fingers start to tingle and I'll loosen it." He frowned. "Normally I'd apply ice, but you're still pretty chilled."

"I feel wonderfully warm, but I'd rather avoid ice for now."

She ate most of her soup but only took one sip of the coffee. She stared into the cup, then looked at him. "I don't think I drink coffee."

She looked startled. It did seem like something she should know about herself.

"I'll get you some water, but first—" Luke set the tray aside, and picked up the flashlight.

"What now?" She sounded amused.

"Looks like you took a pretty nasty tumble, could have a mild concussion. I want to look at your pupils." He tipped her head up and flashed the light in her eyes, watching her pupils react. "Did you lose consciousness?"

She smiled at the question. She'd lost more than consciousness. "Oh, yeah."

"It's not unusual for the noggin to be scrambled after a fall."

She watched him sit next to her, felt his big, warm hands cupping either side of her face. His face was close enough for her to see the texture of his skin as he carefully probed her scalp for injuries. The words craggy and weather-beaten came to mind first. He looked like a man who lived much of his life outside. He wasn't exactly handsome, but she felt an unexpected flicker of attraction flare where he touched her.

"Besides the bump on your temple, there's another here, above your ear."

"I've got one on the lower occipital, too," she said, touching the base of her head with a wince. He looked surprised as he checked it out.

"That you do. I'd say you did a top over tail today." He sat back, his hands dropping away.

To her annoyance, her skin felt cold, almost bereft without his touch. You know nothing about this man, she reminded herself. But that wasn't the worst. She knew nothing, literally nothing, about herself, except that she had an occipital. And a parietal, frontal and temporal. Very weird. It was as if she'd begun her existence when she opened her eyes a short time ago. She hadn't even known what she looked like until she saw herself in the mirror. It was an odd feeling to meet yourself for the first time. By most standards, even with the bumps and bruises, the face that had stared back at her would be considered beautiful. She'd felt no pride of ownership; no sense of *I am a beautiful woman.* No sense of herself at all. She'd fingered her clothes. They were of good fabric, but sturdy and serviceable, rather than glamorous. No perfume, cheap or expensive lingered on her skin. She'd sniffed again. Soap. Just soap. And the smell of pine. Judging by the amount of pine needles she'd shaken out of her hair, the smell of pine was inevitable, rather than revealing.

Her hands, beneath the scratches, were cared for. Her fingers were long and shaped. The nails that weren't torn were neatly filed but unpolished. To her surprise, despite the signs she'd taken a very nasty tumble, she felt relieved, as if she'd laid down a burden. Beneath the uncertainty, she felt free. If she had no past, that left a future full of possibilities.

"What do you remember?" he asked.

A better question would be, what am I trying to forget, she thought. She shrugged, then wished she hadn't. The movement upped the pain quota enough to make stars sashay across her view.

"Let's start with something easy, like your name?"

Her name. Everyone had a name. For a moment, she had an impulse to make one up. To write something onto the blank canvas in her head, but her mind refused to play. It didn't cough up a single consonant, let alone a whole name. She pushed at the gray mist and it pushed back. It did open enough to let out a single emotion. Panic. It spilled through her like a tsunami, threatening to sweep her away. As if he sensed it, he grabbed her left hand, held it, a lifeline pulling her free of the dark undertow.

"You really did scramble your brains, didn't you?" His voice was kindly amused, as if not knowing your own name was no big deal. "How about I call you Goldie for now?"

"Goldie?" From the jumble of letters in her head, the name formed into a row. So she did know the alphabet, in addition to the parts of the head. That was something.

He curled a strand of her hair around his finger and held it up for her view.

18

To her surprise, she felt a slight, possibly mischievous smile curve her mouth at the edges. "I wonder if it's the real thing or out of a bottle?"

He chuckled, drawing her attention to his broad, nicely constructed chest. When he went for the first aid kit, she'd noticed he filled out his jeans nicely. He walked with a relaxed, but determined stride, and he had kind eyes, with a hint of sad lurking in their depths. He was taller than she and had an air of calm competence. She'd never trusted really handsome men, though she had no idea why that was.

"Even if it's not natural," he said with a grin, "you reminded me of Goldilocks when I found you sleeping on my couch."

"Are you one of the three bears?" He was big and woolly enough. His hair was dark and unruly, with the shadow of a heavy beard on the lower half of his craggy face. At the base of his throat, where the collar of his flannel shirt exposed the strong column of his neck, she could see a tuft of thick dark chest hair. No question the sum of his parts had a distinct teddy bear quality. A teddy bear packing a gun, she reminded herself.

"I growl a little in the morning," he admitted.

"Goldie does seem to fit." She examined the name and found she didn't mind it. At least there was no big, bad wolf in the story. "It's nice to meet you, Luke."

"Nice to meet you, Goldie." He held out his hand.

Without thinking, she reached out with her injured right arm, but felt such a stab of pain from the movement, everything went black for a few seconds. From a distance, she heard Luke ask, "What's wrong? Is the wrap too tight?"

"No. Higher up, I think." A few deep breaths cleared the haze, but the pain stayed, clinging to her arm like a pit bull. She saw a tear in the dark fabric of her tee shirt. Around the tear, the material was stiff with dried blood and stuck to her skin. She saw Luke holding a pair of scissors and covered the spot protectively.

"Going to have to cut the sleeve of your shirt."

His steady gaze reassured her. She nodded and lowered her hand.

She wanted to look away when he inserted the blade of the scissors under the edge of her sleeve and began snipping, folding the soft cotton back as more and more of her arm was exposed, but she couldn't. Whether she liked it or not, it was another piece in the puzzle of who she was. Up past the elbow he ran into the stuck-on material and, to her relief, stopped.

"You've bled a fair bit," Luke said. "You must have sliced your arm when you fell. Hang on."

In a minute he returned with a pan of warm water. He wet the material until he'd bared her arm to the shoulder, exposing an angry gash in the flesh of her upper arm.

There was something not right about the wound, something that stole the warmth from her body, replacing it with the chill of fear. She looked at Luke, hoping he'd reassure her, but his face was grim and worried. A cop's face, she realized. He picked up her discarded jacket and examined the tear that matched the wound in her arm. She saw him sniff it, the worry in his face deepening.

"What?"

"It's—" he stopped, then said, his voice as grim as his face, "it's a bullet graze. I can still smell the gun powder." He handed her the coat.

Eyes wide, Goldie took it and sniffed. Someone shot at you. Close range, if she could smell residue. In her head she could see the words, but they didn't make sense. Nothing did. What kind of person got shot at? How did she know about residue? No wonder she didn't want to remember.

"What . . . do we . . . do?"

Luke looked toward the window. "Tonight? Nothing we can do. We're completely shut off until the storm clears. When it does, my truck's a four-wheel. I have a few contacts with the Estes Park cops."

"But . . . I don't remember anything! What will I tell them?" Panic slipped its leash again. She could hear it in her voice, but was too weary to do anything about controlling it.

Once again, Luke rescued her. He grabbed her uninjured hand and caught her gaze with his.

"We'll figure it out in the morning. Your memory can come back at any time. At least, that's what the TV doctors say." He smiled. It was a nice smile. A safe smile, a confident smile, but also a sexy smile with its thin upper and full lower lip, and a flash of even white teeth in between.

"Well, they must know." She found herself smiling back as her body relaxed again. Something intimate and unsettling entered the space between them. She looked away, in the direction of her wound. Right now it was less scary than looking at Luke, so she studied it. "Looks like it plowed along the top of the epidermis. Shouldn't even need stitches. It should heal quickly if infection doesn't set in."

There was a moment of silence. She looked at Luke.

He grinned. "Maybe you're a TV doc?"

Or a real one. She strained against the gray mist inside her head, but it resisted her with painful firmness.

"If I am, my brain isn't giving it up. It's like . . ." she stopped.

"Like what?" Luke's attention was focused on wrapping the white bandage around her arm, but his voice invited her to go on.

Goldie had a feeling he was always the good cop. The urge to confide was almost irresistible. But what if she was confiding herself into jail? Was she a good guy? And if she was, what was she afraid to remember?

"It's like . . ." she hesitated again, but the need to put it out there, see if what she felt could sustain itself in the light of examination, overcame her qualms, "there's two separate . . . issues." That wasn't the right word, but nothing better presented itself. "On the one side is this . . . relief. An incredible lightness of being." She smiled wryly, wondering who she'd just plagiarized. "I'm new and the world is full of possibilities."

"And on the other?" Luke finished his work and sat back, his gaze—sober and encouraging—fixed on her face.

"On the other is . . . dread. Confusion." She closed her eyes and out of the mist heard angry voices . . . *Who am I?* And why did it feel like a question she'd asked before? She groped toward the voices, but they faded into the gray. She shook her head in frustration. "It's gone."

"Don't try so hard. Memories like to be coaxed."

"What if—" she clasped her hands together, "what if I'm mixed up in something illegal?"

"Do you think you're that kind of person?" Luke asked, putting his hands over her clasped ones. His grip was warm and light. It gave comfort without confining.

"No!" The word burst out of her without a second's thought. She probed deeper. Maybe it was wishful thinking, but it felt like the dread came from the outside in, not that it emanated from inside her.

"I don't know much about amnesia, but I do know about people. I see all kinds. The ones with character and the ones without. You're all right, Goldie."

She stared at him for a long moment as relief flooded through her, but felt compelled to ask, "What if you're wrong?"

For just a moment, his eyes showed he'd already asked

himself that question. He seemed satisfied with his own answer, though, because he grinned. "I'm never wrong, though my brothers might disagree." His gaze studied her face, then he added, "Relax. While this storm is controlling the board, trouble can't find either of us."

It was a happy thought. The knot in her stomach eased, allowing relief's return.

He stood up. "I'm going to see if I can find you something to change into. We need to check you for any other . . . injuries." He caught her chin and looked at her eyes again. Not like a man looking at a woman. "Headache?"

"It's hard to isolate my aches to any single area." She touched the sore area at the base of her neck. It felt bigger than the last time she'd touched it. "I think I will try some of that ice, though."

He nodded, then made a beeline for the stairs. She watched him because she couldn't help it and because it was a distraction. She had the weird sense that a guy in tight jeans was a rarity in her life. Maybe she was a nun? Her brain immediately produced, "We are troubled on every side, but not in despair."

Appropriate, but not exactly significant. And didn't nuns have to cut their hair? Luke was almost out of sight, which seemed a pity.

"Luke?"

He paused, one foot on a stair and turned. "Yeah?"

That was better. "Where am I?"

"I told you. Our cabin—"

"No, where in the world am I?"

"Oh. Colorado. Not far from Estes Park and Rocky Mountain National Park."

"Oh," she said.

"Ring any bells?"

"North American continent. Between forty-one and thirty-seven degrees north latitude and one hundred and two and one hundred and nine degrees west longitude. Thirty-eighth state—" She stopped the flood of words, though more minutia hovered on the tip of her tongue. More about Colorado, plus the fact that Rocky Mountain National Park was founded in 1915 and was part of the front range of the Rocky Mountains. She also, apparently, knew that Estes Park was located at the east entrance to the park.

Despite the mini-flood of information, none of it gave her a sense of place, of where she was in the larger tapestry of life.

Outside the storm raged against their beachhead of warmth. So far the cabin held its own against a wind that howled at the door and rattled windows that had frost building from the corners out of its panes. Away from civilization and city lights, the darkness was deep and impenetrable. She could be anywhere. Even on the moon, she realized, and she wouldn't know it.

Goldie smiled weakly. "At least I know what continent I'm on."

"I'll say," Luke said. He looked amused and bemused. "Maybe later we can play Trivial Pursuit, see what else you know."

A name floated into the front of her brain. "Oh. I remember something else! Carmen Sandiego!"

Luke laughed. "It's a game, Goldie. *Where in the World is Carmen Sandiego?* I'll bet you kick ass at it, too."

He left her alone, feeling silly and frustrated. Why could she remember skin layers, streams of facts and games, but not her own name? And why the peculiar sense that she'd never known who she really was?

Unsettled, she padded over to the window and peered out. All she could see was her own, unfamiliar reflection staring back at her. She smiled, watching it appear on the stranger's face in the window. Visibility was zero. Outside the window and inside her own head. She turned and looked at the stairs where Luke had vanished. Unbidden, against her wishes, a thought worked its way to the front of her head. What was he doing out here away from everyone?

All she knew was what he told her. The wind rose in a howl outside. A howl that sounded too much like mocking laughter.

Chapter Two

The moon was a recent memory in the night sky. A few stars broke the cloud cover that added a layer of cool to the shrubbery surrounding the laboratory. The night smells of shrub and flower filled the air, a symbolic reminder of what they were there to protect—Mother Nature herself.

GREEN ONE, a darker shadow in a sea of shadows, scanned the area through his night vision glasses. A guard strolled around a corner, pausing to light a cigarette. Not far from him, ONE could see GREEN TWO's heat signature, also waiting for the guard to move on. When the guard resumed his patrol, ONE moved forward a few steps, crouched for another scan of the area, then forward again. Against the side of the building, TWO and THREE joined him. FOUR was elsewhere, neutralizing the electronic security system.

No one spoke. No one needed to. They had their assigned target inside the laboratory. Only he knew the real names of the members of the team. This was a world at war, with too few soldiers signed up on Mother Nature's behalf. GREEN was his brain child, his underground army, modeled after the French Resistance of World War II. At first, GREEN had been small with few cells, hitting environmental polluters in a few isolated incidents and then vanishing into the night, but it had grown rapidly in the last five years. Gore had made it "in" to be green, and it had also helped his cause when he established a legitimate non-profit front that lobbied Congress, raised money, conducted peaceful protests—and found him recruits for his more aggressive goals. Gore was gone, but it didn't matter now. GREEN was a mighty oak now, with strong, deep roots able to withstand the winds of change.

From his unique perspective as its gardener, it had been fascinating to see his sapling grow and flourish. The battle was like a living chessboard, with him controlling the white pieces and big business in charge of the black. The government tried to referee this unequal match, but the money that flowed from the anti-green forces to the open hands of elected officials had neutered it. Soft money for softer brains.

Despite the power inequity, he controlled his forces with a single purpose, while big business was controlled by many minds with diverging goals. He couldn't save the world, but he could focus on the small piece of the earth he could save.

He wasn't strong on patience, but he'd been forced to learn it. When patience wasn't possible, he worked off his restless energy by freeing prisoners of war. He needed only to be patient a little longer. Even as he and his cohorts moved in on their objective here in California, other players had opened a new offensive back in Colorado—one that would strike a serious blow for the world's green stuff and, as an added bonus, royally screw his father. The best of both worlds.

Like him, dark figures moved through the guts of his father's favorite company, Merryweather Biotechnologies in Denver. This time their special task force would be successful in securing the prototype and the technology data. This time they wouldn't fail, because this time they knew when and where to strike. Knight would fall, he thought with a grin, on the technology and on good old dad. And Knight's daughter would play her role, then die, too. Everyone knew trouble came in threes. Dad was going to get a pointed and painful reminder of that little truth.

Though he was GREEN ONE, for tonight's diversionary

attack he followed FOUR's lead. This team had been pulled together from three separate cells to minimize risk to himself. He was careful to ensure that even if the Feds tracked one of his cells back to himself, they wouldn't believe he was the leader of, let alone the mastermind behind GREEN. They'd believe his carefully projected image of a rich, rebellious dilettante playing at environmentalist. He smiled slightly. Only one person knew the truth, and he'd never tell. Their mutual passion and their mutual secret bound them more securely than any oath of loyalty.

His earpiece crackled. TWO, using the latest in stealth technology, verified that FOUR had taken down the security system. TWO breached the door. They were armed, but with tranquilizer guns, not bullets. Lost lives could cost them the PR war, which was almost as important as their hidden battles to free the hostages to technology. Distraction and delay weren't as inspiring as big headlines in the short term, but they were in this for the long term.

They padded down the hall with THREE on point. A guard rounded a corner, and THREE fired. The guard collapsed without a sound. When they reached the labs where the POWs were caged, they split up. ONE entered his target lab and headed straight for the windows. After opening them, he turned to the cages. His lab was a prison camp for several apes used in medical research. No wire cutters for his teams. They were all armed with the latest in high-tech, portable lasers that cut through wire and padlocks like butter.

In minutes he'd freed the POWs and herded them out the window. He followed, then crouched and stared across the lawn for a last scan of the area before jogging across the lawn. He'd almost reached the cover of the trees when he heard a shout. ONE turned toward the sound, firing a tranquilizer in the guard's direction as he ran backwards. The dart hit the guard in the chest. He stumbled forward a few steps and then fell on his face. Without further incident, ONE reached cover, the trees closing round to shelter him from hostile eyes like the loving arms of his mother, had his mother actually had arms even remotely loving.

The small wooded area was alive with the chatter of their freed POW's. ONE smiled. It sounded like he'd suddenly been transported to the jungle. He jogged deeper into the trees, glad for the night vision goggles. He didn't want to step on any of the freed hostages, darting about as they adjusted to their new freedom.

He didn't see the others on his team. It wasn't part of the plan. There'd be no risky rendezvous to gloat or celebrate. Just a swift, silent strike and a swifter, more silent retreat, with each man disappearing into the night.

At the edge of the woods, not far from the Los Angeles estate where his dad was being honored yet again for his rape of the environment, Leslie Merryweather shed his gear, stuffing it into the duffle he'd left stashed behind a rock. In a short time, he was back in his tux. He pulled the flask from the pocket and sprinkled a bit on his clothes, then drank a bit, gargled and spit it out. He'd parked his car with the rear toward the trees, so it was a simple matter to unlock the trunk, stow his gear and close it again without being spotted by any of the valets working the host's party. This lab hadn't been on their original strike list until he'd seen its proximity to the gala. Sometimes fate was kind.

He adjusted his tie to a crooked angle, mussed his hair, and then staggered unsteadily out of cover. A young woman in an absurdly transparent dress spotted him.

"Looking for a place to puke, Leslie?" Her gaze raked his tall, dashing figure hungrily. She turned so the light hit at the right angle to highlight her breasts.

He lifted the flask in a mocking toast. "Love the new boobs, darling. Who did them?"

"Go to hell." She turned and stalked away, her hair—and the new breasts—bouncing in agitation.

He laughed, then pretended to take a drink. A white coated man approached from the house.

"Your father is looking for you, Mr. Merryweather."

"Is he?" Leslie straightened up. "Tell him . . . I've already left. I have a golf game in Denver tomorrow." Had to keep up his image as a useless waste of space. And he wasn't sure he could keep the triumph out of his eyes in his dad's presence. The old man was an asshole, but he'd always known when his only son was up to something. This wasn't the time. Soon, but not yet. He veered back to his Jag. Inside, with the motor racing, he applied serious pressure to the pedal, spewing gravel at the parked cars as he sped away. Once out of sight of the house, he slowed. Not the night to get picked up for driving drunk, not with what he had in his trunk. His plane waited at his father's private airstrip. At the other end, not far from another airstrip, his new chess piece should be waiting for him.

"I'll see what I can turn up, but a storm is shutting us down as I speak," Bryn Bailey said. She looked at her watch and winced. She was already late for the Kirby clan dinner party, and the storm would slow her down even more, assuming she ever got on the road. "Whole city may be closed tomorrow."

Bryn had been with the Bureau since graduating from college twelve years ago and could have been their poster girl—had they had one. Vigorous and driven, she was beautiful, but much less high gloss after a year in the wild, wild west. Her power suits had given way to designer jeans that were comfortable and had collected an impressive collection of wolf whistles. The spiked heels were now snakeskin cowboy boots that had changed her walk from stabbing to kick-ass.

She told herself it was the wind that had softened her sleek, dark hairstyle, but her dark, less-steely gaze couldn't be explained away by wind gusts. Bryn blamed it on Jake Kirby, a colleague and a friend, despite his choice to join the US Marshals Service instead of the FBI. And riding herd on Dewey Hyatt. The two of them had managed to take the edge off her "take no prisoners" approach to law enforcement. She'd never expected to feel comfortable in a West she'd considered irretrievably chauvinistic. At first she'd put a penny in a jar every time someone called her "little lady," but quit when she realized that it was a habit, not a put down. Inherent in their recognition that she was different from them was an appreciation for that difference that she liked. Amazing, but true, if she hadn't partnered with Jake a year ago, she'd still be in D.C., bitching her way through her usual cases.

She didn't miss it. She liked that she didn't have to act like a man to succeed here. Whatever perks she lost by being female were balanced by the benefits of being female. There was a growing satisfaction in doing her job without worrying about who was ahead of her and who was closing in from behind.

Not long after she moved here, she'd felt a tectonic plate shift inside as she realized that having it "all" was driving her crazy, not happy. She even sang along with the country music station, the only thing her new SUV seemed able to pick up as she drove down the freeway and she had recently learned how to "push her tush," something Dani Kirby, Jake's sister-in-law, insisted was the key to happiness.

After a few more assurances to the voice droning in her

ear—why did men have to say the same thing three ways before they could move on?—she was able to ring off. The reports coming in on the lab strikes were brief, details scarce, but her gut, her instincts were telling her there was more to this than the usual grandstanding. If only the facts backed her up.

Phagan had told her he thought GREEN was planning an offensive for later this year, but hadn't learned what. After six months, he still hovered on the outside of their magic inner circle. Outside that circle, GREEN operated in tight, isolated cells. It wasn't clear which cell member was the contact with their control either. He was impressed with their security—and Phagan wasn't easy to impress.

Not the result she'd hoped for when she inched out on a limb for him a year ago. He'd contacted her online, inviting her into VR—virtual reality—as was his habit. That time, though, there'd been a difference. He came, not to court, but to ask a favor. A huge favor.

"I need access to Pathphinder," he told her. Pathphinder was the Internet "handle" for his former partner in crime, Phoebe Mentel Kirby. Like Dewey Hyatt, Phoebe was on probation for those criminal activities. She was also Jake's wife and Jake wasn't about to let any unhallowed contact with her former partners jeopardize her probation. He liked having her around too much.

"Yeah, Jake will let that happen," Bryn said, "when real-time hell freezes over." She added the "real-time" adjective because the last time she'd said this to him, he'd turned their VR world into a frozen-over hell. The guy had a puckish sense of humor. "The only time Dewey sees Phoebe is when he's with one of us. You know contact with you would violate her parole."

"That's why you'll have to be our go-between."

"And why would I risk pissing Jake off like that?"

"Because it could be my ticket—and yours—into the inner circle of GREEN."

GREEN. How the hell had he found out she was investigating GREEN? For months she'd been trying to plant someone inside this elusive and crafty environmental action group. It was as if GREEN had a sixth sense for Feds. Or a contact in their office. She didn't like to think it, but it had happened and would again. There was always someone who needed money more than their integrity. Maybe it was time to step outside the official box . . .

"If I help you, you're in?" she asked, stalling as she mentally reviewed the pros and cons. Pros were obvious. Phagan wasn't a Fed. Cons were obvious, too. If he wanted access to Phoebe, it was her B&E—breaking and entering—planning skills he was after. Phoebe had earned her path "phinding" rcp planning B&E for Phagan and Dewey. Her probation required her to stop illegal acts, not encourage them.

"Like flint," he said.

"What's the job?"

"You know I can't tell you that, darlin'. You'd have to do something about it." He gave her a virtually sincere look. "When the time is right, I'll deliver the goods. Until then, well, you'll have to trust me."

Trust him. Like a wish before dying, the last two years of contact with him streamed through her head. Every taunt, tease, and love note. And with the teasing, had been solid leads to crimes committed by some very nasty characters.

As if he followed her thought processes, a tiny angel of herself appeared on her right shoulder, with a diminutive devil on the other. She looked at the angel. It smiled in a very unangelic way.

"You know you want to," it said.

She looked at the devil.

"You want to bad."

She looked at Phagan. His virtual smile was wide and hopeful, his teeth unrealistically white and glinting in the sun behind his head. It invited her to forget reason, to forget caution and listen to her heart. She'd never been very good at listening to her heart, but her reasonable, logical brain knew there was a time for caution and a time to leap into the abyss.

So Phagan and Phoebe had done some path "phinding"— with Bryn as go-between. It had been an education to see Phoebe go after a system. She had a genius for finding weak spots in security. She also had an instinct for finding the strengths of a system and using that against them, too. It was fortunate that Jake kept her on a very short leash. It almost drove Bryn mad that she couldn't tell who or where the system was housed. Phagan's VR world was stripped of all identifying marks.

And then nothing. As near as she could tell GREEN hadn't used the information. There'd been no report of a break-in that remotely resembled Phoebe's plan.

So why hadn't GREEN used the plan? Instead, everyone seemed to be in a holding pattern. Until tonight. Were GREEN operatives even now moving on an unsuspecting lab with information she'd helped provide? And where was Phagan? Since her last contact with him, he'd been ominously silent.

It wasn't like him. He liked to touch base with her every day, even it if was just an email smiley. She hated to admit it, but she was worried about him. Could GREEN suspect him? They'd managed to smoke out every other person she'd sent against them but this time she was the only person who knew Phagan was working with her. Six months had passed since Phagan began his online dance with someone called "Forest for the Trees," and still no face-to-face meet with any of the GREEN leadership to show for giving Phagan her trust six months ago, except a few more wrinkles around her eyes. This was the first time she'd stepped outside the lines. If Phagan failed her, it could mean her career.

Out there, somewhere past her personal worries, her brain gnawed at the few facts she'd learned. Why the hell had GREEN chosen tonight to act? In the past, their operations had coincided with environmentally significant days, like Arbor Day. Was there something else that she'd missed in her obsessive monitoring the past six months?

There was no way to know what this change in their usual *modus operandi* meant. Not with the paucity of facts she had and using a brain too tired to produce more than a boatload of unanswered questions and lots of unease. Her last cup of coffee had faded from her system a couple of hours ago. The clock sounded loud in the quiet, empty office. Somewhere there was someone on night duty, but not here where all the smart agents left for home ahead of the storm. Usually Dewey stayed until she left, but he'd had to report to his parole officer before they met for dinner with the Kirbys. It annoyed her that she missed him, that she liked having him working with her as a pseudo-partner.

To escape her thoughts, she grabbed her purse and rose to her feet in one smooth, determined motion. Moping around the office was as useful as hitting herself with a two-by-four. She could at least be with friends eating good food and great desserts. She snagged her coat as she passed the rack. Out in the hall, she hesitated long enough to hear the door click closed behind her. As she rounded the corner, she heard the elevator ping and picked up the pace, but checked when she saw someone waiting in the elevator. It was instinct to reach for the weapon in the holster nestled in the curve of her back, even as she recognized him.

Donovan Kincaid raised his hands above his waist, the palms out so she could see they were empty. "You've gone country. I wasn't expecting that."

And I wasn't expecting you, she thought. She didn't wonder how he'd gotten in the closed building. To be a specialist in keeping people out, you first had to know how they got in. She shrugged. "Stuff happens."

"That it does," he said. "I knew the storm wouldn't scare you home early."

Did he? Bryn arched her brows. "I'd planned to be, but something came up."

"Something always does."

Donovan Kincaid studied her without embarrassment, so she returned the favor. He still looked like Harrison Ford and had the charm—and a rakish air of mystery packaged with military bearing—to match the rugged good looks. He was a man who could make a woman feel feminine and fluttery, even when she was pointing a gun at him. She'd never understood the younger woman/older man attraction until she met Donovan. She'd been tempted, though not enough to join the parade of women that sighed after him. She remembered liking him, but not trusting him—because of what she knew about him and what she didn't.

Back then, his dossier placed him in Vietnam as a sniper, but he wasn't a loner and seemed to be free of "issues" and posttraumatic stress disorder from his three tours of duty in Asia. He did have issues with peacetime, she recalled. He was a natural-born soldier with a romantic streak that helped him with women. He loved the life, the danger. Not surprisingly, he'd turned mercenary, selling his skills to those he perceived as the good guys in the world's various conflicts. A few blank spots hinted at some CIA involvement. Then he turned up as a security specialist for a government contractor, which is how she'd met him. She believed that it was Kincaid who'd sent her the information that nailed his employer—once it became clear that that employer wasn't on the side of the angels. He had to be on the right side, even if he wasn't an angel himself.

She hadn't kept track of Kincaid because of the flare of attraction that hummed below the surface every time she was around him. That might have been a mistake, she decided. Did his presence here mean he'd set up shop in Denver or was he just passing through?

"I like the new you," he said with a smile that warmed the cold hallway. "Can I buy you a cup of coffee?"

"I'm late for a dinner appointment."

"Really?" His smile turned intimate. "You have changed."

A year ago, her hackles would have popped up, but after hanging with the Kirby men, her hackles were plumb worn out.

"I live in interesting times."

His chuckle was sexy as hell.

You'd think that being interested in two men would give you some immunity, she thought ruefully, and wondering, for the thousandth time, how a pair of criminals had become yin to her oh-so-legal yang?

"How about I walk you to your car?" His manner was easy, but as she entered the brighter light of the elevator, she could see the worry in the back of his gray eyes that had a few more lines than she remembered fanning out from them. Snow still dusted his brown hair, which had been mixed with a bit of distinguished gray as long as she'd known him. He topped her by at least five inches. The navy coat he wore with casual confidence looked expensive. He smelled expensive, too, nicely dispelling the odor of pizza and sweat that usually prevailed in the elevator.

She propped a shoulder against the metal wall, her arms crossed over her chest. She chose the defensive pose deliberately. He shoved his hands into the pockets of his dark, wool pants, his attitude that of the supplicant, which was a far cry from his usual take-charge approach. Which meant he was more than a little worried.

"What's up, Donovan?" The clock was ticking in her head, but curiosity drowned it out.

He hesitated, as if not sure where to begin. "I could be crying wolf," he admitted.

She didn't state the obvious, that he usually *was* the wolf. He shifted restlessly, as if he felt claustrophobic in the small box.

"Why don't you start at the beginning and move quickly to the end?" She punctuated this with a pointed look at her watch. If he didn't get to the point, she'd miss dessert. She hated missing dessert.

He nodded. "I'm working for Merryweather Biotechnologies. The usual security consulting, only professional and personal this time. Their work is cutting edge, some of it top secret and under government contract. Earlier today, one of their top scientists, John Knight, collapsed and was rushed to the hospital. He died two hours ago."

The elevator doors slid open. Bryn stepped out into the lobby and stopped, facing Donovan.

"I'm sorry," she said. "But—"

"It's complicated." He hesitated again, then said, "His daughter, Prudence, accompanied him to the hospital, but now she seems to be missing."

His tone had changed when he said her name, though she couldn't isolate just how. Bryn felt her instincts ramp up as his gaze avoided hers.

"According to the nursing staff, there was some kind of argument. She left looking—" he stopped.

"Looking?"

He hesitated. "Agitated. Real agitated."

"And the father? How did he look?"

Donovan's brows snapped together in a scowl. "Pleased. The nurse said he looked pleased."

"That's hardly a federal offense," Bryn said, though gently.

"I know." He sighed, shaking his head. "And it's a good reason to take a time out. But Pru—Miss Knight is more than his daughter. She's his research assistant. And critical to his work. His highly classified, very valuable work. And she's not the kind of person to ignore a page."

"And your gut is telling you that something's wrong?" Bryn had learned to appreciate the value of the twitching male gut, though she liked hard facts the better.

"Her car's in the parking lot outside the hospital," he said, his gaze avoiding hers.

Bryn looked out the lobby's glass doors at the blowing snow. "Has she ever gone AWOL?"

His face told her that she'd hit on a question he didn't want her to ask. He nodded again, this time reluctantly. "He keeps—kept her on a short leash when he was around, but he traveled a lot. Conferences and stuff. And she has some money of her own from her mother. When he's gone, she takes off, too. Though not like this. She parks in a garage downtown and disappears in the mall, sometimes for several days."

How did he know? She held back the question, sensing he wouldn't answer it anyway. It was clear that he had more than a professional interest in Miss Knight. When a woman was involved, he usually did. Maybe that was what was making him twitch. "I have some contacts in the DPD," she said, thanks to Jake's brother, Luke, who was a homicide detective. "I can ask a few questions. I might get some answers."

Or she might not. It was too soon to know much and the storm would complicate more than Donovan's problems before it moved east.

"Do you have a picture?"

He pulled a manila envelope out of a pocket and handed it to her. "Here's her vitals, car stats and a picture." He waited until she took it. "Also my personal cell phone number. Call me if—"

"Of course, but I can't promise much, Donovan."

"I know." He held her gaze for a long moment. "Thanks."

"Sure." She tapped the envelope. "I'll be in touch."

She left him standing on the sidewalk, an improbably forlorn figure with the storm for his backdrop. In the garage, her SUV was cold and reluctant to start. As she waited for it to warm, she thought about her arrival in Denver with Jake just over a year ago. Her skirt—and her attitude—had been so tight, Jake had had to lift her into the cab of the truck he'd rented.

Donovan was right. She had changed. But not completely. She didn't wait to open the envelope. She pulled out the sheets and found the promised vitals on Prudence Knight, along with a picture that was even worse than the usual driver's license mug shot. Probably her company ID. She had that "deer in the headlights" look. Her stats put her at five-eight, but the unkind camera shrunk her a bit. Her hair, blond, was pulled sternly back off her face, and she wore a pair of large, studious glasses perched on the end of her nose. According to her birth date, she was young enough to be Donovan's daughter. Which had never stopped him in the past. Not his usual squeeze, though, unless she looked better in the flesh. From the picture, she could get no sense of who Prudence Knight was or how she felt about daddy's short leash around her neck, but there must be something there. She'd not only managed to break free on occasion, she'd managed to lose Donovan, which Bryn knew from personal experience wasn't easy.

That brought her back to wondering why Donovan had been following Prudence Knight? If she were so critical to her father's research, why would he risk pissing her off? Without answers, all she could do was speculate, which she could do just as well at her destination. She stowed the information and backed out of her spot, then turned truck and self in the direction of the restaurant. With a little luck, she might make it in time for dessert.

Goldie, buried in a mound of quilts, had slipped into a light slumber. Earlier, she'd found one of Dani's flannel nightgowns and a pair of Phoebe's Snoopy slippers for her icy feet. Luke was uneasy with the question of a concussion still unresolved. The last time he'd checked, her pupils were normal and responsive to light, but she also had three nasty bumps on various sides of her noggin. He'd feel better when she could be checked into the hospital, but for now the storm had settled in over them like a broody hen.

He should phone his mom or she'd pin his ears back for making her worry. He could feel it, even with miles and Mother Nature between them. He felt strangely reluctant to call her or his brothers. He hadn't planned this. So why didn't he want to talk about it?

He tried the words out in his head, but nothing sounded right. Just thinking about telling his mother made him feel exposed, uncomfortable. Because he was an adult, he pressed himself harder. What was he afraid she would pick up on?

It wasn't hard to figure out. Against his better instincts, he felt attracted to Goldie. He'd have to be made of rock not to feel his senses stirring under the circumstances. He was a man, alone in the wilds with a beautiful woman. Trouble was, he'd come here to find closure, not to rev his motor over someone who didn't even know her name.

Plus, he didn't want to get teased about it. His brothers could squeeze more mileage out of random chance than anyone he knew. They'd sense his guilt and like sharks who smell blood, they'd be after him with about as much mercy. He needed to know more about Goldie before he exposed them both to that. He didn't like questions without answers.

It was damned odd, her showing up here on the same day he happened to be coming. The only person he'd told he was leaving a couple of hours ago was Dani. If there was a malignant purpose in Goldie's presence, it wasn't likely to be directed at him.

Had she really lost her memory? When he looked into her eyes, he believed her. Now that her remarkable eyes were closed . . . he wasn't so sure. It was time to start thinking like a cop. The only clues he had, except for the lady herself, were her clothes. Or what was left of them.

He picked up her blue jeans. The fabric was soft, comfortable, and well worn. No laundry marks or tags. Nothing in the pockets but some bits of lint. Not surprising, since most women carried a purse. She'd probably lost it when she fell. Her shredded cotton tee shirt was also soft from multiple washings and without pockets. An experienced hiker, she'd spent her money on her jacket and boots, which looked worn but cared for. The boots were scuffed from her tumble but had survived better than the jacket. In addition to the bullet hole in the sleeve, he found more rips than he could count. The pockets yielded a set of keys and an innocuous shopping list.

He studied the handwriting. It was precise and graceful, very legible, and kind of old-fashioned. The list looked like what he'd buy for a high-energy hike. The keys were hanging from a Harry Potter key ring. There was also an anonymous security card key, but no identifying initials, either personal or professional. Two of the keys could have been house or apartment keys. A car key and a computer lock key. The rest were too anonymous to speculate about.

He started to toss her jacket back onto the chair, but stopped when a hard object banged against his leg. He felt the body of the jacket and found it in the lining. An inside seam gave way when pressure was applied. Velcro closed the opening. He pulled it open and found a nifty looking personal digital assistant. It looked a bit like the PDA Dani had bought for Matt. Dani loved technology toys like Harry Potter loved Hogwarts. He flipped open the cover and found a power button. When the screen flickered to life, a password prompt appeared, denying him access to its contents. For the first time in a year, he wished he had Dewey Hyatt close to hand. If anyone could crack this puppy, it was Hyatt.

Interesting that she'd stowed it inside her coat like that. Why hide it—unless she had something to hide? And if she was faking her memory loss, what did she gain?

Time, which the storm gave her anyway, but she hadn't known that when she woke up.

Freedom from explanations? If she were involved in something illegal, finding herself alone with a cop would be a lot of motivation to play dumb. With those eyes and that face she could convince Clinton to be good. He may be too old for her, but he wasn't immune.

There was no way to think his way to a solution. He had no facts and precious few clues. Unless he quit thinking like a cop and turned into a psychic—which wasn't likely to happen.

All roads led back to Goldie. As if on cue, she whimpered in her sleep, her head whipping in one direction, then the other. She moaned, her movements increasingly more frantic in the short time it took him to reach her side.

He hesitated, then touched her shoulder, afraid to wake her too abruptly.

"Goldie?"

She gasped once more, then her eyes popped open. "No!"

"You're safe, Goldie," he said. "It's just a nightmare."

"Oh. Of course." She blinked at him, for a moment not sure who he was or where she was. Luke. Cabin. Mountains. Colorado. Right.

She rubbed her face as images from her dreams slipped around in her head, too fast for her to hold onto specifics, leaving behind the sense they'd been menacing.

She inched her way upright, her muscles protesting. A faint, minatory voice from out of the mist ordered her to sit up straight with her knees together. She knew that voice, but before she could name it, it retreated back into the mist, satisfied she was behaving like a lady.

"How's the head?"

"It's fine, thank you."

"Can I get you anything?"

"No, thank you." The feelings from the dream were fading, though she wasn't eager to risk sleeping again. The firelight flickered, casting shadows on the walls and on Luke's face. It was peaceful, comforting, and intimate. "Don't let me keep you awake. It must be very late."

"After one and I can't sleep either." Luke settled in the chair closest to her. "Want to try your hand at Trivia? Might trigger a memory."

She nodded, despite a reluctance to trigger more memories. *What are you afraid of, Goldie?*

She watched Luke unearth the game from a chest in one corner. He switched on the light, sending many of the shadows scampering into the far corners. She didn't mind. She could see him more clearly. She enjoyed the way he moved and the confident sway of his shoulders. That voice from the mist tried to censure her, but it was faint and easy to ignore. He turned, almost catching her staring. She hurried into distracting speech, "You said something about brothers earlier, didn't you?"

Luke pulled the coffee table between them and opened the box. "Two. Both younger than me."

What if she had brothers or sisters? Or parents still living? Would they be looking for her? Worried about her? She felt alone, but that didn't mean that she was. That there weren't people who needed her, loved her. What if it was family that was the burden she was escaping from? Goldie chose her piece. It felt odd and unfamiliar in her hand. Did that mean she'd never played the game before? "Tell me about them."

Tell me about you, was what she wanted to say. She didn't know this man. He could be the reason she was here. Part of some elaborate plan. Of course, that assumed she was important enough for a plan, elaborate or not. She didn't feel important. Or dangerous enough to shoot at.

All she had was her instincts, and she didn't know if she could trust them. Had they let her down in the past? Or steered her right? Did she have common sense? Or was she an airhead who was lucky to get from point A to point B? There was no way to know. She could resist the attraction that pulled her toward Luke. She could, but she didn't want to. She didn't want to feel responsible; she wanted to be free.

Free of what? Or was it who?

Was she married? Her mind rejected that vehemently. A glance at her hand reassured her. No ring and no sign there'd ever been a ring, though some people didn't wear rings. She didn't feel married. She felt . . . new. It felt lovely to be here, to smile at Luke while he talked and rolled the dice. She liked his laugh. It was deep and infectious. She laughed with him. It hurt, but felt good, too. She needed the endorphins.

Endorphins? Maybe she was a doctor.

Chapter Three

Bryn paused in the doorway to shake the snow off her coat before handing it to the coatroom clerk. She was glad she'd traded in her lethal high heels early in her adventures in the Mile-High City. In honor of the storm, she'd also traded in her cowboy boots for snow boots with deep treads because she didn't intend to break her neck, or any other bone, crossing an icy parking lot.

Her coat dealt with, her gaze swept the restaurant, looking for the Kirby table. Her nose greedily inhaled the yummy food smells filling the wonderfully warm air. It was easy to spot her group. It was the largest in the room, dominating a large portion of a corner that had probably been quiet before it was invaded. The table had a finished-eating look that didn't bode well for her empty tummy—which promptly grumbled.

Two empty chairs drew her attention. One, she knew, was hers. A frown started between her brows until she spotted Dewey Hyatt. Part of her expected the other empty chair to be his. Though he wore an official bracelet on his ankle, it would be easy beans for him to shed it. For the first few months of his electronic probation, tension had coiled her insides like a malignant snake as she waited for him to vanish. Disappearing was his specialty. It was hard to believe he could give up a habit so deeply ingrained into his psyche.

Against the odds, there he sat, a high-tech thief at a table full of lawmen. Lanky and rather nondescript, he managed to look appealing next to the highly "descript" Kirbys. The charm helped, of course. He was loaded with it. It brightened his brown eyes and disguised a face was so ordinary it verged on homely. His mouth was mobile and nicely shaped, with an infectious grin and a dimple that magically appeared in his left cheek. In a perfect world, the fluidity of his face and body could have put him in serious contention with comic Jim Carrey. Dewey had an instinct for comedy and for expertly mining her sense of humor. She'd grown accustomed to him and even let herself enjoy it occasionally, despite her best efforts not to.

She told herself she had him working with her to try and trick him into exposing Phagan, but Bryn couldn't lie to herself forever. In a year long campaign, Dewey'd managed to move her past mere liking and into the dangerous territory of warm regard. She'd even pondered various possible, and even some impossible, happy endings.

Jake's career had survived his marriage to the paroled Phoebe, but he was a man. Men could do some things that a woman in law enforcement couldn't. It wasn't fair, but it never had been. She knew that going in and had figured it was worth it. Now, though, when she looked on the happiness of Jake and his brother, Matt, she wondered if a girl could sacrifice too much for a career.

With Dewey present and briefly mooned over, she turned her attention to who wasn't there. She could see Matt with his Dani, their son on his lap instead of in the high chair the restaurant provided. Dani was still packing a few of her pregnancy pounds, but the extra weight suited her. She'd had a few pounds too many shaved off her during her ordeal as a government witness. Mark looked like he was going to be a chip off his dad's block, but Dani didn't look like she minded. Happiness suited her.

Phoebe still glowed, too. Bryn remembered the first time

she'd seen her, just over a year ago. She'd been singing in a band in a bar in Estes Park. Her eyes had a "no trespassing" sign posted in them and so much sad, it was painful to look at her. Jake had torn that sign down. Jake was always cheerful, but now it was biggie-sized, with a huge dollop of contentment. If she felt inclined to jealousy, she had only to remind herself of what both couples had suffered to be sitting there together.

Debra Kirby sat at the head table, her eyes slightly worried as they studied the empty chair. It still startled Bryn how much Jake and his mom looked alike. Both were light skinned, compared to the dark-visaged Matt and Luke, who everyone said took after their dad.

Luke. That's who was missing. Luke, who they were pretending this gathering wasn't for. Just like they were pretending they'd forgotten it was the anniversary of his wife Rosemary's death. Luke was so easygoing, so even tempered, she sometimes forgot he'd lost his childhood sweetheart to ovarian cancer seven years earlier.

Bryn dropped into the seat between Debra and Dewey and touched her hand. "Your firstborn working tonight?"

She smiled, but there was strain in it, as she shook her head. "He's eluded us. Told Dani he was going up to the cabin. Now the storm has moved in, and he's got his phone turned off or it's not receiving."

"Men." Bryn could feel Dewey watching her, waiting for her attention to turn his way. She ignored him, though she didn't pull away when his hand found hers under the table and squeezed it. When had she moved from rejecting his advances to accepting them? How long would it be before she was returning them? Dewey had been patient and persistent, but he'd upped the tempo of his pursuit lately. Cheeky devil, she thought, then caught her breath as the tip of his finger traced a heart in the palm of her captured hand. Okay, so maybe there was something more than warm regard in her feelings for Dewey, but she was *not* in love with him.

"You're late," Matt said, moving a steak knife out of his son's reaching hands.

It could be either a comment or a question. The Kirby men were like that, she'd found. The choice of what and how much to share was her responsibility. She never got to claim anything was dragged out of her, but they were free with their assistance and never tried to take all the credit.

"Had a couple of calls before I could get clear," she said, adjusting the volume of her voice so it reached only the ears at their table. "GREEN hit six research labs tonight. East and west coast and a couple in between. Turned a bunch of lab animals loose. Graffiti on the walls about freeing the POWs and hostages. The usual stuff, only this time somebody died."

Jake frowned slightly. "Deliberate?"

Bryn shook her head. "They used a tranquilizer gun on one of the security guards. Shot him in the heart. Guy had a heart condition and couldn't take it. We've been tracking sales of the darts because they always use them, so we know this one came from our area. They want us to check it out." She looked at Dewey. "GREEN did their usual pre-screw of the computers. Our guys were wondering if you could fly in and contain the damage once the weather clears. I told them you could."

"Am I allowed out of your sight?" Dewey smiled at her, the charm flowing out of him to wrap around her heart like a favorite chocolate.

"No. That's why I'll be going with you." She tried to keep her expression and her tone noncommittal, but it wasn't easy with Dewey's fingers creeping up her thigh. She grabbed his hand and returned it to his own lap.

Dewey arched his brows wickedly as his hand gripped hers. She could have pulled away, she knew. He knew it, too.

"You got a couple of calls?" Phoebe asked, as if she knew Bryn needed rescuing. "Don't people know when to go home?"

Bryn chuckled. One call had been a report on a right-wing paramilitary group, the Colorado Irregulars, operating out of one of those weekend, "let's shoot paint balls at each other for fun" camps being investigated, but this wasn't the place to mention that, since it had also proved difficult to infiltrate. "Sometimes I'm not sure Alexander Graham did us any favors when he invented the telephone. Then I got tagged leaving the office." She looked at Jake. "Did you ever meet a mercenary named Donovan Kincaid when you were in D.C.?"

Jake frowned. "Ran into him once. Interesting character."

"Well, he's being 'interesting' here in Denver these days. He's a security consultant for Merryweather Biotechnologies. Either of you had dealings with them?"

Both Jake and Matt shook their heads. Jake, as if he couldn't resist it, said, "Sounds like a place that would interest Phagan."

"Almost everything does." Dewey looked amused, as if he knew something no one else did. Except maybe Phoebe, who choked.

Jake looked a question at her, but thought better of it and kissed her instead. Wise man. See no evil, hear no evil, ask no questions and marital harmony is preserved.

Bryn eyed Dewey. "Any idea what might have interested Phagan at Biotech?"

He looked delighted to have her full attention. "They dabble in a lot of different stuff. Been messing around with genetically engineered foods and done some interesting stuff with protective gear."

"Such as?" Debra asked.

"Well, they developed a jump suit that mutes the body's heat signature," he said, winking at Phoebe. Her eyes widened, then she looked away, a smile tugging at the corners of her mouth. Once again Jake looked curious but restrained himself. Marriage to Phoebe was teaching him a lot about self-control, Bryn decided with an inward grin.

"I also heard they were doing some interesting research in protective body armor," he went on. "They have some super brain, name of John Knight, in charge of the research."

Bryn twitched slightly at the name, earning a quick look from Dewey. He hesitated, then continued, "If he succeeds, it could impact more than personal protection. And be mega-valuable."

"How?" Bryn asked, though she knew she shouldn't.

"Well, who wouldn't like body armor that was light and cool and could beat cop-killers?"

Bryn nodded thoughtfully. Armor-piercing bullets were the bane of law enforcement existence.

"Why would a biotech company be working on body armor?" Debra asked.

Bryn looked at her with respect. It was a damn good question.

Dewey shrugged. "Buzz is Biotech is looking to Mother Nature for a solution to the problem of protection and weight. Nature kicks butt when protecting itself from predators."

"Did they do it?" Bryn asked. "Did they succeed?"

"I don't know. I promised this judge I'd be good," Dewey said, his arm finding its way to the back of her chair, his smile worming its way into her heart.

Did that mean he wasn't in contact with Phagan? She

wished she could ask him. Or Phoebe. She'd be damn glad when they weren't on parole anymore. If she lived that long.

"What did Kincaid want?" Matt asked. It was typical of him to bring the conversation back on point.

Bryn related the gist of Donovan's visit and handed over the envelope. "I was hoping to hand it off to Luke."

Though now she was wondering if she should. Was it possible Prudence Knight's disappearance was the beginning of a move on Merryweather? Could it be connected to GREEN's other activities this evening? It could be a coincidence, she supposed, but biotech companies were a favorite target of GREEN.

Matt glanced at the contents, Dani taking a peek over his shoulder, and then he handed them to Jake.

"If she is playing hooky, the storm would complicate things for her," Jake said thoughtfully as he took his turn at the contents, the pages angled so Phoebe could see them, too. "I wonder how close Knight was to succeeding?"

"Want me to find out for you?" Dewey asked, giving Bryn a provocative look.

Bryn kicked him with her foot, then gave Jake a pointed look. "Is your gut twitching?" She had enormous, though reluctant, respect for Jake's gut.

Jake shrugged, his mischievous gaze catching Phoebe's. "Not about that." He jumped as if Phoebe had kicked him and asked Bryn, "Any other trouble signs?"

"Not that Donovan mentioned. Gonna be a bitch to investigate right now. They were saying on the radio that the storm is going to shut us down for at least twenty-four hours."

"Longer in the mountains," Debra said, her look of worry deepening.

"Luke's a big boy, Mom," Matt said. "He can take care of himself."

★ ★ ★ ★ ★

The Colorado Irregulars was one of his more brilliant inspirations, Leslie decided as he relaxed in the leather seat of his private jet, even in a host of brilliant ideas. Who'd look in a right-wing paramilitary camp for the leaders of the GREEN? Most of the men who patronized the camp were weekend warriors looking to play soldier with guns and paint. A few were extreme right-wingers with a grudge against a government they felt no longer listened to them. They were inducted into the secret sections of the camp and encouraged to play soldier for real. Grady O'Brien, the camp commander and Leslie's second-in-command inside GREEN, had recruited a couple of right wingers to run the public section of the camp. Because Grady encouraged them, they thought the camp was a cover for plotting the overthrow of the government.

Leslie had met Grady in college. If they both hadn't been straight, they'd have been lovers, so instantly had they been drawn to each other. The friendship they'd forged was stronger than any sexual bond could have been, despite their vast differences.

Grady was the brilliant son of poor parents, attending Yale on a scholarship. Every course of study to which he turned his attention came as easily to him as a hooker with a pimp to pay. He'd wandered between colleges, trying this discipline and that course. So quickly did his ability to learn outstrip the teachers ability to teach, that he'd be bored before the semester was half over and move on. When he finally flunked out, Leslie left with him. It was a great way to piss off his father, his main goal at the time, and besides, he'd learned more from Grady than any program could teach him. Their passion to change the world flowed naturally into the cause of the environment, but neither could settle for throwing money at politicians and whining to the media. They both wanted to change the world.

During the cross-country drive from the East Coast to Colorado, they'd planned and brainstormed a long-term plan for taking back the world from the techno-tyrants. Ironically, they'd applied for and received a government grant for their initial start up.

When Leslie appeared at the camp, usually before an op, the men treated him with rough contempt, which suited him. As long as they saw him as a wealthy dilettante playing soldier, they wouldn't put their tiny brains together and figure out his real purpose—and theirs.

When he discovered his father's research project, it was to Grady that Leslie turned for help. He'd talked to John Knight at the company party to annoy his father. Old bird looked like he wished he were anywhere else. Leslie had first flashed his charm on the old man's prim and proper daughter, but she was apparently dead from the neck down. She'd blinked a couple of times and then excused herself to find the lady's room. The lady's room. Who talked like that now? After the party and when he was in town, Leslie made a point of stopping in to see Knight in his office, mostly because he knew it would bug his old man. One day Knight had let him sit in on a test of the prototype of his biotech body armor. Why shouldn't he? Leslie was the boss's son.

The experiments his father and Knight were conducting were unnatural. How dare they attempt to merge living organisms and technology into a design to protect man from his own violence? It was an affront to nature, as unnatural as any experiment of Dr. Frankenstein's. He'd known then, even as he smiled at the dried-up old man, that he was going to kill him. First, GREEN had tried to steal SHIELD to prevent his father from continuing after Knight's death. That's when he'd discovered how important the Knight's daughter was to their plan and to Donovan Kincaid.

Donovan Kincaid.

It had been a stroke of luck, a gift from Providence, though Leslie hadn't realized it when he had first met Kincaid, the newly hired security consultant, at that same party. Another environmental group had been sending his father threatening letters and emails when Biotech acquired animals for research. It was this kind of rampant stupidity that kept him from merging GREEN with any of the environmental groups. Why would you warn someone before striking?

Leslie hadn't found Kincaid interesting at their first meeting, except as someone to joke about later with Grady. Kincaid reminded him of a paranoid Indiana Jones. He dressed like a solider, though his uniform belonged to no army on this planet, and he had that "corncob up the ass" bearing, too. The ladies seemed to like him, even though he was pushing sixty.

When Kincaid showed up at the Colorado Irregulars camp, Leslie had wondered if his father had found out about it and sent Kincaid to infiltrate them, but Kincaid had asked no questions about him or anyone else. It seemed he liked to play war. He and Grady let Kincaid shoot paint at the other players, while they considered whether he might be useful to them. When anyone appeared at the camp, they were rigorously, but quietly, investigated. The Feds had attempted infiltration several times without success.

Grady had an instinct for finding out interesting facts about people and a gift for getting them to tell him their secrets. He was almost a male version of that empathic woman on Star Trek, the one who could adapt herself to the personality of the man she was with. It was Grady who'd turned up

Kincaid's odd interest in Knight's daughter. Grady had noticed Kincaid's reaction when Leslie had mentioned Prudence Knight and had had Kincaid's apartment discreetly tossed. The search turned up hundreds of photographs of her. What they couldn't figure out was why. It didn't appear Kincaid had done more than wish her good morning, but the photos proved he was obsessed. It would have been interesting to know why, but it didn't matter to their plan. She was his pressure point and that was all that mattered. When Leslie saw Kincaid's full dossier, the plan had exploded in his head, with most of the pieces already in place. GREEN ought to have its own expert marksman/sniper—especially one who could be traced right back to his dad and Merryweather Biotech.

As he looked at his watch, the plane hit an air pocket and dropped with a jolt, then popped up again. He buzzed his pilot. "Gave me a bit of a jolt there, Harry."

He'd spent a lot of time building a reputation as an idiot. Not even an air pocket would make him to break character.

"I was just going to call you, sir," Harry said. "There's a storm in Colorado. We'll have to divert."

"Well, find someplace interesting. You know how I hate being bored."

Leslie closed the intercom with a frown. He'd have to postpone his meeting with Kincaid's girl, it seemed. He grabbed the onboard phone and dialed Grady's private number. It was late, but he'd be up. Grady never slept.

"Yo."

Leslie grinned. Grady had his own deceptive persona cultivated through years of practice. "So, how did it go?"

A silence was his first intimation of trouble.

"I don't know yet. The boys got grounded by the storm."

And they'd agreed on radio silence for security purposes.

Too many people had scanners these days.

"Right. Well, damn." He tapped the table top. "Storm's shut me out, too."

"Gonna be a couple of days before it clears," Grady said. "Where you gonna be?"

"Someplace fun."

"Why am I not surprised?" Grady chuckled. "How'd it go in California?"

"Barrels of fun. Dad's pissed at me as usual. And I made some new friends."

"Well, when we're all swinging from the trees again, we'll need 'em. Night, Les."

"Night." Leslie leaned back in his seat, stretching out his long legs. He pressed the intercom again. "Where we going?"

"Vegas."

"Very good." Vegas. He could use a woman tonight. Maybe gamble a bit. Reinforce his image as a useless waste of space. Damn it. Maybe he should have blown that lab to hell instead of messing with their heads. What he really wanted to do tonight, he realized with a shocked thrill, was to kill someone himself, not just order it done. He wouldn't, but he wondered how long he'd felt like this and not realized it.

Chapter Four

Luke knew it was morning because it was light and stormy instead of dark and stormy. They'd played Trivial Pursuit and Goldie had whipped him thoroughly. Then, in a moment of weakness, he'd shown her how Phoebe's karaoke machine worked. What she didn't know about popular music and popular musicians was as interesting as what she *had* known at Trivial Pursuit. Neither of them had a wonderful singing voice, though he was the only one who knew it at the start. He'd been too tired to let it stop him, and truth be told, he was glad he hadn't.

He grinned as he remembered how bad they'd sounded. He admired her. She had no instinct for music, and she'd forged ahead, her warbling not exactly awful, but not wonderful either. Despite her lack of memory, he felt he knew her. She didn't fling herself into risk, but she didn't back away from it either. There was a buoyancy and a delight for life beneath that rather prim exterior.

He frowned, straining for the right analogy, like it mattered, and then it came to him. She reminded him of the space shuttle breaking free of gravity. As it strained up, it shed those tiles, as if it had to shed weight to make it. That's what she reminded him of, someone straining to break free.

The effort had cost her. She'd sank onto the couch, laughing one minute and the next she was asleep, the transition as swift as a child's. He'd lifted her legs up and covered her with blankets, resisting the impulse to touch the smooth curve of her cheek. Her soft sigh had shaken him enough to make him retreat to the other side of the coffee table.

Eventually he fell asleep, too, waking to find the fire dying and the power gone. He felt as stiff as his high school English teacher—and about as cheerful—from falling asleep in his chair. When he managed to unbend his body, he built up the fire again, filled the coffeepot with water and hung it over the heat.

He knew a watched pot never boiled, but he watched it anyway and dang if it didn't boil. God bless the altitude. He poured water in his cup, added instant coffee and drank it down in two gulps. It scalded all the way to his stomach, then kicked his butt from the inside. That's when he allowed himself to look at Goldie.

He'd wondered if he dreamt her, but there she was, her position almost unchanged from when he'd tucked the blankets around her last night. Sometime in the night, she'd tucked her uninjured hand under her cheek. The injured wrist clutched the edge of the quilt as if to keep her from falling. The temperature in the room had dropped enough that each breath from her parted lips puffed white into the air around her face. In the storm-pale morning light, he could see the bruises and scratches standing out in sharp relief against her pale skin.

He looked at the flakes beating against the window and realized he didn't feel trapped. He was glad the storm had kept them here. He hadn't felt this alive since . . . the day he met Rosemary. He'd been young, but he'd known she was right. It scared him so much, he almost took off. As if she knew it, Rosemary had gripped his hand and smiled at him. He forgot about taking off, forgot about his plan to hitchhike around the world, forgot everything but the pleasure of looking into her blue eyes.

This wasn't the same as that, of course. Goldie might be

married or at least involved with someone. And she was too young for him. She was maybe in her early thirties. Maybe. He revised the number every time her eyes changed. Bottom line, he wasn't looking to feel young again with a young wife. Looking down the barrel of fifty didn't scare him. He'd earned his years the hard way.

That didn't mean his parts had quit working. Or that he was immune. He was human. He looked at her lying there, the blanket covering her chest rising and falling with each breath. Okay, make that damn human.

She lifted her lashes, and he found that her eyes had changed again. Now she looked younger than his earliest estimate. Maybe it was the hint of shy in her eyes, as if she'd never woken up with a man before.

"Good morning."

Her voice was husky, and he could tell she didn't quite know what to do. Or, maybe she couldn't move. He'd had the odd injury stiffen up on him.

"How do you feel?"

"Like . . . road kill." But she smiled as she said it.

Her smile stole the breath from his lungs and most of his wits. He smiled back and knew his expression was stunned and probably stupid looking, but the connection between his brain and his mouth seemed to be temporarily out of order.

"Can I get you something to drink?" he managed.

"What I'd really like is to get from here to there." She indicated the bathroom with her eyes, most likely the only part of her that didn't hurt.

"I can help you up, but it's still going to hurt."

"Yeah, I know."

When she didn't move, it occurred to him that she probably didn't want an audience. "I'll go rustle up some grub."

After a detour to the bathroom to make sure she had water

for the commode and washing, Luke headed for the kitchen. He braced for expected sounds of distress and pain, but there were none. After a time, he saw her pass by the doorway in tiny but determined steps. She may not know her own name, but the girl had guts. A hot bath would have helped, but there'd be no hot water with the power out. They had some liniment somewhere, but he wasn't going to offer to rub her down. A good woodsman knew when not to add kindling to a fire.

Thanks to a gas stove, he had a decent spread for breakfast ready to eat when she emerged from the bathroom after a period filled with the typical sounds of splashing and flushing. Good, she'd figured out what the bucket of water was for. He looked up, relieved.

"Bad?" he asked, noting that she was moving easier, but with a look of concentration on her face.

"Only when I breathe." Her smile was brief but impish as she lowered herself into a chair. She surveyed the eggs, bacon and toast with surprise. "This looks good."

"It won't disappoint," Luke said with mock seriousness. "My mom taught me that food should taste as good as it looks."

"My compliments to your mom."

Luke noticed she was using her right hand this morning. "How's the wrist? And the arm? And the head?"

"The edema is down in the wrist. The arm feels like someone set it on fire. And my head feels like the pendulum part of a bell going ding dong." Despite her aches, pains and lack of memory, Goldie still felt an odd contentment. Luke was excellent company, and it had been fun last night. She felt embarrassed at how she'd abruptly fallen asleep and it still bugged her that she could apparently recall an almost endless array of useless trivia, but seemed to know little about popular music.

What she felt like, since feelings were all she had for clues, were three different people. There was the one who was scared, not just of losing her memory but of the danger she felt lurking inside the fog blanketing her memory. Someone had shot at her, as amazing and unbelievable as that seemed from her admittedly limited perspective. The next person was the one who felt freed from a burden she couldn't remember. Inside the fog, not far from the fear, was a murmur of criticism, a voice that shot orders at her in a continuous stream. It was growing weaker and she was glad of it. It felt good to throw off the constraints of the voice. To feel more free, and well, not so prim and so worried about correct and proper behavior. Then there was this, well, *woman*. She couldn't know for sure, but it felt new to feel like this. To be so aware of what was feminine about herself as Luke jumped up to refill her cup of hot chocolate—which she found her taste buds preferred to the coffee of last night. To be so aware of what was masculine about Luke.

It was a pleasure to look at him, though she was careful not to let him catch her at it. She liked the way his hair lay back from his face, exposing its planes and angles. His eyes fascinated her, too. Had she ever studied a man's eyes? Had she ever considered all the colors and the constantly shifting emotions? She'd seen them warm, seen them turn cool and wary, seen them grow dark and dangerous. He wasn't a man to cross, but she felt in her aching bones that he was a man she could trust.

She wished she could feel the same about herself. Could she trust herself? She hovered next to the fog, trying to peer into it, even as she longed to leave it undisturbed. Sometimes people didn't recover from amnesia. Maybe she should accept it as a gift and let the sleeping past lie?

Breakfast done, Luke told her to the leave the dishes for him and braved the cold bucket wash. Part of her wanted to take him at his word, while some part of her felt that to walk away would be a betrayal of . . . someone. It also felt rude to let him do all the work, so she struck a compromise with her selves. She washed, using some of the water he'd pumped and put to heat on the stove, but didn't dry.

Their confinement was so intimate, cozy and comfortable. So very domestic. Luke in the bathroom. She in the kitchen. Almost *sans* shoes, since Snoopy slippers hardly counted. It was also natural, she told herself, to cling to this present, since she had no past. What she felt right now was as fleeting as the situation. Like a patient with a crush on her doctor. Not that she had a crush on him. She was enjoying being with him. That's all.

The last pan washed, she pulled the plug on the sink and watched the water drain away from her hands. Soap bubbles dotted her arms as she swirled the water against the sides of the sink. As the moisture on her arms slowly dried, the tiny, transparent soap bubbles popped one by one. It seemed sort of symbolic, though if she'd had to put into words why, she couldn't have. She pumped water into the sink, enjoying the jump into the past and rinsed the remaining bubbles—and any symbolism—down the drain.

Feeling restless, she went into the main room but couldn't settle down. Her discarded clothes lay tossed across the chair. Her boots under it. She had an urge to straighten, but a stronger surge of rebellion swept it away.

A long, gray case on the rough-hewn coffee table caught her eye. Next to it was a set of keys on a Harry Potter key chain. She picked it up, because snooping suited her mood better than playing maid. The minatory voice squawked in shock. Goldie stuck her tongue out at the voice.

"Harry Potter." The books had been fun to read. She could remember the plot of all of them. How come she could remember his name and story, but not her own?

Who am I? A cosmic question in search of a personal answer. Intriguing juxtaposition. The big versus the small, unless you believed man to be the center of the universe, which she may or may not.

Nestled within the cosmic, the search for personal identity. Bits and pieces of identity theory drifted around in her head, like birds pecking at scattered seed. Nature versus nurture. Ids and egos. Optimists and pessimists. Interesting, but not terribly productive, since she had no research material. Most of the theories depended, at least to some extent, on a study, or at least awareness, of a past life.

Which brought her back to the second question of day— how the hell did she know all this? She couldn't seem to spontaneously produce information. If she tried to remember something, it stayed just out of her reach. However, if triggered, she could riff along an information trail at an amazing rate. She'd certainly had a large store of odd knowledge last night while playing trivia. Knowledge that crossed back and forth between the liberal arts and the sciences. It didn't give her many clues, other than the possibility she was an encyclopedia in her other life.

She dropped the keys back on the table with a slight sigh and picked up the gray case. It stirred up nothing but a feeling that she had an aversion to gray. To her surprise, though, her fingers slid across the cool surface as if they belonged there— or they'd been there before? Did this belong to her? As if in answer, her fingers found the lid and popped it up. It looked like a small computer with a miniature keyboard. She turned it over and found the power button. The small screen flickered, then resolved itself into a password prompt.

"Great."

"That's as far as I got, too," Luke said.

Goldie started. She hadn't heard him come out of the bathroom. She turned to find him standing with his feet planted, his hands in the pockets of a fresh pair of jeans that hugged him like they needed him to survive. He'd pulled on a navy blue sweater that clung to his chest and arms. It seemed to like him a lot, too, and did wonderful things for his skin and eyes. His hair was still wet. The dark strands clinging to the bold shape of his head had a bit of natural curl when wet.

He walked up next to her and added, "I found it in your jacket. Ring any bells?"

Was there a hint of suspicion or skepticism in his voice? Since she couldn't admit she thought it was his and was snooping, Goldie shrugged. "My fingers seem to remember it, but my brain is proving recalcitrant." She shut it off and closed it with a loud snap. "I don't suppose you have something here I could change into? I promise to be very easy to please."

"Upstairs. Both my sisters-in-law have clothes here. Help yourself." He stepped back. "Let me heat some more water, and you can take a sponge bath. The water is . . . chilly."

Goldie shot a wry look in the direction of the windows. "I can only imagine."

It felt good to wash, even in a pot. The clothes fit pretty well, though the jeans were a tad short. Did that mean her legs were rather long or the sister-in-law's legs were rather short? The sweater felt wonderfully soft and warm, once she'd navigated her bandaged arm into the sleeve. When she rejoined Luke, she found him eyeing his beeper like it had just snapped at him.

"Trouble?"

"My brother Matt. I knew I should have called my mom last night." His mom wouldn't tell him off, but his brother would. He'd bet money his mom had called Matt to see if he'd heard anything. He dug through his stuff until he found his phone. He didn't remember shutting it off, but he must have. He turned it on and when it was ready, started to punch in the numbers, but stopped. "Damn, I started thinking about it, and now I can't remember the number. She had the number changed last week, after she got some obscene phone calls."

Started thinking about it. Goldie watched him close his eyes, try the number again, and then stop with a disgusted sigh. "It's no good. I'm trying too hard to remember."

She looked at the PDA, then back at him. Saw his gaze refocus on her, then sharpen as his thoughts began to track with hers. He set the phone down and grabbed the PDA. "It's worth a try. Try not to think about it at all, let your thoughts drift . . ."

He opened it, then handed it to her. "Just keep looking at me."

It was easy to look at him. Her eyes liked it a bit too much, and she was afraid they were showing it to him. Dang body language. Soon she'll be tossing her hair and leaning in to him like at teenager with her first crush.

"Don't look down," Luke said.

He made it easy for her by catching her gaze with his and holding it in a way that was almost physical.

"Don't think about anything but me."

Well, since he told her to . . . she upped the level of her scrutiny, finding a tiny cleft in his chin that she'd somehow missed before. A tiny scar above his right brow . . . a heat in his eyes that warmed her insides nicely. Beneath the surface, she felt the bubble of desire waiting to flare, sensed that he was a passionate man who had put passion on hold for some reason. That he was able to do this told her was a man with a great deal of self-control.

There came that urge to lean in again, to feel the warmth, maybe stir it up into a flame to fill the blank places inside herself.

In odd contrast, the surface of the PDA felt cool and impersonal where she gripped it, as the temperature in her body spiraled up her middle like smoke up a chimney. Distantly, she powered it up again. Her gaze started to turn down, but Luke called it back with a soft, "Keep looking at me."

She was going to do more than look. Her body felt languid and inclined to lean his way. And even more inclined to linger. For the first time since she opened her eyes, her aches and pains faded to a dull murmur, while her body turned warm and fluid.

As if he knew it, felt it, too, Luke reached out and brushed a strand of her hair off her face, the brush of his knuckles against her cheek light but tingle inducing. Her lips caught the tingle and parted before she could stop them.

"Now," he said, softly.

It felt like a glider being cut lose as she broke contact and looked at the keyboard. Her hands were already there, in proper position to type. Since they seemed to know what to do better than her, she watched with a sense of detachment as they tapped five keys in slow succession. She took a deep breath, trying to clear the constriction in her chest, then pushed "enter."

The screen flickered to life.

"We're in," she said.

"Any word?" O'Rourke asked. O'Rourke was a thin, wiry Irishman and Grady's second-in-command. If he'd led the sortie, Prudence Knight would be secured in a remote cabin as planned, but Grady had wanted to limit the camp's—and his—exposure by using Larry, an independent contractor.

Grady O'Brien turned from the window, his body burly but graceful, his coloring out-of-control Irish. The prospect outside was not encouraging, as the wind and snow were still a thick, impenetrable curtain, despite a sun that was out there somewhere. No sign of what was usually a bustling, rustic-looking camp, with its rough log housing laid out in military style against the hillside. Grady was careful to keep operations straightforward, open to scrutiny by federal agents who regularly tried to infiltrate them, though there were areas on the land they owned that were not for public scrutiny. His covert, illegal operation was hidden in this area.

Inside it was more pleasing, though still a place with an air of military discipline. The furniture was big and rustic, but comfortable, too. Grady didn't see any reason why he shouldn't be half as comfortable as Leslie. If needed, blackout blinds could cover the windows and special stealth insulation in the attics of some of his cabins protected their heat signatures from the infrared satellites that regularly passed overhead.

Man could plan, but Mother Nature was impervious to the grandest of stratagems, he knew. On the upside, the storm was keeping Leslie away. The guy had no "off" switch on his mouth and since he liked to sound like an idiot, most of what he said made Grady want to slap him silly. Or blow his head off. He'd almost done him during their cross-country trek from Yale, but even then Grady had the ability to see beyond the moment and the emotion. Leslie had money and access to people with money. At the time, Grady had needed that access more than he needed peace and quiet.

Beneath Grady's semi-pleasant exterior was a man who

was both brilliant and highly disciplined. He possessed an innate ability to convince people that they were important and interesting to him. Like many brilliant people, he believed he knew better than anyone else, and that his superior intelligence gave him the right to make decisions for other people—even life and death ones.

When Grady met Leslie, he'd realized Leslie was a man in search of a cause—to piss off his old man. Les didn't give two hoots about the plight of woodland creatures and the environment. Like most fanatics who wanted to do someone dirt, he needed to feel virtuous while doing it. Since his dad was an "evil" businessman bent on destroying the environment, it was easy for Les to find his "cause." With a little nudge from Grady, of course. Grady didn't think the environment needed help. It had done pretty well at taking care of itself for millions of years. But if people thought it needed saving, they were more inclined to donate money. His real cause—himself—required lots of money, but was, surprise, far less popular than the environment.

As far back as he could remember, he'd known he wanted lots of money. Enough to be listed among the top ten millionaires in the world. Enough money to make God sit up and take notice of him.

He'd made progress. He'd skimmed from the money Les donated for the cause. More came from using the camp to train terrorists in an underground area that even Les didn't know about. Grady didn't care who the terrorists hated, as long as their money was good. But the big score, the one that would put him on the rich list, had eluded him—until Les had arrived full of his big plan to finish off dad and score one for nature.

As soon as Les told him about the experiments with the ultimate body armor and that Les wanted to destroy it and everyone associated with it, Grady knew he'd found his personal mother lode. There wasn't a government, drug cartel or terrorist group on earth that wouldn't pay dearly for it. He was still trying to decide whether to sell an exclusive or just start selling. Either way, everyone would win. Hell, he'd even sell it to his own government if they'd cough up the bucks. Though they might be a tad pissed, since they'd already paid for its development. That wouldn't stop them from ponying up again, though—not if they wanted to be "competitive" with other world powers.

By the time the dust settled, Grady would be in the undisputed top spot for richest man on earth. He might even own a couple of countries.

Grady hadn't mentioned to Les the sidelines he'd added to the camp's activities. Les wouldn't like finding out that Grady didn't give a rat's ass if technology took over every piece of green space there was—as long as he got lots and lots of money. He was willing to let Les go forward with his plans—to a point. No way he'd let him kill the goose that could lay his golden egg. But his plans would create enough confusion for his discreet withdrawal to a country with no extradition treaty with the US. It hadn't hurt Marc Rich any to be an expatriate, and maybe he could buy himself a pardon, too.

He could have it all once he had his hands on Prudence Knight. It had been a year of setbacks. Phagan had delivered the promised foolproof bypass of Merryweather Biotech's security—for all the good it had done them when they went in. Who'd have thought the old man would be so paranoid about the technology that he was using to create the body armor? No vaults, safes or computer filing for this bird. Oh no, he kept it all in his daughter's head. His men had left the lab untouched, with no trace of their passing. Grady had cursed his luck, then regrouped and come up with a new plan. A better plan.

Prudence was her old man's weak link. His quiet, unobtrusive little weak link.

From the carefully rustic desktop, he picked up a couple of the photographs his man had lifted from Kincaid's apartment. One was a standard ID photo and told him nothing, but the other, a candid of Prudence Knight, was far more interesting. Her hair, her clothes were not that different from the ID shot. It was her eyes that had changed. They were excited, filled with anticipation, and her mouth curved into a sly smile, as if she had a secret. Interesting that she'd also be the key to controlling Kincaid. She was doubly valuable—and he had used this to convince Leslie they needed her alive. He was looking forward to meeting her. If Mother Nature could be persuaded to move her rampage further east. In the meantime . . .

"Anything from Phagan?"

O'Rourke shook his head. "Nothing yet." He hesitated, then asked, "Why do you want to risk a meeting with him?"

"If he's not with me, he's against me." Grady turned around. "And I'd like to know why he wants to meet me."

"Does he? Seemed to me like he didn't want to meet you."

"Exactly."

"I see. He should want to meet you."

O'Rourke was slow, but he got there eventually. If Grady laid the clues out in front of him and then explained them. It would be a pleasure if Phagan had a brain almost equal to his own. Be nice to meet someone not his intellectual inferior. He was pretty sure he was going to have to kill him, but he'd still like to bump brains with him.

"Well, so far he isn't biting."

"No, he isn't, is he?" It was always possible that Phagan

didn't want to meet him. Not just pretending he didn't. But that wasn't what his gut was telling him. What was holding him back? Phagan had been clever at hiding his tracks, but the FBI was still after him. Did he know something Grady didn't? It was hard to believe that Phagan was cleverer than he. If he was, though the thought still boggled, Phagan had to be with him. If he was against him, well, he'd have to be eliminated.

Chapter Five

Goldie stared at the neat row of mini-Windows icons pitted against the huge void of her foggy gray cells. It wasn't a fair fight. Or maybe she didn't want to blot the empty landscape inside her head with personal facts. She felt more painter than scientist or researcher, with an empty palate to do with as she pleased. She wanted paints in vivid colors that she could splash on with abandon, not tiny icons waiting for a keystroke. It was so tidy, so controlled. It didn't seem like *her*, even though she didn't know who or what *her* was.

"Do you believe in nurture or nature?" she asked Luke, her fingers resting on the plastic keys that had warmed from her touch. If nurture had been wiped out, did that leave only nature or did nurture linger in the unconscious and wield a hidden power? Is that why she felt pulled two ways? Was her nurture in conflict with her nature? Had it always been? Is that how she'd ended up here with her memory wiped out? Is that why she felt like she'd been at this place before, wondering who she was?

If it frustrated him to wait on her caprice, there was no sign of it in his voice or eyes.

"I don't know. I guess a little of both." He frowned a little, his gaze turning distant. "I do think people make choices that go against their nurturing, good and bad ones. I've seen people out of good families screw up unbelievably and seen kids you'd never give odds on, turn out fine."

He reached for his wallet, extracted a picture and handed it to her. She took it, not sure what this had to do with her question. Happy to delay opening the first piece of the puzzle of her life. The snap was a happy one. The couple filled the small picture. She wore white, he a tux. They could have topped a cake.

"My brother's wedding last year." He paused, then said, "I helped him arrest his wife, Phoebe, a month before the wedding."

Goldie stared at him. "I guess that's one way to get a wife."

Luke chuckled. "Jake's way, anyhow."

"Are you—" she stopped. Funny she hadn't thought of this before. She'd just assumed he wasn't married.

His smile didn't disappear, but it shadowed. "I was. My wife died a few years ago."

"That's why you're here, isn't it?" Goldie didn't know how she knew. That also explained the tamped down passion.

"I didn't come here to brood, Goldie. Life has its ups and downs, as my three favorite women will tell you—all of who've faced some pretty tough situations. Something happened to you, something traumatic enough to wipe your hard drive. There's not much either of us knows about you, but I'll tell you what we do know."

"What?"

"You've got guts. And determination."

"How could you know that?"

"Because you're not dead." He covered her hands, still holding the photo. Strength flowed from him.

"Those ladies would also tell you, if they were here, that life's not something you can hide from. Not even inside your own head." He looked around him, his eyes both distant and warm. "This is a good place to heal what ails you. A safe place. And for the moment, a place where no one can get to you."

The slow bloom of her smile took his breath away. Her shoulders straightened. Her chin rose. Her mouth straightened into a firm line. Her eyes, her amazing purple eyes, thanked him, then turned down to the PDA.

"Looks like it runs on Mini-Win. Let's take a look at the programs it's running." She picked up the PDA again, popped up the list and studied it. Luke moved next to her, so he could see over her shoulder. "This looks interesting."

"What is it?"

"Looks like some kind of e-book reader. Here's the book list." She looked at him with delight. "I read romance novels."

Luke arched a brow. "Most women hide it like a secret addiction."

"Do they? Maybe I do, too. It's just that—"

When she didn't finish her sentence, Luke prompted her, "That?"

"I keep hearing this distant, priggish voice in my head telling me to keep my knees together and act like a lady. I was afraid it was mine. Nice to find evidence it isn't." She brought up one of the books. "Oh, it's a Dani Gwynne! And there's a Kelly Kerwin, too."

"E-books. I didn't know Dani was so cutting edge," Luke said.

"You know her?"

"She's my other brother's wife," he admitted. "The one that isn't on probation. I'll introduce her to you when we get out of here."

"Then I'd better find out what name to tell her." Goldie tapped more keys and an expense account program appeared on the screen. While interesting, it didn't tell them her name. "I just remembered something." Goldie frowned. "On a regular computer, a program asks for registration information as it loads. You always give your name."

"Yeah, I know that," Luke said, trying to breathe more shallowly, so he wouldn't inhale her personal scent mixed with the soap she'd washed with. He was failing miserably, of course. It was as if his lungs had a mind of their own and had chosen slow and deep for maximum smelling.

"I wonder if it's the same for something like this?"

Did she realize, Luke wondered, how comfortable she was with the PDA? She clearly knew her way around a computer. In some ways, she reminded him of Phoebe. Even on the little keyboard, her fingers moved almost faster than he could follow.

He liked her hands. The fingers were long, like her legs, tapering to competent tips. In his mind's eye, he could see her fingers intertwined with his. Knew that her hand would feel right nestled in his—even though it wasn't right. For a second he felt angry with Rosemary for leaving him alone, for leaving him to cope with feelings like this about anyone but her. Gut-twisting guilt followed on the heels of anger. He was used to it. It had been his most persistent companion since Rosemary died. It rose in crest, then subsided to a dull grumble.

He felt her stiffen, was close enough to her to feel the shudder that went through her, to hear a soft sigh slip out her parted lips.

She sagged back against him. It was natural, inevitable even, to put his arm around her. The weight of her body started a slow heat building from his mid-section. It had been so long since he'd had a woman in his arms. Felt a woman's body heavy against his. His heart started to pound slow and deep, the rhythm an ancient and pagan one as old as man and woman. He tried to tell himself he was feeling fatherly, or like a protective big brother, but the simmer of attraction made a liar out of him. Goldie wasn't his sister or his daughter. She

77

was an attractive, desirable, very confused woman.

He gave himself a mental shake to clear his head. If he kept reminding himself how confused she was, he might survive without embarrassing them both.

"Did you . . ." He paused to clear the huskiness from his voice. "Did you find something?"

"My name." She swallowed, the sound dry in the intense silence of the cabin. "My name is Amelia. Amelia E. Hart."

"Amelia." It would take time to get used to. She was so . . . Goldie to him. "Amelia E. Hart. Almost like the pilot. Is there an address?"

"An apartment. In Denver." She toggled the screen back to the expense report. "I'm guessing, but these look like expenses related to the apartment. Electricity. Water."

"Phone?"

She paged through the list. "No. No phone."

"Maybe you use a cell phone," Luke suggested.

"If I do, I'm not recording it here. No phone at all."

Luke grinned. "Maybe you didn't pay the bill, and it got shut off."

She chuckled. "A deadbeat. No wonder I wanted to forget my life."

"Anything else?"

"Well, I don't seem to have bank information on this thing, but that might be in the apartment. And it looks like I like to play Solitaire and Mahjong."

"That would make you normal," Luke said with a strained grin.

She looked up at him, her nose less than an inch from his. Worse, the movement had put her mouth closer than that to his. He could feel the soft tickle of her breath against his skin, smell the mint toothpaste that was kept in the bathroom. Her eyes were purple, but within the iris were endless variations and shades. She was close enough for him to know when her heart sped up to match his. To feel when her breathing stopped, then started slow and deep. She inhaled when he exhaled, their bodies pressed together for an endless moment. The retreat was far too brief.

His fingers spread across her back and a tiny gasp escaped from her mouth, parting her lips for contact. He started to bend toward her and felt her back arch toward him. A light brush against the satin surface parted her lips a bit more. Everything faded but the need to taste, to explore her silken, female mouth—

The shrill summons of his cell phone blasted them apart like a bomb detonating.

Luke stared at her, but couldn't think of a thing to say, except, I'm sorry, which he wasn't. Well, he *was* sorry for the interruption.

"It might be your mother."

Goldie—no, Amelia, he reminded himself—looked as dazed as he felt.

"Right." He rubbed his face, then eyed the ringing phone like it might bite him. He picked it up, cleared his throat and pressed the button.

"Kirby."

Amelia studied him, feeling a bubble of laughter trying to sneak out her closed lips. Lips that still tingled from the light contact of his mouth. She realized her toes were curled up and straightened them. Her thoughts weren't so easy to straighten. For all she knew, this was her first kiss. With a man she hadn't even known for twenty-four hours. It felt good, but it wasn't. There was too much about herself, about her life, that she didn't know.

Luke had been right that she couldn't run from her past,

not even inside her own head. And she couldn't start a future, or even an interlude, with anyone until she'd sorted it all out. What she was feeling may feel real, but it wasn't. It couldn't be. Real feelings evolved from knowledge, from long association, not from proximity and isolation.

Besides, any intimate involvement would hardly be pleasant right now, with her many bumps and bangs. Though it showed how powerful the proximity of Luke was, that'd she'd forgotten it during that very heady brush of lips.

Thank goodness for self-consciousness, she decided, as she tried to clear the languid, heavy desire from her system before Luke got off the phone without diving head first into a snow bank. It helped that his mother appeared to be chewing his butt. Laughter was a good antidote for desire.

He turned his back on her, his shoulders hunching, and she swallowed another giggle. It seemed polite to pretend she wasn't listening, so she turned back to the PDA, studying the address it had coughed up. Almost immediately she could see a city map in her head, the address circled in red and not far from the university. Odd that it was a map she saw and not streets and buildings. It was as if her brain refused to be personal.

Little bits of Denver trivia floated out of her brain. Mile-high city. Home of the Broncos, Rockies and the Stanley Cup-winning Avalanche. She could see the winning game, but she couldn't *see* the city itself, had no sense of having ever been there. She pushed harder at the fog and was rewarded with a sharp, stabbing pain and backed off fast. It seemed her amnesia had rules that must be followed. She rubbed her aching temple. Pretty bad when your own brain was against you.

Behind her, Luke finished his call without, she noticed, mentioning her. She could feel him watching her. She heard his measured tread against the wooden floor coming toward her, and her heart sped up. Heat built up in her middle again, but she stamped it out as she turned to face him with a bright, bland smile.

"That was my mom," he said, his eyes blank, his voice forced.

"Oh." Amelia hesitated, then asked, "She okay?" She couldn't look away from him, though part of her felt she should.

Luke nodded. "I didn't mention you because, well . . ."

"I know. I'm kind of hard to explain." For the first time she saw past the moment, the now. She saw a future without him and felt a chill. And fear. It's just because he's all you know right now, she told herself. But she didn't believe it. Her life had been turned upside down. She'd been changed, and she'd never be the same again. With an effort, she turned away from him, getting up to stare out the window. "Looks like the storm is breaking up."

"It does?"

The low blanket of clouds—cumulus congestus?—had been a thick, gray blanket, but it would be breaking up soon or at least moving off. She looked at them, wondering what else she knew. "The wind is shifting from northeast to north-west and already starting to fall off."

"It's interesting what you know and what you don't," Luke said, the curiosity in his voice creating a different, but attractive timber. "Interested in doing some word associations? It might prod your brain."

So he wanted some distance, too. She should feel relieved she wasn't going to have to fight him off. She should.

"Sure. Why not?"

"You know what a word association is?" he asked.

Amelia thought about it. "You say a word and I say the

first thing that comes into my head?"

Luke nodded.

She passed up the couch and chose a chair across from him. On a side table next to it was a carabiner. Absently she picked it up, slid it down on her thumb and turned it slowly in a circle.

"Carabiner," Luke said.

"Rock climbing."

"Harrison Ford."

"Henry Ford's grandson?"

"He's an actor. *Star Wars.*"

"Missile defense system."

"No, he was Han Solo in *Star Wars*. The movie. Dani claims it's the myth for our generation. Or maybe she read someone who claims it's our myth." Luke's forehead creased as he tried to remember.

"A myth is a traditional story of ostensibly historical events that serves to unfold part of the world view of a people or explain a practice, belief or natural phenomenon. Or it's a popular belief or tradition that has grown up around something or someone. It can also be a person or thing having only an imaginary or unverifiable existence."

She realized Luke was giving her an odd look, but all he said was, "Star Wars would probably come under the last one, since it was made up."

"Oh."

There was a moment of silence, then Luke cleared his throat. "Movie."

"Motion picture." There was more, but Amelia felt odd saying it. No question the words sounded unnatural, but she couldn't seem to help it.

"So you know what a movie is?"

"Apparently."

"Cary Grant," he said.

"Actor. Very cute."

"Jim Carrey."

"Not a clue," she admitted.

"Katharine Hepburn."

"Loved Spencer Tracy."

"Brad Pitt."

"Um . . ."

Luke chuckled. "Okay, so you like older movies. Let's try this. *Breakfast at Tiffany's*."

"Audrey Hepburn. *Charade. Roman Holiday. Funny Face. Desk Set*." Amelia could see more names, but decided enough was enough. It felt so odd, having lists appear in her head. "To name a few."

"*Independence Day*."

"July Fourth."

"Not aliens blowing the hell out of the Statue of Liberty?"

"They did?" Her eyes grew so wide he almost fell in them.

"In the movie." Luke looked thoughtful. "I wonder if you watch television? *Third Rock from the Sun*?"

"Earth."

"I'm going to take that as a no." He thought for a minute, then said, "Let's try politics."

He took her through a list of names, state and national. She seemed to know names, but her own political convictions were out of reach. The fact that she winced at the mention of Bill Clinton was not particularly partisan. She knew the names of all the Presidents, in order, and recited enough of the Declaration of Independence to convince Luke she knew it all. She knew there'd been two world wars and knew dates and places from the War for Independence, but drew a blank on David Letterman and Jay Leno. She knew Leonardo da Vinci, but not Andy Warhol. Even worse, trying to figure out what she knew was pushing the boundaries of what he knew. He was pretty sure she knew how to split the atom and seemed to know a lot about the Big Bang theory and black holes. Also knew more than he did about biology.

Her beautiful eyes stared at him with the innocence of a child, while her mouth spouted facts and figures like a freaking computer. It was damn eerie. It was almost as if . . . no, he wasn't going to go there.

"Go where?" Amelia asked.

He'd spoken out loud. Great. "Anywhere. Are you tired? I know I am."

He stood up.

She stood up, too, her gaze opening him up like a laser.

"You were going to ask me something."

He opened his mouth to deny it, but she stopped him with, "Don't lie to me. Please. I *hate* lies."

She said this with enough intensity to startle them both.

Luke hesitated, then said slowly, "I was thinking the word . . . android."

"A robot in human form." Her gaze was thoughtful, even a bit amused. "Is that what you think I am?"

"No, of course not." He'd seen her bleed, for Pete's sake. Had felt her heart beat against his chest, her warm breath on his face, her mouth—

He turned away from her. If this storm didn't end soon, he was going to be in real trouble. Serious trouble. Deep, brown stuff up to his neck. Or higher.

"It would certainly explain some things, though not how I can bleed or urinate."

Luke turned back. "See, that's interesting."

"What?" She took a step back.

"The words you use. Urinate instead of pee."

"I'm . . . sorry."

84

Luke rubbed his face. "No, I'm sorry. I'm just saying you're kind of formal, almost scientific in the way you say some things. It's . . . it's a clue to who you are." Not a good clue, but a clue.

"Maybe I like to read the encyclopedia and don't get out much." She grinned at him, looking so many years younger than him that he felt like a pervert. She sobered immediately. "What's wrong?"

"I'm sorry about what happened. Almost kissing you, I mean." The words burst out of him.

"Why? We're both adults."

"Are we? You look about eighteen right now." He didn't mean to sound grumpy, but he couldn't help it. If the storm didn't break soon, he'd be doing time in a snow bank. That's when he realized the wind wasn't howling outside anymore. He'd been so intent on Amelia, he hadn't noticed the sun was breaking through the dark clouds moving slowly to the east. She knew her weather.

He saw her follow his gaze, saw her turn to look out the window.

"The storm's moving off," she said, her voice strangely expressionless.

She didn't add, "And taking our safe haven with it." She didn't have to. He could feel the fragile peace leave, feel foreboding settle in its place. Even now, the trouble that had taken Amelia's memory might be gathering itself for another try. He needed to get her to a place of safety.

"I should see if my truck will start." He found he was shifting from one foot to the other, like a high school kid asking for his first date. He started toward the door, then stopped.

"I'll gather up my things." For a minute she stared at him as her eyes turning old again as fear bloomed in their depths.

85

Then she turned away from him, her shoulders back, her head erect.

If she'd been older, he'd have fallen in love with her right then. He didn't. But if—

Chapter Six

Larry, a tough and intense man of Welsh ancestry, put the chopper in the air as soon as the wind died down enough to risk it. He'd noted their coordinates when the Knight woman had jumped out of the chopper and headed in that direction as directly as he dared. He still couldn't believe she'd done it. Gutsy. Stupid as hell, but damn gutsy. He'd freelanced for Grady long enough to see some pretty amazing things, but this took the prize. Of course it wouldn't mean jack to Grady if he came back without her, dead or alive.

It had been a lucky break for him when she came boiling out of the hospital as if she had a rocket up her ass. She'd been so upset, she hadn't been able to find her keys in her purse. Didn't hear him behind her. Didn't struggle long either, not after he stuck her in the neck with Grady's fancy knockout shit. He'd made sure they took her purse—which is all they had of her now, and he pretty much regretted it. Her beeper and cell phone hadn't shut up until he turned them off. He'd thought about having one of his guys drive off in the car but decided against it when a bunch of nurses came out the door. Who knew what a bunch of women might remember?

Only—Grady's shit should have lasted longer. Had he given her the full dose? He'd pulled the needle out when she went limp because she'd been lighter than he'd expected. Maybe her lights went out too quick? She'd been so gone, he hadn't bothered to tie her up. Grady'd kick his ass for that, but he'd been trying not to call attention to them. The bound and gagged tended to do that. And then he forgot when they got her on board the chopper, because once again they were trying not to be around long enough to attract attention and to beat the storm.

It surprised them all when she suddenly came to life. Gave Hickey a respectable and well aimed thrust to his nose that broke it and he fired his weapon inside the chopper. Not smart, but no harm except for another hole in the side. Got Bigsy in the balls with her hiking boot, then dived out the door before he got his wits about him. He'd had to leave Bigsy behind this morning. Couldn't trust him alone with the girl, if they did find her alive. He wanted to kill her or hurt her for putting his future children at risk. Bigsy was an optimist. Larry hoped he was right, that Hickey hadn't hit her.

Be a long shot if she was still breathing with the storm, but if she survived the fall, she might have managed to find one of the cabins that dotted the area. That's what he was hoping for. She'd fought to escape them, maybe she'd fight as hard for her life.

It had seemed like such an easy snatch-and-transport to the camp, but no, here he was, fighting the wind left behind by the east-moving storm, and trying to find a needle in a damn snow stack.

"We'll put down in that clearing and see if we can turn up her body!" he shouted to Hickey.

Hickey lowered the binoculars he was using to scan the area and nodded.

"This the spot where she went out?" he yelled.

"Dead on," Harry said, hoping he wasn't being prophetic. He pointed at a huge pine tree with several newly broken branches as they sped by it.

He circled the area, using the whirling blades to blow away some of the snow from the clearing and from the path they'd have to take back to the tree. Didn't want to dig through more than he had to. The snow fall had been heavy. In a moment, they were on the ground.

Larry checked his pockets for more of Grady's sleep shit, then grabbed a Luger and a long pole to prod the snow with. Outside the chopper, they both pulled on snowshoes and goggles. The sun was killer bright now that the storm was moving off. The snow looked like diamonds. Even with the path he'd cleared, it wasn't easy. Hickey puffed and cursed with each step.

"Grady wants her alive," Larry said, "but alive just means not dead. We can blame any bruising on her jump."

Hickey grunted in what might have been satisfaction. It was hard to tell. He was so winded, he was puffing like an old woman. So much for all their "training" at the camp.

Whey they reached the tree, they prodded all around it with their poles, but nothing felt right. Something glinted in the sun a few feet higher than Larry could reach. He climbed up and liberated the glasses she'd been wearing when she went out. Big, ugly square ones with cracked frames. Above his head he could see the broken branches that had slowed her fall through the tree. It might have slowed her fall enough to save her life. Just above his head, there was a brown smear on the trunk that could have been blood. He dropped to the ground.

"She was here for sure." He showed Hickey the glasses. "Let's spread out."

They checked a wide circle in both directions but the deep snow refused to give up any more clues to the girl's fate. Finally Hickey stopped, his chest heaving for a full minute before he managed to say, "This is shit. She's not here."

Larry nodded. "Let's head back to the chopper. Maybe she made it to one of those cabins."

The trip back to the chopper was marginally easier, since they could follow their own trail. Once inside, Larry adjusted his flight pattern, swinging south, then curving west in a tight loop. He gradually widened his flight path until he spotted the first cabin.

Luke pushed open the cabin door, bringing an icy blast of air with him. He'd stamped his feet on the mat outside, chunks of snow falling off his legs like mini avalanches, but remnants of white still clung to his jeans well above the knee. He'd managed to brush most of the snow off on his chest and arms, acquired while attempting to clear his windshield.

Amelia rose, turning to face him, her gaze dancing across him, before moving past him to the truck visible through the open door.

"Trouble?" she asked.

He closed the door. "Battery's too cold to start. I need a jump." If he'd been on his own, he'd have strapped on skis. It was only about ten miles as the crow flies to the highway, where the snowplows would be out.

"So we're stuck?" Her tone was neutral, giving no indication of how she felt about it. She'd been busy while he was outside. She'd not only gathered up her stuff, but everything he'd brought was packed and stacked neatly by the door.

"Well, I noticed a chopper in the distance. Was thinking I'd call and see if I could get patched in to the pilot, see if he'd pick us up—" He stopped when he saw the color drain from her face.

"I can't . . . not a helicopter."

"Afraid of heights, maybe?" he asked, remembering Dani, who's fear of heights had been severely tested on Long's Peak two years ago.

"I don't know." She dropped onto the arm of the couch,

90

her rapid, shallow breaths veering into the hyperventilation zone. "I just . . . feel so . . . I can't!"

Luke grabbed a sack out of one of the boxes, dumped the contents and knelt down in front of her. "Breathe into this."

The bag over her face, the color soon returned to her face. Finally she pushed it away. "I'm sorry."

"No problem." If it weren't for her injuries, he'd call one of his brothers and wait for help to arrive, but his gut told him they should move. He'd tell his gut to get real, except for the bullet graze across her arm. Whoever had shot at her could be near by. "There's an old sled in the wood shed. I could probably pull you out on it, but it would be damn cold."

"Why can't I just use a pair of those?" She pointed at the skis propped by the door.

"You can ski?"

She moved her feet like they had skis on and were testing the snow, her hands curling around imaginary poles. "I . . . think so."

He hesitated, frowning as he considered the risks. "It's about fifteen miles by the road to the highway, all of it down hill, but—"

"But what?"

"Well, your wrist for one thing."

She held it out, flexing it gingerly. "The swelling is down and the pain is manageable. The other wound feels better, too."

Right. And there was this bridge in New York for sale. He sighed. "If you have a concussion, this could be such a bad idea."

Her gaze met his. "You're as uneasy as I am, aren't you? About staying, I mean? I wanted to stay at first, but now . . . we need to go."

He knew she was right, but wasn't ready to admit it yet.

She looked fragile, so breakable as she sat in a ray of sun shining in through the window opposite. The scratches on her face and hands, the bruises turning to rainbows, all a pointed reminder that something had gone seriously awry.

"I can do this," she added. She smiled. "You said I was tough."

As if to nudge him into a decision, the thump-thump of the chopper grew steadily louder.

"All right. I'll find you some snow gear. In the front closet there's an emergency pack and an empty one. Make sure you gather up all your stuff," he finished. It would be best if no one knew she'd been here.

For a weighted moment her gaze met his, then she nodded.

Their orderly departure preparations gave way to a mutual sense of urgency. At the door, Luke handed Amelia, now wearing one of Dani's snow suits and a pair of Phoebe's boots, a small radio transceiver.

"Very cool," she said. "You just happened to have it around?"

Thanks to Dewey. "We use them to keep in touch when we're rock climbing or skiing."

"How hi-tech of you."

Luke grinned. Once he'd shown her how to use it, she inserted the ear piece and tucked the receiver in an inside pocket of the snow suit.

"Testing, testing," Amelia said, in a deep, mock-important voice. "We're moving into position now."

"Now we know you like playing spy," Luke said. "Ever read any Tom Clancy?"

"*Hunt for Red October?*"

"I'll take that as a yes." He pulled on the emergency pack, with two pairs of snow shoes strapped to it, just in case. She pulled on the spare pack with her few belongings tucked inside. "You sure you got everything?"

"I didn't bring that much with me."

Luke locked the door, then joined Amelia in the clearing. Despite her obvious worry, she smiled with delight as she moved her skis in the deep, white powder.

"The snow is perfect." She stopped, her brows arched in mischief. "At least, I think it is. Which way?"

He looked in the direction of the chopper. It had dropped out of sight for a while, but was now airborne again and heading their way. If it was looking for Amelia, they were going to be hard-pressed to lose it with the newly fallen snow taking an imprint of their every move. "Normally I'd take the road, but I think it's better to stay under cover. If they really want to track us, we're going to leave damn big tracks in the snow."

Her face had paled again, but she nodded and moved her skis like she was waiting for the judges signal to burst out of the slalom gate.

Had she raced? He didn't remember seeing her at any of the local events, but that didn't mean much, since he didn't make every one. Racing seemed at odds with her old fashioned formality. She pulled her goggles down over her eyes and gave him a thumbs up.

He pulled his down and said, "I'll take point."

He pushed off, feeling the familiar rush of excitement as his skis sliced through the deep, white powder across the clearing. Skiing fresh powder was a different experience from skiing the packed snow of a resort. It was slower going, and he had to keep his weight back, rather than leaning into the rush forward. But it was also more magical. The closest he could describe it was that it was like floating. His skis sank deep into the powder, while his lungs pulled the crisp, cold air into his lungs. He didn't know why it was so, but the combination of cold and movement sharpened all his senses. His eyes took it in—the images sharp, the color vivid. He heard and processed sounds, too. His skis slicing through the snow. Amelia following on his heels. The clatter of the chopper.

He took the shortest route toward cover, turning with a powerful swivel of the hips that lifted the skis up for the turn. They cut deep into the powder, turning him into the trees and heading straight down the mountain.

"You all right?" he asked. He couldn't risk even a quick look back. He wished he had a rear view mirror on his goggles.

"I'm great." She sounded like she meant it. Her voice was breathless, but he could also hear the same exhilaration he was feeling as the chopper sounded louder and closer.

"We'll try to avoid clearings, where our tracks will be more obvious," he said. Even as he talked, his mind was running ahead, trying to remember the last time he'd skied this way. The hazards, the best route—

"Can you jump?" he asked, suddenly remembering an unavoidable ledge about twenty meters ahead, unless they wanted to turn back toward the road, a lengthy detour from where they were now.

"No clue," Amelia said, cheerfully. "Let's assume I do and hope for the best."

He didn't know whether to laugh or cry, so he said, "Stay on my six . . ."

". . . and pray," she finished for him.

He turned to avoid a large boulder, the branches of a pine tree beating against his face as he passed by it. He burst into the clear and beyond it saw the drop. He had a heartbeat in which to change his center of gravity, and then he shot out into space, hanging in the air briefly before dropping toward the ground. He tried to balance his weight again, but one ski bounced over a rock buried in the snow. He wobbled, then went down, skidding sideways toward a tree.

Hickey saw the half-buried, half dug-out truck and the deep tracks heading into the trees before Larry. He grabbed his arm and pointed down. Larry nodded, turning the chopper toward the clear space beyond. The whirling blades blew the snow in all directions as they landed. This time, Hickey took the Uzi with him, though he concealed it inside his coat which he left hanging open, as they trotted toward the truck. The wind from the spinning blades whipped up the snow, but not enough they couldn't see that someone had tried to dig the truck out, then given up. The chopper blurred the ski tracks, but it didn't matter, since the tracks couldn't tell them who had made them.

They cautiously approached the front door. Two sets of tracks didn't mean someone hadn't been left behind. Hickey took up a position against the wall, Uzi still hidden, but quickly accessible, as Larry banged on the door.

No one answered so he tried the door. It was locked, but he had his pick out, and the door open before Hickey could suggest they kick it in. Supplies were stacked neatly by the front door, ready to be loaded in the stranded truck, but there was an air of emptiness about the cabin, the silence complete.

Still, it paid to be careful. Larry took point, his gun out, but barrel down as he moved into the living area. The fire was out and none of the lights worked, but the cabin didn't have that stale smell usually associated with being closed for a long time. The air was rich with the scent of the bacon and eggs someone had cooked for breakfast.

"Check all the rooms," he directed Hickey. "See if there's something to tell who was here." He didn't want to waste time tracking them down if Knight wasn't one of the two. Upstairs he found drawers rifled through, as if they'd left in a hurry, but nothing to tell who the cabin belonged to.

A shout from Hickey had him trotting back downstairs.

"I found this in the trash." He held up a tee shirt. One sleeve had been cut past the elbow, stopping at a jagged tear surrounded by a brown blood stain. "Told you I got her."

"They're heading for the highway. Let's see if we can cut them off."

Grady stared at the empty sky, a deep frown furrowing his brow. It had cleared up hours ago and still no word from Larry. News of Knight's death had rated a short mention on the morning news out of Denver. Leslie's dad must be shittin' a brick about now, he thought, with a grin. His top scientist dead, the research assistant missing. Unless she wasn't? She hadn't been mentioned on the news, either as the grieving or the missing daughter. No way to tell what that meant. No mention of the robbery yet either, though that wasn't too surprising. They'd counted on the confusion of Knight's death to disguise the theft of the SHIELD prototype for a few days. He planned to have the information out of Prudence and be out of the country before Merryweather, and Les, knew what had hit them.

He looked at the empty sky. Maybe radio silence had been a bad idea. Of course, there was another way to find out if Prudence Knight was missing. Donovan Kincaid would know. Maybe some judicious bluffing was a good idea right now. If his guys hadn't picked her up last night, then his call would tip Kincaid off that she was a target.

It wasn't like Larry to botch a job. Grady had sent his best man. Larry could have had engine trouble, or it might not have cleared where they were. Except his gut was telling him that something had gone wrong. But, how wrong?

He turned. If Larry had mucked it, it would be a major heads up to Kincaid and he'd already be on the alert. This wasn't the time to hesitate. He grabbed the phone, activated an anti-trace device, put an apparatus over the mouthpiece to disguise his voice and dialed Kincaid's number. It was answered on the first ring.

A good sign. So was the worry in his barked, "Kincaid."

"Lose something?"

"Where is she you bastard? You hurt one hair on her head—"

Bingo. Or, as Leslie liked to put it, check and possibly a mate. Now he needed to find out where Larry was. Unless—

A sudden thought put a cold chill down his back. Had Leslie found out his real plans and bought his guy? Leslie, who didn't need the money, wanted her dead, all traces of the technology destroyed. He'd only agreed to keep her alive to put pressure on Kincaid. Could he have diverted delivery somewhere else?

No, there'd been no sign of it in Les's voice the other night. Les couldn't hide his dark side from his good buddy, Grady. He'd have turned bi if Grady had asked him to. The hero worship was sickening, but useful. It would be a relief when he could end it.

Chapter Seven

Bryn had barely walked into the office when her cell phone and her desk phone rang at the same time. Hers wasn't the only phone getting a jump on the day. Everyone seemed to be either on the phone or answering one, the empty desks of last night a memory. She dropped her purse in a drawer, bumped it closed with her knee, then dumped the pile of messages and files the assistant had handed off to her on the top of her desk.

"Give me a royal break," she muttered. She grabbed the desk phone. "Hold, please." Pushed the hold button and answered the cell. "Bailey."

"Someone grabbed her. I just got the call from the bastard who has her," Donovan Kincaid said in her ear.

It took Bryn a minute to figure out who he was talking about, then her brain clicked in. "They make any demands?"

"Not yet. Just asked if I'd lost something and then hung up."

Not much to launch an investigation on. She did a little mental cussing. His voice was grim and strained. Clearly this wasn't just a job for him, but what was it? What was his interest in Prudence Knight?

"Hang on." She muted the cell and picked up the desk phone. "Bailey."

It was Matt. "I called Luke's contact in the coroner's office this morning. Knight died of unnatural causes. Looks like someone slipped him a digitalis Mickey. Did the girl turn up?"

"Kincaid's on my cell phone. Looks she was

grabbed." And I've got a headache. She rubbed one temple with her free hand. "Shit. I'm supposed to be on a flight to California in an hour with Dewey. I only came in to grab some files." She'd already packed. A swimsuit tucked guiltily in one pocket. The thought of some sun time was too appealing to resist when faced with the arctic view outside. "Hang on."

To Donovan she said, "I have information Knight was murdered."

"Son of a bitch. Did your source tell you Miss Knight is now the only person who can deliver Knight's research?"

"How can that be?"

"Knight was a weird old bird. Didn't trust computers or vaults. Kept all his research data in Miss Knight's head. She has a photographic memory. If they are after his work, all they need to do is dope her up and it's theirs." She heard him sigh. "I'm meeting with Merryweather in an hour. He's flying in from California now that the storm has cleared. He's got to do whatever it takes to get her back and I'm not sure he knows that. But he will. I gotta go pick him up at the airport."

"Kincaid, wait," Bryn was tired, but not so tired she couldn't see the huge flaw in his reasoning. "Why did they call you?"

"Merryweather's out of town—"

"Bullshit. They're looking to put pressure on *you*. Why?"

"I don't—"

"Liar." She sighed in frustration. "Damn it, Donovan. You came to me, remember? Be straight with me *now,* or I can't help you."

"Can't? Or won't?"

"Both." She paused, then said grimly, "I got someone waiting on the office line. Make up your mind or I'm hanging up."

She heard his growl. Donovan did not like to be pushed, but right now she didn't care. Too much was happening too fast for her to worry about protecting his love life.

"She's my daughter, okay? She's . . . my daughter."

No question it was a pop in the chops. She tried to gather her scattered thoughts.

"And they know?"

"I don't know how. Probably think she's my girlfriend. Like you did."

"Well . . . you're sure?"

"Not blood test sure, but she's the spitting image of my grandmother. And I knew her mother at the crucial time."

And all that really mattered was what he believed, she realized. "Are they after Knight's work or you, Donovan?"

"I don't know. But I'll do whatever I have to, Bailey. Whatever I have to do to get her back."

"Don't lose your head now, Donovan. You and I both know it's too late for that. Don't go down that road—"

But he'd hung up.

"Shit." She didn't realize she'd picked up the other phone until Matt spoke.

"How deep?"

"Deep. Real deep." She gave him the short version of what she'd just learned.

"Deep indeed. I wonder what they want him to do?"

Bryn felt a cold chill snake down her back. "Matt, he used to be a sniper."

"Damn. You gonna put someone on him?"

"For all the good it will do. If Donovan doesn't want to be followed, he doesn't get followed. Look, to be on the safe side, can you find out if anyone important is coming to town?"

"Will do."

"Thanks." She sighed again. "I'd better go. I've got to arrange a babysitter for Dewey." It was wrong to be disappointed about not getting to go with him. It was business, but business in the sun seemed so much more appealing than business in snow drifts.

"He'll love that," Matt said, before ringing off and leaving her with her thoughts.

She talked to the agent in charge, who agreed she had to hand Dewey Hyatt off and stay on top of the situation here in Denver. It didn't help that the only agent free to leave on such short notice was a cute little red-head who flirted with Dewey every time she passed by Bryn's office and found Dewey in.

Oh man, she wasn't feeling jealous, was she? Why should she? The best thing that could happen is for both Dewey and Phagan to find someone else and leave her the hell alone. She was glad Dewey was heading to warm, balmy California without her.

Really.

Leslie sat on the bed watching the news. Next to him, the woman lay face down, her face no longer the lovely alabaster that had attracted his attention as he drove by her street corner. Her clothes had been classier, though still more revealing, than her companions. She'd taken one look at his car, given him a quick advance preview of her breasts and jumped in the car when he thrust open the door.

She'd been adequate in the sack, but last night adequate hadn't been enough. As she labored to satisfy, he'd wrapped his hands around her neck. He'd taken his time, squeezing until the thrashing of her body slowed, easing up, then squeezing again, until she quit moving.

It was odd how easy it was to kill. Far easier than he'd

imagined. He didn't know why he hadn't waited. He felt better than he had in a long time—maybe since the first time his father had belittled him.

As if his thought had conjured up his father, his cell phone rang, the display showing his father's private number. He didn't really mind. It would be amusing to talk to his father while sitting next to a dead woman.

"Bob's Bar and Bordello," he said into the phone.

"How soon can you fly into Denver?" his father said, in that dead, but important tone he used with his son and other lesser beings.

"Why?"

"John Knight died last night. I believe you two were friends." He said the words but the tone of his voice said he didn't believe it.

The old man was no fool, though Leslie hoped to make him feel like one before he was finished with him. "I'll take off as soon as I find my pilot—"

"I already talked to him."

Leslie felt that familiar frustration rising, but one look at the woman he'd killed and it subsided. Bet the old man had never killed anyone. At least not a human. He'd managed to off plenty of animals.

"You can leave any time," his father went on.

Leslie fondled the woman's hand. "I have a few things to take care of first, but I'll be there as fast as I can. Thanks for letting me know, Dad—"

But his father had already hung up.

Leslie shrugged. He'd have to postpone his visit with Miss Prudence. Odd the old man hadn't mentioned her disappearance, but then he might not know that old Knight was using her for a storage cabinet. And how come Grady hadn't called? Had the snatch gone as planned? So many questions without answers, and no time to puzzle them out. He had a body to dispose of.

How did the average, yet brilliant, murderer get rid of the odd, dead body?

He heard a sound in the hall, padded to the door and looked out. The maid was cleaning the room next to his. On the floor by her cart were bundles for the laundry. It seemed fate was determined to deliver him a way out.

He waited until the maid went back in the room, then grabbed one of the sacks. As he started stuffing her into the sack, the news story he'd been waiting for aired. The only surprise was the death of the security guard. He stared at the television, until the anchor moved on, then looked at the woman, partially in the bag.

"Sorry, darling, I guess you weren't my first, but so far you're the most satisfying."

He was going to have to tell her, Dewey realized, staring down at his half-packed suitcase. Ever since he'd gotten the invitation to meet GREEN's leadership from his contact, he'd been trying to find a way around it, but even he couldn't be in two places at once. Face-to-face with the GREEN leader while wearing his electronic jewelry was not possible. It would be noticed, which would seriously mess with his mysterious and invincible image.

He'd examined the problem from every direction and had even asked Phoebe, his Pathphinder, on the QT—a direct violation of his parole and hers—if she could see another way. Her response had been incredulous to say the least.

"You've got to be kidding," she'd said. "Even I can't figure out how to make you into two people outside of VR."

It wasn't just this situation bringing it all to a messy head. He'd spent the last year trying to find the right way to tell

Bryn that he was Phagan. She was going to be so pissed. At him *and* Phoebe. The fact that Phoebe hadn't known but guessed right after they had gotten arrested wouldn't matter to her. Lucky for him that Jake had never asked Phoebe about Phagan. No way she'd give him up, though she threatened to when he pissed her off. Jake was smart. He knew what to ask and what not to. He knew there were things he didn't want to know. If only Bryn could be more like him.

Every time he got close to spilling his guts, he chickened out, mostly because he liked his head where it was. And he was afraid he'd never see her again.

He'd thought about not ever telling her. Phagan could disappear. But he didn't want her to think he was the kind of guy that would lead a girl on then just vanish without a word. She'd really hate him then.

Of course, she'd probably hate him and Phagan when she found out, he decided glumly, as he looked through his stuff for his swimsuit. He didn't have a lot to look through. His digs were a far cry from his usual when on the run. Spartan *and* middle class. He was sure Bryn had put him here on purpose.

He didn't mind, not when it gave him daily contact with Bryn, but it was hard to believe she'd want to share any of it with him. It was difficult to be optimistic about a happy outcome, despite hanging around Matt's romance writer. The trip to California would be a good chance for them to talk. She couldn't kill him in public, and he could sound her out first on where she was with Phagan. It felt damn odd to be your own competition. He'd even felt jealous of himself, which was weird. If his life ever approached normal, he wasn't sure he'd be able to handle it.

The phone rang. He knew it was her before he answered it. Her rings were always imperious and sort of royal.

"Hyatt's Megalomaniac Criminal Enterprise."

"Ha, ha."

"Miss Bailey?" It was so cute the way she insisted he call her that, as if the formality would keep things from getting personal. "Oops. I thought it was one of my criminal co-horts."

"I don't have time for crap, Hyatt." She hesitated, then said, "Someone else will be picking you up and . . . escorting you to California. Something has come up here that I have to deal with."

"Which someone?"

"That red-head, Carlotta something or other."

She was jealous. He could freaking hear it in her voice. This was too great. She didn't want him to go without her. She'd never admit it, of course. They'd be celebrating their fiftieth wedding anniversary, and she'd still be claiming she'd only married him to keep an eye on him.

"As charming as it would be to travel anywhere with Carlotta something or other," he said. "I can only go with you, Miss Bailey. I only belong to you, Miss Bailey."

"You only belong to the United States Government until your parole ends."

"Why don't you see if Phoebe can go? Or that Sebastian guy that does Matt's crap for him?"

"They asked for you."

"It's flattering, of course, that they think I'm the only one that can do this, but Phoebe's actually better at unraveling computer viruses than I am. Besides," Dewey took a deep breath and then took the first step into the abyss. As Phoebe was wont to point out, there was no going back, only forward. If he hadn't wanted it to come to this, he should have stayed out of GREEN's business. "I need to talk to you about Phagan. As soon as possible."

The silence was so long, he thought she'd either hung up on him or fainted.

"I'll see what I can do."

Then she rang off. With a loud enough snap to make him wince.

Phoebe kept telling him that love would find a way, but he had the feeling Bryn regularly kicked Cupid's butt. A world of women to fall in love with, and he had to fall for a Fed. He should kick Cupid's butt, too.

Amelia's wipe out hadn't been nearly as spectacular as Luke's, but it had taken her further down hill from him. By the time she'd collected her poles and skis again, she'd heard him shout her name from the tree he'd disappeared under. He'd lost his nifty radio headset, too. She hoped they weren't too expensive to replace, since she had no idea if she had any money.

"Down here!" she called. "You all right?"

"Fine. You stay there. I'll come to you."

She was happy to stay put. The snow came up around her waist. She'd practically had to swim through it to get her stuff gathered and was now clinging to the side of a boulder like the tide might sweep her away. She was pretty sure she couldn't swim uphill, but would have tried if he'd needed her.

The chopper had dropped out of sight again, but even as the thought formed in her head, she saw it rise above the tree line and start in their direction.

"Luke!"

"I hear it. Can you get under cover?"

She was only a few feet away from cover, but it was all deep-snow feet.

"Yeah!" No time to get her skis on, but maybe . . .

She maneuvered her skis around until they were parallel with the mountain and facing the trees. The chop-chop-chop sounded closer. Panic crawled through her head, but it seemed to sharpen her thinking. She worked her way onto the skis, turning them into a modified surfboard. A quick look over her shoulder. The chopper grew larger in the sky. They'd soon be close enough to see her. She grabbed her poles, tucked them under one arm, then dug her hands into the snow and slid forward. The chopper made a jog away from her, then swung back, flying directly toward her. She dug into the snow again and slid under the branches of a huge pine tree. As the branches brushed against her face, brief, painful flashes of memory sparked inside her head.

Branches slapped at her, clawed at her as she tried to grab them . . . but she kept falling . . .

"Amelia!" Luke's call pulled her back to the present. "Are you hidden? They're almost here!"

"Yeah!" The roar of the chopper drowned out anything else she might have said. Through the deep green of the branches, she watched the chopper sweep in, make a wide turn, and come back, hovering like some huge, ugly bug. She buried her face in the snow, tried to burrow her body in, too. Cold closed around her until it was all she could feel. It crept inside and wrapped around her heart, slowing it to a steady thud. Ice wrapped around her from the inside out and the outside in, freezing her in place.

The chopper hovered above, as if it could feel her fear. Out of the fog in her head, it reached for her. Or maybe it was hands that reached for her. Their touch hurt, the pain stabbing out from her eyes. A roar from the chopper popped her eyes open. The dark shadow it cast against the white of the snow moved persistently in her direction, kicking the snow into a mini-blizzard, preventing her from seeing who was in the chopper.

They were going to find her.

Amelia covered her ears, burrowing into the snow. Disjointed pictures in her head, like incomplete snapshots . . .

Shouts . . .

Shots . . .

Falling . . .

"Amelia?" Luke touched her shoulder, scattering the fragments of memory like waking from a dream. "They've moved off. I don't think they know what they are looking for. Thought sure they'd see our tracks."

She lifted her face from the snow, inhaling great gulps of air. It felt like she'd surfaced from someplace deep and dark. She ripped off her goggles, feeling a sudden claustrophobia and blinked in the bright light.

"Are you all right?" He'd had to slide under the tree on his stomach to reach her, his concerned face close to hers. He smelled good, like aftershave and pine and fresh air.

"I should be asking you that. That was a pretty spectacular landing," she said, trying for a light tone. Did pretty good at keeping it, too, except for those two little quavers when she lost control of her voice.

"I've had better." He grinned at her and ruefully touched the lump swelling on his right temple. "A couple more and we'll match."

An indescribable feeling of warm delight filled her up, starting from her middle and moving out until even the tips of her fingers tingled. It erased the chill that had invaded her and freed her from her frozen thrall.

If this is some kind of crush, she thought, I like it. Hardly aware of what she was doing but knowing she needed to do it, she leaned toward him. Her free hand curled around the sturdy column of his neck and she kissed him. That minatory voice in the fog gave a shocked squawk, but it couldn't compete with the pure pleasure of her mouth against Luke's.

He tasted as good as he smelled, though his mouth was very cold. It warmed up fast. Real fast. Despite her lack of memory for any comparison, she was, nevertheless, convinced it was the best kiss she'd ever participated in.

They both eased back at the same time, and Amelia felt the world rush into the warm space they'd created between them. The voice expressed shock at her unladylike behavior, but what did that matter when his brown eyes were close enough for her to see gold flecks in the brown? He smiled shakily and his gloved hand trembled just a bit as he reached out and tucked a strand of her hair back into her hood.

"Who are you, Amelia?" he asked, his voice husky.

She rolled onto her back, staring up through the branches at the sky. It was so deeply blue, the branches so green, her chest felt tight with pleasure. Did she often look at the sky or was she seeing it for the first time?

She was scared, no question about that, but despite it, she felt a wonderful sense of anticipation—as if she'd only been set loose in a world full of possibilities. That minatory voice in the fog was fading more and more with each passing moment. She felt alive, all her nerve endings singing like they'd just woke up from a long sleep. What defined a person? What gave them their identity? Who they were or who they'd been?

"What are you thinking?" Luke asked.

Amelia looked at him, found his eyes kind and curious. "That I'm happy to be alive. That I liked kissing you." He looked worried, making the sky slightly less blue. "Is there someone else?"

He shook his head. "Not since my wife died. It's just that—"

"What?"

"You're so young."

"We don't know how old I am," she pointed out. "I could just be well preserved."

He chuckled, but his eyes were still serious. "What if you're committed to someone?"

Amelia looked away from him. "It had occurred to me."

"And?"

She shrugged. She didn't know how to explain to him that all the feelings she could remember were about trying to get away from, not back to whatever her life had been. If she were committed to someone, wouldn't some part of her know it?

"The truth is, Amelia, you don't know who you are or what you want. And I'm not a man who can take things lightly."

Amelia looked at him then. "Are you telling me that you're a man who *wants* to commit?" Even with no memory, she knew that was rare.

His grin was wry. "Something like that." He sat up with a slight groan. "We'd better come up with a plan before our friends in the chopper come back."

Amelia watched him gather their gear together, her thoughts spinning inexorably to one, inescapable conclusion—Luke Kirby was a very nice guy. The fates had been kind to drop her in his lap. She must remember to thank them.

Grady turned from the window. He's been staring out it, but not seeing the snowy wasteland. He saw Paris. London. Cannes. Madrid. The world. It would all be his if the phone would just ring . . .

It did. The summons shrill and welcome. It didn't come by cell or radio, but on the land line.

"Turn on your scrambler," Larry said. His voice sounded resigned and discouraged in Grady's ear.

Without comment, Grady activated the scrambler, then listened while Larry updated him. When he was done, he knew Larry expected him to chew him a new butt hole, but there wasn't time for that. Not if he was going to save his world. He had the prototype of SHIELD in his possession already. His men from that job had arrived as the storm left. He fingered the supple, mesh-like fabric, amazed that it could stop anything, let alone a bullet. He'd have to conduct a test before he'd believe it, but in the meantime . . .

"I'm sending you some help," he said. "I want that highway covered tighter than a hooker's ass. Also the towns on either side. No telling which direction they'll head. You said there was blood? Put someone on the hospitals between Estes Park and Denver and have everyone use their police scanners. Monitor all activity. Also, get back to that cabin and get me the license plate number on the truck. If we miss them on the highway, they'll eventually head for Denver. If we have to, we'll take them before they get home. We can't let her get back to Kincaid. Our only chance is to take her on the road."

"I know. I'm sorry."

"Be sorry later. Get me Prudence Knight. And get rid of whoever she's with. We can't afford to leave witnesses behind."

He hung up quietly. Now was not the time to give into the rage and frustration trying to crawl out of his gut. This was his time, his big chance. She would be found. She would be found or people would die.

"Feeling better?" Luke asked.

"Yes, thank you." Amelia leaned back with a sigh, pushing the empty bowl away from her. The tortilla soup had been wonderfully hot and spicy, sending tendrils of warmth down into the chilliest spots of her aching anatomy. Anyone who said downhill was easy had never tried what they'd just done. Amelia had thought she'd identified all the muscles in her body, but this trip had found new ones. It was amazing that a body could hurt like this and still function. And the aches were mild compared to the fire in her wounded arm. She suspected it had started bleeding again. It was hard to be sure, but the creeping warmth in the midst of that fire sure felt like it.

When they'd reached this little town clinging to the edge of the highway, she'd wanted to weep with relief, but she was too tired. Amelia hadn't known she had it in her. Of course, she hadn't known she didn't have it in her either, which made it impossible for her to quit.

As tired as she was, her surroundings fascinated her. Luke had chosen a dark corner booth of the little restaurant for them, providing them with a view of all the tables and anyone entering or leaving. He'd done it for safety, but it was also entertaining. Couples had flowed in and out, some so familiar with the place they could ask for the usual. The others, strangers who looked at the plastic menus and flinched.

Some teenagers had boiled in and surrounded the juke box. Amelia didn't know who was singing, but she liked the song about the bug or the windshield. She knew which one she was right now. That song was followed by one about feeling lucky. She could feel her spirits lifting, despite the aches and pains her body persisted in reporting to her brain. Her feet started tapping, but a look at Luke convinced her he wasn't open to trying out the tiny square of dance floor in front of the fireplace with the moose rack over it. And after the other night she didn't blame him. She hadn't exactly demonstrated a talent for music, let alone an ability to dance.

112

The demands of her stomach satisfied, Amelia felt a pleasant lethargy stealing through her aching body. It went up and down and around, then added lead weights to her upper eye lids. Her eyes were dry and tired from the strain of seeing past glare to the trees and rocks dotting the mountainside. A yawn forced its way up her throat. When she tried to cover her mouth, her muscles protested painfully.

"Sorry."

"Fresh air makes me sleepy, too." Luke was quiet, a frown creasing the area between his dark, slashing brows. Amelia wanted to kiss him again, but she didn't think she could move. Or that he'd let her. "Why don't you stay here while I try to scare up some wheels? I'd like to reach Denver before dark."

Amelia nodded. Not moving was good. Sleeping would be even better. But when he was gone, she found that she couldn't sleep without him there. She felt too exposed, too vulnerable, even in her corner of the murky room where the only light came from an odd looking, three dimensional picture of a waterfall, which was between a mounted bear head and a velvet painting of dogs playing poker.

She had no idea what the guys after her looked like, so every time anyone came into the room, her adrenaline would spike, until whoever it was settled at a table away from her. It was a small town, she decided, maybe she could find Luke, but once outside on the street, a sign caught her attention.

Carol's Cut and Curl.

Had she always yearned for a haircut? She touched the thick braid of hair hidden by the hat she'd borrowed. The weight of it dragged her down and increased the throbbing on all three sides of her cranium.

Made her more identifiable, too.

113

If only she had some money . . .

Then she noticed a smaller notation in the corner of the window.

"We Pay Cash for Your Long Hair."

Chapter Eight

Bryn had refused to meet Dewey until dinner, legitimately citing piles of work to plow through, but now she regretted her attempt to not appear eager, when she was the one in torment. To make matters worse, she'd told him to stay home and work his way through the dummy corporations and find the actual person who'd bought the tranquilizer that killed the guard.

It was hardly a good use of his time. He'd probably finished it in an hour and was now playing some shoot 'em up computer game on the government's time. The other day she'd found him deep in it with a kid from Japan and a lawyer in New Orleans. When it became apparent the kid was whipping both their butts, Dewey had logged off with that half-impish, half-sheepish smile that turned her heart into something foreign in her chest. She didn't like thinking about it much, but when she did, she couldn't get away from knowing it was a soft, squishy feeling, almost . . . tender. She hadn't felt like this since sixth grade when she got her first kiss. Even now it grossed her out to think she'd swapped spit with a kid who grew up to be a mortician.

At some point, she'd realized that the men in her life weren't going to take her seriously. Ever. They wanted to kiss her on the mouth, maybe feel her up if they could get away with it. She wanted more. She'd always wanted more. Maybe that's why Phagan had made the inroads he had? He may or may not have been attracted by her body—who knew if he'd ever seen her in real time?—but he sparred with her *brain*. He teased her, drove her crazy, made her laugh . . . made her feel alive, right down to her toenails.

And Dewey? What did he intend to tell her? He'd said he needed to talk to her about Phagan. Did he mean he was going to tell her who Phagan was? Or was it personal? And if he was going to finally talk, why now? Was it because he felt personal?

She didn't want him to tell her, she realized. It was sobering to have to admit it because she was supposed to want to catch Phagan. It had been her primary goal for four years. And as Phoebe liked to point out, all God's children needed a goal.

She pushed back her chair and paced over to the coffee machine, dispensing a cup of hot black liquid that she didn't really want. It didn't help her escape realizing she didn't want Phagan in jail. It wasn't just that she'd miss hunting him. She'd miss . . . him.

She added sugar and cream, which she normally didn't add, just so she could stand there and think with her back to an office stuck in a middle-of-the day frenzy.

So where did that leave her and Dewey—besides *not* on the plane to California that was now carrying Jake and Phoebe toward the fun in the sun that should have been hers. He wasn't the handsome prince she'd imagined when she was little and still believed in Cinderella. He was kind of cute, in an annoying sort of way. He had nice eyes. And a nice mouth. And she liked the way his hair flopped on his forehead. It had sorely tried her self-control, not to smooth it back during the hours they worked together. Would his hair feel as soft as it looked?

Even now, with him not even close, the pads of her fingers tingled at the thought of touching not just his hair, but his skin, his face, his mouth. She rubbed her own mouth, which had parted in anticipation and sighed.

How could she feel this way about two men? Was she some kind of aberration?

Before she could answer that, the agent at the desk next to her called her name. When she turned, still holding her tasted coffee cup, he held up the phone.

Back at her desk, she said, "Thanks," then picked up the call. It was Matt.

"We need to talk."

"You can come up—" Bryn began, but he cut her off.

"It's lunchtime and I didn't get breakfast."

"I'll be right down." She hung up, opened a drawer, put in her worries and took out her purse. "I'll be back in an hour," she told the secretary.

Soon she was seated across from Matt at a restaurant a short walk away. The crisp, cool air had filled her lungs and swept away the remnants of her anxious thoughts, leaving behind only the longing. It was nuts, wasn't spring the time for a woman to have fancies? It was the freaking dead of winter.

She ordered, then turned to Matt. "What's up?"

"Had to call in a few favors, but I got us a name of a possible target." He took a sip of coffee then said, "Albert Gore, former vice president."

"What? He's coming here? I thought he was teaching somewhere in the East?"

"Fundraiser with some environmental types is on his agenda for this week. My source says some of those types have also planned a protest of Merryweather Biotech and a few other labs in the area who engage in animal testing."

"Really. Hang on a minute." She rang Dewey's number. When he answered she asked, "You find out who bought that tranq?"

A pause. A sigh. "Yeah. Trail eventually led to some guy

named Merryweather. Hamilton Merryweather. CEO of—”

“Merryweather Biotechnologies.”

“You want me to run him through the big mill and see what else falls out or do you have psychic powers now?”

“Run him. Thanks.” She hung up, trying not to smile about the brief contact. Time was, that kind of comment would have made her grind her teeth. She had changed.

Matt had that look he got, the one that was expressionless but menacing. “Merryweather would be stupid to use his own employee.”

“Yeah, or terribly clever. He has someone grab the girl, then it looks like someone else is applying pressure. Stupid to let the tranqs get traced back to himself, though. I wonder if he is stupid?”

“Could be stupid. Or a player we haven’t met yet.”

She knew Matt hated jumping to conclusions. He liked the facts, just the facts before he made up his mind. Usually she was the same, but something about this situation was making her edgy. Uneasy.

“You ever seen a Gordian knot?” she asked.

“Not for a couple of years,” he said. “You think someone’s trying to play you?”

“I think,” she grinned at him, “I’ll keep the scissors handy.”

Matt grinned back. “Smart girl.”

Luke had intended to talk to the local sheriff, but as he walked along the main drag, his gut started twitching like it had a condition. It had been pretty quiet when they arrived, stashing their skis behind a boulder for later collection. Now he noticed trucks of hunters parked at each end of town. And a set in front of the police station. Another watching the local truck stop. And yet another had the local motel staked out. All seriously packing.

They didn't seem to be doing anything in particular, but there was a watchfulness about them that tightened his gut. He strolled by one set and noticed that they had a police scanner inside the cab of their truck, the power light glowing.

Hell and damnation, he thought, what was he up against here? Who could be after Amelia? Who might unleash this much activity, this fast? And how the hell could they get out of town without being followed and stopped? No way his Glock would be enough against the firepower he could see waiting in all those gun racks.

He saw a pair of hunters enter the place he'd left Amelia. He should never have left her. These guys were hunting. He followed, trying not to look like he was in a hurry. Inside, it took a minute for his eyes to adjust to the light. His two guys were heading for the corner where he'd left Amelia, then they veered off and he could see the older couple sitting there, reading the menu.

She was gone.

He grabbed their waitress as she passed. "Did you see where my friend went?"

"She left not long after you did."

"Alone?" The waitress, her face puzzled and impatient, nodded. "Which direction did she go?"

"Sorry." She pulled away.

Luke went outside, looked one direction, then the other, feeling frustration spike in his gut. What was she thinking—

"Luke?"

It was Amelia's voice, but when he looked at her, she didn't look like the Amelia he'd left. Her hair was short, almost boy short and clinging to her head in fluffy little curls. The difference was amazing. Without the hair, the clean, classy shape of her bones was visible. She must have found some make-up, because her scratches were pale shadows under her skin. Her eyes were bigger and purpler. And her mouth was red and moist and slightly parted—

He gave himself a shake. This was not the time to lose his focus.

"Where you been?" He stopped. It was obvious where she'd been. Having her hair cut. He noticed the bags she was trying, but failing, to hide behind her back. "Shopping? You just went . . . shopping?"

Her smile was a delight and full of mischief. "And I enjoyed it. I was quite shocked at myself."

He swallowed a couple of times. "I thought you didn't have any money?"

"I sold my hair. They gave me a hundred dollars and didn't charge me for the hair cut or the make-over. I told them I'd wiped out skiing. I was going to look for you, but—"

"You went shopping."

"Your sister-in-law's jeans were so short . . ."

Now that he looked, he could see she her jeans now reached all the way to her borrowed boots. And they had some kind of embroidery on the hem. They fit her like a glove. A very affectionate glove.

"I didn't think I needed the snow pants anymore. I didn't lose them. They're all in the bag." She held it up. It bulged like a pregnant woman. Obviously, she'd bought more than pants.

Dani, he remembered, had shopped while being hunted by a hit man. Not to mention that she gone dancing. "I'll never understand women," he said. "Never."

Her smile almost made him not care.

"That's the way it's supposed to be." She looked around. "So, did you find us some wheels?"

He saw one of the sets of hunters driving slowly in their direction and took her arm, turning her away from them. "Let's walk and talk."

"Is there a problem?" Amelia pulled her ski cap back on, covering her shorn locks.

"Maybe. Not sure." He told her what he'd observed as they stopped in front of an antique shop, and he pointed at something in the window.

"What are we going to do?" She didn't look at him, but he could see the two worry lines appear between her arched brows.

"There's a bus that comes through. Runs all the way to Denver."

"Where do we get tickets?"

"Over there." He gestured over his shoulder as he continued to point at different things in the window. Amelia looked casually in that direction and saw, right in front of the gun shop with the bus station logo in the window, a pair of hunters.

Because he had no description of who Prudence Knight was traveling with, Larry had focused on the woman. Her photo wasn't a lot of use, so he reminded them that she was probably scratched and bruised from a fall. She had long, blonde hair and would probably squint a bit, since she'd lost her glasses in the fall through the tree. She was traveling with someone else, so look for people in pairs. He figured that was good enough to turn her up, once they emerged from the woods.

They'd seen where they went into the woods, of course, but had been unable to find any other signs of them. Too many miles to cover and only one chopper to do it with. It had seemed wise to abandon the air search and focus all their attention on places where the pair could get transportation. At least until Grady got them an ID on the truck and possibly a picture of the owner.

He couldn't fault the support Grady had sent him. It was an education and, if he were truthful, a bit troubling. He'd had no idea Grady had this level of support at his fingertips. It was damn near an army.

At first he'd thought about heading into Estes Park. It was closer than Boulder and would have a hospital and more transport options than most of the smaller towns, but it was away from Denver, and Grady said that's where they would head. They could still be on skis, of course, maybe still heading cross country, but they'd have to take them off eventually, and he was pretty sure they had them boxed in. How could they not?

He noticed a couple looking into an antique shop across from the bus stop. It was pretty cold to be window shopping. Maybe he'd just check them out . . .

He turned in behind them. If they were expecting trouble or the girl had gotten a look at his face, the situation could get hot quickly. On the other hand, he didn't want to pull out the guns on a town street. Just wanted to ID them, then follow them and take them somewhere quieter. He pulled out a map and studied it, like he might be lost. Then he rolled down the window.

"Excuse me." The couple didn't move. He opened his truck and hopped out, approaching them from behind and forcing them to turn. The woman was still partly in shadow from the overhang, but as soon as he got closer, he could tell she wasn't his gal. Even in the shade, her *short* blonde hair poked out from under the edges of her ski cap. And no sign of bump or bruise on her model-perfect face or a squint. Prudence Knight had been severe and a real geek with pulled back hair. Couldn't stop now, though. He held out the map.

"I seem to have taken a wrong turn somewhere. Can you tell me how to get to Allenspark?"

The guy, his air of authority enough to jump Larry's heart, took the map from him and spread it out on the hood of his truck. His mind raced as he pretended to follow the man's directions. Where could they be? And why had he chosen a cop to ask directions from? He'd remember his face, and he was sure, from the piercing look he got in return, that the guy would remember him.

"Thanks. Don't know where I went wrong." He took the map and looked at the girl. "Anything interesting there? My wife likes antiques, and she's got a birthday coming up."

"Slim pickings here, I'm afraid," the girl said, with a slight, lovely smile. "Ready, honey?" she said to the man, then to him, "My husband is going to buy me my very own hand gun. I know a Glock isn't usually considered a lady's gun. What do you think?"

Larry didn't know what to think. He backed away. "A Glock's very nice. As are others . . . well, thanks." He climbed into the truck and watched the pair cross the street and enter the gun and tackle shop. Maybe someone at the local eating places had seen a woman with a scratched face.

Inside the gun and tackle shop, Amelia looked at Luke. "Do you think he was one of them?"

Luke frowned. "I don't know. He made sure he saw your face. Good idea to cover up the scratches and cut your hair. If he was after you, he didn't recognize you." His frown deepened, but he didn't share what was worrying him with her. "Let's get those tickets."

Tickets to Denver in hand, they supported their cover story by looking over the stock. Amelia picked up a hunting rifle, surprised to find it felt . . . familiar. She lifted it, the butt against her shoulder and looked down the sight. The fog opened for a flash, giving her a glimpse of something . . . or was it *someone?* A bullet piercing a dark silhouette.

Who am I? What am I?

She lowered the gun so fast, it clattered against the counter.

"Are you all right?" Luke asked, his voice distant and hollow. He wavered in front of her eyes, then steadied.

She took a shaky breath. "Just felt dizzy for a minute."

His hand gripped her arm. "Maybe you should sit down. I should have taken you to the hospital—"

"No. I'm fine. Really." Her vision had cleared. Fear did that, it seemed. "Look, our bus is here."

It blocked their view of the street but also gave them some cover as they boarded. Luke directed her to the rear of the bus, where they kept low until they were clear of town. In a few minutes, they were on the highway, with no signs of pursuit.

Luke relaxed. At least for now they were safe, though Amelia's color still worried him. Adrenaline had sustained them both this far. To his relief, the movement of the bus had her head nodding. In a few minutes her head drooped, then slid onto Luke's shoulder, her head tilted back so that all he had to do was turn his head a millimeter to have her full, pouting lips in easy striking distance.

What was happening to him? He'd spent less than twenty-four hours with her and he was already wondering how to keep her. There was so much he didn't know about her, but his heart didn't seem to care. It felt oddly right to have her next to him, her body supported by his as the miles slipped past.

He felt sleep tugging at his eyes, but he still hadn't decided what to do once they reached Denver. It would be easy to call one of his brothers, but what if their pursuers had made him?

If they were as organized as they appeared to be, they'd be running the plates on his truck and may have his name. That meant anyone with the name Kirby could put Amelia and his family at risk. For now, he had to avoid the family.

He felt alone, isolated, cut off, even if it was his own choice. On the upside, this meant he wouldn't have to explain Amelia. He wasn't ready to share her with his brothers yet, remembering Matt's reaction to Phoebe a year ago. His middle brother didn't like women with mysterious pasts. Besides, he wasn't ready to have to answer their questions when he had no answers for them. He'd find out who and what Amelia was, then he'd be ready for introductions. Maybe.

Bryn would help him, he knew, but he couldn't see her and Amelia together. Kind of like pairing a kitten with a wolf. Though Amelia was tougher than she looked. Besides, Bryn would ask a lot of questions. He'd never met anyone so unrelentingly suspicious.

He hated to admit it, but Dewey seemed like his best option. There was no obvious connection between them, and he wouldn't be leaving Amelia alone while he checked out her apartment.

He eased his cell phone out of his pocket and made the call. Dewey sounded surprised but amused. Typical.

At some point, Luke fell asleep, too. He woke to find his arms wrapped around Amelia, his face buried in her silky, provocatively short hair and his lungs inhaling her scent.

He'd gone up the mountain to deal with his past, to let go of Rosemary, not for this. Rosemary wouldn't grudge him happiness without her. That wasn't the kind of person she was. It's just, well, if Amelia had only been older, it wouldn't seem like such a betrayal.

What could he possibly have in common with someone so young besides the physical? He'd had true companionship with Rosemary, the kind with shared interests and shared memories. He couldn't settle for less than that in his life or in his bed, no matter how attractive the package. All he was really sharing with Amelia was a mutual sense of danger. He was feeling protective. Easy to mistake it for warmer feelings. It wouldn't be the first time a victim had mistaken gratitude for . . . whatever, and it probably wouldn't be the last. Once Amelia was restored to her life, her memories, she'd be embarrassed by that spontaneous and amazing kiss. She'd return to her life and he'd go back to his.

One thing he was sure about, his heart wouldn't be busted again. He'd lost Rosemary and almost hadn't gotten over it. No way he'd fall headlong into a situation that painful, not when there was no chance of a happy ending.

Amelia stirred in his arms, murmuring and his heart jumped in his chest, reminding him that hearts didn't always act in their own best interests. A wise man would put distance between them as soon as possible.

He sighed, as his arms tightened around Amelia.

No one he knew would call him a wise man.

Chapter Nine

A cop. Grady couldn't believe it. She dives out of the chopper on a freaking mountainside and lands in the lap of a cop? It was over. No way they'd get their hands on her now.

Except . . .

Why hadn't Kincaid known she was safe? He hadn't sounded like a man trying to set a trap. He'd sounded frantic. Grady knew how to read voices, to read the nuances, body language and eyes. He could smell intentions, feel motives. Home in on weaknesses like a smart bomb on a target. Something wasn't tracking right. But what?

Faint heart never won fair lady.

It didn't exactly fit. Prudence Knight wasn't fair, and his heart was careful, not faint. He pushed back his chair and walked over the window. The sky had cleared, leaving behind a view that was postcard perfect. If snow and mountains were your thing.

They weren't his. He wanted sun. He wanted heat—the sultry, rich kind of heat where he could buy himself a new future and erase his past. A place where he could avoid people like Leslie if he wanted to.

Leslie. What an asshole. Had he heard he'd made his first kill? He hadn't called to whine—or gloat—yet. Grady had a feeling Leslie would like it. A destructive rage lurked beneath his sunny, idiot-son surface, but Grady'd bet it wouldn't stay down for long, now that Leslie had taken first blood. He might need to remove Leslie from the picture sooner than planned. Some monsters, unleashed, raged out of control.

Leslie was weak and impractical. Everything he did was driven by emotion—mostly rage and jealousy for those in control.

How long would it take for Leslie to turn on him? he wondered. When would it occur to him that Grady controlled him as much, or more, than his father? Yes, it was time to eliminate Leslie from the board. A pawn who thought he was king was too dangerous to have around.

Which did nothing to help him figure out where Prudence Knight was or what Luke Kirby planned to do with his catch of the day.

Maybe he should toss in a line and see what he could pull out?

He dialed Kincaid again. He answered on the first ring. Even in the single, tersely snapped, "Kincaid," Grady could hear that the fear in his voice had built, not lessened. So he didn't know. He hung up without comment. Now was not the time to deal with Kincaid, not without the girl in hand.

Which left him with the multi-million dollar question. Why hadn't Kirby phoned home? Since he couldn't answer it, he'd do what he could to make sure he couldn't get home with the prize.

He knew they'd skied out of the mountains, so Kirby was innovative and willing to switch gears when necessary. He looked at the picture his contact in the police department had faxed to him. Strong, determined, stubborn. A worthy opponent. He stared at the map. What would I do if I were in the hop and not sure what was happening or who my enemy was?

For sure he'd trade in the skis as soon as possible. But they hadn't rented a car. No contact with any of the police or sheriff departments between the cabin and Denver. They had the bus stations covered, too.

Where are you? And how do we smoke you out? He

frowned, then reached for the phone again. A few calls and some judicious faxing. Had any of his army seen this man?

The wait wasn't long before the phone rang. It was Larry. "I saw this guy, but the woman he was with didn't look nothing like Knight. And not a scratch on her." He sounded frustrated and aggrieved. "I think they got on the bus."

Bingo. In a few minutes, he had his army moving in on Denver like locusts bearing down on a field of grain.

"Okay," Luke turned from the bus window and looked at Amelia, who was reapplying the make-up that covered her bruises. "We got a spot of trouble. The dogs seem to have beaten us to town."

Maybe he was paranoid and maybe he wasn't. But there were too many guys hanging around, looking like they *weren't* looking for someone. And one of them was the guy who'd approached them on the street just before they'd boarded the bus. He seemed to think he was being very discreet behind that newspaper. The guy would recognize him for sure and may already know he belonged to his truck abandoned at the cabin. He frowned, his mind racing. How to get Amelia safely to Dewey, who he hoped was out there waiting.

"We'll have to get out separately. I'll go first, try to draw them off you. Leave your jacket off, and reverse the hat. Tuck all your hair under it. Stuff the jacket in your bag, out of sight." He handed her his beeper. "If I get clear, I'll beep nine-one-one. Dewey should be waiting not far from the exit." He described Dewey. "Head straight for him. Pretend you know him. If I send you nine-nine-nine, forget Dewey, get into a stall in the bathroom and stay there until you hear me or see a police badge shoved under the door. Okay?"

She nodded, her face calm but pale. "Will you be all right?"

He looked up from checking his weapon. "They need me to lead them to you."

It was the second hardest thing he'd ever done, walking away from her. He stepped ahead of a woman about the same age as Amelia. When he stepped down, he turned and offered her his hand. She smiled and thanked him. When she walked inside, he followed her, close enough that it looked like they were together. Like magnets and nails, he noted he was pulling the surveillance inside with him, including the one who'd seen Amelia. So far, so good.

He pulled out his cell phone and dialed Dewey. Be there, he thought, the relief intense when Dewey answered right away.

"Where are you?"

"Outside, by my car," Dewey said. "Why?"

"I seemed to have picked up a tail. I need you to get Amelia. She should be in the ladies room." He didn't dare look back or draw his tail's attention to her in any way. He gave him a quick description of her. "Get her out of here."

"What—"

"No questions. Just do it. If it looks safe, call my beeper and punch in nine-one-one. If it looks dicey or you feel something's wrong, send a nine-nine-nine, then call the cops and get security in there to keep an eye on her. Okay?"

"Okay."

Luke rang off, stowing the phone and strolling toward the men's room. With a thrill of adrenaline, he noted that at least two of them were following him inside. The lady he'd used as a decoy was greeting a husband and kids, leaving the rest of his tail with nothing to do.

Amelia stared at herself in the mirror of the gritty bus station ladies room, surprised to find she was very good at hiding her feelings. None of the turmoil she felt at being separated from Luke was apparent on her face. Not even her eyes betrayed the feelings churning her insides. They were tranquil, purple pools, an odd contrast to the scratches and bruises she knew lurked beneath the make-up and the pounding of her heart. She'd seen men follow Luke into the bathroom, but not all of them. She hoped he was right, that they'd leave him alone as long as they believed he'd lead them to her. No one had given her a second look. The last off the bus, she'd attached herself to a small group of chattering women, making a beeline for the ladies room.

Panic had bubbled up inside her, but it seemed unable to break through to the surface. The calm façade appeared impenetrable. This ability to disguise her fear might have pleased her, if it weren't for the flash of memory from the gun shop, the flash of her pointing the gun at that shadowy figure and pulling the trigger. The bullet speeding toward the dark silhouette. The rifle had felt comfortable, normal in her grip. If it had only been that, she might have been able to shrug it off as a hobby. This was the wild, wild West, after all, but her head was a veritable treasure trove of statistics about guns, and not just the ones in that shop. She could have lectured at length on the history and development of weapons but had managed to contain the urge, thanks to a throat dried with panic.

Who was she? What was she, that she knew so much about guns? And how could she be so calm and controlled? On the inside it felt like she was fetal with fear. And it wasn't just the fear she couldn't see on her face. The pain wasn't there either. There was lots of pain to be there. She'd stiffened like mud in the sun while slumbering in Luke's arms. It wasn't natural. It wasn't normal. What if she was some paranoid paramilitary type with a huge stash of guns? Or a hit woman?

And what would Luke find when he went to her apartment?

If only she could remember, but every time she tried to pierce the veil of her memory, she got slapped back by the pain. You can't hide from the past, not even in your own head, Luke had said, but how could she fight what she didn't remember?

Luke's beeper vibrated in her pocket. She pulled it out. Nine-one-one. Time to emerge. Well, she looked around her. There was nothing more to learn about herself in this place. She turned and left, the last glimpse of her face still eerily serene.

Outside, the scene was moderately chaotic and intimidating, as her gaze swept the crowd for a glimpse of Luke, or his friend, Dewey. A man, tall and kind of lanky, waved at her cheerfully, a charming smile nicely breaking up the ordinary in his face. His brown hair fell across his forehead with small boy insistence, and he walked toward her as if his body couldn't quite keep up with his thoughts. He fitted the description Luke had given her. She started to smile. She had just a moment to process the sudden wicked look in his brown eye, before he swept her into a hug and planted a kiss on her shocked mouth. She resisted for a moment and he whispered in her ear, "I'm Dewey. Play along. We're being watched."

So she hugged him back and found the tension in her stomach ease.

"Darling, welcome home." He kept one arm around her waist, turning her toward the exit. "Denver was a desert without you."

"A very cold desert," Amelia said, a bit dryly.

There was no sign of Luke anywhere. *Please let him be all right,* she prayed, then she wondered if she believed in God.

Larry nodded for two of the men to follow Kirby into the

bathroom, while he figured out what to do. He hadn't expected him to get off the bus alone. As soon as he'd seen Kirby's picture, he remembered seeing him with the looker outside the antique store. Could the Knight woman have changed her looks that much? Didn't seem possible, and not just the upgrade in the babe factor. He hadn't seen a scratch on her.

He'd explained the problem to Grady, who had dispatched someone with a digital camera to discreetly snap all the women getting off the bus. He was so discreet, in fact, that Larry couldn't tell who it was. But that only worked if she'd gotten off the bus. It was possible, she'd gotten off en route to Denver. Kirby didn't look like a fool. Wouldn't be that hard to lose them here, then double back and pick her up somewhere. He signaled a couple of the boys.

"Check the bus. Make sure everyone got off."

They nodded and left. After a moment's hesitation, he realized he needed to whiz. Always nice when the body and the brain were in sync, since he was curious to see what was happening inside the crapper. What he found was Kirby calmly washing his hands. And no sign of his men.

Two stall doors were closed. Surely they both hadn't needed to take a dump right now? Larry stepped back and tried to see if there were legs under the doors.

"Lose someone?"

He turned to find Kirby's chest inches from his nose. He looked up. Kirby's face was blank but dangerous. Definitely not a fool.

"Um, my friends came in here . . ."

"Two guys went into stalls. I'm sure they'll be out soon."

"Um. Thanks." Larry stepped back. Tried not to look nervous. The guy was built like a tree. He raised his voice slightly. "I'm sure they will be out *soon*."

Kirby smiled, but there was no amusement in it. "And I'm sure we won't be seeing each other again."

Larry tugged at the neck of his shirt, which had suddenly gotten tight. "Uh, no. Definitely not. I'm catching the bus out as soon as—" he nodded toward the closed stalls.

"Right." Kirby turned without further comment and walked out.

Larry sagged back. "What's with you two? Get the hell out here!"

Nothing.

Uneasy again, Larry approached one door and pushed. It opened. Guy one was laying next to the toilet, his jaw rapidly swelling, his lights out. In the next stall, Guy two was dragged across the toilet. He wasn't showing lights either.

Maybe it was time to find a different business.

The door let a blast of cold air swirl around Amelia as she and Dewey exited the station. Outside the sun was high and blindingly bright. The snow might have been a pretty white blanket, but the city had wasted no time in dirtying it up as it went about its business. The heaped piles of snow were pushed to the side by plows where they'd melt slow and messy. The car he directed her to was small and rather battered, but it warmed up rapidly once Dewey got the motor running.

"Luke said you're probably hungry. Drive-through all right?"

After all the cloak-and-dagger, it seemed sort of anticlimactic, but she *was* hungry. She nodded, still a little bemused by the current of energy he radiated like a mini-sun. He plunged the car into traffic as if he were piloting a craft in space. To her surprise, Amelia felt a kick of excitement as the car fishtailed taking a corner. Maybe she raced cars in her other life?

It was a strange feeling to have traits, or maybe it was personality quirks, floating to the surface of her mind like this. She felt like one of those bubbling pots of mud in Yellowstone Park. Kind of murky, with hidden depths and globs of information erupting at unexpected moments—none of which made sense, even taken all together.

Her computer-like brain. Working knowledge of wounds and anatomy. Extensive knowledge of guns. An apparent inclination towards thrill-seeking. Bullet graze on the arm. A feeling of betrayal. A longing to be free—of something. Maybe that prim, annoying voice urging her to behave? And her, well, warm feelings for Luke. The cop. It was all very troubling.

"I'm under strict orders, with the potential for painful retribution, if I ask you any questions or tell anyone about you while you're staying with me, so anything you want me to know, you'll have to volunteer it. Luke has promised to reimburse any expenses I incur, so if there is anything you need, just tell me and your wish is my command." He punctuated this by speeding up to make a light, the rear of his car fishtailing again before the wheels dug into the snowy street. She also noticed that he checked behind them regularly, as if watching for a tail.

"I've been separated from my luggage," Amelia said, "so a stop where I could buy some basics would be helpful."

"Wal-Mart, okay?"

Amelia hesitated. "Is it inexpensive?" She only had a few dollars left of her hair money.

He looked surprised. "Downright cheap. How—oops, that would be a question. I'll just *observe*, for the sake of my knees, that you must be from out of town—possibly even out of country."

Amelia met his curious look with a bland smile. It was interesting that Luke trusted Dewey to transport her for him, but he didn't trust him with her story. For now, she would follow Luke's lead, though she felt he was being overly careful. Dewey seemed okay to her and was very entertaining. She had a feeling she'd never met anyone like him before, but what she knew of him, she liked.

They were just parking at Wal-Mart when Luke's beeper sounded. The quick, annoyed feeling she felt told her she wasn't a stranger to a beeper's summons. One more thing to add to the bits and pieces of disconnected facts. She pulled it out and showed it to Dewey.

"What should we do?"

"That's his work number. I'd better call and tell him." He pulled out his cell phone. "I'll call. You grab a cart."

She didn't move until she heard Dewey say, "Luke-ster, you got a beep." He gave him the number, then asked, "You all right?" A pause. "Good-o. We'll catch you later then."

He was okay. Amelia gave a huge sigh of relief and grasped the handle of a shopping cart. It was icy cold from the outside air and sent a thrill through her, similar to kissing Luke, but not quite that good. She rolled it forward, then back, testing the wheels. All she'd wanted was to clean up and stop moving. But now she felt energy flowing back into her body at the feel of the cart. She pushed it toward the doors, which swished open at her approach. It was lovely. She felt important. It was even better inside. Goods stacked almost to the ceiling. Aisles to explore. Time slowed down. Exhaustion faded. Aches and pains dimmed to a dull murmur. It was just her and a big store full of things to see and buy.

Dewey looked at her, his expression slowly turning resigned. "Luke owes me more than money for this gig."

"Sorry I had to interrupt your day off, but it's an odd case, no question, buddy." Luke's partner, Mannfred Gage was short and stocky, with a bright, cheerful gaze that saw everything, but gave nothing away. They'd been partners since Luke transferred to homicide and Luke wouldn't have it any other way. Mann was solid as a rock with a puckish sense of humor and great instincts. Though he was a little quick with the beeper. "Not much to go on."

An understatement, Luke thought, setting aside the file on Dr. John Knight as they pulled into the parking lot at Merryweather Biotechnologies. So far it was a thin file, mostly because of the blizzard that had shut down the city for most of the day. Basically they knew he was dead and that he had worked for Merryweather prior to his death. A preliminary coroner's report listed the cause of death as an overdose of digitalis. Knight's personal physician had requested the autopsy. If he had an unexplained heart attack, he wanted this guy to be his doctor, Luke decided. Very quick on the uptake. Merryweather had only arrived back in the area an hour or so ago, so maybe now they'd learn something useful. Not that Luke wanted to be here. It felt wrong to be dealing with the dead, when Amelia was alive, in danger and with Dewey. It also frustrated him to wait to visit her apartment. To himself he could admit he hoped it would answer the big question, the one he shouldn't want to know—was she involved with someone else?

Damn duty called. It was a hard habit to break. And he did need his paycheck.

"Let's go shake some trees, see if we can plump this file up some," Luke said, opening his door. And put a quick end to this, he silently added.

The place looked quiet, almost deserted, but they knew the owner, name of Hamilton Merryweather, was waiting for them. Mann had called and set up the meet while he waited for Luke to join him.

Dark was settling in fast as he walked with Mann to the entrance. He glanced around and thought for a minute he saw a match flare inside a van, but decided he was seeing things. Easy to do in the near-dark.

Inside, a guard waved them to an elevator. The place oozed money. Marble floors in the hallways. Lots of chrome and crystal and thick carpets in the offices. The elevator swished them quietly to the top floor, the doors opening with a discreet hiss.

The lower floors were expensively equipped, but they were nothing compared to the opulence of the boss's floor. The gray carpet was so thick and deep, he felt like he was sinking in it up to his knees. Mahogany desks, original paintings and fancy sculptures. Place was like a museum and proclaimed a very important person worked here.

What Luke found most interesting was how cold it felt, as if it all had no soul, no life. He almost expected to find a corpse inside the big, double doors Mann was pushing open.

He wasn't far wrong. Hamilton Merryweather would have made a great mortician or corpse. Tall and slightly wilted, despite being impeccably dressed, he had a long, pale face, his expression appropriately mournful for the occasion. Graying, thinning hair was combed carefully back off a high, well-bred forehead. His brows were so light, Luke thought he had none until he got close enough to exchange a chilly handshake with him.

"Luke Kirby." Luke showed him his badge, then nodded toward Mann. "My partner, Mannfred Gage."

"This is my son, Leslie," Merryweather said, the careful neutrality of his tone revealing a great deal about their relationship.

"Gentlemen." Leslie shook hands, trying too hard to

achieve the right level of firmness. He had the look of his father, but with the life stamped out of him and a weaker chin. Luke wondered how long it would take him to give up the unequal battle for supremacy with his father. A slight air of decadence told him the rot had already set in.

"I presume you're here about Prudence?" Merryweather said, leading them to a frosty looking conversation area off to one side. Leslie strolled over and assumed an attitude of casual alertness against the bar. A certain watchful look in his eyes put Luke's antenna up. He exchanged a look with Mann, before taking a seat across from Merryweather.

Mann pulled out a notebook and pencil and looked at Merryweather, "Prudence?"

"Prudence Knight." Merryweather looked at Mann, then at Luke. "Isn't she why you're here?" His voice was as funereal as his aspect. "I know she hasn't been missing forty-eight hours, but under the circumstances, I think we should move ahead."

Luke felt a chill snake down his back when Merryweather said, "missing," but this Prudence was, well, Prudence. Not Amelia. It was strange, though. A missing girl. A found girl.

"When did she go missing?" Luke asked, earning himself a surprised look from Mann. He thrust his hands in his pockets, his fingers closing around the keys he'd taken so he could check out her apartment.

"Yesterday morning. Outside the hospital. I believe her vehicle is still there."

This has nothing to do with Amelia. Focus on the job, damn it, he mentally muttered, annoyed with himself.

"Kincaid says he turned over the vitals to the FBI," Merryweather was saying.

Luke looked at Mann, who gave a slight shake of the head. "Kincaid?"

"My chief of security. He should be joining us soon, as soon as he checks on some items for me."

"Here, Dad," Leslie said, the concern in his voice perfectly pitched, as he handed his father a drink.

Something about him rubbed Luke the wrong way.

"Can I get something for either of you?" Leslie asked, with a charming smile.

Did the guy ever hit a wrong note?

"Coffee for me, if you have it," Luke said.

"Same here," Mann said. "On duty and all that."

"Of course." He picked up the phone and in a few minutes a secretary entered with a tray and cups. When she'd poured and left them, Leslie perched on the couch behind his father, causing a small flicker of annoyance to break the expressionless expanse of his father's face.

What had it felt like to be his son? Luke wondered. There were worse things, it seemed, than losing a father.

"We will, of course, be doing all we can to find Miss Knight, but we're here to ask about Dr. John Knight," Luke said, watching both men. Merryweather's brows arched, he noticed. Leslie's did, too, but just a beat too slow. Or maybe Luke was looking for it because he didn't like him?

"We're with homicide, Mr. Merryweather," Mann said.

That got the father's brows up some more. Leslie's look narrowed. And his cheeks flushed faintly, as if he were excited.

"Homicide? Are you saying," Leslie asked, "that Dr. Knight was murdered? I thought he died of a heart attack?"

"He ingested a lethal dose of digitalis," Mann said. "Not the preferred method of the suicidal."

"An accidental overdose—" Merryweather started to protest.

"Hard to accidentally take something that wasn't prescribed to you," Mann pointed out. "It was his personal physician that called us."

"Can either of you think of anyone who would want Dr. Knight dead?" Luke asked.

Leslie straightened, a look of diffidence on his face. "I hate to be the one to point out the obvious, but doesn't this put a new spin on Miss Knight's disappearance? And Dad, shouldn't we verify the . . . integrity of the project Dr. Knight was working on?"

His father frowned. "I hardly think Miss Knight—"

"She is his next of kin," Leslie said.

For just a moment, Luke thought he saw amusement—or was it satisfaction?—in the son's eyes, before he replaced it with one more suitably sober. He and Mann exchanged another quick look. "Do we ask what the project is?"

"It's a highly classified project that Knight was working on. Miss Knight is his assistant." Merryweather seemed like he wanted to say more, but didn't.

"You'll have to tell them, Dad. We need to be truthful or the police won't be able to do their job," Leslie said, earnestly cooperative. Merryweather didn't say anything. He might have been thinking. It was hard to tell.

Leslie sighed. "Dad." He looked at the two men. "Miss Knight was more than an assistant. She was Knight's, well, filing cabinet."

"Filing cabinet?" Luke frowned and Mann looked up from his notes with a puzzled look.

"She has a photographic memory. All his research, all his data is stored in her homely little head."

Luke felt a strange sensation in his middle. A photographic memory. That would explain Amelia's unusual ability to pull up facts at a whim. But the name—an icy chill slid straight down his back without passing "Go" or collecting money. Amelia was the one who'd produced the name and address. He'd never seen the information on the PDA. If she had killed her father and stolen classified material, then a loss of memory would be pretty handy, particularly if you happened to land in the lap of a cop.

Get a grip on yourself, he told himself. You don't know Amelia and Prudence are the same person. This time he did finger the set of keys. There was the computer access card, but he was reluctant to pull it out. It would be hard to explain how he happened to have it. And he definitely didn't want Leslie to know he might know where their missing tech was. Something about the guy gave him a chill. He'd been quick to point the finger at her. Real quick. No, he wouldn't pull out the card. Not now. Not until he'd had a chance to talk to her.

And there was another way. Merryweather said her car was still at the hospital. Even without the personal added incentive, they'd need to check it out.

"I'd say that gives her a rather obvious motive for murder," Leslie continued, "particularly since they had a fight before she left the hospital and vanished."

"Interesting that you'd feel the need to throw suspicion on Miss Knight, Leslie," a voice said from the doorway.

"Donovan," Merryweather seemed relieved to see him. "Gentlemen, this is my head of security, Donovan Kincaid. Detectives Kirby and Gage. Homicide detectives. It seems Dr. Knight was murdered."

There was a palpable shift of power in the room at Kincaid's entrance. Merryweather got paler and Leslie got . . . shiftier. And shorter. And slightly annoyed, if the pulling together of his brows was any indication.

A big man with the air of a soldier, despite the businessman clothes, Kincaid exuded crisp and competent and had an air of mystery that Luke would bet women found irresistible. At the moment, his fists were clenched, like he'd like to pop Leslie, but he was willing to wait for later. And he didn't look surprised to hear Knight had been murdered. Who had been talking to him?

Leslie stepped behind daddy. Luke wasn't sure he was aware of the movement. Leslie hadn't taken his eyes off Kincaid, though that look of secret amusement was back. Did he like trouble or did he have a particular interest in *this* trouble?

"I'm not trying to throw suspicion on anyone," Leslie protested. "They asked who might want Knight dead. The relationship between John and Prudence has always been . . . kind of 'daddy-dearest.' It would be dishonest to pretend otherwise."

"It's my job to assess the character of the employees. Miss Knight is a person of impeccable character." Kincaid pinned Leslie with his gaze.

He was out-gunned, but he held his ground long enough to be interesting then turned with a shrug and poured himself a drink. All kinds of undercurrents. Luke hated undercurrents. Made an investigation about as much fun as swimming in quicksand. And about as safe. Just because he didn't like him, Luke put Leslie at the top of the suspect list.

Kincaid cut across the room to Merryweather, bent and whispered something in his ear. Merryweather's perfect gentleman façade cracked momentarily. He recovered, but when he lifted his drink to his mouth, his hand shook a little. He looked at the two detectives then turned a looked at his son.

"Could you fetch the personal files on Dr. Knight and Miss Prudence, Leslie?" He turned back to them. "Is there anything else you'll need from us?"

"We'll need a list of everyone who worked with Dr. Knight. Addresses and phone numbers," Mann said. "Also, who was working with him yesterday when he collapsed? A picture of the missing daughter. For starters."

"Leslie?" Merryweather didn't look at his son this time.

Luke did. Leslie stood irresolute, obviously annoyed, his air one of a small boy who knows he's being gotten rid of while the grown-ups talk.

"Fine." He stalked out, closing the door with a snap behind him.

Luke was careful not to look at Mann. Not polite to chuckle under the circumstances.

Merryweather jumped to his feet. He didn't creak, but Luke wondered if he'd moved that fast in years. It wasn't natural for him. He nodded to Kincaid then went and poured himself another drink.

Luke looked in Kincaid's direction and lifted a brow.

"I've just informed Mr. Merryweather that the prototype of Project SHIELD, which Knight was working on, is missing from the vault. Whoever did this had to be a damn Houdini. I've never seen anything like it."

"Really." If Pathphinder and Hyatt weren't in retirement, Luke thought, he'd be talking to them next. "You're sure it wasn't an inside job?"

"An insider," Merryweather said, turning to look at them, "would know that the research wasn't complete. SHIELD isn't ready. I don't understand why they took it—unless it was to stop our research."

"And I," Donovan said, "have been contacted by the person who grabbed Miss Knight."

Both Luke and Mann sat up straighter. "Did he make any demands?"

"Not yet. I think he just wanted me to know he had her." Kincaid turned away from them, striding over to glare out the window.

If Prudence Knight had been kidnapped, that meant Amelia was Amelia. He should feel better, but why had the kidnappers contacted Kincaid? If they were after SHIELD, then they had it, didn't they? He was very curious to see Prudence Knight's picture. Very. And he needed time to think. And to talk to Dewey. Right now was not the time to lose track of Amelia. Now he wished he'd gone with Bryn as caretaker for Amelia.

"Could I use your restroom?" he asked. Merryweather indicated a door off to the right. Once inside, Luke pulled out his cell phone and dialed Dewey.

Chapter Ten

Grady's photographer had emailed him the pictures he'd taken at the bus station. Thanks to high speed access, they'd downloaded quickly, but the process of studying the pictures and comparing them to the two pictures he had of Prudence Knight took more time. Some of the pictures had to be cleared up before he could even begin to compare them. As picture after picture was examined and rejected, he began to wonder if they were chasing a phantom. Larry's premise that Prudence Knight was with Luke Kirby was based on a bloody tee shirt and a lot of hope. Maybe too much hope?

Grady had rallied his private army to track the pair and turned up nothing to indicate that Prudence Knight hadn't died from her fall from the chopper and been buried under some snow drift on the mountainside.

To further trouble him, Leslie hadn't phoned in. It wasn't like him. Had he somehow picked up on Grady's plan to shaft him and made a counter play? Leslie prided himself on his chess playing and Grady had let him hold onto that pride, though he could have kicked his butt a million times over in every game they'd played over the years. Ego stroking was hard work, a work he'd grown weary of.

Only three pictures left. Three little files on which his hope was pinned. If they'd lost the trail, he had no clue how to find it again. The first was clearly not her. But he frowned at the second one. It didn't look at all like her, except for something in the jaw? A feeling in his gut? Wishful thinking?

He pulled up the picture he'd scanned and put them side

by side. In the shot from the bus, the woman was wearing a hat that hid her hair. Larry had said the woman with Kirby had short, blond hair and was too much of a looker to be Knight.

He took the picture of Prudence Knight and removed the heavy, dark glasses. Almost immediately the severity of her looks softened. Okay, let's pretend she cut her hair. He took off the severely pulled-back hair and replaced it with short and blond.

"Much better. Moving into the babe zone." But how had she hidden the scratches and bruises she had to have acquired during the dive from the chopper? "Maybe the same place she got the hair cut?" He'd seen stuff on TV infomercials that was used to cover up massive disfigurement. Why not a few scratches?

He took the altered Prudence and put her next to the woman from the bus.

"Gotcha."

Amelia learned two more facts about herself in Wal-Mart. She loved to shop, and there was no way she was going meekly to Dewey's apartment to wait for Luke to sort out her life. She needed to be proactive. She needed to be . . . spunky? Yeah, she needed to be spunky. Women who waited for life to happen to them never found true love. Or self-fulfillment, which was more important than true love, though possibly not as fun. She didn't know how she knew this, so she could be wrong, but she didn't feel wrong. She felt right.

The shopping and the need to be spunky were connected in some way, though how wasn't clear at the moment. Maybe it was a female imperative, a way of accessing her inner power through shopping. Oh, it had felt good to have Luke's big, strong shoulders to dump her burdens on. She'd felt safe around him and it felt good to feel safe, but she was stronger now. She'd rested, the aches were healing. Mostly.

She didn't want Luke to find out she was a bad person. Better to find out the truth about herself and then decide what to do about it.

She could probably persuade Dewey to take her to her apartment, but that was still relying on Luke by proxy. It wasn't spunky. She hated to ditch him when he'd been so nice, but it had to be done—for the good of all womankind.

Luke had her keys, but she could ask the super, couldn't she? Surely he'd let her in. He must know her. Or maybe she was one of those people who left a key under the mat or in a flowerpot. Luke had told her she needed to face her past. What she really needed was to face it by herself. Because if it were ugly, she didn't want to face him again.

Dewey wasn't hard to lose. He kept getting distracted by things on the shelves and then totally stopped by some sort of computer game. She waited until he was deep in a game that seemed to involve blowing up aliens before they blew up him, abandoned her cart of stuff, and slipped away. Leaving her stuff was the hard part, but surely she had things at her apartment? Outside, a cab was dropping off an old lady. He didn't mind picking up a young one.

The drive through the streets was as peculiar as anything she'd felt. She could see the streets, but like a map, not like real places. She watched the driver take the turns, but had no sense of belonging to any of it. Did she even live in Denver? Or did the lack of personal connection mean she did live here? It seemed to be the personal that had been wiped out.

She asked the driver to drive past the apartment building first, but didn't see anything untoward. No hunters or even anyone lurking suspiciously in or out of a car. Instead of feeling better about it, it made her more uneasy. They'd seemed to have all the bases covered. Why not this one?

Amelia paid the man with the last of her money and got out. It was quiet. Still no sign of lurkers or watchers. No feeling of danger. No sense of coming home. Just a knot in her chest about what she would find in Amelia E. Hart's apartment.

Someone was going out as she reached the door, so she didn't have to worry about being buzzed inside. The stairs were straight ahead. She climbed them slowly, the wood of the banister cooling her sweaty palm. She wasn't feeling nearly as spunky now that she was here, but there was no going back. She didn't know how to get a hold of Dewey now, even if she wanted to. Which she didn't. Not really.

Her door was the third one down. Still no feeling of familiarity, no sense of recognition. Without stopping to think, hoping her subconscious would lead her past this hurdle too, she approached the door. She thought it wasn't going to work, but then she reached up, as if by habit, and snagged a key above the door.

"Not very original," she muttered, fitting it into the lock, turning it and pushing the door open. She started to return the key, but stopped and tucked it in her pocket instead. The dogs may have lost her scent, but that didn't mean they wouldn't find it again.

It was dark inside, with patches of light slipping past dark window coverings hinting at a larger room past the minuscule hall. The light from the hall semi-illuminated a switch. She flipped it, leaving a dim circle of light in the hall, enough so she could step in and close the door. She looked up. Not much wattage there. Did that make her cheap? Or poor?

It was a weird feeling, so disconnected and not quite real to be here, wondering who and what she was. Maybe it was some wacky dream. She'd soon wake up and resume her real life. She leaned against the cheap door, her eyes drifting closed as she reached out with all her senses and felt . . . nothing. And yet in these walls were, hopefully, the keys to her past. A few steps in the dark, but a huge leap into the void for her. If only there weren't so much to fear from finding out.

As if her own subconscious was eager for her to get on with it, some words of someone called Krishnamurti—how the heck could she remember *that* name and not her own?— floated out of the fog: *Without freedom from the past, there is no freedom at all.*

Freedom from the past would only come with facing it, not ignoring it. Okay. She took a deep breath and opened her eyes. To her left a door stood open. A bathroom. She flicked on the light. Saw a toothbrush and toothpaste. Well, she already knew she had teeth, but not that she preferred Colgate. Kept her hair brush relatively free of long, blonde hairs. Shampoo waiting by the tub. Strawberry. Conditioner, too. Suave. Some body wash from The Gap called Dream and a white loofah. The matching Dream lotion rested on the toilet tank. The towel hanging over the bar was rust colored, thick and soft. Matching hand towel and washcloth. Cheap shampoo and expensive towel? It appeared she had priorities.

And what wasn't here? This was almost as interesting as what was. There wasn't the clutter of makeup and other odds and ends she'd noted in the bathroom of Luke's cabin. No bottle of Tylenol. No mascara. No lipstick. Not even a tub of lip gloss. Just the bare hygiene necessities.

She flicked off the light and turned her attention to the main room.

She found a small room with wooden floors partially covered by a fake, Persian print rug. Against the outside wall was a big, comfy couch. To its left were an unfinished wood desk and a small lamp. She turned on the lamp and immediately the room looked warmer, friendlier in its gentle glow. Most wattage here, she noted. There was a boom box on the floor next to the desk. Nice, but not a Bose. She turned it on and country music softly filled the empty spaces. The little stack of CDs stacked next to it didn't reflect a single preference. Some jazz, some blues and blue grass. Something called Zydeco and a couple of rock collections. Aaron Neville and Linda Rondstadt. Hmmm. No classical, though she could pull up a list of classical pieces in her head without even straining.

She straightened and looked around, trying to sort through the feelings welling up inside her. Despite the paucity of the furniture, she liked this place. There were pictures on the wall of places that must mean something to her if she'd put them up. Some mountain shots, a couple of cliff shots and someone standing by an airplane. She stepped closer and realized she was the person standing by the plane.

She wore a gimme cap and some bits of hair had escaped their severe confinement. She was smiling with delight, but she still looked buttoned down.

"Way past time for that hair cut," she muttered, fingering the strands of her shortened hair with a sigh of relief. No other people in any of the shots. Did that mean she was friendless? Alone in the world? She had no answer, so she continued her survey of her odd little domain.

Books were stacked around the room in little piles that probably meant something to her when she had all her faculties. She squatted down. Action-adventure. The Tom Clancy she'd mentioned to Luke. All four Harry Potters. Romance. Mysteries. Some nonfiction piles devoted to flight and rock climbing. No self-help. Did that mean she felt okay or that she was beyond help?

A closet held a few clothes. Jeans, sweaters and tee shirts.

A couple of jackets. In the corner behind the jackets, she found a little black dress that sent her eyebrows up. She fingered the silky material, wishing she could wear it for Luke. He wouldn't think she was a kid in this.

A cheap set of plastic drawers held knickers, jams and socks. On the floor was a pair of cowboy boots next to pairs of climbing shoes, snow boots and running shoes. A pair of strappy black heels, presumably to wear with the dress, huddled in the corner partially out of sight. A couple of pairs of skis and rock climbing equipment propped in the opposite corner. Nice stuff. Expensive stuff. There was also a little pile of bedding neatly folded on top of the makeshift dresser. Apparently she slept on her couch.

There was also a sort-of kitchen area. A few cupboards, a tiny counter, a half-size refrigerator and a mini-microwave oven. The food in the fridge was fossilized. The cupboards held a few spices, a couple of single-serving microwave meals. One had a stash of candy, chips and cookies. Did that make her a junk-food junkie or very hospitable?

The desk drawers were a bit more interesting. Bank statements and paid bills were neatly lined up in one drawer, a partially used checkbook at the front. In another, she found a purse with a wallet with her driver's license (awful picture), a bus pass, discount cards for several bookstores and a pilot's license. According to the driver's license she was thirty-four. And beneath the purse was an envelope with—

"A thousand dollars in cash? And I leave the key on the jamb above the door? I must be nuts."

To her relief, she'd found no sign of weaponry of any kind. She turned her desk chair to face the room. There was no phone, which was kind of odd, since she'd found no sight or sign of a cell phone. Maybe she hated phones?

It looked like . . . a hideaway or a retreat, not a place where someone lived. A few clothes, enough toiletries and food to make do. Something to read. A pad on the desk had a shopping list started. A few doodles around the words.

"I doodle?" She tilted the pad, studying the doodles. She'd made the words at the top into little, quirky people. "Not bad."

But if she had another residence, wouldn't her bank statement reflect it? She pulled out several, but the only expenses seemed related to this apartment. Nor did they indicate how she earned her money, what her job might be. What deposits she'd made all seemed to be in cash and most of them just enough to pay the bills. The bank statements went back only two years.

So what did she do for a living? If she was a hit woman or a criminal, she didn't seem to be a particularly successful one. Could she be hiding from something? Like the law? Or was it someone?

She remembered that feeling she'd had when she said she hated lies. It had surged out of the fog in her head, the pain of it far deeper than the merely physical. For just an instant, her heart had hurt, too, like someone was squeezing it.

Okay, what do I know, she asked herself, pulling the pad of paper toward her, she flipped a page and grabbed a pencil.

I hate lies, she wrote at the top, under the logo that took top billing.

She frowned. But who doesn't? Maybe a liar, but that would be it. Okay, so maybe someone she'd cared about lied to her. And then she got kidnapped or something and had been shot at. That could give anyone traumatic amnesia.

I hate helicopters, she wrote next. But not planes, since she seemed to be a pilot of some sort and climbed rock walls. It couldn't have been a fear of heights that had prompted that brief panic attack on the mountainside. For an instant she could hear the chop-chop of the blades and feel the panic rise again, choking her, driving her—

She had brief sensation of . . . flight.

She hesitated, then shook her head. Not flight. Falling. She couldn't fly, at least not without a plane. Unless she was the alien or cyborg Luke had wondered she was. If she was a cyborg, would she know it? She felt the bump at the back of her head. Take some clever engineering to make her bruise and swell. Okay, let's forget flights of fancy and stick to what you know.

You're afraid of helicopters. Why?

The fog in her memory gave her nothing but a stab of pain in response. She rubbed the spot, doodling with the pen on the pad. Doodling a tiny cartoon of Luke. Did that mean the other people were people she knew? She flipped the sheet back and studied it. Little faces that might of meant something—if her brains hadn't been scrambled.

All the sudden she froze, as she realized that there was something behind her doodles, like a shadow. A logo and an address of a company.

Merryweather Biotechnologies.

It may mean nothing. No way to know. At least it was a place to start. She looked at the cheap clock on the desk. If it was right, then it was something to do in the morning. Suddenly, more than anything, even finding out who she really was and where she belonged, she wanted a shower and then bed. Well, couch.

She stared at the couch, wishing Luke were sitting on it. Missing him was a new ache to add to her others, this one right in her heart. This was their first night apart. At least, it was her first night. It was better this way, but it didn't feel better.

It was probably good that she didn't know how to get in

touch with him, since Dewey had kept the beeper. She remembered the number it had beeped, but Dewey said that was his work number. What message could she leave him? I miss you. That would go over big at his work. Apparently she didn't even have a phone book, which made sense when she didn't have a phone. She stood up. A hot shower would help wash away some of the aches. Help her take back herself.

The water felt as wonderful as she'd hoped it would, and her jams were soft flannel that hugged her comfortingly. Almost as good as a friend to talk to—

A knock at the door cut that thought off at the knees. Amelia peered through the peep hole and saw a dark-haired, multi-pierced young woman in a caftan of many colors. Cautiously she opened the door.

"You're here! Cool!" the woman said as she surged inside, sweeping Amelia aside, then pulling her in her wake. "I'm so in the mood for a girl's night in. Hilly's popping the corn, and I made cookies and *An Affair to Remember* is in the machine." She spun and faced Amelia with a wide, friendly smile. "We could order some pizza?"

As if on cue, Amelia's stomach rumbled. "Let me get my key."

"Hey," the woman caught Amelia's chin. "What the hell happened to you? Though I must say, I love the new do."

Amelia smiled. "I ran into a tree."

"Better than a door, hon. Hey, Hilly!"

A head topped by riotous red hair peeked around the corner. "Oh, hi, Melly. Tweeks thought she heard you in here. You coming?"

Tweeks. Hilly. Amelia grabbed her key and some of the cash. This could be interesting, but wasn't that how life was supposed to be? "Of course I'm coming."

Tweeks looked at Amelia's couch before following her out

the door. She shook her head. "Wish you had a TV and VCR. I love that couch."

"I'll see what I can do," Amelia promised. She locked the door and pocketed the key, feeling her spirits lift as she followed Tweeks and Hilly to their apartment next door.

She had *friends*.

Dewey's cell phone rang, ruining his aim. The alien mutants took advantage of his distraction and blew him out of the sky, chunks of him and his craft raining down on the surface of Mars.

"Your ass is ringing, mister," one of the kids glaring at him pointed out.

"Right. I'm done anyway." Dewey stepped back, and a ring of boys crowded into his spot. Dewey pulled out his phone, wondering if his pay would stretch to pay for the game system. Maybe if he cut back on roses and stuff for Bryn. She never thanked him for his offerings anyway. She always thanked Phagan, but he wasn't paying for the stuff. Life was so not fair.

"Hyatt?" Luke's voice cut across his musings. "You and Amelia all right?"

"Yeah, sure . . ." Dewey trailed off, as he looked around and realized Amelia was nowhere in sight. That might not have been too troubling, she'd been wandering off without him since entering Wal-Mart, but she'd never abandoned her cart the other times. He eyed the cart, with its carefully selected little pile of woman stuff, with rising anxiety. It was possible that Luke would kill him well before Bryn got a chance at his ass—"Oh shit!"

He looked at his watch. He was late meeting Bryn.

"What's wrong?" Luke asked.

"Everything," Dewey said. They say confession is good for

the soul. He hoped to hell "they" were right, whoever "they" were. "Look, I'm late for an appointment with Bryn. Got something important to tell her—"

"You're finally going to tell her?"

"Tell her . . . you knew?"

"Let's just say I suspected. If I'd known, I'd have had to do something about it." Luke sounded amused, but his voice was serious when he added, "Why don't you take Amelia to a hotel?"

Dewey took a deep breath. "She ditched me. Sorry about that."

And he hung up. He didn't need to hear him swear. Bryn filled that function for him. He dialed Bryn's cell.

"Bailey."

"It's me." Silence. "I'm really sorry. Luke asked me to—"

"Luke?" A hint of curious took the edge off annoyance in her voice. "Is he back from the mountains?"

"Oh yeah." He'd promised not to mention Amelia to the brothers Kirby, but Luke hadn't said anything about Bryn. Not that he knew a whole lot about Amelia, but what he did know, he'd throw out there in hopes of saving his ass—at least until he'd had a last meal. "Very interesting, very mysterious. Tell you when I get there?"

A sigh. "I'll give you twenty minutes."

God bless curiosity. It may just save his life. Then he'd have to hope Bryn's lust for access to GREEN would do the rest.

As the reports came in from his men, Grady grew more and more perplexed. No sign of Prudence Knight at her home or at the office, which Luke Kirby and his partner had just left. No sign of her at his brothers' or his mother's place. She hadn't left the bus station with Kirby, but none of his men had noticed who she had left with because they weren't looking for her. They were looking for Kirby. She hadn't left by cab, like Kirby. His men had checked.

Kirby had called someone. That had to be it. But who? Certainly not one of his brothers or his mother. He'd gone straight from the bus station to the police station where he met his partner. Maybe another cop? Details on the contact were sketchy and would take days to pull together. What he really needed was access to Kirby's cell phone records. He needed to know who he'd called. Those files were tough to get into, but an obstacle was just something to go around. And he knew just the man to do it. He reached for the phone, but it rang under his hand.

"Yo."

"Hey, man." It was Leslie. "Why are your guys watching my dad's company? I don't remember that being part of the plan."

Grady hesitated, then trotted out, "They're watching Kincaid. Don't want him going to ground now, do we?"

"Really." He was quiet for a short beat. "Odd that they didn't follow him when he left. And the two Feds did. Did you forget to tell them who they were after?"

"You know how hard it is to get good help, Les," Grady said soothingly, as his mind raced. Feds? Following Kincaid?

"We should bring him in. We don't want the Feds jumping on him. We need him," Leslie said, an edge to his voice that hadn't been there before.

That was the basic problem with Les. He looked at the surface of people and thought that's all there was.

"We don't need to bring him in. He'll come to me," Grady said.

"How will he know?"

"He'll know, once he starts thinking," Grady said. Something you should try, Les. "So, you've been with your father?"

"Yeah." Grady could hear him struggle with wanting—and not wanting—the change of subject. Les was easily distracted. "My old man is starting to spin. He knows SHIELD is gone. Though Knight's doc was smarter than we gave him credit for."

"What do you mean?"

"A couple of homicide cops paid him a visit. I was brilliant when they asked who might want him dead. Mentioned prim Prudence."

"Clever of you. Muddies the water nicely." Grady smiled, even as his thoughts spun too fast to collect. Homicide detectives. It couldn't be, could it? "You catch the names of the homicide dicks?"

"Oh, um, one was named Corby or—"

"Kirby? Luke Kirby?"

Leslie's voice sharpened again. "You know him?"

"Heard of him. You sure you covered your tracks? He's got a rep for getting his perp." It felt good to twist Leslie's nerves a bit. Grady didn't like feeling out of control.

"I'm sure that all roads lead directly to my old man. Or prim Prudence, who isn't exactly around to defend herself, now is she?"

Grady flicked an amused look at the pic he had of homely little Prudence. "No, she's not." Though he didn't know why the hell not, if Kirby had her, why hadn't he produced her? Unless he also suspected someone inside Merryweather? Wouldn't that be an unexpected hoot. And absolutely true.

"I can't wait to meet her." Leslie's voice turned dreamy, with an unbalanced edge to it as he added, "I did it, Grady. With my own hands."

"Who?" he asked. Trust the idiot to risk releasing his serial killer instinct now.

"No worries. Just some hooker."

"Where is she?"

He chuckled, like a small, bad boy. "Sent her out with the laundry."

"Can they—"

But Leslie cut him off. "I did my homework, Grady. I know what to do. It's taken care of. No worries. None."

Grady released a silent, frustrated sigh. "Just don't do it again—wait until the op is finished, okay?"

"Aren't you forgetting something?" Leslie sounded dreamy again. "I finish the op with it. I want to do her myself, Grady. Me. Alone with prim Prudence."

"No problem, Les." Grady didn't worry about that promise. He didn't expect Les to be around to keep his date with Prudence Knight. Funny how getting what he wanted was unraveling Les.

He hung up the phone thoughtfully. It was useful to have him on the inside, tracking the players, but it was obvious he didn't plan to wait long before trying out his killing skills again. If he found out that Grady didn't have her, he wasn't sure what Leslie would do.

It wasn't a feeling he liked.

Chapter Eleven

Luke considered himself a patient man, thought he'd learned the hard way as Rosemary wasted away before his eyes. Now he realized it was easier to be patient in the face of death, than in the face of life. Death was the rock and the hard place. It didn't move much, sometimes in increments toward you or your loved one. Sometimes it pounced, but it was always an absolute. Life, on the other hand, was fluid, shifting, and constantly in motion. You thought your feet were firmly planted in patience and then the ground shifted, taking your feet right out from under you.

He didn't like being stuck with this investigation right now. Knight was dead, Amelia was alive and needed his help. He was sure she'd headed for her apartment. Now that he thought about it, he understood why she left. He'd have a hard time waiting for someone else to look into his life, his past. Of course she'd go there. He just wished she'd taken Dewey along with her. Unless the apartment address was bogus? That was a reason to give Dewey the slip. Damn, his head was spinning with unanswered questions and he didn't like it one bit. His heart was telling him that she wouldn't, that she couldn't, lie to him. His head, the cop part, called him a fool.

When he and Mann left the stifling air of the office building, his head was aching. He inhaled the crisp, fresh air with relief. Merryweather Biotechnologies was not a happy place, despite all the money spent making it look pretty, which should have suited his mood but didn't. Not much would.

"Think we should check out Merryweather's native son," Mann had said as they crossed to the car. "I don't like him. And we need to go to the hospital. See if we can find out what the fight was about."

"We should check out her car, too," Luke said, fingering the key again.

"Don't want to find her in the trunk," Mann said, cheerfully, "but it would prove the little bastard wrong."

Luke bit back a sharp retort. It wasn't Mann's fault Luke couldn't appreciate his gruesome sense of humor.

The trip to the hospital seemed slow. With the setting of the sun, the streets were slick and treacherous. Donovan had given them the same info he gave Bryn, so Luke had a description of Prudence Knight's car, the plate number and its general location. He looked at the picture of her again. It didn't seem possible this could be Amelia. Prudence Knight wore glasses, while Amelia had shown no sign of needing aids to her vision. No way she could have skied down the mountain if she needed glasses that thick. The chin could be hers, though. The picture was so bad, it was hard to tell anything from it.

When they pulled into the hospital parking lot, Luke said, "You go on inside. I'll check the car."

Mann nodded. He wasn't sorry to get out of the cold. He never was. He always talked about heading south when he retired, but Luke doubted he would. Mann wasn't a guy to make big changes in his life.

Luke retrieved a flashlight from the jockey box and started across the lot, checking the rows of cars until he found a gray Neon. A sturdy, reliable car, no flash, no dash. Went with the picture of Prudence and the name, but not with Amelia. In his mind, he saw her sailing through the air, her untidy landing, and the way the cold had flushed her cheeks. They couldn't be the same person, could they?

All he'd thought about during the drive across town was finding out the truth, but now that he was by the car, Amelia's keys in hand, he hesitated.

He wasn't naïve. He knew there were all kinds of truth. He'd have sworn on his dad's grave that Amelia's eyes had spoken the truth. The pursuit was real. The wound he'd dressed was real. And the kiss? Well, that had been real, too. Very real. Was he letting emotion cloud his judgment? Or did his judgment need clouding? Jake had had every reason to doubt Phoebe, but he'd followed his instincts, trusted his feelings over the facts that were piling up. In the end, both the facts and his instincts turned out to be right. She had been a thief, but a good thief.

But Jake had been in love. He'd fallen like a rock the minute he saw Phoebe.

Luke wasn't in love. He was just feeling . . . chivalrous. She needed help, and it was his job to help her. Unless she was a criminal. Then it was his job to stop her, to arrest her if she had conspired to eliminate her father and steal the oh-so-secret SHIELD—which she must know wasn't completed. Did she think she could finish it? Have a secret "green" agenda to stop it? A grudge against her father? Or was she an innocent victim?

He rubbed his face impatiently. He felt like he was looking at Amelia through an out-of-focus camera lens. It would explain some things if she was Prudence—but others? Not even close.

He hunched his shoulders, took a quick breath, and shoved the key in the lock. A single turn, and the lock popped up.

It didn't seem possible, it made no sense, but somehow, some way, Prudence Knight and Amelia Hart were the same person. Unless Amelia had somehow gotten possession of Knight's keys? Yeah, right. She'd lied to him. That had to be it.

It was a bitter pill to swallow. He looked at the keys. The apartment was probably bogus, too. Still had to check it. A good cop always checked his facts. And if it wasn't there? Then he'd add Prudence Knight to his suspect list and do his job. There was one absolute where the Kirby family was concerned.

They always did their job.

He leaned against the car and wished, more than anything, that he could ask his mom what to do when he didn't want to do his job.

Donovan Kincaid watched his tail take the corner just the right distance behind him. They were good, but he'd been expecting this. Bryn was determined, and she was smart. She'd figured it out before him. He'd been so busy worrying about Prudence, he'd quit thinking. Only one other time that had happened, and Prudence had been the result. How often had he told his men to forget feeling and focus on thinking? It had seemed so simple when he had no ties, no daughter to feel connected to.

Maybe he'd always known that ties were, well, ties. He'd tried to avoid them. He was a soldier, a man on the move. Then he'd met Prudence's mother. She'd been beautiful, he couldn't think of anything but her. For two weeks she'd belonged to him. He thought it would be forever, until the morning he woke up, and she was gone. He'd tracked her down, found out she was married. That's when he went over seas. It had been a dark time for him. He'd done some things he wasn't proud of, but he'd never crossed a line he couldn't cross back over. When his head cleared, he came back to the states. He hadn't meant to look her up or even keep track of her, but he was curious. Maybe he'd wondered if she was sorry. Maybe he wasn't as over her as he'd thought. Whatever the reason, it had been a shock to find out she'd died not long after giving birth to a daughter.

It wasn't hard to do the math and figure out she was his daughter, not John Knight's. He'd kept track of her through the years. Eventually she finished school and went to work for Knight. He'd kicked around some more, then started working in D.C., where he'd met Bryn. He hadn't tried to seek out Pru, as he called her in his mind, but as his reputation as a security consultant grew, he moved closer to her, until the day Hamilton Merryweather came to him. He should have stayed away, but the compulsion to connect with her had been stronger than his common sense.

It had been part pleasure and a lot of pain to be so close to his little girl. John Knight was a cold, unfeeling man who lived only for his work. Donovan thought he'd crushed the life out of her until she gave him the slip the first time he was following her. Since he couldn't talk to her, he started photographing her. When she was going wherever it was she went, there was a look in her eyes that told him the fire she'd gotten from her real father was burning inside her.

A hundred times he almost told her. A hundred times he didn't. He told himself he did it for her, but it wasn't true. He held back because he was afraid of being rejected, of losing the right to at least see her. It didn't help that she had herself wrapped in an air of reserve that turned him mute every time he was within ten feet of her. He'd been all over the world, talked with kings and leaders without fear or favor, and here he was afraid to talk to his own daughter.

And now he might not get the chance. Who had her? They

had SHIELD and if they had Pru, how long would it take them to find out it wasn't ready? And what would they do when they did? John Knight had thought he was so clever, hiding it all in her head. He'd just made it easy for someone to take him out and put Pru at risk. And somehow, he had put her at risk, too. Someone had smoked out his interest in her and was planning . . . what? They already had SHIELD, so what else could they want that he could deliver?

Whoever it was had seriously underestimated him, and he had an idea of just who that might be. He'd known when he met Grady O'Brien that he was a dangerous man. That's why he hadn't gone back to that camp. Even that small contact appeared to have given O'Brien ideas.

He looked in his rear view mirror. Time to lose the tail. Then he needed to do a little recon of Grady's camp. Grady wasn't the only person who could come up with a plan and execute it.

Dewey entered the restaurant in much the same way a Christian might have entered an arena full of lions. It was odd to be in love with someone that scared him, but he could no more change that than he could change the way the moon moved through the night sky—in the real world. In VR, he was captain of his fate, master of his soul and ruler of the skies. In this world, Bryn was master of his fate, ruler of his electronic parole bracelet and the ruler of his heart.

If only she could figure out her own heart. Didn't Bryn know she loved him? Hadn't she figured that out yet? And if she did, what would she do about it? He knew a lot of things about Bryn, but he didn't know that.

He saw her before she saw him. She'd brought her work with her. Smart girl. He was usually late. She frowned down at the paper she was holding. A file lay open on the table in place of her plate. The two little wrinkles between her brows made his heart jump in his chest the way it had the first time he'd seen her. She'd been so uptight she crinkled when she walked. And that walk, well, that made his heart jump, too. She had a great ass and this side-to-side move that just about knocked him over when he saw it. And don't get him started on her legs. Man, the good Lord knew what he was doing when he gave women legs. He'd been thinking about giving her an ankle bracelet, but wasn't sure his libido could stand it. If he went up in flames, he'd never know if they could make it as a couple.

He approached her slowly. This might be the last time he walked toward her, so he wanted to savor what time he had left. Of course, he probably should have been thinking about how to tell her instead of his little stroll down memory lane.

He'd thought about doing it ala *You've Got Mail*, but he didn't want to add plagiarism to his list of crimes. There was always the direct approach.

"Hello, Bryn. I'm Phagan." Then his head gets lopped off, it rolls across the floor, to rest against a wall with his eyes staring blankly at the ceiling. With his luck, his body would keep on walking for a few minutes, before slumping to the ground. Besides, the direct approach sounded so Al-Anon-ish, so twelve steps waiting in the wings. "My name is Dewey Hyatt and I'm a Phagan."

If confession was good for the soul, why was it so hard to confess? No, the direct approach was just too . . . direct. Which left the indirect approach, whatever that was—

He saw Bryn stiffen, then turn in her chair to look at him, and he knew that she already knew. He just didn't know how she knew.

Bryn watched Dewey stop, tug at the neck of his shirt, then walk up and drop in the seat opposite her. He looked like a man on his way to the death chamber.

She almost smiled, but her body was still in shock. Thank heavens she'd brought the file with her, so she had something to pretend to look at while her thoughts spun in crazy patterns inside her head.

"How . . . when . . ." his voice trailed off.

The "when" could be counted in moments. How was a little harder. On some level, she realized she'd always known. Or she should have. It had been in front of her face for the last year. It was as if her brain had finally arranged all the pieces into a recognizable pattern.

She'd been thinking about both of them all the way to the restaurant, listing their good and bad qualities in her head. Oddly enough, the lists had come out the same. The odds of that happening were as great as two strangers having the same DNA. That's when she had the blinding flash of illumination. She wasn't in lo—interested—in two men. There was only one, and she might have to kill him.

Dewey knew it, too. He looked at her like a man who'd played his last card and knew it was a loser. His shoulders slumped and for the first time, he looked serious.

Like a small, bad boy whose world was ending in a crash.

Against her will, her heart softened. She didn't let it reach her expression. There was just too much happening too fast for her to give ground right now, especially not when it was crumbling under her feet. At some level, she knew she wasn't making sense. How could she when her head was spinning with rage?

And relief.

Okay, she admitted it. She was relieved. She wasn't looking at three choices: Phagan, Dewey or neither. Just two. Do I or don't I? And if I do, how do I make it happen? Making it not happen would be easy, so very easy.

This deception could end Dewey's parole in a heart beat. It had been based on truth in elocution. He hadn't lied, but he'd left out the mother of truths. If he'd said anything, tried to defend himself or charm her, it would already have been over. But he didn't. He just sat there looking at her. Totally in her power.

But not.

He reminded her of Phoebe the day she'd been arrested. Not fighting her fate, but not giving in either. Self-contained, relieved everything was on the table. All the burdens at someone else's feet. Later, she'd asked Phoebe what she would have done if she'd got jail time. Phoebe had looked at her as if surprised at the question.

"I'd have done it. Running isn't all that fun, sugar."

Phoebe always got more southern with her, Bryn had noticed, or when anyone asked about her life of crime. It was a defense mechanism from her years of shifting identities. It was her own fault, Bryn realized. She hadn't forgiven Phoebe for getting away with her crimes. Or was it her happiness that Bryn was jealous of? Probably both. And Phoebe sensed it, hence the auto-defensive southern-ness.

It wasn't easy to realize she wasn't a nice person. Not only had Phoebe paid a heavy price for crimes committed by her father, she worked hard to give everything back, to atone. And if Bryn were honest with herself, which apparently she wasn't, Phoebe had never been a criminal in her heart or her soul—she had always hated what she did.

And Dewey? He was always joking about being a criminal mastermind, but he'd been remarkably docile in his captivity. He'd tweaked her with his past, but she probably deserved it. She thought she'd loosened up, but not nearly enough. She was still holding something back, even with people who gave everything to her without reserve.

When did I lose my sense of humor? My sense of balance? Was it the agency or a character flaw? A man had loved her enough to give up everything. And his everything was a lot. He really was a criminal mastermind with uncounted resources at his fingertips. Enough to get himself out of that dive he lived in now, for sure.

Instead of being impressed or even grateful, she'd been annoyed. Of course he hadn't told her. How could he trust himself to a woman who trusted no one? Not even herself.

He leaned toward her but didn't touch her, to her disappointment.

"Why are you so sad, Miss Bailey?"

"Are you hungry?" He shook his head. "Neither am I. Let's get out of here."

She pushed back her chair and stood up. He stood up, too, his expression troubled, worried. There wasn't just a world between them. There were two, hers and his. But there was nothing between them that hadn't been between Jake and Phoebe.

She took a deep breath and then held out her hand. It seemed to take a long time for it to reach the halfway point between them. In painfully slow motion she saw Dewey look at the hand and then look at her.

Don't crack a joke, please, she prayed.

He didn't even smile. Just slowly—very slowly—took her hand in his.

He'd touched her before of course, but it had never been like this. She'd never . . . initiated the contact. Had always shooed it off. Who'd have thought the mere touching of hands could be so shattering? The slide of his flesh against hers. The slow meshing of fingers. The full palm contact. The click of two wrongs uniting into an amazing right. She felt like she'd exploded and was now reintegrating as someone else.

Someone she didn't know, but felt a lot more comfortable with.

They turned together and walked outside. They must have stopped to collect coats. She didn't remember. Was just glad to find herself outside on the sidewalk with Dewey. It must have been cold, but she didn't feel it. She was wrapped in warmth, all of it flowing steadily from their two joined hands.

Out of the light from the restaurant, they stopped and turned to face each other. There was so much to say, so much to wade through, but none of that seemed to matter. His hand holding hers tightened. His other hand touched her cheek. Chills feathered down her body from the contact. She caught her breath. He started to bend his head towards her, but his cell phone rang. He stopped, then shook his head slightly.

"It might be your parole officer," Bryn said, not recognizing her own voice. It was so breathy, so husky.

"Right." He pulled it out, giving her a shaken, crooked grin before saying, "Dewey Hyatt's Criminal Enterprise."

For once she wanted to laugh at it. Finally she wanted to laugh.

He waited a minute, then said, "Hello?" He stowed the phone. "Wrong number, I guess. Now where was I?"

"You were about to kiss me," Bryn said. "And I was about to let you."

His grin curled her toes. When his arms slid around her, her insides opened like petals in the sun. He picked her up and twirled them in a slow circle.

"You . . . amaze me, Miss Bailey."

"Good," she said.

Grady hung up the phone with a frown. Dewey Hyatt's Criminal Enterprise? Obviously it was a joke, but had he got the real name? Where had he heard that name?

171

He turned to the computer and did a simple google search, just to see what he'd turn up. His first hit was a newspaper story about a year old. About a pair of high-tech thieves getting parole and community service hours—if they'd help the government fight computer-related crime. Along with the article were pictures, mug shots, of the pair.

Grady studied both pictures. He wanted to be able to recognize them if he ever saw them again. He spent the most time on Hyatt. Was he, he wondered, the genius who had unraveled the viruses Grady created? He'd cracked the last one in under an hour. Pity he'd changed sides. He could use talent like that on his team.

What he found even more interesting than the pictures, though, was the name of the Deputy US Marshal involved in the case.

Jake Kirby. Brother of Luke. That was one law enforcement infested family, but he was only dealing with one of them. And Luke wasn't federal. A simple homicide detective. No problem.

Despite the lateness of the hour, Luke couldn't go home without checking the address Amelia had given him. To his surprise, and relief, it was there. What did it mean? It sure as hell wasn't the address listed on her employment records. He could postulate that the PDA belonged to a friend, but how had she gotten the keys? It made his head hurt to think about it.

He looked at his watch. It was after two in the morning. If she was in there, she'd be asleep. If she was in there, he needed to know she was all right. He needed to look at her with the Prudence photograph in mind. He sighed. He just needed to see her again. Oh boy.

Finally, he tapped lightly on the door. When there was no

answer, he tried a couple of the keys. One released the lock, letting him push the door open.

"Amelia?"

Nothing. He didn't want to blind her with a light, so he pulled out a pen flashlight, but the precaution wasn't necessary.

She wasn't there.

There were, however, signs she'd been here. The clothes she'd been wearing were in a small heap on the bathroom floor. The towel was still damp. The smell of soap and lotion still hung in the air, teasing his nostrils with memories of what it had been like to be close to her.

It didn't take him long to look around her apartment and conclude it wasn't a place where someone lived their life. The pictures on the wall were an odd combination of Amelia and Prudence. Amelia, in a Clark Kent/Superman motif, didn't wear glasses. The bank statements and driver's license said Amelia Hart, but he *knew*, didn't he, that Amelia was Prudence Knight? So why the apparent double-life?

The license put her age at thirty-four, which made his heart do a little jump. Not as young as he'd first thought. A thought he shouldn't be having right now. Face it, man, if she had been planning to kill her father and steal SHIELD, establishing another identity was the logical, first step.

While his cop side argued against her, his heart sided for the defense. This place didn't really look like a hideout. It looked like a retreat. A place she'd come to read, listen to music, maybe to be alone?

The next question was, where had she gone? She must have known he'd come here as soon as he was free. So why wasn't she here? Unless he hadn't been too good at keeping this secret? And whoever had been after her had caught up with her again? There was no sign of a struggle, but they could have taken her as she left. Where else would she go? She didn't know where he lived. Hadn't made it to Dewey's apartment to know where that was.

He sank down on her couch, sinking back into the comforting softness and releasing another cloud of her scent into the air around him. He was tired. And afraid he'd never see her again.

He hadn't wanted to feel this way about a woman ever again. Ironic to find himself back, almost to square one, just a few hours after he thought he'd achieved freaking closure.

Damn ironic.

Chapter Twelve

Bryn leaned back with a sigh, holding Dewey off with one hand. With much kissing and some embarrassing giggling, they'd managed to make their way to his apartment. Each kiss was deeper and more mind spinning than the last. As fun as it was to be necking with someone on a couch, they had some air to clear before it went any further. "Sit over there. I can't think when you're this close."

His lazy, satisfied smile took her breath away, and undermined her resolve to get back to work. If he'd pressed the issue . . . but he didn't. He also didn't move across the room. Instead, he drew in his body until the width of one couch cushion separated them. He ran both hands through his hair, adding to the disarray her hands had done, and took a deep breath. She trembled when she saw him shudder, feeling powerful and humble at the same time.

She'd given up wondering how it happened. How someone had managed to steer a heart-whole course through thirty-three years only to fall, with a thump, in love. It had happened, so now she dealt with it. Her life had changed. She didn't know what she was going to do about Phagan. It was Dewey in front of her. Phagan was, and probably always would be, virtual. He was something she'd have to think about, but not now when her lips were still swollen and tingly from kissing Dewey. To avoid the issue she went to make coffee, asking over her shoulder, "So what was the big mystery with Luke?"

Dewey seemed to gather himself in a bit again. His smile

was as wide and as sexy, but he also seemed to have retreated just a bit. It seemed the elephant—his legal status—was back in the room with them. Would they be tripping over it forever?

"He asked me to meet him at the bus station today," he said.

"Bus station?" Bryn paused in her preparations. "Something happen to his truck?"

"Got snowed in the mountains. He skied out." Dewey paused, then added as if it were an afterthought, "Had a damsel in distress in tow."

"Really?" Bryn added the grounds to the machine. "Well, his mom has been wanting him to meet a nice girl. Was she . . . nice?"

"I guess. Sure was a looker."

That got her attention. He grinned and the elephant shrunk a little for a moment.

Her grin felt rueful. "Really. And in distress. Sounds . . . irresistible."

"And hard to keep track of. I lost her in Wal-Mart. I'm hoping you can protect me from Luke."

Bryn propped her elbows on the counter and stared at him. "She gave you the slip?"

"Yeah. I saw some burly types after them. A couple of them followed him into the men's room. Saw a couple more get on the bus and search it."

Bryn straightened with a frown. "Luke okay?"

"Yeah, other than being pissed at me. He got called into work on some murder or other."

Bryn could guess which murder. Clearly she needed to talk to him about the various nuances she'd turned up. In the morning. She poured them both a cup and sat back down beside Dewey.

"So why did you want to talk to me about Phagan?" She didn't look at him. The elephant was back and sitting between them. She took a sip out of her cup and then set it down. She didn't want it. She wanted Dewey.

"Forest for the Trees wants a face-to-face meet."

She looked at him then.

"This is it. Your line into GREEN. If you can get me disconnected from this." He held his foot out, the one with the electronic bracelet.

A stab of fear followed a surge of elation. Dewey wanted to walk into the fire of undercover and take both her guys with him. If something happened, she'd lose them both. She took a deep breath.

"I can get you disconnected. When?"

"Let's find out." He crossed to his computer and logged on. She watched him type, then hit return to send the email on its way. "Guy's good," he said. "I've tried to track him every way I know how. No go."

"And what about him? Has he been able to track you?"

Dewey looked hurt, except for the expression in his wicked eyes. "Miss Bailey! How can you even ask?"

"Sorry," Bryn said, smiling, but feeling the muscles around her heart tighten. "So."

His eyes turned tender. "This is the only way."

"I know," she said.

Almost as if Forest for the Trees had been waiting for him, he got his answer. Bryn looked at him.

"Tomorrow. He wants a number he can call me. Will tell me when and where then."

"Don't give him your cell phone. He could check it out. Do you—"

"Have a clean number? Well, yeah."

She waited until he'd sent his response with the clean cell

phone number and logged off. When he turned to face her, there was no sign of amusement or triumph in his face. "I wish—"

"What do you wish, my darling Miss Bailey?" He came and sat down beside her, taking her back in his arms.

She sagged against him, her head against his heart, which was beating slow and steady. Persistently—like his courtship.

"I wish—" she almost couldn't say it. It was the ultimate admission of weakness. And what if this wasn't a courtship, but an affair? She'd just assumed, because she thought the whole premarital sex issue nuts, that he would, too. What did she really know about him or what he believed? He'd been living out there on the fringes of the law abiding world. He and Phoebe—well, she'd always wondered how close they'd been. Phoebe had said once that Phagan had loved her sister, Kerry Anne. It was her death that had brought them together, had launched their pact to avenge her death.

She wasn't jealous of Kerry Anne. How could she resent a dead girl? First love was first love. Even she had one. Sweet, unrequited, tucked away in the moth balls of the past. Phoebe, on the other hand, was very much alive and in the present.

"Were you and . . . Phoebe ever . . ." She couldn't even say it out loud, couldn't look at him as she asked.

Dewey cupped her chin, turned her face to his. "No. Never." He sighed, his gaze turning distant. "When we met, we were both . . . snarling balls of grief. I did love her sister, as much as I could love someone then."

She smiled. "I know. What was she like?"

Dewey sighed again. "Broken. Inside and out." His grin was crooked and absent of joy. "I would have married her. I thought I could fix her. Instead . . ."

"It wasn't your fault she died. You were just a kid."

"Yeah." He didn't sound like he believed her. "She's part of who I am. She always will be. I've made my peace with it. And it brought me to you. We might never have met if I hadn't met her and got the notion I could fix what was wrong with her world."

His look was rueful, resigned, and a little sad. It made her love him more, want him more. She covered his hands with hers and looked at him. "Then she's part of us. And always will be."

If there would be an always?

His mouth widened into a grateful, faintly awed smile. "You're so beautiful, so . . . everything. I can't believe we're here. We're now. I—"

He stopped.

"What?" she didn't know whether to be puzzled or afraid.

"I don't want it to end. I want—it all." He changed the position of their hands. Now he held her, with hands and his anxious, eager gaze.

"All?" She knew what her "all" would be, but his?

He hesitated, like a diver at the edge of the board who now realizes how deep the water is and isn't sure he can jump.

"All." He took a deep breath, closed his eyes, then opened them again and leapt. "Marriage. White picket fence. Kids. Mortgage. Lawn to mow. All. With you."

Relief took all the stiffening from her body. She sagged into his arms.

"Oh, Dewey, so do I." She snuggled against his chest, listening to the pounding of his heart and reveling in feeling like the "little woman." His hand found her chin and tipped it up, so his mouth could find her mouth. Her mouth was very happy with this arrangement, as was the rest of her. When they stopped for air, she murmured, "I wish we could get married before you have to go."

"Well," Dewey turned her chin up again, the mischief back in his eyes, "we could. I've been carrying this around for the past month. And there's one of the those mail order preachers next door . . ."

"You were so sure?" Bryn felt her hackles rise, even as a thrill coursed through her.

"Never," Dewey said, with a tender smile, "but as Phoebe is always pointing out, all God's children need a goal."

Hackles subsiding, Bryn took the paper he held out and looked at it. It was a marriage license. With his and her details already filled in.

"Is it—"

"Legal? Of course it is, darling. There are some things in this life you don't counterfeit. Ever."

"How did you know?"

He shook his head. "I never knew. Ever. I just lived in . . . hope."

Warmth swept through her, sweeping away her doubts and her fears. Hope was all any of them had. Or its opposite— fear. She wasn't going to live in fear anymore. Bryn pulled away from him.

"Well, don't just sit there. Go get him. I have to be to work at eight a.m. That doesn't give us a whole lot of time to conclude our . . . business."

Dewey's smile took her breath away. "Yes, ma'am."

Amelia woke lying on the floor of Hilly's and Tweek's apartment. She remembered Hilly handing her the big, comfy pillow, but not the quilt that now covered her. An arm trailed off the edge of the sofa a few inches from Amelia's nose. Tweek's arm, judging by the tattoo circling the wrist and the exotic perfume, faint but enduring.

Amelia looked around and found Hilly hanging off three

sides of an overstuffed chair. The smell of pizza still lingered in the air and a pile of crumpled tissues testified to their satisfaction with the movie.

Pizza, Amelia decided, was a perfect food. Right up there with chocolate. It hadn't stopped her missing Luke, but it did fill the hollow spots in her stomach. If she couldn't be with Luke, this was sure as heck the next best thing. She didn't remember Tweeks and Hilly, but oddly, she did. Or maybe it was the feeling of companionship that her brain was reluctantly releasing? It was the first sense of the familiar she'd had since she woke up in Luke's cabin, and she welcomed it.

She hadn't talked much, since she didn't know what to say or not, but they hadn't seemed to notice. Was this how it usually was? She'd wanted to ask them about herself, but Luke's caution held her back. They felt okay to her, but what did she really know about anything or anyone right now?

With a sigh at the world and its fears intruding into the moment, she tossed the blanket back and got up. Neither Hilly nor Tweeks moved. If they did have sinister intentions, they were disguising them very well behind snuffling baby snores.

Amelia smiled. They were probably around the same age, but she felt years older than them as she tucked the blankets around them both before letting herself out of the apartment. The clock showed the time as brutally early, but she couldn't get back to sleep. Her heart was pumping with fear and anticipation at what she would find at Merryweather. It could be everything. It could be nothing. And she wasn't sure what she wanted it to be.

She took another shower and dressed in warm, comfortable clothes. Her heartbeat was slow and heavy as she stowed the driver's license, some cash and the bus pass in her coat pocket.

181

Odd that the license hadn't been with her, but she didn't seem to have a car, so maybe that explained it. Maybe she just used it for ID. But hadn't there been a car key on the set of keys Luke kept? At the thought her head began to ache again, as if to punish her for trying to sort it all out. Her brain just didn't seem to want her to remember, which meant that part of her didn't want to remember.

Her last act, before pulling on a warm hat, was to take the top sheet of the Merryweather note pad and tuck in her pocket, too. Then she let herself out of the apartment, locking it securely behind her and keeping the key as she headed down the hall. She'd sort of been hoping that Luke would show up. In the living room, she had the odd feeling she could smell Luke, but it had to be wishful sniffing. She'd tried to listen for any sounds of him arriving last night, but hadn't heard any movement in the hall before she fell asleep.

She didn't know what to make of it. He'd had to work, but all night seemed a bit excessive. Maybe he was annoyed with her for giving Dewey the slip. She couldn't blame him for that, though she'd sort of hoped he would understand her need to find out for herself. She'd decided not to rely on him. He had other priorities. And he'd said he took things seriously. He'd probably needed to pull back a little, in case she got too serious. That's all. He'd protected her. Done what was needed and now he had his own life. And his work, if that beep was what Dewey had thought it was.

She'd eat some breakfast to ease the hollow feeling in her middle, then see if she could figure out the buses. She'd noticed a McDonald's on the next corner as they were driving in. And, not being a man, she wouldn't hesitate to ask directions.

Luke decided to make another run by Amelia's apartment

before meeting Mann, but he had to stop by his mom's first. She'd made that quite clear last night. He entered cautiously. As the oldest, the "experimental son" Debra Kirby liked to call him, his relationship with his mom was complicated. Unlike his brothers, he never seemed to know when his mom was fake mad or real mad.

He was just finishing up at the academy when his dad died and he found himself thrust into the role of man of the house. More than his brothers, he knew how hard dad's death had hit their mom. He'd stood outside her room some nights, listening to the harsh sound of her sobs. He'd noticed the shadows under her eyes, despite the determined smile she had for her boys. Sometimes her eyes would meet Luke's across the room and pain would flare, stark and raw.

He knew why. He and Matt were the image of their dad. He'd sometimes wondered how he'd felt if Rosemary had left a miniature of herself behind to haunt him. And his dad had left two of them. But back then, Matt had still been in development. Not like him. The day before his dad died, Luke had stood back to back with him and his mom had declared them equal in height. If his life were a Greek myth, that would be why his father died. The defeat of the old in the face of the young. For a long time he thought he was to blame.

Eventually, he realized that wasn't so. A perp on a high had killed him. Acceptance of it took a long time. He'd tried hard not to *be* his dad, while still trying to fill his shoes. His Mom had needed him to be the support, to be there for her and his brothers.

It was Rosemary who helped him sort it all out. She would look at him, one brow arched as if to ask, "What the hell are you doing?" and pretense dropped away. She'd ask him about his dad and in talking about him, understanding had emerged. He'd forgiven his mom for feeling pain when she looked at him, but a part of him still braced for that first look when he came into a room where she was.

This morning, his mom looked relieved. Her arms wrapped around him. She had to stand on her toes to do it, though she was a tall woman and thin, like Jake. Luke kissed her on both sides of her narrow, clever face and ruffled the hair he'd watched turn gray all those years ago. She looked happier these days. The shadows of the past almost erased. She was dating their dad's best friend. He wasn't thrilled about it. None of them were, but they all agreed she had more than the right. And in light of his recent feelings about Amelia—on the anniversary of his wife's death, no less—he understood a little better about how things happen.

"What's wrong?" she asked, taking his face in her hands. Her look, as always, pierced his surface shields and started digging around his insides.

"Got a case dumped on me last night," he said, still hoping to bluff.

"The one on the news? The scientist?" Luke nodded. "Okay, now tell me what's really wrong."

"What makes you think—"

"Don't even start. You have the same look in your eyes Jake had a year ago—you've met someone. And it's not going well." She stepped back, her hands on her hips, daring him to say she was wrong.

Even if she was wrong, which she wasn't, it was a violation of the mom/son relationship to say your mom was wrong. It was like stepping on the flag or dissing baseball.

He hunched his shoulders and shuffled his feet.

"What's her name?"

He had to look at her then, his mouth twitching into a sheepish grin.

"You don't know? What is with you and Jake?"

184

He rubbed his hair. "It's . . . complicated."

"Love always is." She studied him so long, he shifted from one foot to the other.

"What?"

"I'd like to meet her."

Now he looked down at his feet. Managed to not shuffle them.

"I can't believe it. You've lost her?" He nodded. "Well. Déjà vu yet again." Her foot tapped for a minute, then she said, "Do you have time to eat before you find her?"

Her confidence was absolute, the love in her eyes without condition. Relief washed over him in waves. He nodded.

"Pancakes?"

"Only time for some toast and coffee." She didn't move, her gaze still locked on his. "What?" he asked again.

"I like looking at my son. Is that a crime?"

He laughed and shook his head, taking the newspaper she shoved at him. He had a feeling she'd been seeing him in a wedding tux. He didn't disabuse her of the notion. When he'd told her it was complicated, the understatement had almost choked him. Besides, his mom wanted him to be in love. That's why she said he looked like Jake. He wasn't in love with Amelia. He couldn't be. It was too soon. It wasn't right either. The way they'd met, on the anniversary of Rosemary's death? He'd always remember that. She'd kissed him because he was there. Maybe to confuse him. Maybe because she was confused. He couldn't, wouldn't let his heart be involved until he knew—and probably not even then.

He arrived at Amelia's apartment later than he'd planned but was glad he'd stopped by his mom's. He felt better, though he didn't know why. Stepping inside Amelia's apartment, it was apparent that he'd just missed her. The shower and Amelia smells were stronger, her towel wetter than last night. And this time some of the clothes in the closet were gone.

Where was she going? What was on her mind? Was she working from a plan or just reacting? Had she remembered something? Or never forgotten anything?

A quick search turned up that she'd taken the driver's license and the bus pass and some of the cash, but not all of it. If she'd been about to run, she'd have taken all the cash. There was one possibility he hadn't explored. If she was conspiring with whoever had taken the SHIELD prototype, that would be a reason to stay put, mainly if she thought she could complete the research—or was in cahoots with someone who could. Maybe there'd been a falling out? A betrayal?

Damn. He rubbed his face. He could invent theories, but convincing his heart to believe them was another matter. He kept bumping up against her eyes. Could anyone lie and look that innocent? Be that believable?

He looked at the desk again, his gaze sweeping past, then returning to the scratch pad. He'd noticed it last night, though not particularly. It had a shopping list started on the top sheet. That was gone now. In its place was another kind of list. He studied it with a frown. It wasn't long, but it was illuminating.

I hate lies.

He remembered her saying that with real passion. What did it mean? It felt like the truth. A struggle for identity, for memory. Almost at once his left brain reminded him she knew he'd be coming here. She hadn't waited. Maybe she felt like she had to continue the charade, while she tried to get her hands on the prototype.

He told his left brain to shut up. Even managed a slight smile at the tiny doodle he recognized as himself, she'd done under the list. There'd been other doodles on the shopping list, he remembered now. Had it sparked some memory for her?

A bit of light worked its way through the heavy curtains over the windows, showing him something he'd missed last night. Stenciled into the background of the pad was a logo and address for Merryweather Biotechnology.

If she really had lost her memory, it would be natural to go there and see if she remembered anything or if anyone remembered her. It might also be a place a co-conspirator would go—especially when she had a handy-dandy amnesia alibi all set up.

Whichever it was, it was where he was going.

Larry was sick of staring at the Merryweather Biotech parking lot and the streets around it. And himself in the rear view mirror. Surely the girl would have showed up by now if she was going to? Kirby had her on ice, stashed somewhere safe while he figured out what was going on. Meanwhile, here he sat like a big, old sore thumb where Kirby could spot him.

As if his thoughts had summoned the guy, Larry saw him turn the corner and quickly ducked down.

"What's he doing?" he hissed at Hickey.

"Turned into the parking lot. Now he's getting out. Walking toward the building. Oh, wait. Now he's stopped. He's looking at the bus that just pulled up."

That was curious enough to encourage Larry to peek over the dash. There was a bus. Kirby was stopped, looking at it. Why? Unless . . .

He did a quick estimate of the distance to the bus stop. He was closer and he had the advantage of wheels. Kirby was walking back, but slowly, as if he wasn't quite sure what he'd seen. Good. If the girl was getting off the bus, he had one chance to grab her before she got to Kirby.

Larry started the engine and eased the van into drive. "Get

ready with the sleeping shit. When I tell you, open the door."

"What—"

"I'm betting he just spotted the girl. Hurry and get ready! We got one shot at this. Don't screw it up or we're done for!"

Hickey, grumbling under his breath, scrambled into the back of the van. Larry rolled forward as a figure stepped off the bus. The bus pulled back into traffic, blocking her for a moment. When it rumbled past him, he got a clear view of her.

It was her, no question about it.

"Get ready, Hickey."

Luke saw Amelia looking out of the bus and felt a surge of relief. He'd beat her here. He could head her off, talk to her. And see if she was honest or the best actress he'd ever met. On the drive over, he'd been thinking about who might be trustworthy inside the company and remembered Donovan Kincaid. He'd sure leaped to her defense when Leslie got cute yesterday. Of the two, he'd put his money on Kincaid having the better instincts. Or did he want to believe him?

He started walking—not hurrying because part of him didn't want to know if the news was going to be bad—toward the street as the bus came to a ponderous stop. His gaze followed Amelia's progress the length of the bus, then lost sight of her until the bus moved off with a smoky roar.

Maybe it was the engine sounds or a prickling on his neck that had him looking down the street. When he saw the van, he froze for an instant, then pulled his piece and started to run. The light was with her, so Amelia started across the street. The van was closer to her than he was.

"Amelia!" he shouted.

She stopped in the middle of the street, looked his way,

then her face broke into a smile and she waved at him. "Luke!"

"Look out!" He gestured as the van sped up. The side door opened. She turned to look, as it pulled level with her. The man crouched in the opening fired off a shot at him. Luke dodged behind a car, started to fire back, but Amelia was in the way. The guy hooked his arm around her waist and lifted her inside. They fell back in an untidy heap on the floor as the van picked up speed. Before it turned out of sight, Luke saw Amelia struggle, then go limp.

She was gone. He rubbed his face in frustration, muttering every swear word he knew. He stopped.

Helicopter. Amelia had been terrified of them. One had been on the mountain the day they'd skied down. In a moment, he was back in his car, heading for the airport, his cell phone to his ear. He'd tried this alone and failed. Now it was time to use his strengths, or in this case, his brothers' strengths. It was time to call in the rest of the Kirbys.

Chapter Thirteen

Bryn padded out of the bathroom in her stocking feet. She kept her eyes down, looking for her boots in the semi-dark, so she wouldn't look at the bed where Dewey lay sleeping. She'd slept about two hours last night, but she didn't feel tired. She felt . . . delicious.

There'd been one moment of panic after he'd carried her over her threshold and set her on her feet when she'd told him, "I've never—"

"Neither have I," Dewey had interrupted. His hand brushing her cheek had been trembling, igniting an answering quiver in her mid-section.

"Never?" She knew why she hadn't. At first there'd been the drive to succeed, then she'd fallen for a guy who presented himself in cyberspace. Once she thought about it, though, it didn't surprise her. He'd told her last night that his first love was broken.

"I was saving myself for you," he'd said. His hands traced her face as if he still couldn't quite believe he could touch her. He stepped close to her, their mouths a breath apart, their bodies touching. "Mating should be more than just bodies squeaking together, my darling Miss Bailey."

"Have you been reading my romance novels again?" she murmured against his mouth, holding off a moment longer.

"A wise man does his research."

She'd laughed, feeling the joy all the way from her toes. She'd never felt this free, this happy.

People who said inexperience was a turn-off were so

wrong, she concluded as she finished lacing her second boot. So very wrong. Despite their mutual lack of experience, they'd managed to satisfactorily do the deed and then again in the time allotted to them. Granted, she had nothing to compare it to, but why should she care about comparisons when her body still tingled with delight?

She stood up, forgetting her resolve not to look at Dewey. He lay sprawled face down in the tangled sheets, the top sheet just hiding his butt. Just to the right of his shoulder, the shoulder she'd traced with her mouth last night, she could see the clock glowing in the dim light.

She was already late for work. She took a shaky breath and turned away instead of diving in and tasting his skin again. Desire was an undertow she fought against all the way to the door. In the living room, it was slightly easier with him out of her sight. Slightly.

She'd take it in stages. Start with some calls. Some good, some bad. Phoebe had managed to disable the virus GREEN had planted in the computers in California and had sent the instructions to the other labs hit that night. Jake sounded lazy and contented, with the sound of the waves in the background. Tough duty.

Her next call was to her voice mail. The men who had been following Donovan Kincaid had lost him last night. She didn't feel too bad. She'd expected it. She'd try to phone him later. Maybe by then she'd have decided whether to tell him her and Matt's theory that someone wanted to pressure him into blasting Al Gore. By then he might already know. Would he call her? Somehow she doubted it. He'd already told her he'd do what he had to. Which meant she'd have to do what she could to stop him.

This morning it was easier to understand how he'd gotten into a mess. It must have been hard for him to live his life

knowing the woman he'd loved had chosen someone else—
and taken his child with her. What kind of woman had she
been?

At least she'd only deceived herself all this time, she
thought wryly. Dewey seemed to have figured her out a long
time ago. She'd fought the good fight and lost, but by losing,
she'd won way more than she lost. She felt no regret for
missing out on the big wedding. She'd never seen herself
walking down any aisle, but her parents would be disappointed. If she gave them a grandchild . . .

She covered her stomach. Her mom had had her nine
months and a minute from after saying, "I do." Unexpectedly
a baby didn't seem nearly as much of a trap as she'd thought,
though parenthood was proving quite the trap for Donovan.

It was unusual that the kidnappers, if they were kidnappers and not conspirators—she had to consider that Prudence Knight stood to the gain the most by her faux dad's
death—hadn't made any demands yet. Time was a kidnapper's enemy. Why the delay? Typically kidnappings were
planned down to the smallest detail, but this one had an on-
the-fly feel to it. Something wasn't right, but she couldn't
figure out what. Not enough data yet.

She pulled a pad of paper toward her and then had page
fright at the thought of her first note to her husband. *I'm a
wife,* she thought, but the idea was too new to track. Oddly
enough, the idea of being mother was a lot easier to process.

She was saved by the bell—well, Dewey's cell phone
ringer. Was it the clean phone number they'd given to Forest
for the Trees? After a very short, mumbled conversation, he
appeared in the doorway. He'd pulled on his jeans, but his
chest was bare and his hair still tousled from their love-
making. His gaze found hers, a hint of worry in the depths.
She knew what he wanted to know. She went to him, feeling

enormous relief as his arms closed around her again.

"Was it him?" she asked, though she didn't want to know. Didn't want to think about him in danger, just when they'd found each other. She could tell herself that she'd always have last night, but she wanted more than a night. She wanted a lifetime with him.

"Got my marching instructions," Dewey said, watching the worry deepen on her face. Phoebe kept telling him to be careful what he wished for. He'd started the dance with Forest for the Trees to please Bryn. Now it was pulling him away from her. He wasn't afraid of the danger. He'd damn near died a year ago. It was easy to think you were bullet-proof, until you started caring if you lived or died. "I wrote 'em down. It's somewhere south, he'll tell me more when I get there, he says. Midnight tonight."

"Not in a hurry, is he?"

"Doesn't seem to be. Clever of him." This guy, and he was sure now it was a guy, reminded him a little bit of himself. Set the right bait and let the fish bring themselves in. No worries, no work. Not much fun for the fish, but then it never was. He wished he wasn't slated to be the fish in this deal. Well, he had until midnight to figure out how to turn the tables.

"A lot to do before then," Bryn murmured, but she didn't pull away from him.

He was content to wait, to hold her, to hold onto the moment. Over her shoulder, he studied her apartment. It was tidy, controlled like he'd thought she was the first time she arrested him. Not anymore, he thought, as he noticed the trail of their clothes leading to the bedroom. It was funny in such a clean room, but he'd known Bryn wasn't the sum of what could be seen.

She sighed, so deep it was almost a shudder. Slowly, but

firmly, she pushed away from him, her smile bright, her gaze avoiding his.

"Let's get this over with so we can continue our honeymoon." A blush surged up her neck into her face.

Dewey turned her face up to his and smiled at her. "With that kind of incentive, how can I fail?"

Hey, fish had brains the size of a nail head and they got away, so why shouldn't he?

Luke stared out the window toward the south, the direction his buddy in airport security had told him the chopper had been flying before it dropped off the radar screen. Behind him, his brother, Matt, entered the conference room. Luke turned to face him, remembering the last time they'd conferred in this room. He was a local cop. How did he manage to keep getting caught up in all this Federal shit?

He should be with Mann, doggedly pursuing leads in the Knight murder and leave this one to those with jurisdiction. He liked what he did, liked his circle of influence and was happy to stay within it. His brothers' jobs gobbled up too much time. He liked to balance work and play. He was the mellow big brother, the one who was around when mom needed her lawn cut or his brothers needed their butts kicked. That was his role, his place in the family and community.

So what was he doing here in this dreary room once again with his gut twisting with worry for a woman he'd known for little more than one day? A little more than twenty-four hours. Busy hours, but still just hours. Dani liked to trot out the whole, no man is an island quote and would probably bring it out now, but even under her stringent guidelines, he'd done his part for the whole and more. He'd protected Amelia. He'd gotten her down the mountain, placed her in a safe place that she herself had chosen to leave. That she was missing was not his fault. That he felt guilt twisting his gut was a choice, not an imperative. Could he have done more? Logic said no, but his heart indicted him.

Jeez, was that *his* brain whining like that? Okay, he was short on sleep and shorter on patience—another departure from the norm, since he was usually the one with the endless supply, but was that any reason to whine?

Worse than whining, instead of patience, instead of calm reason, there was this pounding, urgent beat driving him forward, muddying his thoughts and tripping his reason. Okay, he liked Amelia, even when he wondered if she was playing him, he . . . liked her. Oh, she was beautiful, but that alone wasn't it. Beauty without character was like cotton candy without sugar, if that were possible. Even with her brain scrambled, she was smart and funny. And she hadn't quit. She'd dragged her butt down the mountain and that had to hurt. Possibly concussed cranium. Held her poles with a sprained wrist and went the distance.

How could he not like her? She'd given off a lot of confused signals during the hours they'd spent together, but some facts were clear for anyone with a brain to observe—something he'd thought he had. She had a strong sense of adventure, felt a real joy in being alive. There was a French word for it that he never could remember, but it fit. Even in pain and afraid, she'd loved the trip down the mountain. He'd seen it in her eyes, in the way her body took the turns, spraying the snow in a joyful arc with each turn when she'd shot past him after their first fall. Had felt himself respond to that joy with some of his own. Much as he loved his private play, it was always more fun with someone to share it with—and a touch of danger to add a little spice.

She was young, though not was young as he'd thought. If only—what? The question made him squirm inside. If she was Prudence Knight, she'd have plenty to deal with when this was all over. Plenty. And if her memory came back, he'd fade to the back of her mind. Order restored, they could both return to their lives.

So why didn't that seem as appealing as it had forty-eight hours ago when all he'd had to deal with was the past? Again a stab of guilt. Nothing like a little lust on the anniversary of your wife's death.

Because he wasn't ready to find answers for any of the questions his bitter brain was producing, he turned his attention to his brother and his companions. Bryn and Dewey had entered with Matt, their mutual glow piercing his preoccupation. Looked like they'd finally settled it—in spades if the discreet gold band on Bryn's finger was any indication. Good for them.

Hypocrite, a voice in his head taunted him. Okay for her to take risks, but not Luke Kirby. There were risks and *risks,* a different voice argued for the defense. Bryn had had to trust Dewey's feelings for her. Amelia didn't know what her feelings were. She couldn't remember them. He wasn't avoiding risk. He was being sensible. And loyal to Rosemary's memory. Before he could stop it, the contrary voice reminded him that this was the kind of loyalty that Rosemary would never have asked for.

"Let's get started, shall we?" Matt said, taking his place at the head of the table.

It seemed off not to have Jake there, challenging Matt's place at the head of the table with his gaze. Those two had taken sibling rivalry into adulthood, which left Luke as the peacemaker. Luke dropped into his chair now, wishing Jake was here. He had a quick brain and good instincts, both of which they could have used right now. And he looked at life differently from either he or Matt. Drove Matt crazy, but it worked. As if Matt heard him think, he said, "Jake's flying in. Should be here before we move out."

"We have to talk fast," Bryn said. "Dewey's got an important date down south."

"I can be fast," Luke said. He leaned forward, his elbows propped on the table as he told his story in terse spurts. Bryn interrupted him just once.

"You had Prudence Knight and you lost her?"

Luke looked annoyed. "I didn't know I had her until after I lost her, okay? She doesn't know who she is." If it weren't so serious, it would be funny, them all running around with bits of the same whole, all thinking they were in control when they weren't.

"Well," Bryn gave him a wry look, "if she was grabbed so she could spill her guts on SHIELD, this could get interesting, since it doesn't work. We should probably talk to a specialist, find out if truth drugs could crack her apparent loss of memory. If she really has lost it?"

Luke tried not to stiffen, not with them all looking at him. "Her injuries were real. I'm just guessing, but I'm thinking she somehow fell out of the chopper, which was probably flying low to avoid getting picked up by radar. Trees would break her fall and people have survived falls from far more serious heights. You say she had some kind of fight with her father?"

"That's what Donovan said." Bryn frowned. She filled them in on what she'd learned from Donovan. "What if Knight knew he was dying and told her he wasn't her father? Then she gets kidnapped, falls. Trauma like that could lead to hysterical amnesia, I would imagine. At least it does on television," she added dryly.

Luke remembered her "I hate lies" vehemence. It seemed she had good cause to hate it.

"It doesn't really matter, does it?" Dewey asked. "You saw her get kidnapped, whether she knows her own name or not, she's in trouble. How do we find her?"

"You don't do anything," Bryn said. "You have a date with GREEN." Luke and Matt looked at her, so then she filled them in on this, fumbling a bit over how Dewey got involved with GREEN. It was obvious to Luke she wasn't eager to clarify much, but at least now she knew who her friends were and told them enough.

What also seemed obvious to Luke was the criminal movement on so many fronts and yet no one seemed to see a connection. Could it be a coincidence that Dewey was meeting GREEN this week, the same week someone tries to kidnap Amelia and use her to put pressure on Donovan?

"What if this GREEN is involved in the kidnapping?" he asked.

Matt sat at the head of the table, slumped in a chair with his feet thrust out. With one hand he beat tapped the table impatiently. "Merryweather is a biotechnology company, a favorite target of GREEN and other environmental activist groups. We've got a biotech conference in town this weekend. Did you see that bit on the news the other night? People dressed up like vegetables and other crap yapping about the evils of technology—after having driven or flown here in their cars and planes?"

Bryn nodded. "I saw it. And we know that's bringing the former VP to town. He's going to speak out at a big counter-demo. He's the most important target in town this week."

"Target?" Luke asked. He'd missed some key points it seemed.

Bryn filled them in on Donovan and his possible role as sniper in the proceedings.

"Would he really turn shooter for them in hopes that

they'll release Ame—Prudence Knight?" Luke asked. "Looked smarter than that to me." In his head, Luke was relieved. It meant they wouldn't kill Amelia as soon as they got what they wanted—or in this case what they didn't want—out of her. On the other hand, they might be dealing with an out-of-control sniper before they were through.

"It does make me think GREEN must be behind the grab. No question she's the key to Donovan's buttons," Bryn added, with a look of worry toward Dewey. "If they are turning violent—"

"—and Dewey's date is our only lead, then how do we make sure we don't lose him?" Matt finished for her.

This wasn't his area, so Luke sat back, listening as the talk turned high tech and technical.

Dewey shook his head when Matt suggested an electronic tracking device. "This guy is smart. He'll be looking for everything, up to and including a wire. I walk in there broadcasting anything, I'm dead. They'll also be looking for tails, advance and post surveillance of the area. Trust me on this. It's what I'd have done before I became a reformed man."

Bryn jumped up and paced to the window, looking over her shoulder to say, "We can't send you in without some kind of backup. Your community service hours don't require you to go on a suicide mission."

"Actually, I already have a plan," Dewey confessed. "Well, Phoebe had a plan, but don't tell Jake or he'll kill me, making this all pointless."

Bryn turned, leaning against the windows, her arms crossed defensively. Despite his worry, Luke found he could grin, though he hid it with his hand.

"Based on the assumption that this guy was beyond paranoid," Dewey said, "he may make me change cars, clothes, even a watch, but who plans for a guy with glasses?"

Like a magician, he produced a pair from his shirt pocket. They were small, wire rectangles. Bryn stalked over and took them, peering through the lenses. "They have a prescription. Can you see with them?"

With a sigh, he nodded. "Unfortunately, my eye doctor thinks I can."

Luke took them from Bryn. "So how do they help?"

"There's a small, but powerful GPS transmitter in one of the nose pads. But it's not active, so if they scan me for anything, it won't read. When I feel safe, or I'm in trouble, I can activate using the other nose pad." Dewey took the glasses back and put them on.

He looked studious and sort of like John Lennon, Luke decided, with an inward grin. Trust Phoebe, the Pathphinder, to find a way to beat paranoid.

"I'd sure like to put a team on the road ahead of you," Bryn said.

Dewey shook his head. "He'll be looking for that. That's why the extended advance warning. He's waiting to see if there's any sudden activity in the area. You do anything and he's gone. I could be wrong, but I'm betting he's been where he is long enough to know who's new and who isn't. This guy is smart." He grinned. "He could be me. If I didn't know I was here, I'd say you should be looking at me."

In the olden days, that remark would have set Bryn off. Luke noticed now she just looked at him, a look so intimate he looked away. His gaze bumped into Matt's, who was also trying not to notice the sudden rise in temperature.

"So what do we already know about the area?" Matt spread a map of the state across the table top. He looked at Luke. "Your chopper headed south, didn't you say?"

Luke nodded. Bryn found the rendezvous point, then used her finger to trace a circle around the area. It was in the direction of the chopper, but a lot was.

"We're assuming that GREEN is the culprit here," Luke objected. "It's kind of hard for me to buy. I mean, if they don't like what Merryweather is doing, wouldn't they be getting rid of SHIELD, not stealing it? Is there anyone else who might be targeting this SHIELD? I don't like concentrating all our efforts in one direction without something more than some guy who wants to meet Dewey. If we're wrong, then it's over."

The words sent a chill down his back. What if he never saw Amelia again? The chill turned into a sick feeling in the pit of his stomach. He had to fight to clear his thoughts so he could focus as they discussed other possibilities, but with the admittedly scant information at their disposal, there wasn't a better lead for them to follow. Bryn promised to direct her team to look for other possibilities, which helped some, but not a lot.

"You know . . ." Bryn's fingers stopped by a town, then moved to a spot at the base of the mountains. "This is . . . odd."

"What?" Luke stood up next to her and frowned down at the map. Where had they taken Amelia? It was a damn big state. Was this how his brothers had felt when their women disappeared? Except Amelia wasn't his woman, he reminded himself, and he should start calling her Prudence. Or Miss Knight. They were the same, weren't they? He just wished he knew where the Amelia persona had sprung from? The same set of keys that had opened her car had also had a key that opened Amelia Hart's apartment. Could she have created an alternate identity for herself? And if she had, why? She'd said something about feeling lighter and relieved. Was that the explanation? She'd been someone trying to find a little room to be herself? Everything he'd heard about John Knight made him sound like someone you'd want to get away from as quickly as possible.

It made more sense than that she was involved in something dishonest. Granted he only had his instincts to rely on that she had been truthful with him. Did he trust them? They hadn't let him down in the past, but in the past his hormones hadn't been in the mix. Didn't seem to matter how often he told his libido to stop it.

He hated feeling like this. Hated feeling out of control. Hated feeling helpless again. It brought back all the feelings he'd wrestled with when Rosemary was dying. He'd promised himself he'd never feel like that again. Hell of a time to find out it wasn't something he could control.

"We're also investigating the Colorado Irregulars," Bryn was saying when Luke tuned back in. "Their camp is right here, near the mountains. They're open to the public on the weekends. You can pay to get hit with paint balls and gripe about the government."

Matt and Dewey both bent over the map, too. Dewey looked aggrieved. "You were investigating them without me?"

Bryn flicked him a look that was straight out of the olden days. "It was need to know."

Luke was happy for the distraction. His thoughts were giving him a headache.

"Odd that two such opposite groups should be working in the same general area," he said. "I'd like to check them out. No question a paramilitary group would want SHIELD. If they were behind this, they sure as hell mobilized a pack of hounds. They had our route covered faster than a fart. And they looked more like right wingers than lefties."

He was going to say more, when he noticed that Dewey was still staring at the map with a peculiar look on his face.

"What?" Luke asked.

"Huh?" Dewey looked up, his gaze unfocused for a moment before it sharpened.

"You have an idea?"

Bryn and Matt were now looking at him, too.

"Do you know who I'm meeting?"

Luke shrugged. "GREEN."

"His handle is 'Forest for the Trees,' " Dewey said.

Luke stared at him. "Forest for the Trees?"

"That's right."

"As in, you can't see the forest for the trees?"

"Yup."

"Damn. Are you thinking what I'm thinking?" Luke asked.

"No, I think you're thinking what I'm thinking," Dewey said. "I thought it first."

"Damn it," Bryn said. "I should have been thinking it a long time ago. I could tell the guy had a . . . quirky sense of humor. Do you really think—"

She stopped, as if she couldn't bring herself to say it.

"Well," Luke stared at nothing as his thoughts raced. It was so bizarre, but in a weird way, made sense. "I can't think of a better place to hide a radical environmental movement than a right-wing paramilitary outfit's camp."

Bryn didn't look amused. "Shit. This could easily turn into another Waco—if we can even get the proof we need to go in." She frowned as the three men watched her quietly. "You know who we need?"

Matt looked wary. "Who?"

"Donovan Kincaid."

"He's gone to ground, hasn't he?" Dewey pointed out.

"Yes, he has. But I'll bet he has his phone with him."

Luke found his thoughts moving in another direction. If

GREEN was behind this move on Merryweather, they'd have needed someone on the inside. They'd need to know how the technology was progressing, access to Knight to administer the digitalis, and someone to tell them Prudence Knight's movements, when and how to make the grab. Someone had jumped the gun. Or chosen to sabotage it? Someone who wanted to screw his father, say?

One thing he'd been right about. He was in the wrong place. His job was the murder. There was a threat to Amelia here, too, and he needed to find it. At least it was something to do while they waited.

"There are some things I need to check. Let me know when you head south for Dewey's date. I want to go with you," he said.

Matt looked up, his gaze sharp. Finally he nodded. He got up and went with Luke to the door. "You all right?"

Luke rubbed the back of his neck, then shrugged. "Sure."

"We'll find her," Matt said. "With the three of us together, we can't fail." He slapped Luke on the back. "Keep your phone on."

The sun shone fiercely, as if to atone for letting the recent storm blot it out, but it was too far away in the winter sky to be felt. All its power turned the deep, mostly unbroken layer of snow diamond bright. Made it hard to hide tracks, even wearing camouflage appropriate to the conditions. What Donovan needed was camouflage that could lift him above the snow. Since he didn't have the capability, he'd had to work his way carefully down the mountainside toward the Colorado Irregular's camp.

On the upside, if anyone down there were to catch a glint of his binoculars, they'd write it off as the sun's reflection. He'd been observing the camp for about an hour, but there hadn't been much to see, though what he had seen convinced him he was on the right track. The weather was keeping the casual inside. Interesting that they'd posted guards when there didn't seem to be anything going on or anything to hide. It had taken him a while to find them. Like him, they were in camo and dug in. It had taken patience and a little luck to spot them. One was about three hundred yards below him. He'd picked him up when his radio sounded. Now he was waiting to see if it would go off at the same time. He needed to know when they checked in, when they changed and how. They hadn't left any tracks in the snow either.

As soon as it went off, he had turned on his scanner and picked up their frequency. They were no dummies, but they were also bored. He got enough from their exchanges to locate most of the guard posts he hoped. Once you knew where to look and you knew what you were looking for, they were as obvious as hookers in a red light district. Perception was the key, even in war.

Despite his worry about his daughter, it felt good to be back in the field. This was where he belonged, pitting his brains and his brawn against the enemies of the weak. And the fear, the worry, would keep him sharp. He couldn't afford to lose this one. Too much was riding on it. With Knight out of the picture, he could talk to Pru, maybe tell her who he was, what her mother meant to him. From what he could tell, she didn't know a lot about her mother. She had the spirit, the will to live her life better than that. He could show her how.

The vibration of his satellite phone interrupted his thoughts. He'd set it to vibrate, since he couldn't afford to be out of touch, if Pru's kidnapper called again. He'd also set it up for hands free. In fact, he was so wired, it's a wonder he wasn't conductive. He wasn't worried about being overheard, but he still kept his voice low.

"You ready to talk, Kincaid?" a digital voice asked him.

"I've been ready the whole time," Donovan said. "Which makes me wonder why you haven't been? And to wonder if you even have Miss Knight."

"If you need proof, I can send you one of her fingers. Or an ear," the voice said.

"Talking to her is so much less messy. And quicker," Donavan said, trying to keep his cool. If this was Grady, he was a dead man.

"Well, she's a little unconscious. I think an ear. Or you earn the right to talk to her."

"And how do I do that?"

"Easy. Prove to me you can follow orders."

"Orders?" Donovan said.

"Didn't I mention that you work for me now? Well, you do. If you want to keep Miss Knight ten-fingered, two-eared, and in the land of the breathing, you'll do exactly what I say."

"And what do you say?"

"Well, no big surprise, no cops or feds. We keep this just between us."

"Not original or surprising," Donovan said. He braced for what came next.

"How are your sniping skills?"

He hadn't been expecting this. It had been so long since he'd used them.

"I can still hit my man." One bullet. One kill.

"Good. Leslie Merryweather. If I hear of his unfortunate demise on the news, you earn a few words with Miss Knight."

Merryweather? "Why him?"

"Okay, let's try this again. Because I say so."

"Fine."

"You aren't going to argue with me?" He sounded genuinely surprised.

"Why should I? Guy's a waste of space."

"I think we're going to get along just fine. I'll be in touch."

And he was gone. Leaving Donovan with a lot to think about. He had gone to a lot of trouble to bump off an easy target like Leslie Merryweather, so he couldn't be the real target. This was what he'd said, a way to see if he'd jump when told. By now, Bryn probably had a good idea of who the real target was, but he wasn't sure he wanted to know. Didn't want to have to choose between that person and his daughter.

What also puzzled Donovan was why it had taken so long to reach this point. Had that first call been a fishing expedition? Now O'Brien sounded confident, though he still wouldn't let Donovan talk to Pru. She could be unconscious. Or she could still be in transit.

As if the thought had given birth to reality, he heard the clatter of a helicopter. Careful not to disturb the snow covering him, he turned, scanning the sky with his binoculars.

"Gotcha." It seemed to hang in the bright, blue sky, growing slowly larger as it flew steadily closer. What it didn't do is stop at the encampment. Instead, it turned toward the mountain, skimming the top of the trees, at one point turning the snow covering him into a small blizzard.

He marked the direction with his compass, then started the laborious job of working his way back up into the trees. Looked like Grady had hidden depths and he intended to find them. He had no illusions about what would happen to Pru once she'd filled her purpose. No way he was flying off the scent now.

As for the problem of Leslie and the deadline, well, be easy enough to have him taken out for him. He was clean, but he knew some mercenaries who weren't. He hadn't lied when he told O'Brien he considered the guy a waste of space. Mostly he didn't like the idea of jumping to O'Brien's tune. Could he get Bryn to help him? She was a by-the-book girl or she had been. She'd loosened up some, but was it enough? Actually, he was surprised she hadn't called him by now. He looked at his watch. He'd give her until he was to the top of that ridge to call him. If she didn't, he'd call a merc he knew. Between Leslie and Pru there was no contest.

Chapter Fourteen

Leslie had planned to wait to kill again. He really had. It was his dad's fault. It infuriated him angry when his father shut him out. He'd planned to be the inside guy, feeding info from the police to Grady. Only daddy wouldn't let him. He'd turned to Donovan instead, sending him off like some damn errand boy.

He'd come storming out of the office, intent on heading for the camp. Grady wasn't going to keep him out of that action, too. He'd been living for the moment when Miss Tight-Ass Prudence found he was the one who had her father killed and had her kidnapped. He couldn't wait to see the look in her eyes when she realized she was going to die, too. Girl that homely, he'd bet she was virgin. He'd fix that for her. Be a shame to send her off without knowing what she was missing.

No way he was missing that. To hell with Grady and his dad. It was his plan and he had a right to be there as it unfolded. But outside he'd run into one of his dad's friend's vapid daughter. Bridget or Britney or maybe it was Barbara. She'd sent out the signal. He'd answered it. Even then, he thought, just dinner. As long as I don't take her home . . .

Then she'd wrapped herself around him while they danced. Had practically crawled inside his pants. What was the problem with girls now? They'd crawl into bed with anyone. Well, she wouldn't do that again.

He looked at her limp body. She looked more surprised than the hooker had, but she was younger and a hooker had to expect that maybe sometime someone was going to kill them.

A hazard of the job, wasn't it?

The purple marks his hands had made on her throat were the same. Guess everyone bruised the same way. He hadn't exactly had a stop watch, but seemed like she took about the same time to die. Maybe one of these times he should time it. Timing might matter at some point.

He frowned. She was going to be harder to dispose of. That was the annoying part. He needed to be more careful here, on his home turf, which was why he'd been determined not to kill here. Didn't want to launch a serial killer task force.

A serial killer.

I'm a serial killer, he thought. The idea wasn't repulsive. Serial killers weren't just about the killing. It was the battle of wits, the planning and execution. It wasn't a stupid man's game.

He looked at what's-her-name. She was a mistake. No wits there, just instinct. And anger.

Which didn't help him with his problem now. Serial killers don't kill people they know. He'd been seen with her last night. Maybe seen leaving the parking lot with her. He felt a moment of panic. How long before someone missed her? This one would take some thought. She'd have to disappear. He'd probably take some heat, but if she didn't turn up . . .

He covered her body with a sheet, arranging her hair over her face as if she were sleeping—just in case one of the servants wandered in. They weren't supposed to, but servants were like women. Only trust them to be where they weren't supposed to be. He pondered the problem of disposal through his shower and thought he had a plan, but before he could get his pants on, or get her out of his bed, the bell rang. He'd have played not-at-home, but his Jag was in the drive.

He pulled on a robe and went to the door. Through the glass panels he could see the two cops he'd toyed with last night.

Let the battle of wits begin.

Amelia woke slowly as the murmur of voices penetrated the strange thickness that held her body immobile. As consciousness returned, with it came little flashes of memory that made no sense. Faces. Voices. People who seemed to know her, but when she tried to bring them into focus, turned away from her, vanishing into the gray mist that pressed in on her from all sides.

Despite her inability to move, she felt the sensation of movement. It was cold for a space, then warm again. Movement ceased. She was lying on something. Something that gave a bit underneath her and was scratchy against her skin.

The voices grew louder, but she still couldn't sort out words. After a struggle, she managed to open her eyes long enough to see she was in a cabin.

Luke? She tried to say his name. Let him know she was awake, but sound lodged in her throat. The effort exhausted and she sank back into the fog with a feeling of relief.

When she woke again, her head wasn't clear, but at least the suffocating fog was gone. She was still in the cabin, but it wasn't Luke's cabin. It had the same split logs for walls, but the dimensions were different. She seemed to be in some kind of bedroom. From her place on the four poster bed, she could see a dresser, a chair, a window liberally coated with frost. The furnishings were what you'd expect to see in a cabin. Rustic and sturdy with lots of picturesque looking knots in the wood.

Her impression was that this was a "guy zone," though she was still too fuzzy-headed to sort out why. The bed was comfortable, but her arm was crooked up at an odd angle. When she tried to arrange it more comfortably, she realized she couldn't.

She was handcuffed to the bed.

With some effort, and a lot of discomfort, she squirmed her way into a position more comfortable for her shackled arm. At least they hadn't cuffed the sprained wrist. She gingerly flexed it and winced. It seemed worse today. Rough handling?

She'd thought it was awful to lose her memory, but this was far worse. She still had her clothes on under the blankets someone had piled on her, which was a relief, but not much. Someone had taken off her coat. She could see it on the chair. She'd been taken, manhandled while unconscious. What had happened to her while she was out? Her stomach muttered unpleasantly. Her head ached, too. The pain, which had been as three-sided as her bumps, had now migrated to a place behind her right eye. Whatever they had used to drug her had left her feeling lethargic and fuzzy-headed. Something thick and nasty coated her mouth, too.

Behind the lethargy was cold, hard fear. Whatever it was that she'd escaped, it had now caught up with her. What did they want? Was this a simple kidnapping or something more?

She managed to push a pillow behind her aching head and sagged back, flexing her cuffed hand to restore feeling. She remembered seeing Luke. He called her. Was running toward her when someone grabbed her. Then nothing.

Nothing? Well, mostly nothing. She had a vague memory of movement and something else. But when she strained for it, her brain slapped her back by upping the pain stakes. With the past still off limits, that left only her very limited present, which could be summed up in one man—Luke.

Is this where being spunky had gotten her? Handcuffed to a bed somewhere, never to see him again? She'd trade all her past memories to see him once more. She didn't expect him to want her in his life, but she could wish for it, couldn't she?

It made no sense. They barely knew each other but she felt like she'd known him forever. Or had she been looking for him forever? Something inside her recognized him as important to her, even if she couldn't remember anything else. It was all she had to hang on to as someone fumbled with the door, then opened it.

A man stood in the doorway holding a tray. A thin man with a ferrety face and a head topped with a riot of shockingly red hair.

"I thought I heard you moving in here," he said. He put the tray on the nightstand by the bed. "Do you need to . . ."

Color ran up his face faster than it did hers.

It helped to feel amused by it. Cleared her head some. She nodded. Nature couldn't be denied, even when it embarrassed.

He undid her cuffs at her wrist, leaving them hanging from the bed. "Wouldn't try anything. We're a long way from anywhere, and it's damn cold out there."

She nodded again. The bathroom had no lock, so she did her business quickly, then took the time to splash water on her face. The face in the mirror over the sink was pale, but composed. What in her life had made it so easy for her to hide her feelings? Maybe it was better not to remember.

Outside again, the man led her back to the room and secured her to the bed. She sat on the edge, her back straight, her knees together, and her hands on her knees.

"You should eat," he said, nodding encouragingly toward the tray, which held a glass of juice, some toast and a couple of pills.

She looked at him.

"For your headache," he said. "Just Tylenol."

He sat in the chair, obviously not planning to leave until she'd eaten. It was hard with him watching, but she needed the food. After a few bites of toast her stomach settled down. She took the Tylenol, too. She needed to clear her head. The orange juice was the best. Cool and slightly tart, it cleared the nasty aftertaste out of her mouth. And it gave her a nice jolt of energy.

Without conscious thought, she realized she'd already decided to resist, to escape if the opportunity arose, despite the cold and the possible isolation. For a moment, the veil over her memory flickered. She'd felt this way before. Maybe not this scared, but certainly this trapped and determined. And she'd done something about it. The veil closed before anything but that feeling could escape, but she drew strength from knowing that she may not know a lot about herself, but Luke was right about one thing. She wasn't a person who gave up—or she'd already be dead.

She finished eating and wiped her mouth, then said in a colorlessly polite voice, "Thank you."

He looked pleased as he gathered up the tray. "Grady'll be along shortly."

The comment had echoes of a doctor's office, which was mildly amusing, unless the trend continued.

"Grady would be my . . . host?" she asked primly, the sound of her own voice surprising her. She sounded like an old-fashioned school marm.

It surprised her jailor, too. He straightened his shoulders, his face turning worried. "Well, yeah. Sort of. I guess."

After such a definitive response, why should she worry?

He balanced the tray with one hand while he opened the door. "Can I get you anything else, Miss Knight?"

Miss Knight? Amelia started to object but stopped herself. While it would be nice to know how they'd made such a mistake, if they knew they had the wrong person, well, letting her go was only one of the options available to them. Unfortunately, the least likely. She needed time to think before this Grady person came in. So much depended on what they wanted with her.

"Some water, please." Her look made him straighten his shoulders even more. It was almost comical. Was she a teacher in her forgotten life?

"Sure." He closed the door. There was sound of the lock being turned, then retreating footsteps on wood. The sound seemed to be going down, as well as away. Was she upstairs? The window was too frosted to see out, though a Monet wash of green left her with the impression of trees outside.

The nightstand had a couple of drawers. In an odd twist, one held a Gideon Bible. The other one was empty. She couldn't reach anything else. Okay, that meant she'd have to catch someone off guard when she was free. He hadn't been armed, but then neither was she. Okay, what were her resources?

She grinned wryly. Well, she had a knee. She'd just have to find the right time to use it.

Luke stared at Leslie Merryweather. Something was going on with the guy, though, not knowing him, it was hard to put his finger on what. There was the obvious, but it was a bit early in the day to be pouring himself a drink. And in a bathrobe with his hair still wet. Unless . . .

He looked around and spotted the discarded heels partially hidden by a plush looking chair near the stairs.

"Very sorry to disturb you," Luke said, dryly.

Leslie followed his gaze to the shoes, then gave a strangely embarrassed laugh. Luke's gaze narrowed. Leslie didn't seem like the type to be embarrassed about much, let alone his own decadence. He exchanged a look with Mann, who shrugged.

"Did you have something particular you wanted to ask me, gentlemen?"

They had a lot they wanted to ask him, actually. After chatting with other employees of Merryweather, he'd secured the top spot on their suspect list. It was all about access and opportunity. Only Leslie, Hamilton Merryweather and Prudence Knight had had the necessary access to have slipped Dr. Knight the digitalis. The major stumbling block was that Leslie hadn't been in town the day of Knight's heart attack, but they were checking the suspected medium of delivery—a special blend of coffee that only Knight drank. According to staff, Prudence didn't drink coffee—yet another link to Amelia.

Unfortunately, Bryn was asking them to hold off on their questions. She'd talked to Donovan, who had reluctantly coughed up his first order from Prudence Knight's kidnapper. Kill Leslie Merryweather. As far as he was concerned, it would save the tax payers money to let him fulfill his mission. Only reason to keep him alive, as far as he was concerned, was if he could tell them where Amelia was. Bryn had convinced Donovan to let her handle the "assassination," hoping it would buy them time. On the up side, once he was in protective custody, they could sweat him a bit, see what fell out.

"Perhaps you should sit down," Mann said.

Leslie looked at him, then at Luke. "Okay." He sprawled in a chair, his robe barely covering his privates. "Now what?"

The look of anticipation in his eyes tempted Luke to pop him. This guy liked trouble—for other people. Well, let's see how he liked trouble for himself.

"We have information that you've been targeted for . . . termination," Luke said.

Leslie twitched slightly and his expression flickered between shock and surprise. It was obvious that this was not what he'd been expecting to hear. He got his face back under control, replacing shock with bravado. Behind the bravado was something else. Worry? Or was it something more? Luke was having a hard time getting a feel for the guy.

Leslie jumped to his feet and freshened his drink before saying, "You must be joking."

"We're not allowed to joke about threats," Mann said, with a straight face even.

"Our information is reliable," Luke added.

"Who?" Leslie's bravado was showing holes.

"Our informant is the man who is supposed to kill you." It hadn't been part of the plan to tell him that much, but now Luke felt compelled. He looked thrown off balance, but not the way Luke had expected him to. His expression wasn't, this is nuts. You're nuts. It was, this is wrong. This isn't supposed to happen.

"And that would be?"

Mann was frowning at him, but Luke didn't hesitate. "Donovan Kincaid is being pressured to kill you. Do you know why anyone would want you dead?"

He went white as the old-fashioned sheet. He lifted his drink to his mouth, his hand shaking. "No, I can't."

He reminded Luke of someone who just found out their girlfriend was cheating on them. "It would be better if you would tell us what you know."

Leslie didn't say anything, just stared ahead. Finally Mann stood up.

"We're taking you into protective custody, Mr. Merryweather. You'll have to come with us." He sounded almost gentle.

That got his attention. He looked like he was going to protest, but must have realized it wouldn't do any good. "I need to get dressed."

"Of course."

Luke watched him walk up the stairs. When they were alone, Mann said, "Thought you were losing it, but he knows, doesn't he?"

"He knows. He's in it up to his eyeballs." If he had helped to kidnap Amelia, Luke didn't want any part of protecting the bastard. He clenched and unclenched his fists as he fought for control.

"He's a light weight," Mann said. "He'll turn."

Luke wasn't so sure. He had the feeling that this betrayal was too personal—

"Shit." He pulled his gun and started for the stairs. "He's going to run."

Mann pulled his piece and followed him up. Luke took the lead as they checked the rooms one by one. The last one was Leslie's. The robe he'd been wearing was a puddle of white on the plush carpet. The closets stood open and looked rummaged through. The window was open, and there was a woman in his bed.

A woman who didn't move when armed men burst into the room. Luke padded over and eased back the sheet, the action reminding him of the first time he saw Amelia. He didn't have to check her pulse to know there'd be no help for her. Her eyes were wide and shocked. Her dark hair covered her neck. Luke lifted the strands and found the bruises on her neck.

That's what he'd sensed about Leslie. Evil. Many in the world didn't believe in evil, but cops did. He should have picked up on it sooner, but like Mann, he'd written him off as a lightweight. Looking at the woman, he'd bet a lot of people underestimated Leslie Merryweather.

"Call in the crime scene boys, Mann. I gotta call Bryn and tell her we lost her victim." Though that wasn't worrying him as much as where Leslie was heading. Damn. He'd put Leslie in the quiver and fired him right at his partner. Who was probably holding Amelia.

Chapter Fifteen

Grady looked up as O'Rourke came down the stairs carrying the tray. Normally O'Rourke hated playing butler for guests willing or otherwise, but he'd been curious to see the recently plucked thorn in their side. "So?" he asked, as O'Rourke started toward the kitchen. "What's she like?"

O'Rourke's opinions were always interesting, even when they were wrong.

He stopped, his face screwed into thinking position. "She's . . . a damaged angel with the soul of school teacher."

"A school teacher?"

"Second grade. Miss Hanlon. Used to look at me the same way. Almost told her the dog ate my homework." He held up the tray. "Gonna get rid of this and she wants water."

Grady gave a half laugh, half snort. "By all means, give her some water."

O'Rourke started to leave but hesitated. "You going to, you know?" He mimed stabbing her with a needle. "Food might make her hurl."

Grady stared at him. "I'm going to give a her chance to give it up without needles. And I have to keep her lucid for her little chat with Donovan."

"Right." He left, leaving a thoughtful Grady behind.

The board over his head creaked. He looked up, suddenly curious about the women who held the keys to his future. She'd been important to him only for what she could give him, but now he found himself interested in O'Rourke's "damaged angel." The school teacher description didn't surprise him. She'd looked like the stereotype of a teacher in her pictures.

Her spirited defense of herself was interesting, though ultimately pointless, and she'd cleaned up pretty good. Even unconscious, a couple of his guys had expressed a desire to spend some private time with her when they hauled her in. He'd quelled them with a glance—he wasn't a pimp or a rapist. If she gave him what he wanted, her death would be quick and clean. But he wasn't above using the threat to catch her attention. With success almost within reach, he'd do what it took to close the gap. Half the pleasure in getting what you wanted was the anticipation—or so he'd heard. If that were true, then getting what he wanted was going to be really great, because he'd been in the anticipation zone for a long, long time.

He pushed back his chair, all of a sudden curious to see her with her eyes open and her mouth closed.

Upstairs, he took the key off the hook and unlocked the door. When he pushed it open, she was sitting on the bed. Immediately he could see where O'Rourke got the school teacher idea. Not only was she sitting primly, but her expression almost made him shuffle his feet. And claim the dog ate his homework. It helped stiffen his spine that O'Rourke climbed the stairs with the requested water. Had an image to keep up. O'Rourke set the water carefully on the nightstand, near at hand.

"Thank you," she said, her voice as prim as her aspect.

She had to be scared out of her mind, but there was no sign of it on her face or even in her eyes. Grady stepped closer, peering into her eyes. Damn, they were purple.

"Why did you hide your eyes behind those awful glasses?" Grady asked, because he couldn't help himself.

"Excuse me?" Her brows arched toward the tousled,

blond hairline. He could see why O'Rourke saw an angel in the pure line of her jaw and the vulnerability of her mouth. What he called teacher in the set of her shoulders, Grady saw as strength. She was lost, but not out yet.

He pulled her picture out of the pocket of his jacket and showed it to her.

"The glasses. You don't need them. Why wear them?"

She studied the photograph, a tiny frown between her arched dark brows. She'd been lovely unconscious, but awake . . . It was a pity he had to destroy her. She was extraordinary. And quite . . . rare. She'd look good on his arm in the South of France.

She shrugged and reached for her water, the movement somewhat awkward because of her cuffed hand. She sipped, outwardly unmoved by the silence growing between them. Her composure was remarkable.

He stowed the picture and dropped into the chair across from her. "You can go, O'Rourke."

When O'Rourke didn't move, he looked at him. "What?"

O'Rourke shuffled his feet and said, "Nothing. I just . . . nothing." He looked at her like he wanted to ask her something, but her steady gaze deflected him nicely, and he turned and left.

"Alone at last," Grady said, more to test for a reaction from her than anything.

Her gaze turned his way, one brow just a little arched. It was a masterly put down and Grady had to grin. Usually his grin put at least a hair line crack in the most determined resistance and he could sense what his victims were feeling. As a rule, but not this time. That interested him more than her looks and, his gaze strayed lower, her nicely constructed body.

She cleared her throat, pulling his gaze back up. He resisted an urge to apologize. It wasn't easy. Her gaze intimidated, something he usually reserved for himself. Time to bring out the big guns. He held her gaze for a long moment, then smiled intimately. His gaze invited her to trust him.

Her expression finally changed. She looked puzzled.

Amelia was puzzled. Did she know this smarmy character? It was an icky thought. He oozed something he mistook for charm, but it was really just ooze. He clearly wanted something from her, but what was it? Despite the leers and looks, she didn't think he'd kidnapped her to be his sexual plaything.

The "let's be friends" look gave way to one more calculating. A serpent with an apple to share. "Would you like to stretch your legs?"

Amelia didn't want to accept even the smallest favor from him, but she did need to find out where she was. "Yes."

He got up. It was hard not to shrink back as he moved close. He had to touch her to free her from the cuffs. She winced. She couldn't help it and he stopped, his brows drawn together in a frown. "Did one of my men do that?"

She was tempted, but couldn't do it. She shook her head.

"Looks like it needs wrapping. I'll take care of it later."

Everything was nice, friendly, and helpful. Such bullshit. Did he really think he could charm her into forgetting he'd kidnapped her? Twice?

The shackle fell away from her wrist. He stepped back, but not enough. When she stood up, they'd be close. Her flesh cringed as she rose. She was almost as tall as him and saw surprise flicker in his eyes at it. Her knee longed to go into action, but this wasn't the time. She needed more data before she acted.

Later, she promised her knee, later.

Did he realize he ran a finger around his collar before gesturing for her to precede him, she wondered? With her back to him, she allowed herself a tiny smile. She may be down, but she wasn't out. Not yet.

It had been a job to maneuver himself into position above the cozy looking cabin huddling on the hillside several miles from the main camp. O'Brien had more patrols up this way, and they were better hidden. Either he expected Donovan to make this move, or he was a very careful man. Maybe both.

After all that effort it was dull work. Once he'd located all of O'Brien's spotters, there'd been nothing left to do but look at the cabin and wonder what it was doing up here, isolated from the rest of the camp, innocuous looking—and well guarded.

Because there was nothing else to do, he scanned the surroundings with his glasses. There was something about the layout that niggled at his mind. The terrain was rugged, much what you'd expect in a mountain camp. Snow lay thickly on everything that wasn't moving. The broad sweep of white was ruffled in the clearing by the arrival and departure of the chopper.

A very big clearing, now that he thought about it. Was that what was troubling him? He tightened the focus on his glasses and did another slow sweep of the clearing. The first time, he didn't see anything. He tried again, this time mentally dividing the clearing into search grids. Even then he almost didn't see the ventilation pipe barely breaking the surface of the snow. Now that he knew what to look for, he picked out more of them.

Underground bunkers?

What if O'Brien was cooking up more than a little discontent toward the government here? He'd seen some training camps like this one in his travels. Terrorist training camps always looking for a way to evade the satellites circling overhead. If he was rubbing shoulders with terrorists, SHIELD must have looked like manna to him.

Only one thing that didn't fit, Bryn thought that some environmental wacko group called GREEN was involved. No way O'Brien was into the environment. Not his style. Donovan hadn't spent much time with O'Brien, but it didn't take long to figure out that the only thing O'Brien cared about was O'Brien, though he did a good job of making you think otherwise—when you had a couple of beers in you. He'd steered clear of the camp because he didn't like the smell of O'Brien. He lived or died on his judgment of men, more often than not a judgment straight from the gut.

He had no problem believing that O'Brien was simply after SHIELD. What he couldn't figure out was why O'Brien wanted Donovan to kill for him. Looking around, it didn't seem like he had a shortage of men available to do that.

There was something missing, some piece of information he didn't have that explained all of it, but all he really wanted was Pru. Let Bryn solve the puzzles. He'd done something that tipped O'Brien off he was interested in her and it was his intention to get her out of it before O'Brien found out she didn't know her own name, according to Bryn, from a hole in the ground. And before O'Brien found out the information in her head was incomplete.

If only he could be sure she was here. He'd studied the cabin windows, but they were too frosted for him to see anything. He needed to look inside. No way he could cross that clearing in daylight. He was good, but not that good.

It was going to be a damn, long day. He hoped that at the end of it, he wouldn't find out he'd been watching the wrong foxhole.

"So, what do you think of my small . . . domain?" Grady asked Amelia as he led her back into the main room of the cabin.

What she thought was that her life expectancy had just been dramatically shortened. She was pretty sure that if he had planned to let her go, he wouldn't have shown her his hidden barracks, told her about his terrorist training program, introduced her to his reduced winter staff and told her his name.

On the plus side, she'd caught a glimpse of a map of the area with the camp marked on it and now knew exactly where she was. Now if she could figure out to make use of the information. There were phones scattered around the underground complex, but they all seemed to be connected to a central switchboard, which he'd made a point of showing her. Perhaps he'd noticed her eyeing the phones? Even if the phones weren't so inconveniently situated, she was quite sure one of Grady's men would happily shoot her if she were so foolish as to try for one.

It was impossible not to compare him with Luke, to contrast this situation with her only other one. Grady evidently thought his mere gaze had some kind of power, the same with his smile, since he trotted it out every other second. He wasn't unpleasant to look at. His sturdy, Irish body was strong and well made, but his face lacked the strength and character that made Luke's face so fascinating to her. There was weakness in Grady's chin and plenty of stubbornness, and she sensed his utter selfishness. Contrast that with Luke, who had so willingly risked his life for her, a stranger with no memory.

Thinking of Luke gave her strength. Did she have character? She wasn't sure, but she hoped so. She hoped she had the strength to resist whatever it was this guy wanted from, or with, her—or rather, from the person he seemed to think she was.

Grady was patient. He'd asked his question, and now he waited quietly for her answer. He seemed sure he would get what he wanted, so perhaps it was easy to be patient.

She turned from him and peered out the heavily frosted window. Before her breath fogged her view, she saw the snow-swept clearing, empty of all signs of the trouble beneath its surface. The sun was fading west, helping her to orient the cabin with the map in her head. She could remember it, right down to the gray smudge in one corner. It seemed she had a very good memory for everything but who she was.

"Nice view," she said finally, dropping the words into the silence between them. He seemed so sure he had the upper hand. It would be satisfying to throw him off his self-satisfied stride. She looked at him over her shoulder. "I suppose the skiing is excellent?"

He chuckled. "Very." He turned the bar. "A drink?"

She had no clue if she drank or not, but this didn't seem like a good time to addle her wits with anything. "Just water, thank you."

He smiled with conscious charm. "Don't you trust me?"

She arched her brows and gave him a politely incredulous look. It was odd to feel this prim and proper person taking possession of her exterior. She turned back to the window as the fog in her head faltered for an instant. Instead of the clearing, she saw a room full of people, laughing and talking. One, a good-looking young man with a weak face, came toward her . . .

Grady chuckled again, shattering the memory into tiny fragments, but leaving the feeling of distaste and possibly fear, behind.

"Stupid question. What was I thinking?"

Behind her was the clink of glass, the sound of fluid interacting with ice. Outside, a man in winter camouflage suddenly emerged from the trees and walked across the clearing. He was smoking and carried an Uzi with casual confidence. He was dressed for the cold, with heavy boots and thick hat pulled down over his ears. His face looked chilled and cruel. He took a last drag on the cigarette, then flicked into a snow drift before disappearing around the corner of the cabin.

"Dinner should be ready soon, Prudence," Grady said. "May I call you Prudence?"

Amelia looked at him.

"No," she said. "You may call me Miss Hart."

He froze with his glass halfway to his mouth. "Miss . . . Hart?"

"Miss Amelia E. Hart." She propped a shoulder against the wall, crossed her arms and waited, curious and nervous about what he'd do with this.

Grady stared at her. What kind of game was she trying on him? No question she was not at all what he'd expected her to be. For one, she was far more interesting. Leslie had once again missed the forest for the trees during his recon. Her composure and her ability to deflect his efforts to develop empathy with her were rare. Damn rare. In fact, she was a first. He'd never met anyone he couldn't sense something about. She was closed, right down to her body language.

She had to be terrified and confused. Must be wondering why she was here and what he wanted. Unless she suspected he was after SHIELD. Even that didn't explain her impressive composure. He'd hoped they could come to an agreement about what was in her head, but he could see that wasn't going to happen. But he'd planned for it and had the drugs on hand.

As much as he wanted to get SHIELD, he realized he was enjoying himself. It had been a long time since he'd met anyone that challenged him on any level.

"It's a gallant try, my dear, but that dog won't hunt."

"I have ID in my coat pocket."

She was really going to play it out? Okay, he'd see where it took them.

"O'Rourke?"

He popped his head around the corner. "Just a few more minutes . . ."

"Could you fetch the lady her coat from her room?"

"Okay."

His footsteps clumped up the stairs, then across the hall. He'd returned with the coat and handed it to Grady, who felt in the pockets and removed a driver's license.

"Amelia E. Hart." He looked at her. "How enterprising of you. But the dog still isn't hunting. You should have used a different picture."

Her expression didn't crack, but he sensed the small break in her confidence. He turned and dug through the desk, pulled out the purse they'd taken off her during the first grab. In a minute, he had her other driver's license. He held them both up for her.

She came toward him reluctantly, and for the first time he was aware of her as a woman. She moved with unconscious grace, her body fluid as a doe. There was something wild as a doe about her as well, something simmering beneath her tidy, controlled surface. This was a woman at odds with herself. Might be fun to be the one to introduce her to that wild side.

She stopped just out of reach, as if she sensed the change in his regard. Or maybe she could just see the change in his interest. A man couldn't hide some things.

He stepped toward her, just enough so she could take the

229

two licenses and made sure their hands touched as she took them. She didn't flinch or in any way acknowledge the contact, but he felt her deepening withdrawal. It was as if her soul had retreated even more deeply inside herself.

Wasn't too hard to figure out who had put the protective hide on her. Les had talked freely about her old man. She stared down at the two pieces of plastic, her face an exquisite mask, even with the bruises and scratches standing out sharply on her pale skin. She may have paled more. It was hard to tell. Her lashes lifted slowly, until she was looking at him.

Damn, she was remarkable. Her composure was complete. This was a woman who could fit into his life. What an asset she'd be, in looks and brains.

"They say everyone has a twin."

He had the feeling she threw that out as a stall, while she considered something, but what was there to consider? He had the goods on her. He held all the cards. He didn't say anything. Just gave her tit-for-tat by arching his brows in disbelief.

She came to a decision. He did pick up that. She tossed the two licenses aside. "Your men grabbed me before."

"That's right. You took a header out of the chopper. Gutsy, but stupid. And pointless, Miss Knight. I'm a man who always gets what he wants."

"And what is it that you want?"

Grady gave her a politely incredulous look. "SHIELD. It was always about SHIELD."

She turned away from him, tracing the corner of his desk with her finger. He had a vision of her sprawled across its surface, naked and waiting for him, her expression no longer closed. Yes, he'd have to give serious consideration to keeping her. Like SHIELD, she was one of a kind.

"I'm afraid I won't be able to help you with that," she said. "Even if I knew what you were talking about. Which I don't."

"You're far too intelligent to play games, my dear." He gave in to the temptation to touch her, a light caress to the back of her neck. That got a reaction. She moved away from him so quickly, his hand still hung in the air. She faced him, still composed, but with an air of being on guard and ready to fight.

"You're right. I am. But you see, I'm not playing anything. Your first attempt and my dive, had an unfortunate side effect. I lost my memory."

"What?" He reared back, sex thoughts vanishing as fast they had arrived.

"You heard me. I have no memory of anything. Amelia. Prudence. You could tell me I was Cleopatra of the Nile and I wouldn't know. It's all . . . gone. For all intents and purposes, my life began a couple of days ago."

Grady stared at her, his thoughts spinning in all different directions. What amazed him the most, was that he believed her. It was more than the sincerity of her voice. It went deeper than that. His damn special sense told him she spoke the truth. And the glint of satisfaction in her eyes, the first crack in her composure. He smiled ruefully. He didn't blame her. It must have been a sweet moment for her. Let her enjoy it. It was possible the truth drugs he had on hand could crack the memory loss. He'd have to do some checking on that while he waited for their chat with Donovan. For now . . .

O'Rourke came in. "You said you wanted to know about, you know."

The distraction was a good one. "Well?"

O'Rourke shook his head. So. Donovan hadn't managed to kill Leslie yet.

"Thanks."

Grady thought for a moment, then picked up his cell phone. Time to twist the tiger's tail again. He dialed Donovan's cell phone number, smiling at his guest in a way that he hoped made her feel very uncomfortable.

"I'm very disappointed in you, Donovan," he said. "More time? We're both running out of time."

Amelia, she still felt like Amelia no matter who Grady said she was, resisted the urge to shift nervously. And who was this Donovan he was talking to? One of the men she'd seen down in the communications area downstairs ran up and signaled to Grady. He covered the mouth piece, leaning toward the man who whispered something to him. He looked startled, then pleased. He said something to the man, who looked at her, then nodded.

She felt suddenly uneasy. Something had happened to shift the balance of power. Grady was no longer patient or relaxed. He wasn't even . . . excited anymore. It was something else.

She was right. The other man grabbed her arm, shoving a Glock into her side.

"Bring her outside," Grady said.

Even with the gun at her side, the fresh air was a welcome change from the heated, deadly atmosphere inside. It also gave her a better view of where she was. As she was dragged into the center of the clearing, she looked around, getting her bearings as best she could.

The man holding her transferred the gun to her head, standing behind her as both men studied the mountainside.

"I know you're there, Donovan. We picked you up on our scanners," Grady said into his phone. "Show yourself or she's dead."

Chapter Sixteen

Luke had spent the day rushing forward, as fast and furious as he could, but at the end of it, his thoughts, like the furies or hell hounds, stayed right on his heels, trying to bring to the front of his mind the one thing he didn't want to admit, acknowledge or feel.

It was natural to feel worried about Amelia. It wasn't natural to feel frantic. Or to feel like his life would be over if he didn't find her again. He'd felt that once, didn't want to feel it again, but it had crept up on him, blind siding him while his defenses were down. If he wasn't already in love with her, he was damn close.

He thought he only got one shot at this kind of love, the kind that wasn't about sex or companionship, but was both and more. He'd found it with Rosemary. He'd known she was right for him right away. The more he learned about her only deepened his sense of discovery and his love for her.

Guess I should have recognized the feeling, he thought ruefully, rubbing his face as he waited in the chilly parking garage for Bryn to start things moving. This was her show and soon she'd have as much at stake in it as he did. As it got closer to the time for Dewey to start his lonely drive south, she got more brittle, more like the Bryn she'd been when she came west. She didn't like feeling vulnerable, and she didn't yet know there wasn't anything she could do about it.

She'd learn, like he had, that love could come into your life, then fade to memories. He knew time was precious and fleeting. That it had to be savored, not run from. She'd learn.

He hoped she wouldn't learn it the way he had.

He stood outside the dim garage lights. With the setting of the sun, the air had turned bitter cold. Inside the garage the chilly air had a metallic edge to it caused by all the exhaust in the closed space.

In the semi-dark, with preparations happening all around him, he faced his own fear that he wouldn't survive if he took another stroll down lover's lane, but that was stupid really. What, was he going to lay down and die? No such luck. The real fear was of living alone again with all that pain. The fear wasn't of *not* surviving, but knowing he *would* survive. Dani, Matt's wife, talked a lot about survivor's guilt. About how surviving wasn't the option, how you dealt with survival was. She knew firsthand that it was damn hard to be the one left behind, forced to have the stiff upper lip and the smile, to tell people you're fine when your gut was on fire with the agony of being left behind, left alone after having it all.

He'd gone up the mountain, so sure he'd figured it all out, so sure he was in control, ready to face the world. Master of his fate. Captain of his soul.

He gave a silent laugh. Yeah, right. It was an arrogant notion, this idea that man controlled his own destiny. All you could really control was your response to what happened to you. Look at that weenie, Leslie Merryweather. Guy was born to money, even had what passed for a brain, and all he can figure out to do with it is kill someone weaker than him. He probably thought he was in control, too, when it was really just his impulses that were running the show.

Which brought him back to his own impulses. He wanted to tear up the countryside until Amelia was safe again and then keep her somewhere safe, but she didn't belong to him. And tearing things up might get her killed. He wasn't some spoiled little shit like Leslie. He was a man, a lawman. An adult. Time he started acting like one.

He straightened and walked over to Matt, who sent him a quick, worried look.

"You all right?"

Luke grinned at the question. It was a hard one to get shed of. "Yeah," he said. "I'm all right."

Matt nodded, then looked ahead. "We'll find her, bro."

Luke wasn't so sure, but he did know Matt would do his damnedest, as would he. That would have to be enough for now. "We ready to rock and roll?"

Bryn had opted for a small team, counting on stealth, rather than force to achieve their objective. Their team consisted of a four man SWAT squad, Jake and Matt, Bryn and Luke—who had a warrant for Leslie Merryweather's arrest in his pocket. Mann might be a little miffed at being left out of the fun—or he'd at least pretend to be. Crawling around in the snow wasn't his idea of a good time. Bryn had been hoping Donovan would join them, but he'd disappeared off the radar after tipping them off about Leslie Merryweather. She'd tried to call him back after Leslie gave them the slip, but he was offline and out of touch.

The plan, such as it was, was for Dewey to set out, assuming he'd be picked up for surveillance at some point along the way. Over Dewey's objections, Bryn had opted to use choppers to move in, flying at low level, to avoid detection, then switching to ground transportation so they could set up a loose, hopefully low profile, perimeter around the meet and only moving in well after the time for the meet. They'd be further back than she liked, but it was a compromise Dewey had insisted on. No question that their target had created a challenge, but it was one they were willing to meet.

Dewey would go in, activating the transponder if he was in trouble, or when he located Amelia or had determined she wasn't there. Any sign of probable cause and they'd move in, and hopefully scoop up all the perps and rescue the girl.

Luke saw Dewey straighten at Bryn's approach.

"You ready, Mr. Hyatt?" she asked.

Dewey's lips twitched, but he responded seriously, "Yes, Miss Bailey."

After an exchange of looks that took some of the chill out of the air around them, she said, "Good luck."

"Thanks." Dewey's grin was crooked as he climbed into his car. He started the engine, gave her a jaunty salute and pulled out. Bryn waited until he was out of sight before she turned and said, "Let's move out."

Luke noticed that everyone gave her a lot of room as they complied. It was nice to know she had as much at stake in this as he did, he decided. And he was damn glad he wasn't the one between her and what she wanted.

"I have you in my sights, Grady," Donovan said, his finger on the trigger of his rifle, Grady's head in his cross hairs.

"And my guy is holding a gun to your girl's head. If I die, so does she. Now get your ass down here, Donovan. Hey, you said you wanted to talk to her."

"So I did." Donovan lowered the rifle. He couldn't play chicken with Pru's life. Damn, he should have figured Grady'd have scanning equipment if he was training terrorists. He wasn't thinking clearly. It was easy to be cool and calm when it was your own life on the line. He couldn't do it with Pru's. "I am going to kill you, Grady."

"It's good to have a goal. Now show yourself." His voice hardened. "I don't have to kill her to . . . hurt her. My men have been dying to . . . play with her."

Donovan's hands clenched into fists. The bastard was going to pay. "You win. For now."

He pushed up through the branches and snow he'd used for cover, noting with satisfaction he'd managed to startle Grady by being much closer than he'd expected. He moved down the hill toward Pru and Grady, holding his rifle by the barrel so Grady's goon wouldn't get jumpy. It was a relief when the goon turned his attention to him, taking his rifle, a pistol, a knife and his satellite phone. He handed the phone to Grady who examined it carefully.

"Nice." He turned it off and tucked it in his pocket. "That everything?"

He knew Pru was watching him, but he kept his attention on Grady. "Hardly."

Grady laughed. "I like you, Donovan. Let's have it."

Donovan removed two more pistols, a sawed off shotgun and another knife, tossing them at Grady's feet. His gaze locked on Grady's, he added, "Sorry, can't remove the arms and legs."

"Point taken," Grady said, taking one step back from him. "But I don't think you'll use them while Miss Knight is at risk?"

For the first time, Donovan let himself look at Pru. He almost didn't recognize her without her glasses and the new hair cut. But her eyes were the same. Cool, deflective, remote. Bruises marred the pale purity of her skin, bringing his insides to a boil with rage. But damn, she made him proud. She stood there, her back as straight as a soldier's, her chin up in cool defiance. No way she was Knight's daughter. A warrior's blood ran in her veins. His blood.

"No. I won't kick your ass *now*," Donovan said. To Pru he said, "You all right?"

Her chin lifted a bit. "Of course. Though the accommodations are—" She finished with a shrug and a snooty grimace.

Donovan bit back a grin. "Good girl."

Grady laughed. "Your girl's a pistol, Donovan. Been tempted to keep her for myself."

Donovan's insides clenched, but he didn't let his face show anything but disdain. "Never happen."

Grady didn't flinch, but his gaze narrowed, even as he widened his smile. "I like your *can do* attitude, Donovan. We're going to get along just fine—if you do what I say."

"Surely you can find people to kill for you," Donovan said.

"Killers are easy. Good assassins," he shrugged, "are expensive. I like having money, not wasting it. Not when I can get two things I want for the price of one." He looked at Pru, his gaze far too interested for Donovan's comfort. "Did your boyfriend tell you he's a trained sniper? Oh, that's right, you can't remember, can you?" He turned to Donovan. "Guess that means you don't get a hello kiss."

Donovan gave him a look and realized that Pru had, too. He had a sinking feeling it was the mirror of his, a feeling confirmed when he saw Grady's eyes widen.

"Well, well, this gets more and more interesting." His gaze traveled between them with unnerving intensity, but to Donovan's relief he merely said, "We should take this inside. I think the lady's cold."

Grady held out his arm to Pru. She ignored it, turning on her heel and sweeping into the cabin as if it were a castle she was taking. Bryn had said she didn't remember anything. If she was right, Pru hid it well. The goon indicated with the barrel of the rifle that Donovan should precede him inside. With inner amusement, Donovan noticed he kept what he thought was a safe distance. Since it was what he wanted to do, Donovan complied, taking his time to let the goon know who was really in control.

Inside Grady spoke to someone he called O'Rourke. "Set another place for dinner." He stopped and looked at Donovan. "You will join us, won't you?"

"I'm feeling a bit peckish," Donovan said.

"I'm not going to have to cuff you, am I? It's such a messy way to eat."

"Not necessary." Donovan didn't mention that he hadn't met a pair of cuffs he couldn't pick. Instead he looked at Pru, offering her his arm. She looked startled, then she smiled. The effect on her face was startling, to say the least. "I like the new hairdo. It suits you."

"Thank you."

Donovan saw her look at Grady, and the shutters went down in her face again. Smart girl. As they walked to the rough-hewn table, he studied her out of the corner of his eyes. That she looked aloof was not unusual, but whatever had happened to her over the last few days had changed her, a change that went beyond the new haircut. She looked . . . lighter, and freer, despite her current captivity. With a jolt, he realized she didn't know that Knight had died. That to her, she was without a father. Had she loved him, he wondered? He'd never seen any sign of affection between them, but he wasn't in their inner circle.

He pulled out her chair in front of a place setting that looked like military surplus. When she was seated, he took the one next to her.

"You look . . . well," he said.

Amelia looked at him and smiled faintly, but her thoughts were chaotic. Was he really her boyfriend? Were they an item? Had they had some kind of relationship? It felt wrong. She felt liking for him, but not attraction. Even if Luke didn't want her, she belonged to him. This meeting from her missing past just made her conviction stronger. She felt guilty and anxious. This Donovan seemed nice and was clearly worried about her, so much so, that he'd been lurking in the snow trying to rescue her. It was an obligation she didn't want and hadn't asked for. The weight of it ignited the trapped feeling that lurked just below her memory.

Grady took the seat at the head of the table, O'Rourke the one opposite her where he smiled at her like a hopeful suitor. It was an odd scene. The firelight from the fireplace flickered off the beamed ceiling as the sun faded from the sky, turning the frost a brief, brilliant gold before it faded to gray. It had all the trappings of a dinner with friends. Except for the lack of friends and the armed men close at hand, one standing behind her with his Uzi trained on her back. Donovan may have been given his parole, but it was obvious that Grady still didn't trust him. She didn't blame him. Donovan had walked down the mountain with such an air of leashed menace that Grady had taken an involuntary step backward. Did he know he was in deep, she wondered?

She peeked at Donovan out of the corner of her eyes. He looked old enough to be her father, which made her think of Luke's concerns about her age. Apparently the same concerns hadn't troubled Donovan. Did that mean she had a taste for older men?

Donovan was handsome. He was better looking in some ways than Luke. His face was more classically handsome, though Amelia preferred Luke's craggy lines and angles to the classical. Just thinking about him curled her toes in her shoes. And Donovan knew how to make an entrance. He'd managed to startle Grady when he'd risen out of the snow like a ghost. His military camouflage, the paint on his face and his erect, soldier's bearing added to her overall impression that here was a striking man—in the literal and figurative sense of the word striking. She could see him appealing to some women, had felt a thrill herself at first sight of him. He had a rakish charm, right out of a romance novel. Even had a scar

240

above one eye. Very dashing and dangerous. If she were Grady, she'd be sweating, not eating. Despite all this, the thought of kissing him or intimacy with him left her feeling a bit nauseous.

Her mouth wanted to kiss only Luke. And the thought of intimacy with him made her shiver. She lowered her lashes, pretending to study the plate of food one of Grady's men placed in front of her. Just thinking about him turned her soft and languid, lifting her out of the here and now to the then with him. Thinking about how he'd tasted heated up her middle better than the fire flickering in the fireplace. She could feel the warmth tracking up her neck into her face. With a hand that only stayed steady with severe effort, she lifted her water glass and drank, sending down the cold mountain water to put out the fire.

This was not the time or place for fire. It was the time for icy thought. Cold planning. Firm resolve. She had to believe she could survive this. Half of any battle began in the mind.

She looked at Donovan. Was he the one who'd said this to her? Was he the part of her past that this had come from? His attitude toward her was so formal and protective—his gaze worried, not heated. His discipline impressed her, but his motives troubled her. The thought that he might want what she couldn't give tightened her chest.

"Not hungry?" Grady said, breaking into her thoughts.

She poked the slab of meat with her fork, arching one brow in inquiry. It had a wild taste and took up more of the plate than she liked. The sad looking veggies were pushed to one small corner, with a huge potato hugging the meat's other side. Also, no sight or smell of a dessert.

"Elk," Grady said. "How do you like it?"

"If I were a bear, I'm sure I'd be in heaven."

He chuckled. "It's probably just as well if you don't eat too much. I'm not sure how the scopolamine will affect you. Not an easy meal to hurl."

Her brain produced the fact that scopolamine was a truth drug, but not much else, which was odd. Her brain had practically been puking facts since she woke up in Luke's cabin. Now it decided to be sparing?

Donovan stiffened. He leaned forward, his face urgent. The guard behind him stepped closer, his Uzi ready.

"Don't do this, Grady." Donovan looked at Amelia. "You have no idea what effect the drug will have on her memory. It could just as easily wipe it out completely."

"It's a chance I'm willing to take," Grady said.

Amelia wasn't surprised to hear this, though her insides cringed at the thought of being out of control again. She couldn't let it happen. Not again. Not now, when Grady's eyes were no longer dispassionate when he looked at her. There was no question that the forces aligned against her were formidable. The cabin was isolated. The weather was hostile. There were armed men everywhere. All she had to pit against this was her resolve.

It would have to be enough. If it wasn't, well, they'd have to kill her, because they sure as hell weren't knocking her out again.

"I can't afford to wait for her memory to return. And I have a feeling that even if she could remember, she wouldn't give up SHIELD." His gaze slid her way, admiring and vaguely frustrated. "There's an unyielding quality about you, my dear. I used to train horses in my misspent youth. I learned to recognize which horses could be broke to a bridle and which couldn't."

She felt him try to reach her again, with his charm and that something more that he appeared to possess, something she didn't recognize, but could feel even as her gaze worked to deflect him yet again. In some ways, it felt like this probing was the greater peril than a sexual attack. This probing sought to reach her mind, her soul.

It was a relief when his gaze moved to Donovan, a look of malicious amusement turning Grady's eyes dark. "Hard to believe that sour old bastard, Knight is your father."

At the word 'father,' Amelia's world tilted briefly, a quick, short stab of pain taking out her sight for a moment. When her vision cleared, she could feel the thin skim of sweat on her forehead and upper lip. The pain was slow to fade, leaving a dull ache behind her eyes to plague her.

She was vaguely aware that Donovan had tensed next to her. And that this amused Grady. Thankfully neither man seemed aware of her distress.

She looked at the meat, felt her stomach roil and pushed her plate away. The water looked good, but she wasn't sure she could lift her arms. They felt weak. Behind the pain, there'd been a flash of something that her mind had quickly flinched away from. If her memory was returning, it had picked a hell of a time.

Grady laughed and lifted his wine glass, breaking the thread of the testosterone moment between he and Donovan.

"Relax, Donovan. We all know that Miss Knight never forgets anything. Well, almost anything."

She looked down, her eyes felt owl wide and Sahara dry. Was it possible she had a photographic memory? That would explain the encyclopedia-like flood of trivia trickling out of her muddled brain. What she knew and didn't know. A buzzing sense of relief took some of the edge off the ache. I'm not a bad person. Not a hit woman or thief.

Grady looked relaxed and triumphant. He thought he was in control—a touch of hubris that might be exploited? He thought he had his bases covered, but Donovan's appearance had startled him. So he wasn't as in control as he thought he was. Her lack of memory had to be a big set back, too.

She became aware that Grady was still talking.

". . . sent Dr. Knight to the hospital . . ."

Pain exploded in her head again. Through tiny, explosions of light, she saw them still talking, apparently not noticing any change in her. Her head felt like it was going to fall off and they hadn't noticed. Maybe all the action was inside. Little flashes of memory appeared and disappeared so quickly she couldn't take them in. Like tiny lights in real fog, they did more to highlight what she couldn't see than what she could.

The flash of ambulance lights.

Feelings of panic.

A man in a hospital bed, his face twisted with pain and rage. His mouth moving with words she couldn't—or was that wouldn't?—hear.

And with each flash of the past, the pain worsened. Not content with rampaging through her head, it spread downward toward her heart . . .

From a long way away, she heard Donovan say, "You don't know what you're messing with. I'm telling you, you could erase her memory permanently!"

Please do. Her lips moved, but no sound emerged.

"It's a risk I'm willing to take." Grady wiped his mouth with his napkin, then crumpled it and tossed it on his empty plate.

I don't want to remember. I don't want to know . . . With that thought, the lights and memory began to fade, taking the pain with them. She realized she was holding her breath, and let it out on a shaky sigh. The two men were still arguing, unaware her universe had shaken so violently. Luke had talked about shock and memory the night they met. They'd both assumed it was the shock of the kidnapping that had erased her hard drive, but now she wasn't so sure. If she was Prudence Knight, then this Dr. Knight must be her father—

Pain exploding again, knocking her off this train of thought with pointed emphasis. *Okay, don't go there. I got that.* She rubbed her temples until the pain eased again.

"But enough about that," Grady was saying. "Let's talk about you. You now know I do have Miss Knight and that I have no qualms about hurting her. The only question left is, what are you going to do so that I won't?"

Donovan looked at her, then back at Grady. If looks could have killed, Grady would be lying on his back, barely twitching.

Amelia stared at him as the weight that had left with her memory, pressed down on her again. She remembered this feeling, even if she couldn't remember why. She remembered it well—the weight of others' expectations. And needs.

"Please . . . don't do anything for me," she said, her voice a desperate thread of sound. If he did this, she'd never be free of him. Her debt to him would be too great to walk away from. "Just . . . don't."

"Trust me. It'll be all right." He covered her hand with his, his touch igniting her panic instead of calming it. Looking in his eyes, she could feel Luke slipping away from her. He looked at Grady. "You bastard."

"Hey, her old man is the one who stuffed his data in her head. Call him the bastard. Oh, you can't, can you?" An edge altered his voice with something Amelia could only call . . . evil. "Too bad he's dead. And not sitting right next to her."

Dead? Her . . . old man? Her brain found this term less inflammatory than that other parental name, though the pain still came.

Donovan surged to his feet, his hands reached for Grady.

His men jumped at him, pulling him back. One raised the butt of his Uzi with the intention of bringing it down on his head, but Grady stopped him with a sharp command.

"He's not hurting me," Amelia lied, looking at Donovan, trying to hold him with her gaze. "I don't remember. I don't remember . . . him." That was a lie, too. She could see a face, a twisted, angry face. Her insides quivered, but she refused to allow Grady to see her squirm. She shrugged, then smiled defiantly. Donovan stared a few beats longer, then his body relaxed. Finally he nodded.

"I'm very sorry about . . . it, Miss Knight," he said.

"Thank you." The pressure, the panic eased. Odd he didn't call her Prudence, though she was glad of it, too. "And please, call me Amelia."

"Amelia?" He looked taken aback.

"It seems little Miss Perfect Daughter had a secret identity," Grady said. He looked like he was enjoying himself. He got up and tossed Donovan the two drivers' licenses.

Donovan studied them for a bit, then looked at her with a charming, crooked grin. "Clever girl. I wondered where you went—" He stopped, then said, "When this is over—"

He stopped again. Maybe because he knew they probably wouldn't be alive when it was. His eyes promised her his best effort, but she didn't want that. She didn't want to owe him her life. She wasn't a good person. She was an ungrateful person.

"I'm touched," Grady said. "Really, but it's time to get down to business."

Donovan stiffened, then he looked at Grady. "So who is it you want me to kill this time?"

Amelia jerked in her chair. Damn, she hoped he wasn't her lover, because it looked like *he* was the hit man.

After a brief moment of elation at eluding Kirby and

friend, Leslie spent the next few hours in fetal position on the cement floor of his dad's old bomb shelter sobbing uncontrollably. He'd stumbled across it as a boy, using it as a private club house, then updating it as he got older. Now it served as his hideout. It was here he kept the equipment he used in the GREEN raids. It was here he'd planned to hide what's-her-name. It was also a bunker in every sense of the word. It was well stocked with weapons, explosives and food. And it had a communications center, but there was no one for him to call. The only person he ever called from here was Grady. Always Grady—who had betrayed him so completely.

Years, years they'd spent planning this, talking about it. Or had they talked? With his recently discovered hindsight, Leslie examined the years with Grady. Mostly, he realized, he'd talked. And Grady had listened. And listened. And listened. Heady stuff to a kid with a father to whom not listening was an art form. He'd never actually heard Grady say he supported GREEN's objectives. He had encouraged setting up the Irregulars, had laughed with him at the irony of it, while he set up the little, armed kingdom in the mountains. And given himself his handle, Forest for the Trees.

Damn. He'd laughed about it, thinking he knew what it meant and all the time, Grady was laughing at him. The bastard had played him with a few words of encouragement, and Leslie had given him his trust and piles and piles of money. No, it was worse than that. Leslie had given Grady his love. Not the twisted love between parent or child, or the sexual crap between a man and a woman. This had been the clean, pure love of friends. Or so he'd thought.

Was it just the money? Or was it something else Grady wanted? Why decide to kill the cash cow now? But he already knew the answer.

SHIELD.

Grady was hoping for a new cash cow, maybe one that didn't talk so much or need so much. It was always about control. Who had it, who didn't. That's what his dad always said. Who had it. Who didn't.

Leslie pulled himself into a sitting position and smiled through his tears. Grady was in for several surprises. He didn't know everything about him. And he didn't know everything about SHIELD.

It was time he found out.

Chapter Seventeen

Dewey was annoyed with himself and Forest for the Trees by the time he reached the rendezvous point. He could be snug in bed with Bryn, his *wife,* right now, not sitting at some God forsaken intersection waiting for a very suspicious wacko. It was dang ironic that he'd started this to get closer to Bryn, and now he was further from her than ever.

He pulled his truck to the side of the road and turned off the headlights. Immediately, the night descended, dark and forbidding. There was little moon to be seen in the sky. Just a thin crescent casting enough light to put an eerie glow on the surface of the snow and make the shadows around the trees deeper.

It looked like he was alone in the universe right now, but Dewey knew better. *He* was out there and he wasn't alone. Dewey could feel eyes watching him. Knew he was being assessed. After being under Bryn's microscope for a year, he wasn't worried. He knew how to hide—even when the hiding was inside himself.

Dewey had decided on a modified geek disguise for the op. People expected it from hackers. Slicked down hair. Plaid shirt. Dockers. Penny loafer shoes. Polyester jacket. Some padding in the cheeks to alter his profile. And, of course, the all-important glasses with tape around the nose bridge. And in case they were suspicious enough to check, he'd even broken them before he taped them, then dirtied the tape.

It would be interesting to see just how paranoid Forest was. And if Dewey had been paranoid enough. This had all been a lot easier when he hadn't cared if he lived or died. He wished he wasn't so cut off. Be nice to have Bryn hissing sweet bitchings in his ear right now.

He'd been out at night, but not in the wilds. He was pretty sure that critters hibernated in the winter. Ninety percent sure. Well, sixty percent sure. Not sure enough to get out of the truck, even though pacing would have been a relief. Instead, he started beating a discordant rhythm on the steering wheel.

The motor was still running, but not loud enough. He reached for the radio knob, hoping for any kind of signal in the boondocks, when a bright light cut the night, freezing him in mid-reach. He shaded his eyes and tried to pierce the light. That's when he heard the chopper approach. It swooped in, its search light sweeping the area before it settled down in a clearing a short distance away. The rotation of the blades kicked up the snow, adding a fog effect to the eerie scene. In the light from the chopper, he could see a jeep with a machine gun mounted in the rear. Three armed men manned the jeep, giving him the odd feeling he'd been transported back in time to the Battle of the Bulge.

"Show time." He shut off the engine, pocketed the keys and slid out, his tennis shoe shod feet slipping on an icy patch under the snow. He regained his balance, then shut the door and walked to the front of the truck, still shielding his face from the bright lights and blowing snow.

One of the men hopped out of the jeep and approached him, tossing a bundle of clothes onto the hood of the truck.

"Take off everything and put these on," the faux Rambo ordered.

Dewey had known it was coming, but being right wasn't that satisfying with the prospect of freezing his family jewels off just when they'd been put into service. He opened his mouth to protest, but closed it again. What was the point? He was just wasting what body heat he had left.

He quickly stripped and donned the other clothes, aware his jewels weren't displaying well in the bitter cold. His teeth were chattering when he finally pulled on a bulky coat. There were gloves and a hat in the pocket. He pulled them on, too. Next time Bryn had a problem, neither of his personalities were going to step up to volunteer.

"Now what?" Dewey asked, stamping his feet and beating his arms against his sides to try to restore warmth.

The guy didn't answer, but Dewey saw two men climb out of the chopper, their heads down, bodies bent until they cleared the rotating blades. Once clear, they joined him at the truck. One guy was tall and covered in winter camouflage. Spooky looking with furious eyes. The other one was Forest. Dewey knew it even before he spoke. He looked and acted like he was in control. It was in the way he moved and in his eyes. He was enjoying all the fanfare and playing at soldier. Odd attitude for an environmental wacko. It was a lovely bit of misdirection that Dewey could appreciate.

"Phagan?" Forest held out a gloved hand. Dewey took it, shook it. "Keys?"

"Huh?" Dewey pushed his glasses up on his nose, falling into the role he'd created for himself.

"To the truck. My friend here needs to borrow it. He'll bring it back, won't you, Donovan?"

Donovan gave a short, sharp nod.

Dewey stared at him in fascination. So this was Donovan. He said, "In my coat pocket."

One of Forest's men searched the coat, then tossed Donovan the keys.

A smaller, Irish looking, heavily bundled guy shifted nervously. "Shouldn't someone go with him, Grady?"

Grady flashed him a quick, annoyed look. "He won't mess with me, will you, Donovan?"

Another short, sharp nod. He went to the truck and opened the door, stopping when Grady spoke again.

"Noon, Donovan."

Donovan looked at Grady. Dewey was glad that look wasn't directed at him. Talk about killing. Grady just smiled.

"Noon. Or else."

Donovan got in and slammed the door. When he'd fired the engine, he gunned it, then spun out, the rear of the truck fishtailing before the wheels found the needed traction.

Dewey thought of several things he could have said, but they weren't appropriate for his persona, so he kept them to himself. He sure missed working with Phoebe. She always knew what he was thinking, even the smart ass stuff, and would give him a look that was as good as a laugh. With a silent sigh for what had been, he turned his attention to Grady. Grady was looking at his glasses.

"You need those to see?" he asked.

"Only reason for wearing them," Dewey said, pushing them up again.

"May I?" He reached for the glasses. Dewey nodded, letting him pluck them from his nose, then peering myopically at him as Grady held them up to the light, then moved them a little, feeling the break in the bridge. "Ever think of getting new ones?"

Dewey shrugged. "Maybe when I run out of tape."

Grady laughed. "I had a feeling I'd like you, Phagan." He slapped him on the back. "Let's go somewhere warmer."

Grady had sent Amelia back to her room before the men discussed their business. It seemed he had missed the women's movement. Donovan had jumped to his feet, taking her hand one more time and squeezing it so tightly that panic crawled up her throat again. She'd longed for time alone with him to find out more about herself, while at the same time feeling relieved to leave him behind.

As O'Rourke directed her toward the stairs, she'd spotted a paper clip on the desk, close to her two driver's licenses. As she passed the desk, she picked them and the clip up with them. She'd held the licenses up.

"Can I take these with me?"

Grady hesitated, as if the question surprised him, then shrugged and nodded. As she climbed the stairs, she heard him asking Donovan if he wanted some brandy. It was all quite freaky. It was as if Grady couldn't make up his mind between genial host and evil overlord.

Back in her room, O'Rourke, with an apologetic air, had secured one wrist to the bed again and then locked her in. As soon as he was out of ear shot, she unbent the paper clip and went to work on the lock. She was still working on it when she heard the sound of a chopper arriving. Anxiety faded with action. She was doing something, not just a staked lamb waiting for the slaughter.

There were cracks appearing in the wall of fog holding in her past. She had a hazy memory of being in the chopper, though none of falling out or struggling to Luke's cabin. It was possible she never would remember that. She couldn't remember where, but she did remember reading something about memory loss from an accident being permanent.

Donovan played no role in any of the little bits of stuff she was remembering. It seemed obvious that she'd had a personal shock of some kind, something related to her father. It was possible that he was part of it, and that's why she couldn't remember him. Just thinking the word "father" sent little frissons of pain off in her head. Something so painful that her brain shied away from remembering it. Not being a masochist—that she knew of—she let that sleeping dog lie and turned to another unanswerable question.

Who was it that Grady was trying to force Donovan to kill? He'd looked so grim, it must be someone important. If he succeeded, his life would be over. He'd either go to jail or be killed. She didn't want, didn't need the burden of that. If you were going to incur a debt, shouldn't you get some say in it?

She pulled the clip out and bent the end slightly, then eased it back in, feeling for the latch that she was trying to release. If she could free herself, then she wouldn't owe him. The point caught on something. Was that it? She upped the pressure and suddenly the cuff fell away from her wrist.

"Not completely useless," she muttered. Freed from restraint, she was able to search the rest of the room. Not that it did her much good. There was nothing in any of the drawers, other than the Bible she'd found before. The window was tightly latched from the outside. With a sigh, she sat back down on the bed, hefting the Bible. As a weapon, it left a lot to be desired.

Outside, the chopper lifted off again. She could hear the clatter of the blades fading toward the north. As it subsided, she realized that someone was unlocking the door to her bedroom. She quickly looped the handcuff back around her wrist, tucking the Bible out of sight under her pillow.

The door swung open, only this time it wasn't O'Rourke or Grady in the doorway. It was the man she'd seen when she looked out the window, the one walking across the clearing. The one with the cruel face. His face was unchanged, except for the addition of an equally cruel smile. There was a look in his eyes that sent her adrenaline surging like a flash flood through a dry creek bed.

He stepped in and slowly closed the door behind him,

bringing the stench of lust and a creeping sense of evil with him. Her mouth went dry as he set his rifle aside, removed his cap and jacket and tossed them onto the chair, then began unbuckling the heavy utility belt around his waist.

The staging area Bryn chose was a bleak, cold piece of real estate enough miles away from the rendezvous to give them a reasonable sense they hadn't been spotted. They were running with little or no lights, keeping their profile low while they waited. And waited. And waited.

Luke spun and started back along the path he was wearing through the knee-deep snow and into the frozen turf. This was taking too long. They weren't accomplishing anything. Everyone was pacing to stay warm, so Luke's pacing didn't stand out, but he'd have been doing the same had it been one hundred degrees out, instead of spiraling toward zero.

Matt approached carrying a hot thermos and a couple of sandwiches. It reminded Luke of a time when it had been Matt wearing the path. A couple of plastic cups hung off one finger by the handles. Matt held out one to him, his eyes daring Luke to refuse.

"Enjoying this?" Luke growled.

"No. Now eat and drink."

"I'll just hurl it," Luke protested, glaring down at the sandwich Matt dropped in his hand.

"No," Matt said. "You won't. You'll feel like it, but you won't. And you'll have the strength to do your job when we get ready to move."

"Any news?"

Matt shrugged. "According to GPS, Dewey's truck is still waiting at the rendezvous. We've got the military tracking any aerial activity in the area. Nothing from them either."

Lucky for them, Dewey's truck had GPS capability, so

they'd been able to track it to the rendezvous point, but it was frustrating to know so little. It was like being blind, only this time his other senses weren't enhanced, Luke decided, with a frustrated sigh. He shoved the sandwich in his mouth and chewed, using the coffee to wash it down. A flurry of activity around the truck had them moving that way.

"What's up?" Luke asked, as Jake jumped down.

"Truck's moving again, back this way."

"What's our move?" Matt asked.

"Bryn wants us to stop the truck."

Luke followed his two brothers to their truck. Matt took the wheel, firing the engine and spinning the truck around toward the road. In a few minutes, they were in position to block the road on Bryn's signal. Luke watched as the headlights, at first pinpoints in the black night, grew steadily larger. When the truck was about a hundred yards away, Bryn signaled and Matt pulled the truck into the road as Bryn pulled her rig in and closed the gap, turning on their headlights at the same moment.

The driver of the truck hit the brakes. The truck fishtailed, then slipped sideways, stopping within inches of their road block. Immediately the truck was covered, as Bryn's men moved in, their guns trained on the cab.

"Get out of the truck," one of them ordered.

Because of all the headlights, all Luke could see was a figure with his hands up.

The driver's door opened with a creak of metal. The driver eased out, careful to keep his hands raised. As he stepped into the light, Luke saw a soldier in winter camouflage.

"Fancy meeting you here, Bryn," he said.

Bryn's gun was already being lowered, even before he spoke.

"Donovan." She rubbed the back of her head. "What the

hell are you doing in this rig?"

"Following orders," he said. He looked at Bryn, and for the first time, Luke saw the expression in his eyes. They were bleak and angry. Close to desperate. "He has her. I saw her. If you stop me, he'll kill her."

Luke pushed forward and grabbed him by the collar, lifting him partly off his feet. He didn't even resist. "Not if we stop him."

Eyeball to eyeball, Luke saw the moment the guy started thinking again.

"Where is she? Where are they holding her?"

He pulled free and straightened his clothes, his gaze curious as he studied Luke.

"Who the hell are you?"

Bryn pushed between them. "Long story. Just tell me, can you take us to where they're holding her? Can we get to her?"

With some reluctance, Donovan looked from Luke to Bryn. "Won't be easy. He's got the place well guarded. He won't kill her until he gets what there is of SHIELD. And I do my job."

"And then he'll kill her anyway," Bryn said, her voice hard. "We both know it. So are you with us or not? Stop thinking like a father and start thinking like a soldier."

She was right, but Luke didn't like thinking about it. Neither did Donovan if his face were any indication. How had she gotten so important to him so quickly? He turned and looked in the direction of the mountains, remembering another time the mountains had hidden someone. They'd seemed so big, so vast when Dani was in them with that crazy bastard, Jonathan Hayes, and they'd managed to think their way to her and bring her back alive. He had to believe they could do it again, or he'd just sit down and cry. Or go off with his head up his butt like Donovan. He turned back to the group, where a tense Donovan still faced a pugnacious Bryn.

Donovan's chest heaved in a sigh. "I'm with you. Of course I'm with you."

Bryn's hard look cracked into a real smile. "Good. I've got a map in the van. Tell us what we need to do."

Amelia winced as he dropped his utility belt, laden with ammo and what looked like grenades, to the floor, only mildly relieved when something didn't blow. More weaponry followed it to the floor, so much she was surprised he had been able to stand upright. Then he sat down and began unlacing his boots. She swallowed dryly as he dropped the first one on the wooden floor, smiling when she jumped at the sound.

Maybe it was the shock that gave her this terrible clarity of thought. Or maybe she just knew she didn't have time to be afraid. She reached and found the cool, heavy Bible she'd left under her pillow. It wasn't much, but its weight and its message offered comfort and support.

He unlaced the other boot and pulled it off, dropping it, too. He unbuttoned his shirt, shrugging it off to reveal powerful shoulders. A tattoo of a dragon marred one side of his chest, the head where his heart should have been. The tail trailed down his biceps almost to his wrist. All that was left was his pants. He stood, undoing the buttons one by one. He had the soul of a stripper, taking them down slowly, then kicking them into the corner.

He didn't say anything. He didn't need to. His body movement said it for him. Amelia looked once, then kept her gaze fixed on his face. It was obvious that he felt in control of the situation as he looked her top to bottom, his eyes stripping her down to cringing flesh.

Her body tensed, adrenaline screaming in her veins. Her

head buzzed with it. Only one clear thought. She had to stop him.

His smile was feral as he closed on her. He grabbed her chin. His fingers digging in with cruel force, tightening until they cut down on her air.

Her head spun. Her vision narrowed sharply as she fought to stay conscious.

His eyes, his touch told her he wouldn't be kind. He was a predator, concerned only with what he could take. With his free hand, he grabbed the neck of her shirt and ripped it off. His eyes raked her exposed flesh, her bra a frail barrier in the storm. His hand went to the strap on her shoulder, his nails raking her flesh as he ripped it down. His mouth swooped toward hers.

She couldn't stand it. The stench of him filled her nostrils; her stomach roiled. She couldn't abide his touch, couldn't stand to have him erase the sweet memory of Luke's kiss with his vileness.

Her knee jerked up with all the force she could muster, plus the adrenaline chaser. It slammed into his groin. His gasp sprayed her with his spit. She flinched away from it, from him. He shoved her away, the force knocking what little breath she had left out of her.

His body curled around his injured member with a wheezing groan.

She could see his neck. It was dirty, like a boy who'd been in mud. She lifted her arm holding the Bible, then brought it down on his neck. The jolt of it vibrated up her arm. Her hand went numb and the Bible dropped. She backed away.

He seemed to hang there for several heartbeats, then fell onto the bed.

She was sorry he'd had a soft landing. Her breathing was quick, panicked, but still distant. As if she'd left her body and become an observer. The air felt cold on her exposed skin. The wounds he'd inflicted throbbed with the frantic beat of her heart. But something insulated her from the full horror of what had almost happened. She edged past the feet sticking off the edge of the bed and grabbed his rifle.

It was an M1 carbine. She checked the clip. It looked like it held at least thirty rounds. She shoved the clip home again and pointed it at him, somewhat startled by how familiar it felt in her hands.

He wasn't moving. He was breathing. A harsh, sonorous sound in the deep silence of the room. It occurred to her that she ought to secure him while she could. Keeping him covered, she retrieved the handcuffs and secured one around his wrist, shoved it through the bedpost and secured the other.

It was awful being close to him. He stank of cheap cologne, sweat and booze. He groaned, and her heart jumped into overdrive again. If he woke, he could raise an alarm. From her safe distance from herself, she watched as she lifted the butt of the gun and brought it down, but she stopped short of his temple.

What are you doing? she asked herself, horrified.

He was going to rape you, she reminded herself.

She lifted it again. This time she closed her eyes and brought it down without stopping. It crunched sickeningly. She opened her eyes. Saw blood bubble up from the wound she'd made and run down the side of his face. It dropped, brilliant red, on the white sheets of the bed.

Her stomach heaved. She could smell the blood. Worse, she could smell him. His smell was all around her. It seemed to fill the room. For a moment, horror broke through the barrier of shock protecting her, but she fought it back. Survival was the most basic human instinct.

She covered him with the blanket and turned away with

relief. She turned her back on him and looked at the door. It was closed, but she was pretty sure he hadn't locked it when he came in. Why should he? He had the guns and the size. Just hadn't had the brain.

She checked. The knob turned. She eased it open, peering out through a crack. The hall was empty. No sounds from downstairs. She could see the key hanging where O'Rourke kept it. She closed the door and leaned against it. She stared at the motionless man, then she picked up his pants.

"Yuck." To get her mind off what he'd probably done in these pants, she measured her foot against the side of his boot. They'd work. It felt good to have a plan. And it kept the horror at bay.

Chapter Eighteen

Luke couldn't remember ever being this cold. It drilled through his gear and plucked at his face with icy fingers as he struggled after Donovan through the waist-deep snow. The world, his world, had narrowed to two goals—keeping Donovan in view and taking the next step. If he just focused on those two goals, he'd make it. Outside of that was everything else. His fears for Amelia and the cold that dug through layers of clothing and skin.

He'd insisted on being partnered with Donovan. He was their point man and the one who knew where Amelia was. Obviously, he was the guy to be with when they hit the camp.

Huge mistake.

The guy wasn't human. Didn't seem to feel the cold. Or tired. If he felt fear, it didn't show. He didn't stop. Didn't hesitate. Went over, under or around. Whatever it took to move forward.

All of the ground had been up, but the terrain abruptly took a downward turn. The burning pressure on his lungs eased. The labor to get air where it was needed eased. He could talk again.

"Why?" he asked, as he drew almost level with Donovan.

He looked at him. "Why what?"

"Why didn't you ever tell her?"

Donovan's stride broke for the first time. "How well do you know her?"

Completely and not at all, he thought. He settled for a shrug. The downward turn got steeper, seriously steep. The straining forward now shifted to straining backward. He grabbed at trees, rocks, whatever he could find to hang on to. They weren't worried about covering their tracks right now, just about covering ground. Luke sensed that Donovan shared his feeling of urgency.

"Then you wouldn't understand." Donovan eased his way around a large boulder, then dropped into a crouch. "We need to be more careful now."

Luke dropped down beside him. Below, a long way below, he could see a cabin with a few lights showing, crouched on the edge of a large clearing.

"We're in the range of his lookout bunkers. I spotted two on this side when I was working my way down today. Must have some kind of underground access, because there's no sign of a trail in the snow," Donovan said. "We'll have to take them both out, or they'll sound an alarm."

"Any idea how many men per?" Luke asked. He was ready for some action. Not the struggling through snow action. The kick some butt action.

"One, maybe two."

"How'd you spot them?" From here the hillside looked serene and untouched, like a postcard.

Donovan flashed him a quick grin, the first Luke had seen break the bleak in his face since he'd met him an hour ago. "X-ray vision."

He could like this guy. Now that they were heading downhill.

Amelia tightened the belt, but it was still too big for her. She undid it and simply tied it in a knot around her middle. The arms of the jacket extended well past her hands, but it had Velcro bands at the wrists that she was able to tighten to keep them in place. The utility belt was heavy. She had to lift it on the dresser, then used its top to support the weight of the belt as she secured it around her waist. She staggered, but then found her balance.

She checked her armaments. Plenty of ammo. She seemed to know all about it but didn't know anything about the grenades. That was odd, but she didn't have time to mull it. There was a silenced hand gun—most convenient—and a vicious looking knife. She kept the gun, but hid the knife in the dresser drawer. In one of the pockets of the jacket, she found night-vision goggles. There was also a pair of regular snow goggles and a pair of thick, warm gloves. There was even a compass and a small flashlight.

She had to hand it to Grady. His men were well equipped.

She used the mirror to adjust the hat on her head, trying not to think about how much grease it had probably absorbed. His gear was mottled white and gray. Snow camouflage, much like what Donovan had been wearing. The usual green and tan wouldn't be much use in this weather. She looked pretty menacing and could probably pass a cursory inspection from a distance. Up close could be dicey.

Something flickered, in the mirror? Or in her head? Instead of the faux soldier, she caught a glimpse of a sober face like hers in the license picture, only this time she was hiding behind dark glasses. Her hair was pulled up and back. If that was Prudence, it was no wonder no one had recognized her. Why had she worn glasses? She didn't need them.

It was time to leave but hard to do. As much as she'd wanted to get out of the room, now she wanted to stay, despite the presence of her gnarly roommate. Briefly she considered the pros and cons of barricading herself in. Unfortunately the cons outweighed the pros. Grady had more men and more guns than she did. And that was just the stuff she knew about. He could have tear gas or some other icky knock-out stuff he could toss in.

No, the fly didn't wait in the web for the spider to find her. She took a deep breath and opened the door. The short hall was empty, a bit murky without its own light. Everything seemed quiet. She slipped out and closed the door behind her. The key gave her a little trouble, since she couldn't bring herself to put her gun down. Her nerves were jumping and her fingers felt thick and clumsy, but finally it clicked into place. She considered keeping the key, but her goal was to deceive and delay. A missing key would be an immediate heads up that something was wrong. She hung it up, but before she could turn, she heard the creak of footsteps behind her.

"Oh, good idea, Ray," a male voice said. "Grady ain't gonna like it that you messed with the girl."

Amelia stared at the wood. Her shoulders twitched, the movement not unlike a shrug. She slipped the silenced automatic clear of the holster and eased off the safety.

"You won't be so cool when he shoots your nuts off, man." He wheezed a couple of times, then said, "So, how was she? Think I could have a go, too?"

Amelia found fear fading in a wave of disgust. Jeez, did any of them have an original thought to rub together? Or anything beyond the most basic of human instincts? Without stopping to think, she spun to face him, bringing the pistol up once she was clear.

"Actually, she kicked his ass," Amelia said. "And now she's thinking of shooting *your* nuts off."

He lost all his color. Apparently, he valued his nuts more than his life. Trembling, he raised his hands.

"Didn't mean no harm."

"Right." Amelia shook her head. "Is there somewhere I can put you that you can't get out of? Otherwise, I'll have to kill you."

My goodness she sounded tough. Course she *had* just kicked Ray's ass. Well, the general region of his ass.

He lowered one hand and opened a closet door.

"Leave the hardware," Amelia said, using the carbine to punctuate the order. "And don't make a sound. Bullets penetrate wood."

He dropped it all with a clatter and stepped inside. "Same key locks it."

In a moment, she had him secured. She looked through his gear, taking anything else she thought might be useful, then hiding the remainder in the other bedroom at the end of the hall.

Her impulse was to creep downstairs but furtive would look suspicious. She had to be Ray, or something like him. She straightened her shoulders. Think military, Amelia. She stepped forward, using what she hoped was a military swagger. The boots helped. So did the clothes.

There was no one downstairs, but as she reached the main door, the darkness outside was cut with the searchlight and the sound of a chopper. Was Grady back?

Grady instructed the pilot to land the chopper at the lower camp. He wasn't ready to bring Phagan into the upper camp. There was something about him that made him uneasy, despite the instant sense of liking.

"Keep the motor running," he directed. He and Phagan jumped out and started toward a huddle of buildings. The men were hunkered down for the night. No sign of the hidden watchers as he led Phagan toward his office. Inside he beelined for the bar set up against one wall. It had been damn cold in the chopper.

"What'll you have?" he asked over his shoulder.

Phagan had stopped in the doorway, his gaze moving unhurriedly around the room. "Uh, beer if you have it."

"In the kitchen, through that door." He nodded to the right. "Won't warm you up as good as this stuff." He held up the whiskey.

"Don't expect to ever get warm again," Phagan said mildly, before disappearing into the kitchen. In a moment, he returned with a cold one.

Grady gestured to a seat on one side of the desk, then sat down, and studied his new guest as his new guest studied him. Phagan wasn't what Grady expected, even though he was. It was a strange feeling. Maybe it was because he was exactly what he'd expected. You never really expect to get what you expect. Not in the real world. Maybe it was because he'd been hoping for something more . . . unique. His reputation sure as hell was. Beyond geek.

He'd been clean though. His men had picked his clothes clean while they made their slow way to the camp, then let him know. So why the prickling on the back of his neck? Was it from the geek? Or somewhere else?

Phagan broke eye contact, his conclusions his own, as he looked around again. "Not exactly what I was expecting."

"And what were you expecting?" Grady asked him.

He shrugged ruefully. "Damned if I know. Maybe the Unabomber with a brain? Or a stainless steel super criminal empire."

Grady chuckled, but also felt he'd heard those words before? Or something like them? The eerie echo of his own thoughts should have reassured him. They didn't, but they should have. Phagan was saying all the right things, doing all the right things. Very cool. Very relaxed. Phagan got up and peered at an elk head above the fireplace. This view of his profile triggered something. A feeling of recognition, maybe?

"We haven't met, have we?" Grady asked. He believed in

the direct approach, where possible.

Phagan looked at him, his light brows arching in surprise. "I don't think so. I don't meet many people."

Grady got up. "Then I've seen you somewhere."

"I don't get out much either. And never get photographed." He shrugged lightly. "They say we all have a twin out there somewhere."

"Shit, I hope not." Grady sipped his drink. Hadn't even blinked. Should he blink? It was hard to say. Most geeks he'd met had no social skills at all. All their energy, all their brain power went to the hack. Was that what was making him twitch? "You do good work. The run on Merryweather was flawless."

"Merryweather?" Phagan looked down his beer can. "That's who it was. You do wonder." He took a drink. "Let's see. Biotech company. Doing some interesting stuff in protective armor. Doesn't seem like your thing, man. Like, anti-green, isn't it?"

"I'm a curious guy. It's a curse."

Phagan's smile was slow, but curiously charming. For the first time, Grady had a feeling that he'd met someone he could actually like. Maybe even respect. But could he trust him? It was time to find out.

"I've got a . . . meeting with someone who can ease my curiosity. Want to come along? I think you'll find her quite as interesting as I do."

Phagan shrugged. "Was just thinking the other day that I need to get out more. Meet some people."

Grady laughed. "Well, you came to the right place."

Phagan stood up, but before they could leave, the phone rang.

"Yeah?" Grady said into the receiver.

"We got trouble, boss. Leslie Merryweather just flew in on a chopper."

"Damn. I'll be right there." He hung up.

"Trouble?"

He looked at Phagan. "Nothing I can't handle."

As Amelia hesitated inside the door, the chopper landed in the clearing. There was another exit out of the cabin, she recalled, but this might be the only opportunity for her. The chopper was blowing snow around, it was dark and cold. Be natural for someone to wait for it. And maybe she could hitch a ride on it. The pilot wouldn't be expecting to be hijacked.

She pulled the hat down, tucking the flaps under the chin to disguise its shape. She pulled on the snow goggles and the gloves, then opened the door and plunged into a night that was a mix of light and dark. The cold bit into her lungs, and she gasped for breath. Had to be close to zero out here. The lining of her nasal passages crisped and her clothing stiffened. A cloud of snow billowed in her face, forcing her to look away, even as she jogged toward the chopper. Before she could get close enough, the chopper's engine roared as it lifted off again, turning its light up and away, then shutting it off. Guess she was going to have to do this the hard way.

As her view cleared, she saw a single figure remained in the clearing, staggering a couple of times as he turned toward the cabin and her. It wasn't Grady, but he looked familiar.

"Where's Grady?" he shouted. "Is he inside?"

Amelia shook her head. The chopper had retreated enough that she could say, while trying to make her voice as deep as possible, "He left."

The man was bundled up, but his face was bare. Handsome but weak, with something in the eyes that reminded her of Ray. She knew him, but from where?

She started to walk past him, but he grabbed her arm. "Where's the girl?"

Amelia froze. Couldn't stop her pulse from doing a jump to light speed.

"Inside."

"Show me," he said.

Amelia's first instinct was to refuse, but she knew any sign of panic now would spell her doom. There were men out there watching. Grady hadn't taken her into the lookout bunkers, but he'd pointed out the passageways below ground, and she'd seen the bunker's layout on the map during her tour. Thanks to her photographic brain, she could probably give her own tour now. She wanted to get away from here before Grady came back.

Which did nothing to help her with her current problem. If she could get him inside, she could use her gun again. She nodded and turned back to the door. The guy waited for her to open it. Clearly, he thought he was important. With her back to him, she got the pistol ready again. Inside, her goggles fogged over as the warm air hit them. She lifted them. Her eyes watered from the change in temperature. She blinked them rapidly and found the newcomer wasn't looking at her. His avid gaze scoured the room. He'd brought with him the smell of something feral. Something slimy and evil.

"Where?"

"Upstairs," Amelia said, glad it wasn't really so. This was not a guy to be left alone with.

"Show me," he said again.

With a sigh, Amelia led him toward the stairs, trying to remember to walk like a soldier. His eagerness, his lust, reached past her, the brush with evil sending a chill down her spine. Unlike Grady, this guy wasn't interested in what was inside her head. They didn't meet anyone and she couldn't see anyone in any of the rooms. Maybe they were all down in the bunker?

"How long will Grady be gone?"

Amelia shrugged. She didn't want to try out her voice in the quiet. It might not hold up to scrutiny.

"How long has he been gone?" he sounded impatient now. Great. "About an hour," she said, gruffly and with crossed fingers. She stopped in front of the door she'd only just left, slipping the pistol clear of the pocket on the side away from him. If the guy in the closet made a sound, the situation could go south quickly.

She released the safety, covering the small click with the sound of the key sliding in the lock. It turned easily this time. Odd how steady her hands were now, when danger threatened. She pushed the door open and stood back to let him enter. The room was much as she'd left it. Ray was still under the blanket.

He stopped, a smile curling the edges of his mouth that chilled her blood more surely than the winter air. He moved forward lightly licking his lips in anticipation.

She brought her gun up, her hand steady as a rock.

He pulled the blanket back, growling in frustrated rage as he turned toward her. His hand reached for his back and what she assumed was a weapon, but he stopped when he saw the gun trained on him.

"Get it. Two fingers. Drop it and kick it toward me or I take out your manhood," Amelia said. She was a quick study on male motivation.

Despite the rage in his eyes, he paled and did as she asked. She kicked it out the door without taking her eyes off him. Now what? How did one back off from a rattlesnake, she wondered.

He must have sensed her uncertainty. He smiled again. She supposed there was charm in it, but it had no effect on her. She'd seen beneath the surface.

271

"Well, aren't you the clever girl, Miss Prudence," he said. "Not just a filing cabinet, after all."

She knew that voice. A flash of memory produced his face, too. It came accompanied by a stab of pain. She'd felt like this before. Felt this odd mix of interest and unease. She didn't strain for the name this time and it came to her.

"Leslie." She didn't know how or why, but she could feel whatever was holding her memory out of contact begin to crack. It hadn't burst yet, but it was ready. It bulged, like a dam under siege. She knew two things with perfect clarity. It was going to be bad. And she needed to be away from Leslie when it went. The flood could sweep away her control of the situation.

"I hate to lock you up and run, but I do want to be out of here before Grady comes back. I'm sure you understand," she said, surprised at how calm she sounded with her insides roiling like a volcano.

He took a half step toward her and she brought the gun up sharply, directly in his face.

"I wouldn't. You know that I know how to use this." Did he?

Apparently he did. He stopped. But he was poised to strike. She stepped back, feeling for the door with her free hand.

"Did Grady tell you what we did to your old man?" he said, as if he sensed that upping the pressure might break the situation his way.

Amelia felt the tremor deep inside. She had to get out now.

"I don't have time—"

"I killed him. He was still alive when you left the hospital, but he's dead now." He smiled again, but this time it wasn't pretty or charming. "Your father—"

272

At the word "father", the first piece of her memory dam burst free of restraint. Her whole body contracted from the pain that accompanied it.

A gunshot. The recoil in her arm. The pain in her wrist. A cry from Leslie.

Through waves of pain, she saw something red splatter on the log walls. Leslie sank to his knees, a surprised expression on his face.

"I'll be damned. The mouse has claws—" He fell slowly forward, sprawling face down on the wooden floor. Almost immediately a pool of blood began to form near one shoulder.

Memory pushed harder. She pushed back, but control was tenuous. The opening widened. More memories slipped out. She was in an ambulance, looking down at a gray, aesthetic face. Instead of a siren, she heard chop, chop, chop.

Was it a chopper? No, there was a chopper coming in. Her vision narrowed to a murky tunnel as she turned away from the present and the past.

Must be Grady. She had to get out before her head exploded. She turned and ran from the room with her memories on her heels.

Chapter Nineteen

Dewey hadn't been joking when he said he didn't think he'd
ever be warm again. The cold had taken up permanent residence in the marrow of his bones. It had, Dewey decided, as
much to do with who he was with as the punishing cold of the
winter night.

Grady was an interesting character. Interesting, even
charming on the outside. Soulless on the inside. The cold
came from him. Like an icy fog, it oozed out of him and
wrapped around anyone near him. Its purpose seemed to be
the freezing out all sense of right and wrong. It sought to store
his conscience in the deep freeze.

Dewey could feel it working on him. There was such a
sense of unreality that it was easy to feel disconnected from
what was real and right. He'd felt this before. He'd danced on
the edge of evil for many years, working to take down some
very nasty people. Grady's evil wasn't as malignant as some
he'd met, but it was by far the most pragmatic. He was more
frightening in some ways. Because he was so brisk and prac-
tical, he seemed reasonable, even logical. He didn't ask for
the leap into the abyss from his followers. No, he just invited
them to join him in hell one step at a time.

Dewey always managed to find the funny-pathetic in
the evil he'd taken on. It helped him keep stuff in perspective, made it easier to dance on that edge, but this time he
wasn't smiling. As the chopper cut its way through the
night sky, he hung on, not just to the strap, but to the
memory of Bryn. She was his fixed point in this slightly

askew world he now found himself in.

In his mind, he reached out to her, taking this short moment of privacy to plunge into the memory pool of their one night together. He'd dreamed about it for so long, it almost didn't seem real that she'd been his, to touch, to kiss, to whisper all the things he'd been wanting to tell her as his hands touched her silken skin. Their mutual exploration had been heady and fun, as they'd let instinct, not experience, guide them in bringing their bodies together.

Caught in Grady's web, he could feel his usual confidence ebbing on the icy flow of Grady's personality. His confidence was so complete, it sucked not just Dewey's confidence, but seemed to suck the life out of the air around him.

The chopper dipped, bringing him back to the present with a jolt. The spotlight blazed from the base of the chopper, lighting up their landing zone. A shadowy cabin stood just outside the circle of light. In front of it, a couple of heavily armed men in winter camouflage waited for the chopper to land.

The chopper touched down. Grady signaled for Dewey to follow him. With his senses screaming a warning, Dewey jumped down, feeling he was right back where they'd started. They'd done the cabin scene already. Didn't the guy have something new in his bag of tricks? His head down, he jogged after Grady. Behind them, the chopper lifted off again. He followed it with his eyes.

"Satellites would pick it up if I left it here," Grady shouted over the whip of the blades, answering Dewey's unspoken question. "I like to keep this place low key."

One of the men opened the door for them. Inside, warmth closed around them without warming him. In the fairy tale, the villain was an ice queen, he remembered. Maybe she'd had a sex change.

A quick glance showed him a pleasant place, but like its creator, it lacked a soul. The two men who followed them in were simple thugs, the kind of men that people like Grady needed to do their dirty work for them.

One of them whispered in Grady's ear. For a moment, his pleasant expression, and his confidence, flickered. His gaze met Dewey's and order was restored, but Dewey felt the crack in his control. Something had happened. Something Mr. I'm-in-control-of-my-universe hadn't expected.

Dewey felt a measure of his own confidence return. Reminded him of that moment in *Lord of the Rings*, when the Dark Lord's control of his minions faltered. The next question, how did he use it?

"Wait here," Grady said. "Help yourself to a drink if you'd like. Or Al here can get you another beer from the kitchen?"

"I'm fine," Dewey said, eyeing Al, who was at least twice his width and half again taller. No surprise that Grady had trust issues. He loosened his jacket and shoved his hands in his pockets.

Grady started toward the stairs, then stopped and looked at him. "Actually, why don't you join me? If you're with me, you're with me. Right?"

"Right." Dewey wasn't excited about going with him, but then, staying with Al wasn't that appealing either. The walk upstairs was short. They turned left, heading for a room at the end of a short hall. Its door stood open. Over Grady's shoulder, Dewey saw another goon kneeling on the floor by someone, his hands bloody from trying to hold a pad over his wound. Blood was splattered on the wall and pooling on the floor. The guy's eyes were open—barely—the lids drooped and his gaze was dull and angry. On the bed, another goon, this one wearing nothing but long johns, lay holding an ice pack to his temple, a murderous rage in his slightly crossed eyes.

Grady stopped between the wounded guy's out flung feet. "Leslie." He sighed. "How bad is it?"

Dewey had heard the name. Must be Leslie Merryweather. Bryn said he'd killed a woman. This was not good, but at least it wasn't the girl, Prudence Knight.

"He'll live," the goon said.

"That's too bad," Grady said. Time slowed as Grady pulled the gun from his waistband and pointed it at the fallen man. The edges of Leslie's mouth curved in a grotesque mimicry of a smile.

"Did I ever . . . matter . . . to . . . you?" he asked hoarsely.

It would have been easy for Grady to say yes, Dewey thought. He was going to kill him. Dewey knew it. On some level, he felt like he should do something about it, but a sort of weird thrall held him motionless as events played out. He saw Grady smile back and knew he wasn't going to do it.

"No," he said. "You never mattered to me."

"Guess . . . you win . . . this . . . round . . ."

"I won them all, Leslie." His finger tightened on the trigger. "You just didn't notice."

It felt like they were trying to sneak up on Grand Central station, Bryn thought, when the second chopper came in. They'd heard the first one arrive as they were approaching the rise, but hadn't been able to see it until it left again.

Bryn had opted not to partner with one of the Kirby brothers. It was easier to be with someone who didn't know her too well right now. Too many feelings churning in her insides to work under the knowing scrutiny of a Kirby. She needn't have worried. By the time she finished fighting her way to their present position, she was numb with fatigue and cold. She hadn't gotten this close to nature since she left the farm. Didn't help that her pride wouldn't allow her to let Joe, her partner, outpace her. She needed to work on her competitive instinct. It was going to be the death of her.

Despite her good intentions, she'd felt petty satisfaction when she noted that Joe sounded just as winded when they dropped into a crouch behind a boulder on the hillside above the cabin.

It was a peaceful scene that met their gaze. The cabin was postcard perfect as it nestled against the snow-covered, evergreen tree-dotted hillside. The clearing in front of it was a bit big for perfect symmetry, but it was a small nit pick in a scene that was mostly charming. The cabin even had puffy white smoke drifting out the chimney. A few lights showed in the windows. She almost expected Santa and his sleigh to appear over the top of the mountain and land on the roof.

She'd pulled out the GPS, but Dewey still hadn't turned on his transponder. It had been too long since his meeting. Did the delay mean he hadn't seen Prudence Knight yet or that he wasn't able to turn it on?

It was hard to feel optimistic. It wasn't in her nature to see the good side, to believe in a happy outcome for anything related to herself. Happy endings were for other people. It was the law of universe. By allowing Dewey into her life, she'd cursed him. If he died in there, it would be her fault.

Joe tugged on her arm then indicated a point a few yards away. He leaned close to whisper, "Kincaid was right. There is a faint heat signature down there. Can you see it?"

Bryn took the binoculars he handed her and studied the hillside. "I see it. You ready?" He nodded. "Right, let's roll."

Joe went first. It was his area of expertise. Bryn rose wearily and followed on his six. She wished she knew how the other teams were faring. They'd decided on radio silence, at least until it wasn't necessary. Donovan had warned them Grady had scanning equipment. They couldn't afford to risk early detection with such a small group. It felt like she and Joe were alone in the wilderness until the second chopper arrived.

They'd dug into the hillside as it swept over the top of them. It turned, a searchlight beaming from the base to light up its landing zone. It seemed to hover for a long time, then unhurriedly dropped into the clearing.

Snow curled up around the spinning blades as two figures jumped out. Their bodies bent, they ran toward the cabin. Bryn had had her glasses on them from the moment the chopper touched down. The first face wasn't familiar. The second was.

Dewey.

She was, she thought, going to kill him for making her worry like this.

"Okay, here's our bad boy," Donovan said, his lips against Luke's ear. "Follow my lead." The sound of the chopper in the clearing was giving them some good sound cover, and they took advantage of it.

Luke had no problem with the procedure. He was a cop, not a soldier. Donovan's attitude troubled him a bit though. At first Luke thought he had a hero complex, but he was beginning to think it was more like a guilt complex. Donovan was an unstable wild card in a situation that was already dicey.

He also wasn't law enforcement, which meant that, for all his training, he wasn't bound by the same rules they were. It had surprised him that Bryn permitted him to join their expedition, even as he realized she probably couldn't have stopped him with a bullet.

They slithered through the snow toward the bunker on their stomachs. It was an odd set-up. Luke couldn't figure out if Grady didn't trust technology or he needed busy work for his men. From what he could tell, they were a combination of a pill box and a hunter's blind. Dug into the side of the mountain, they must have cave access of some kind inside, since there were no footprints or trails anywhere outside. The top was a circular piece of cement or something like it, with what appeared to be netting thrown over the top, then camouflage added to hide the location. It had to be damn cold in there, though they must have some kind of heat source, since the bunker gave off a slight heat signature, which was how Donovan had located it and not x-ray vision, though Luke didn't call him on it.

The construction provided the guard inside with a three hundred and sixty degree sight line—in theory. But with all the angles of the mountainside, the camouflage and snow cut down that advantage. Donovan had a canister of knock-out gas with him. Luke didn't ask him where he got it. He didn't want to know. How could they deliver it before the guard could sound the alarm?

"I'm going to try to cut through the netting," Donovan hissed in his ear. He started to move away, then Luke caught sight of what looked like the barest wisp of smoke from the center of the bunker top.

"Wait. Look." He pointed to the smoke. "Ventilation, maybe?"

Donovan smiled. "When I give you the signal, pull the pin and drop it in. Don't forget your mask."

Luke took the canister, pulled down his mask and climbed as quietly as he could onto the bunker top. Behind him the chopper was rising again. He dropped down, pressing into the bunker roof, as it swept his way, the search light on its base still on, but just before it reached him, it went dark again. Luke used the racket to reach the ventilation pipe. He popped the top. A faint glow from the light deep inside was no competition for the moon. A puff of warm air fogged his mask briefly and he heard the muted sound of a radio.

He looked at Donovan, got a thumbs up. He pulled the pin and dropped it down the hole. It hissed like a pissed off snake. The guard coughed, staggered around a bit, and then fell with a crash.

Donovan disappeared from sight. Soon Luke saw him wave up at him, then signal him to move on. Apparently the idea of staying with your partner was alien to him. And he couldn't call him on it without breaking radio silence.

The shot was loud in the tiny room. Leslie's body flinched, then even the dull light in his eyes faded to nothing.

Shock held Dewey immobile. It wasn't the first time he'd been in the presence of violent death, but it wasn't something he planned—or even wanted—to get used to. If you devalued life, even scummy life, then you became one of them.

Grady holstered the pistol and looked at his men. "Do we know where she is? How long she's been gone?"

"Not long," the kneeling goon said, rising to his feet. When he was upright, he towered over Dewey and Grady. "He's only been here maybe ten or fifteen minutes."

Jeez, Dewey thought in an oddly distant way, didn't goons ever come in small, or even medium? Was this where they'd kept Prudence Knight? It appeared she'd managed to have affected her own escape, if she was the "she" they were referring to. And he had no way to let Bryn know. And wasn't even sure he knew something.

Should he trigger the transponder? The deal was, he set it off when he found her, or was sure he wouldn't find her. They hadn't planned on an option number three, the I-don't-have-a-clue option.

He needed space, a little time to think. "Mind if I get myself a beer?" Again. He hadn't drunk the last one. Trying to keep a clear head, but it wasn't easy.

Grady looked at him sharply. Dewey just stared back. His face gave nothing away. He knew because this was how his face felt when it gave nothing away. He hoped.

"You still with me?" Grady asked, his eyes a laser cutting through the layers of disguise Dewey had put on.

It took everything he had not to look at the body. How would Grady expect him to act? He hadn't planned this part of the disguise. He needed his pathphinder, but she wasn't here. All he could do was wing it.

He shrugged. "Why wouldn't I be?"

It must have been the right answer. Or Grady was too smart to show disbelief. Why should Grady worry anyway? Al was downstairs. And who knew how many more like him were scattered about the area?

"I'll be down in a minute. Get me a cold one, too. I'm thirsty," Grady said.

Dewey turned and left, finding the air outside the room better than inside the room. Blood did smell. So did fear and . . . he fumbled for the right word, but all he could come up with was malicious intent. The room had reeked with it.

Al looked up at him as he came down the stairs.

"A beer?"

He nodded toward a door, but to Dewey's relief, he didn't follow him through it. He got the beer, then leaned against the counter with a sigh of relief. He popped the top and drank just enough to get the taste of that room out of his mouth. Then, despite the cold in his bones, he held the cold can to his head. It helped some, as much as anything could when you'd just witnessed an execution.

He couldn't say when he realized he was being watched. It came over him like fog in a swamp. Creeping up on him from the ground. The feeling full-blown when he finally noticed it. He tried not to stiffen but wasn't sure if he succeeded. He lifted the can again, using it to block his face as he glanced right, then left. The only place someone could be hiding was in the shadows of the open pantry. He tried to quiet his thoughts, sort through the vibes, but his thoughts were too chaotic to pick up on them. He took a step in that direction and the barrel of a rifle popped out of the shadows, pointed directly at his chest.

He hesitated, then said softly, "Miss Knight?"

There was a small gasp in the darkness.

"I'm a friend. Dewey Hyatt."

The barrel wavered, then lowered slightly. "From Wal-Mart?"

"Yes—Amelia?"

"Did you win your game?" Amelia asked, her voice spooky sounding.

He'd have to thank Bryn and Luke for not mentioning that Amelia and Prudence Knight were the same person.

The single shot from inside the cabin sent Bryn's adrenaline surging.

"Break radio silence?" Joe asked.

"Hell, yes." She sounded calm, in control, but inside her stomach was churning. She should never have let Dewey do this. He wasn't trained for this kind of infiltration. Okay, so he was good at pretending to be someone else, but this wasn't his usual operation. He didn't have Phoebe in the trenches with him this time and they were too far away to be much help if the situation in the cabin had gone south.

283

Dewey, she mentally reached out to him. *I'm here. Hang on. Don't get killed now. I need you, damn you. I need you.*

This was surrender indeed. Last night she'd let herself want him, but need? She'd thought need was weakness, but she didn't feel weak at all from needing him. Vulnerable, yes, but weak? If he was in danger, she'd leap mountains to get to him. Or kick any butts she had to.

And if he was already dead? The thought was a kick in the teeth. And filled her with cold resolve. She rarely colored outside the Bureau lines, but if Dewey was dead, someone would pay for it tonight, not years from now.

"Let's get in there," she said. She didn't remember pulling her piece, but it was in her hand.

"Wait." Joe grabbed her arm, pulling her back to the ground. "Look."

The back door of the cabin opened and two figures in camouflage emerged. They talked for a minute, then, their weapons ready, started walking in the direction of the road.

"What do you want to do?" Joe asked.

"Let them go. We can't get to them without being seen. If they raise the alarm—"

But they didn't have to. Someone inside the cabin was raising it for them.

Chapter Twenty

It was like a pot suddenly coming to a boil. One minute the scene was quiet, almost serene under the scant crescent moon, the next it was alive with moving figures and lights as about twenty men poured out of the cabin and fanned out in a search pattern.

Bryn and Joe looked at each other.

"Definitely time to break radio silence." Her team agreed with that assessment.

"What the hell happened?" Matt said in her ear.

"Who knows," Luke said. "Any idea how many we're up against?"

"I can see about twenty men," Jake said.

"Donovan?" Luke asked. "Where are you?"

There was no answer.

Bryn felt her heart jump. "Where is he?"

"He went into one of those bunkers and I haven't seen him since," Luke said.

"Without backup?" Bryn swore silently. "What do you think? Can you go after him?"

"Sure. I've always wanted to backup Rambo." Luke's voice was dry, but resigned. "If you lose contact with me, you'll know it's the bunker and not us."

"Somebody's kicked the ant hill up good. Call in your backup, Bryn," Matt said. "And let's get our butts in gear."

"Right." She sent the signal to the additional men she had standing by. They'd moved into their previous staging area when she and her team had moved out. She realized she couldn't see the two men who'd been walking down the road. "Did you take out the two guys walking toward the road?" Bryn asked.

"Didn't see two guys," Matt said, "but got about six heading our way."

"Take 'em," Bryn said. "Joe and I are going to check out the cabin."

She slipped and slid down the hill ahead of him. At the door, she paused so Joe could open it, then went in, low and fast. A kitchen. Someone had conveniently left the light on. She did a sweep, then signaled for Joe to come in. As she was heading for the next door, she stepped on something and looked down.

It was Dewey's glasses.

Grady ran down the echoing halls of the underground bunker. He'd emptied it of men to join in the search for Phagan and Prudence as soon as he found Al, dressed only in his long johns, holding his head in the kitchen. He wasn't sure they were together, but it was an interesting coincidence that they were both missing. Or that Phagan would take off after so much effort to arrange the meet. It seemed his instincts about him were right, just a bit slow to get going. And now that he thought about it, he remembered what it was that Phagan had said that started his instincts in high gear. Something about a criminal enterprise. Dewey Hyatt had said that when Grady had called his number. Did the Feds know, he wondered, that Dewey and Phagan were the same person? That little tidbit hadn't been in any of the news reports, but it wouldn't be if they were planning to use him undercover.

His instincts—like those of a deer scenting danger—were telling him it was time to cut his losses and move on. He took a sharp right into his communications center and sat down.

Right off he noticed some of his monitors were down. Had his security been breached? He pressed a switch.

"Bunker one, come in. Bunker one, come in." No answer, and it was the monitor to that hallway that was down. He brought up an outside camera. Cameras and motion detectors weren't his primary security system. He knew, thanks to Phagan, how easy electronic surveillance was to breech. It was useful in moments like this however.

Right now he was glad of it. The grainy picture showed his men kneeling in rows. A quick count only turned up five figures covering them, but he'd bet his ass there were more out there.

He leaned back in the chair, his thoughts racing. It had to be Phagan who'd brought the hounds down on him. Only way they could be here so fast, but how? He'd stripped him to the skin.

Except for the glasses. Damn, the guy was good. He'd won the round. Now how to keep him from sweeping the field? There wasn't much time, but he could buy a little more for himself if . . .

He grabbed the secure phone and dialed. When O'Rourke, who'd stayed at base camp, answered he didn't waste words. "We're busted here. Get a chopper in the air, ready to pick me up." He gave him the coordinates for pick up, then shut down the connection.

With a last look at his men, he turned for the door. He'd miss them. He'd taught them well. Not bright, but good men, willing to work hard and kill on command. But there were more like them out there. Some he'd already trained here and had move on. Others he'd find. Or they'd find him. Their kind always found each other the same way water always found its level.

Just like he and Leslie had found each other? No, that had

been an anomaly. Leslie wasn't his kind. The world, particularly Grady's world, was a better place without that waste of space. Stupid of Leslie to put killing women over the plan. If he could have learned a little restraint, but that wasn't in his game book. He'd have escalated the killing. Could see that coming like a big, old truck and no way to stop it. Leslie's frustration had been stronger than his head. Always. No regrets really, though Grady would sure as hell miss the steady flow of money Leslie had provided.

He checked his weapon, then gave a quick look down the hall. It was clear. He moved out, his weapon down, but ready if needed. He knew the corridors, knew where he might run into trouble. When he got there, he eased up to the opening, his senses stretched out. He sniffed the air, caught the faint whiff of evergreen in the current. He edged back, bringing his gun up—

A blur of movement.

The jolt to his chin crossed his eyes and started stars wheeling across his horizon. He fell hard, the wind knocked out of him. Before he could recover, Donovan was on him, his hands around his throat and squeezing. One chance . . .

One hand fighting to break Donovan's grip, the other edged down his leg and closed over the hilt of the knife. The world was growing dark. His head felt like it was going to explode.

He pulled the knife out.

Air. He needed air.

With one last, desperate flail, he stabbed Donovan in the back.

Immediately the pressure on his throat eased, though Donovan wasn't out yet. Grady thrust up with his legs. Donovan fell back, but almost immediately was after him again. Grady rolled away and rose in crouch. They both saw his fallen pistol at the same time.

Donovan started for it, but Grady sliced the knife through the air in front of him, catching Donovan's arm with the tip. When Donovan fell back, Grady grabbed the gun. Quick as a cat, Donovan flung himself around the corner at the same moment Grady fired.

Grady thought he got him, but didn't wait around to find out. He still remembered the look in Donovan's eyes when they said good-bye.

In a few minutes he was in his office. He pulled the key out of the neck of his shirt and stuck it in the lock on the panel. Once it was open, he started inputting the self-destruct codes. One half hour from now the whole side of the mountain would blow up. Not a bad finale for someone who'd started his life as poor, white trash.

Luke heard the shots and ran forward. He found Donovan down in an intersection of hallways and did a quick sweep before approaching him. Still keeping watch, he checked Donovan's pulse. Luke tried his radio, but some quality in the bunker blocked his signal.

"Damn."

"I'm not out, just a little down," Donovan said weakly. His lids raised and he managed a faint grin. "Little bastard is good. Has the instincts of a wolf."

Luke helped him into a sitting position, but when he tried to check him for damage, Donovan pushed him away.

"Don't waste time with me. Go after him."

Luke hesitated.

"Just go. I'll start working my way down this main hall. See if I can find a way out. Maybe I'll pick up a first aid kit along the way."

"I suppose you can bandage yourself, too?" Luke asked.

Donovan's brows arched. "Of course. Can't you?"

Luke grinned. "I'll be back as quick as I can."

Donovan grabbed his arm. "He's good. Reacts like prey. I heard him sniffing the air."

"I've done my share of hunting." Luke stood up, checked his weapon, and then with a wry look at Donovan, sniffed the air. "That way, I think."

He moved down the corridor, but Donovan's voice halted him one more time.

"Just what are your intentions toward my daughter, Kirby?"

Luke stared at him. "I'll—" He shook his head. "—see you in a bit."

He shook his head again to clear it, then took off. The corridor stretched out, straight and empty. He could see places where it branched off. He checked a few of the rooms as he went along. Found rooms with bunks. A dining hall. Armaments rooms. Place was an underground military base. In a class room, he found posters on the wall diagramming bomb construction and deployment.

Looked like Grady had a side-line training terrorists. He heard a sound out in the hall and padded silently to the door. His back to the wall, he pulled out the "toy" Dewey had slipped him before he left. It was a small video camera on the end of a flexible extender—the kind used by hostage rescue to see into a room. Crouching, he eased it barely around the corner, his eyes fixed on the monitor.

Grady was standing in the hall, his head tilted as he listened. Luke saw his head lift, as he sniffed the air. He also saw something that chilled his blood.

Bryn taking a quick look around the corner behind Grady. He saw Grady pick up her scent. Saw him start to pivot in her direction.

"Don't move! I've got you covered!" Luke shouted. As expected, Grady spun back in his direction, but Luke was already taking his shot. It took him in the shoulder. Luke didn't want to kill him. His gun spun free, as the blow of the bullet spun him around. A second shot from Bryn's direction brought him to his knees.

He held his shoulder with his good hand.

"Hands on your head," he called.

"Cross your ankles," Bryn added as she slowly emerged from cover.

While Luke covered him, Bryn patted him down, then cuffed him. Grady's face was pasty. Now Luke could see where Bryn's shot had entered as blood spread in a widening stain across his middle.

Luke hustled him into a chair, then cuffed his feet together, too. Still Grady looked like a snake about to strike. Luke could feel his hackles rise in warning. What did he know that they didn't?

"Did you see where he's been?" Luke asked.

"He came out of a room a couple of doors down. Why?"

"Watch him," Luke directed. "And see if you can raise some help. Donovan's hit, I left him about a hundred yards that way." He started out the door, then stopped. "And try to find out where—"

Bryn gave him a look. "I do have a brain."

"Right. Sorry." He jogged down the hall, glancing in rooms as he passed. The second door down was locked. His pistol to the lock ended that. He pushed the door open and found himself looking at what had to be Grady's office. To one side was a map, no it was a layout of the compound. To the other was—

"Oh, shit!"

Luke had done a short stint with the bomb squad—until

his mom pointed out how much Rosemary hated it. He didn't have to ask anyone what that timer, showing barely thirty minutes, meant.

Bryn grabbed Grady's chin. "Don't pass out on me now, you little bastard."

"He won't talk," Donovan said behind her. Bryn turned, found him hanging onto the door jamb. His color was worse than Grady's, and he was leaving a blood trail that would have made a vampire dance for joy. "Not without some persuasion."

"I can't—" Bryn began.

"I know *you* can't. Leave me alone with him for a minute."

His eyes burned with the same fire eating away at her gut. If only he knew how bad she wanted to let him have at the little prick. She looked at Donovan and saw that he saw what was in her heart.

"Just walk out the door. Go to the bathroom—"

"We don't have time for it," Luke said, popping up beside Donovan. "We gotta get out of here. Place is gonna blow in under thirty."

"We can't leave without Pru," Donovan said, hoarsely.

As one, Bryn and Luke turned to look at Grady. His grin was ghastly. Blood leaked out between his teeth.

"Gonna be bigger than Waco," he said between labored breaths.

"Get Donovan out of here," Luke said. "Start clearing your people out of the area. Way out of the area. He's got enough armament to bring down the mountainside."

"But—"

"I'll be right behind you."

His face was calm. His voice was beyond calm. So why did she feel so . . . chilled by it? "Luke—"

292

"Bryn," he spun to face her. "You don't have time."

"You can't leave him here, no matter what he's done."

"I don't plan to. Now go."

After a long hesitation, she nodded. She slid her arm around Donovan's waist, but he didn't move. He stared at Luke for a long moment, then he nodded and turned away.

Luke listened to the shuffle of their footsteps down the corridor, then turned to Grady. "Where are they?"

He lifted his chin, his head lolling to one side. "Who?"

"Miss Knight. And your passenger on the chopper."

That ghastly smile again. "Oh, him. He left. Very rude, I thought."

"And Miss Knight?"

"No idea what you're talking about."

Luke knelt in front of him, his gaze holding Grady's. "I know you think you're going to die an anarchist's hero, but you're not dead yet."

He stared into Grady's eyes. He'd never stepped over the line. Never. Not even when it twisted his gut with frustration. He believed in the law. He believed in those rights he had to read, even to pukes and perps and low lifes. The judging he left to the courts, even when he didn't like what they decided.

But it had never been this personal before. Amelia was his girl, even if she walked out of his life. He loved her and a man protected his own. It was that simple. It wasn't about rights. It was about what was right. Grady might want to die, but he had no right to make that decision for anyone else.

Luke held Grady's eyes, saw them widen as Luke pressed his thumb into the wound. The gray surged into his face. Luke didn't feel so good himself, but he didn't stop. Not even when the blood bubbled over his thumb.

Beads of sweat bloomed all over Grady's face. Luke could see his struggle, saw his surrender in his eyes even before the guy knew he was going to cave.

"All right. All right."

Luke stopped pressing, but left his hand in place. The clock was ticking. He wasn't going to be jerked around by this little puke.

He managed to lift his chin, the shadow of a real smile edging his mouth.

"She got away. Couldn't . . . believe it. Kicked Ray's ass. Took his clothes and his gun. Locked Bub in a closet. I'm . . . guessing she just . . . walked away . . . looking like one of us." His chest heaved with the effort, then he added, "Unless one of your Feds shot her or something. Not knowing."

Luke's fist shot out, but he pulled back at the last moment, just popping him enough to put his lights out. Then he slung him over his shoulder and headed out at a jog.

Chapter Twenty-One

Bryn and Donovan emerged from the underground bunker to a scene of orderly confusion. Her backup had arrived in several choppers. She saw Matt and Jake standing at the edge of the mayhem talking to Joe. When they saw her, all three of them ran over and took Donovan's weight off her.

"We've got to evacuate. Now," she panted out. "Place is rigged to blow in about twenty minutes."

"Where's Luke?" Matt snapped.

"He's coming. With Grady." She avoided eye contact with him or Jake. "He had a couple of questions for him." She cleared her throat, then asked, "Have you seen Dewey?"

They both shook their heads. "Maybe you should check the prisoners?"

Their eyes filled with sympathy, but without another word, they both turned for the entrance to the bunker. She stared after them for a minute, for the first time wishing she had a sibling. Then she turned back to Joe.

"Get him on a chopper and let's start evacuating," she snapped. Joe took charge of a protesting Donovan, leaving her alone for a moment in the center of the storm. She looked around. Where was Dewey? She rubbed her face. Where the hell was he? In hope and fear, she started for the line of prisoners. Please God, let him be there . . .

"You know," Dewey said, helping Amelia over a snow-covered log, "this could be the real hell, with that whole fire and brimstone shtick a smoke screen. Because I wouldn't mind fire or brimstone at all right now, so where's the incentive to not go to hell?"

Amelia crawled over the log and sat down so abruptly, Dewey almost fell back over the log.

"Let's take a break, shall we?" He sat down next to her. She was scaring him. She hadn't said a word since they left the clearing behind. At intervals she'd checked a compass and made course corrections, but it had all been done silently. He thought she was crying, too, though he couldn't be sure with the snow goggles covering her eyes. Just seemed like she had an extra accumulation of ice around her goggles. And her breathing was harsh and labored, whether they were going up dale or down hill.

It worried him how silently she cried. She seemed lost in grief and he didn't know how to help her. After a brief hesitation, he covered her gloved hand with his. "What's going on, Amelia?"

At first he thought she wasn't going to answer. Then she gave a huge sigh, one that quavered going in and out. She pulled off her goggles and looked at him, her eyes huge and sad.

"I remember," she said.

"And?" he said gently, remembering another time when he'd faced a woman's devastation. Phoebe's eyes had looked like Amelia's when she told him that Kerry Anne was dead. Looking at her brought it all back in a rush of pain and regret. He didn't feel any wiser now than he did then. Would he fail her, too?

"I wish . . . it had stayed gone."

"I understand," he said.

"Do you?"

For the first time since he'd found her in the pantry, he felt like she was seeing him. The amazing part, she'd taken out Al without even blinking, even in that state. Been nice if the guy hadn't fallen on him, but those were the breaks. Bryn was going to kick his ass for losing the glasses. If he could see her again, he didn't mind. She could kick away with his blessing and cooperation. He reined his thoughts in. Man, he was seriously losing it.

"Yeah, I do," he said. "When I was . . . younger, I met this girl. Her name was Kerry Anne. She was . . . I, well, you know. And she was murdered."

Now Amelia covered his hand with hers. "I guess you do know." She sighed again, but it didn't sound so ragged. Her eyes had quit running, too. "We should get moving."

Dewey nodded, pushing up with an inaudible grown. He started to move out, but stopped and looked at Amelia. "Where are we going anyway?"

Amelia crouched and drew a fairly detailed map with her gloved finger. "We're around here somewhere. The camp is over here, the lower camp here. We're heading for a little town that is approximately here."

"You saw all that flying in?"

"I was unconscious when I flew in, but Grady gave me a tour. He had a map on the wall of his office."

"Uh-huh."

Amelia smiled. "I have a good memory."

"No shit." He crouched down next to her. "Which way is Denver?"

Amelia marked it. "Why?"

"Because Bryn and the brothers Kirby, are somewhere that way." He pointed to a spot on her little map. "Somewhere here. Not far from the highway. Might be closer than this town. And downhill."

Luke? He was near by? Amelia studied the map, on the ground and in her head. If Dewey was right, they were closer.

The problem? Grady's camp stood between them. It would be tricky, but worth the risk to end up safely with Luke.

She'd been worried about something in her past standing between them, but now she knew. She wasn't involved with Donovan. She barely knew him from work, though she'd found him interesting. She wasn't involved with anyone. She was old enough for Luke. And she was Prudence and Amelia, though Amelia was an assumed identity. She had her own money, from her mother and that's how she'd used to get away from her father who wasn't her father. There was a lot to sort through in her head and now wasn't the time for it. Besides, she didn't want to sort through it. She knew in her mind she was Prudence, but she didn't feel like Prudence anymore. Amelia may have been a figment of her imagination, but now she felt more real than all the years as Prudence.

"Okay. Let's do it."

"You rested enough?"

She managed a smile for him. "I'm fine. Let's just hope they don't take us for Grady's guys and shoot us."

Dewey stared at her. "You just had to say it, didn't you?"

Her smile widened. She looked at the compass. "I think we should take a straight line this way for a few miles, so we don't end up back in Grady's arms."

To Amelia's relief, the straight line was mostly downhill. She'd thought skiing was painful with her bruised body, but wading through snow, some of it nearly waist deep, was far worse. Dewey looked pretty happy about it, too.

"So, who's Bryn?" Amelia asked breathlessly. There was a bit of moon, enough to brighten the clearings, but under the trees, the shadows were dark and menacing. The tiny flashlight illuminated the compass, but not much more. The snow was deep and delivered a double whammy with each step. It both slowed her progress and was treacherous under foot. Luckily it also cushioned her many falls. The cold bit into her lungs, making each labored breath that much more painful.

"Bryn," his voice was as breathless as hers, but edged with tender. "She's . . ." He stopped. "Do you hear something?" Amelia stopped. "Choppers?" In the distance. Still, anxiety spiked in her gut. She started forward again.

"No, something closer. Like water running. I wonder if there's a stream near by. Could use a drink—"

A stream? Her brain sent the warning one step too late. Her weight shifted to her front foot. The snow under her gave way with a rush that pulled her forward in a dark void. The fall was short, the landing wet and icy cold.

Luke was glad to see his brothers running to meet him. With them sharing the burden, they made good time out of the bunker. They emerged to a scene far different from the one they'd left.

Bryn had half the men and prisoners evacuated. Matt and Jake loaded Grady on a departing chopper and then rejoined Luke. Bryn looked unusually grim, even for her, before Luke gave her the rest of the bad news.

"Did you believe him?" she asked.

"I don't know . . . yeah, I did. I think they got away. They could be anywhere out there, and the whole mountain is about to go up." Luke rubbed his face. Exhaustion dragged at him, at his thoughts.

"It gets worse," Bryn said. "Did some checking to make sure there were no other dwellings in the area. Guess what's just above us, just waiting for a loud noise to set it off?"

Luke looked around. He'd skied enough to recognize a potential avalanche situation. "Damn, if it weren't for bad luck, we'd be out of luck." He looked at his watch. They had ten minutes, maybe less, to find them and clear the area before it blew. "We gotta get in the air."

Bryn nodded. "We commandeered Grady's choppers. One's coming in now. We can take it up." She looked at Matt and Jake. "You get yourselves out on the next one."

Matt gave her a crooked grin. "We'll look, too, in the next chopper. Get going and . . . good hunting."

Jake slapped him on the back. "I'll see you all at the staging area. Don't get lost. Mom'll have our heads."

Luke grabbed Bryn's arm and ran with her to the chopper. He helped her in the front, then climbed in the rear. As they rose into the sky, he tapped the driver on the shoulder. "I need to broadcast!"

Pilot nodded and handed him the mike, switching it to the outside speakers.

"Go this direction," Bryn shouted. She looked back at Luke. "I remember seeing two guys walking this way. They came out the back door and then I didn't see them anymore. It was right after the shot. Could have been them, damn it."

"Go!" Luke shouted. He cleared his throat, then said into the mike, "Amelia, Dewey. It's all right. We've got the area secured, but we need to find you ASAP. Move into a clearing ASAP. If you can, signal us." His voice boomed outside, oddly amplified by the delivery system and the mountains. He repeated the message, using night vision goggles to search the horizon for a sign, any kind of sign.

"You need to leave me," Amelia managed between the shudders shaking her body. "Hypothermia. In this temperature, I won't make it."

"I'm not leaving you," Dewey muttered. He'd managed to pull her out of the stream without getting too wet himself. The stream was shallow, but bitterly cold. Amelia would have been all right if she'd hadn't landed on her belly. Her clothes had provided some protection, but not enough. The water hadn't soaked clear through everywhere, but it had in enough spots to lower her core body temperature dangerously. "We need to move—"

Amelia shook her head. "Exhaustion . . . will finish it." In the penlight, her lips were already turning blue. "Need heat."

Another shudder shook her. He could almost see it drain her scarce energy reserves. "What do I do?" She didn't answer. He flashed her face with the light. Her eyes were closed. He shook her. "What do I do?"

He could see her struggle to remain conscious. "Most . . . popular . . . cure . . . get naked . . ."

Her smile was faint, but still impish, fading quickly in another bout of shivering.

"What if we burrowed in the snow?" He had to shake her and repeat the questions again.

"Tell Luke . . . sorry," she murmured.

"No!" He shook her sharply. "You're not pooping out on me now."

"Chopper . . . coming . . . don't let . . . get me . . ."

Now Dewey heard it, too. He turned and started digging frantically at a bank of snow. "We'll hide. They won't get you—"

He stopped as Luke's voice boomed into the forest night and jumped to his feet.

"Here! We're here!" He turned in frustration. No matches. Wet wood all around. How could he signal?

"Grenade . . ." Amelia gasped.

"Of course. Stupid of me. Sorry." He grinned. Hope had taken a little of the edge off pale in her face. He could see her struggle to remain conscious as he tugged at the utility belt she was still wearing. He got a grenade, but hesitated.

"Never done this before," he admitted.

"Just . . . remember . . . to . . . throw . . ." Her attempted smile was a grimace. She turned her head away from him. "So . . . cold . . ."

Dewey pulled the pin and tossed it.

They were heading away from the camp in a straight line when he heard the blast. The forest ahead of them flared then faded, leaving a trail of smoke behind.

"There!" he shouted.

"I see it!" Bryn cried. The pilot adjusted course. The forest they swept over was mostly dense. No clearings to land in. Five minutes. Maybe less.

The chopper hovered just above the tree line as it raced the clock. The smoke from the blast was blown away by the rotation of the chopper blades. He and Bryn searched the ground as the chopper circled the point of the blast.

"There!" Bryn cried. Luke followed her pointing finger. The search light did, too, picking up one figure waving madly in a small clearing. Next to him, another figure sat or lay next to a half buried tree stump.

"We can't land there," the pilot shouted. "We'll have to use the ladder."

The chopper stopped over the figure, the searchlight a golden circle around him blowing the snow up from the ground in a curling wave. It was Dewey. Amelia, it must be Amelia, didn't move. Luke grabbed the ladder and dropped it down.

"Hurry!"

Dewey, he could see him now, cupped his hands and shouted, "She can't climb! Hurt!"

Without stopping to think, Luke started down the ladder, jumping into the snow when he was close enough. "Get up

302

the ladder," he ordered Dewey. "Mountain's going to blow!"

"Shit."

Luke didn't stop to see if he'd do as he was told. In a heartbeat he was kneeling next to Amelia. Her eyes opened. In between shudders, she said, "So . . . sorry . . . tried . . ."

"Don't give up on me now, sweetheart." He gathered her up, slinging her over his shoulder and ran for the ladder. Dewey was almost up. Bryn reaching out to grab him inside.

Luke grabbed the ladder. He thought she was out, but she struggled. "Let me—"

He turned her, so she was holding the ladder, but also held her between him and the ladder. Each step seemed agonizingly slow. Over head, Bryn leaned out and pointed at her watch.

"Hold on," he said, hooking his arms around the ropes and locking his hands together. "Go!" he shouted.

The engine roared as they rose. As soon as they cleared the trees, the wind hit them like a wall, trying to tear them off. He pressed close, hoping to give her some of his body heat to hold her until they could reach help.

The rope ladder danced in the air currents, almost shaking them free in its demented game of crack the whip. He thought he heard her cry out, but the roar of the engine was all around them as the pilot bee lined for safety.

He probably shouldn't have looked down, but he couldn't help himself. It had to be down to seconds before it blew—

It was. Luke had the best view in the valley. The earth erupted upwards, forever it seemed like, not just once, but over and over as the munitions Grady had stockpiled detonated sympathetically. Armament was still going off like a geyser when the avalanche started. The snow pack peeled away from the cliffs, slowly at first, but gravity had its way and the snow mass quickly picked up speed. The roar of it joined the roar of the chopper and the detonations until it seemed like the whole world had lost it. Snow, out of control and packing the punch of a freight train, roared toward the eruptions of earth, engulfing it in a white embrace.

The explosion sent a turbulent current of air and the chopper danced in response. Luke felt his hands start to slip. The pressure on his arms was almost unbearable. Amelia was a dead weight now as the wind sucked energy and heat from her body. If it had just been his life, he might have let the force of it tear him from his perch, but it wasn't. He wouldn't, he couldn't lose her. Even if she was never his, he needed to know that she was somewhere in the world.

Caught in a wind tunnel, Amelia strained to stay conscious, strained to hold on. Luke's arm encircled her, his body trapped her against the unyielding rungs of the ladder. It hurt, but she didn't care. It meant she was still alive. If she could hang on a little longer, maybe she could tell Luke she loved him. Didn't matter if he loved her. Didn't matter if he didn't want her or her love. She could live with that, but she couldn't die without telling him.

Through a haze of pain and cold, she watched the dust and snow settle into a new pattern.

She knew just how it felt.

Chapter Twenty-Two

The evacuation area looked like a kicked up ant hill with all the figures swarming over it. As they drew closer, Amelia was vaguely aware of some method in the madness. On one end, a row of men were on their knees, their hands clasping the backs of their heads, with armed-to-the-teeth federal agents watching them. At the other end, ambulances dealt with the wounded. The press had found them. She could see them being briefed in an area that looked like a disco because of all the lights. There seemed to be a steady flow of people between the various groups. One end of the road was clogged with a variety of vehicles. The choppers used in the evacuation had settled along the other end of the road like dragon flies waiting some secret signal to take to the skies. It was toward this area that their chopper swooped.

The ladder touched down before the chopper. Amelia's legs wouldn't work, so Luke swept her up in his arms. Her view had narrowed to his face above her and the jolt of each step he took.

As the world closed in on her, she could feel the different eddies, the varying currents of movement around her. One was taking her down and down into a sea of unconsciousness. As she sank into it, she also sank inside herself like a log in quicksand. Prudence, and her tightly constricted life, closed over Amelia with the suffocating insistence of long established habit.

She fought it, fearing she would lose Amelia in the dark, the way she'd lost Prudence. If she lost Amelia, she lost Luke or at least the memory of him. She tried to reach out to him as he walked beside the stretcher, but her arms no longer responded to her commands. She could hear him telling the EMT she had hypothermia, hear them reassuring him that they had something called a Hot-Sack and Res-Q-Air. Just before the current closed over her head, she felt Luke take her hand and bend and kiss her cheek.

"Don't give up, Amelia," he whispered.

I'll try, she thought, just before her world went dark.

Luke stood out of the EMT's way as they fitted the Res-Q-Air over her face and started warm, humidified air circulating into her lungs. It was important they warmed her core temperature, he knew from the times he'd helped out in a search and rescue. Her chances of survival were good if they could get her warm her from the inside out. Next they stripped off her wet outer clothes and got her wrapped in blankets, then started a warm IV, temperature controlled by a Hot-Sack.

In a few minutes, the EMT pronounced her ready for transport and he had to watch as a chopper once again carried her away from him.

He turned away to look for his brothers and almost tripped over the stretcher that held Grady. He looked terrible. His face was gray, his eyes were sunk back in his head and surrounded by brown, bruised skin. Bubbles of air mixed with the blood oozing out of his mouth. He was dying. He could see it in his eyes and feel it in the air around him. Despite the dullness of his eyes, Luke could see intelligence, even a hint of charm in them as they returned his gaze. He had a sudden vision of what he could have been. He didn't know what drove Grady, but it had abandoned him now.

His lashes fluttered up. "Did . . . she . . . make . . . it?" he asked, more bubbles of bloody air emerging with the words.

Luke nodded. There was only one question he really

wanted to know. He crouched down next to him. "Why did you go after SHIELD now?" he asked. "Why didn't you wait until the research was complete?"

His eyes widened slightly. "Damn Les . . . said it . . . was done . . ." He gave a half laugh that came out a wheeze. "Glad . . . I . . . shot . . . bastard."

His voice faded, his lashes pulled down by an imperative stronger than his ability to resist. Luke had the odd feeling that he might have liked him—if everything in Grady's life had been different. He'd been in law enforcement a long time and it still puzzled him why people made the choices they did. He hunched his shoulders against the cold and turned to find his brothers. At least them he understood.

Bryn stood in the midst of the chaos, basically directing the traffic, in between giving the SAC a report on everything that had happened. It seemed to take forever. And it felt so unimportant. It was over. Wasn't that enough? Okay, so half a mountain got blown up. It wasn't her fault. At least no one died in the explosion. Any comparison to Waco would be weak.

Grady was out of business. Order would soon be restored.

The SAC turned away to answer a question from another agent, and Bryn used his distraction to fade into the crowd, her gaze scanning for Dewey. She didn't have to scan long. Dewey was behind her, cutting her from the mass as neatly as cowboy separates a heifer from the herd.

The touch of his hands on her waist, even through her bulky coat, turned her legs to rubber. Tough agent faded into pliant woman, though she tried not to let it show on the outside until they reached the relative cover of some vehicles.

She turned to face him, her arms sliding around his neck. She didn't care who saw her now. He was alive. She patted

307

the parts of him she could reach, just to be sure.

"You going to kick my ass for losing the glasses?" he asked, rubbing his forehead against hers.

He smelled like outdoors and pine trees and himself. Heaven.

"I did think about it," she admitted, as he unzipped her coat and slipped his arms inside. "But I came up with something better to do with your ass."

She smiled at him, figuring now they'd kiss, but he held back, his gaze serious.

"I love you," he said, his voice breaking slightly. "I . . . love you."

He'd said it. She'd said it back, but she hadn't, she realized, completely surrendered to the situation. She'd held something back. Maybe she'd been afraid to trust him. Or maybe she was afraid of the power it gave him over her. In her world, power wasn't something you gave up easily. And you were always careful who held it. And now here she was, the thief and the lady agent. It made no sense at all. And it made perfect sense. She knew what he wanted to know. She eased back in his hold, so that he could see her eyes.

"I love you, too," she said. There was more that she didn't say. She hoped he knew it was implied and as binding as the vows they'd taken before the JP. Things like, *I'm there for you, with you for always, no matter. I trust you. With me. With your choices. We're partners now in every way.*

She knew he knew what she meant by the way he sighed. His body shuddered with the relief of that sigh. He sagged into her, his face against her neck, his breath warm against her skin. Bryn stroked his hair as one tear tracked slowly down her cheek.

Dewey Hyatt, aka Phagan, had finally come home. And so had she.

★ ★ ★ ★ ★

Luke had the chopper he hitched a ride on drop him at his truck, still stuck in the snow outside the cabin. Jake and Matt helped him dig out and get it running, but took the chopper back. Their wives were waiting. Luke didn't mind. Once again he was glad to be alone with his thoughts. Before leaving, he loaded the supplies that Amelia—he should call her Prudence but he didn't know Prudence, only Amelia— had before their flight such a short time ago.

Three days? Was it only three days? He wasn't sure. Didn't even know what day of the week it was anymore. Knew it wasn't much more than that since he'd driven up here to find his closure. Looked like he'd taken the big fall in- stead. Standing in the doorway remembering how Amelia had looked in her skis—so scared of what she couldn't re- member, but willing to take it on—he faced the facts. He was in love. He had it bad.

How could he not? She packed a double whammy. That cool, little smile she'd part with like she was doing you a favor and that looked like it wouldn't be warm and never would be. But when contact was made? Beneath that cool was a lot of warm.

He rubbed his hot face as his memory reproduced, with every nuance, the kiss under the tree.

His nose missed the scent of a woman. His arms missed holding one in the night while he slept. He missed the inti- mate exchange of glances in a crowd and in the bathroom. He sighed. And he missed the sex. He was only human. God was right. Men weren't made to be alone.

Dr. Laura—who his mom listened to religiously and passed her wisdom on to her sons—would say they hadn't known each other long enough, that they didn't know the im- portant things about each other, but he wasn't so sure. In the furnace of danger, he'd learned that she had courage. That she didn't quit. That she had a sense of humor.

That she never forgot.

And she could kick some serious butt.

He grinned. She'd fit in well with his sisters-in-law.

If she wanted to.

His grin faded. What happened when she got her memory back and her world expanded from him to everyone she'd known before? How could a girl like her not have someone in her past? What would she be like then? What would she want? Would there be some place for him?

And if there wasn't, what then? He'd deal with it. It's not like you could choose not to deal with life. Okay, it was going to hurt, maybe as bad as losing Rosemary, but he wasn't sorry he'd met her. He'd never be sorry he met her.

"You taught me that, Rose. And I finally learned it," he told the silent cabin. "I'm going to be all right."

Then he closed and locked the door, got in his truck and drove toward Denver.

Chapter Twenty-Three

"Yes, I remember," Amelia said. "I remember almost everything." The details of the kidnapping were still hazy and incomplete and probably always would be. It was a huge relief to still remember Amelia. To wake knowing, even if it hurt. It was a relief to have faced the void, to know what was behind the fog that had been her memory. It had been ugly, that last, terrible scene when her father told her he wasn't her father, had never wanted to be, but it hadn't killed her. She was still here.

So was the question, who am I?

Amelia seemed to be locked firmly inside Prudence, but the fit was a bad one. It was like wearing a straight jacket. How had she endured it all those years? She knew why she endured it now. The people who flowed in and out of her hospital room were more comfortable with tidy, controlled Prudence. They didn't even see Amelia peering out of her prison. Until the day Luke came.

If he'd come alone . . . but he didn't. He brought his partner Mann with him. And Bryn, the FBI agent. While Prudence smiled politely and invited them to sit down, Amelia studied her with interest. She was also tidy, controlled, but seemed to simmer with a secret satisfaction.

"How's Dewey?" Prudence asked, her voice cool. Amelia noted the color that bloomed in Bryn's cheeks at the question.

"He's fine," Bryn said, looking down at her notes instead of at Prudence.

Amelia noticed Luke hide a grin behind a cough. Amelia

was used to the secret world that simmered beneath outward lives. She'd spent many unnoticed hours people watching. It was easy when people didn't really see her. It was this awareness that had emboldened her to launch her own secret life.

The truth will out. Her infallible memory failed her when she reached for the source of the saying. Maybe she never knew it. Well, the truth was out now. And with a new question? *Who will you be? Prudence or Amelia?*

The doctors had decided to keep her under observation for a few days and had her talk to a shrink about her memory loss. She'd done as they asked, her Prudence façade polite and reserved. They'd pronounced her healed. Why shouldn't they? She looked all right. Mostly she was. She was rested now, stronger and ready to face her demons—if she could just get shed of all the people trying to help her. Well, all of them but Luke. Amelia yearned for him. Prudence, and his closed face, held her in check. Had she dreamed the words she thought he whispered to her on the mountain?

Don't give up. What had he meant? Don't give up on life? Or on us?

She had her release in hand, was dressed to find her answers, but they'd arrived needing her statement to wrap it all up. How easy it was for them, she thought. They type it up and file it neatly away.

Her job was much harder. John Knight's death had left ragged edges and hanging threads that needed to be sorted out. Her guilty secret? She was relieved he was dead. She wouldn't have to face him again.

She sat like Prudence for them, feet together, hands on her knees, and answered Luke's questions delivered in a cop voice with answers in her Prudence voice, while Amelia studied Luke hungrily from behind Prudence's calm gaze.

He was so cute, but so distant. The time at the cabin might never have happened if she just looked at his face. When she let her gaze stray beyond that, she noticed the pulse beating in his neck. Beating fast. Inside Prudence, Amelia smiled wickedly. He wasn't as calm as he looked.

She'd seen the power a woman could have over a man, but this was the first time she could feel that power in herself. Like a baby bird flexing its newly hatched wings, she looked at him, then slowly licked her lips. He twitched so briefly she'd have missed it if she hadn't been watching for it and then tugged at his tie.

Warmth swept through her, delight, too. Both loosened Prudence's hold on Amelia.

Mann cleared his throat, drawing Amelia's attention away from Luke. Prudence regarded him politely, one brow arched in inquiry. "I'm a little confused about the Amelia persona?"

"It did confuse the issue, didn't it?" Amelia said, prudently. She hesitated, then said slowly, "I . . . respected . . . John Knight . . . but he was a . . . difficult man to live with. Amelia was a way for me to . . . explore . . . those facets of my personality that didn't fit in his life without the media making a connection that would cause him distress."

"You did a good job of that," Luke said.

Amelia looked at Luke, her eyes wide. "I always try to do my best at anything I take on, Detective."

Luke swallowed dryly. He gave a good tug on his tie. Damn, he wished he knew what the hell was going on. She looked so cool, butter couldn't melt in her mouth if it tried. So why was he seeing her in his bed? Was he hoping the comment was double-edge or was it really double-edged?

"And you say Leslie told you," Bryn asked, "that he killed your father—"

"He's not my father," Amelia said, with composure.

Bryn looked up from her notes, exchanging a quick look with Luke. Amelia's gaze narrowed sharply, as if she sensed he knew something she didn't.

"Have you spoken with Donovan Kincaid then?" Bryn said.

It was Amelia's turn to look puzzled. "No."

"Then how—"

"My father told me in the hospital. I realize now that he knew he was dying. I guess he wanted to make sure I knew."

There was no sign of how she'd felt about the revelation, though his heart contracted at the thought of how it must have hurt her. He understood her better now. Only when she felt safe did her reserve fade away. Knight had tried to stamp out the life in Amelia. That he'd failed was a testament to the resiliency of her spirit.

"Why would Mr. Kincaid know he wasn't my father—" She stopped, a flare of awareness in her eyes, before the shutters came down again.

Luke wanted to gather her in his arms and hold her while her mind, and hopefully her heart, made the adjustment to this new reality. Mann leaned toward him and whispered, "What am I missing here?"

"Later," Luke mouthed.

"Donovan is here, on another floor, Miss Knight," Bryn said. "He was injured in the action at the compound. He was hoping you'd stop by." Her smile was slight and wry. "I don't think he believes that you're really all right."

She blinked twice, then nodded. "Of course. If you're finished taking my statement?"

"I'm done," Bryn said. "You done, Luke? Mann?"

"I'm done," Luke said. Mann echoed his agreement. They rose in uneasy concert.

Bryn held out her hand. "Thank you for you help. I hope—well, take care."

"Thank you. I will."

Luke thought he saw a weighted look pass between them as they shook hands, but he could have been wrong. He often was. Mann shook her hand, too, then it was Luke's turn.

"When you're through with—your visit, I can run you home." He hesitated. "I'll be waiting downstairs."

Her smile was polite, but he thought he saw something in her eyes. Or maybe he just hoped he did. Maybe when they were alone, the woman who'd kissed him under the pine tree would return.

"Thank you." Now it was her turn to hesitate. "I'll try not to be long."

She walked past him out the door. He stared after her, until he realized Mann and Bryn were both staring at him, trying not to grin.

"What?" he asked.

They shrugged, looked at each, grinned and walked out of the room. Luke followed them, glad of the time to think before he was alone with her again.

He'd told her he took intimacy seriously. That had probably been an understatement, he thought ruefully. He'd hid it well, sometimes from himself, but he'd been that way from the time his dad died. The jovial surface was a smoke screen he threw up to protect himself from getting hurt again, he realized.

It was interesting that he'd chosen an occupation filled with risk, had hobbies that were, too, but was so unwilling to take one with his heart now. Was his heart less valuable than his life?

He sighed, rubbing his face. He hadn't slept well since he'd gotten back to town. Mostly he paced, mentally reciting the pros and cons of telling Amelia that he loved her. She wasn't as young as he'd first thought, but she had lived a very sheltered life. Didn't he owe her time to find her feet, to find out who she was?

The elevator opened without him realizing they'd moved. He followed Bryn and Mann into the lobby. Bryn said her good-byes with a nearly straight face. Mann just shook his head and said, "You got it bad, buddy," before following her out the door.

That was one way to look at it, he supposed. Or you could say, he had it good.

Donovan Kincaid hated being in the hospital. It wasn't the first time and it wouldn't be the last. Soldiers of fortune earned their scars one at a time.

This was a hard time to be stuck in a bed. Bryn said Pru was fine, but he needed to see her with his own eyes. He needed to find a way to tell her—

It had seemed easy up in the mountain, in the heat of action. Now it didn't seem so simple. Her memory was back and she'd learned the man she'd called father all her life was dead. She needed time to mourn his loss. If he told her the truth now, she'd lose her father twice. She'd taken so many knocks in the past few days. How could he hit her with one more?

He shifted restlessly in the bed. His back hurt, where the knife had entered. Grady had damn near killed him. A pointed reminder he'd gotten soft. It was time for him to get out of the security business and go back where he belonged— in the heat of battle. Surely there was a war somewhere he could dive into.

A soft movement in the doorway caught his attention. He looked up. It was Pru, looking at him with her usual aloof, far too serious, gaze. She was dressed in something drab that tamped down the spirit he now knew was there. His heart hurt just looking at her. Before he could stop himself he said, "Damn, you look like your mother."

Her smile broke across her face like the sun broke over the mountains. "Really?"

"Didn't . . . he tell you?"

She came closer, her walk as fluid as her mother's had been the day he met her.

"He never told me anything." She sank into the chair by the bed.

Her face was even with his. Her eyes were her mother's. They didn't welcome him the way hers had. Despite the smile, they stayed cool, but interested. They saw him. He didn't think that had ever happened before. He shifted uneasily. Her eyes made him aware of all things he hadn't been—like in her life.

"Who am I?"

He drew in his breath sharply. It hurt like hell. "You're—"

"—not John Knight's daughter. He told me that day."

Donovan scowled. "What a bastard." He hesitated, then asked, "Did he tell you who—"

She shook her head, but the most amazing thing happened. Her eyes . . . opened. The shutters lifted. He could see her soul.

"I think," she said, her hand lifting to lightly rest on his gripping the blanket, "that I'm a little like my dad, too."

He covered her hand with his and gripped. "You're a lot like your dad. Sorry about that."

She gave a sigh that trembled a bit and laid her head on his shoulder. "No apologies necessary . . . Dad."

Prudence was losing the battle of the personalities when

Amelia got off the elevator and saw Luke waiting for her. She'd been so long, she'd wondered if he'd still be there. He was. He looked like he'd taken root near the window.

His expression was closed, maybe a bit brooding, but it brightened a bit when she appeared. He didn't say anything, just looked at her across the lobby and her heart stopped. When it started again, it felt new, like it had never beat quite like this before. Her knees were different, too. Weak. She wasn't sure she could get from where she was to where she wanted to be. She didn't know who she was yet, but she did know what she wanted.

Him.

She knew he wanted her, but did he *want* her?

She took a step and her knees held, so she walked over to him.

"Ready to go home?" he asked.

She nodded. Did he know that home wasn't a place? It wasn't where she'd lived. It was him. And her dad.

In his car, they didn't talk, but the silence wasn't awful. She wanted to lean her head on his shoulder and tell him what it felt like to meet her dad for the first time, but the width of the seat seemed like the Grand Canyon between them. She peeked at him out of the corner of her eyes, wondering how she could cross it. Wondering if he wanted her to try.

Luke felt her watching him, but couldn't get a read on what it meant. She was quiet, a little subdued. He wanted to ask how the meeting with her dad went, but the right words wouldn't come. He wanted her to move closer to him, but she didn't. How had he managed it in high school? He couldn't remember. It was as if all his life had ceased but this moment. He could feel the heavy thud of his heart and the deep ache in his gut from wanting her.

He stopped the car in front of the Knight house. It was

austere and unfriendly. Even the winter stark shrubs looked like they could repel all boarders. Home, sweet home—when hell freezes over. He hated that she'd lived here with a man who not only hadn't appreciated her, but had tried to kill her spirit. No wonder she'd fled this place when she could.

He got out and opened Amelia's door. The bruises were mostly faded on her face. Her hair lay against her head in soft curls. The long hair had been nice, but short, her eyes were huge and deep enough to fall in. He'd never seen eyes that color or that careful.

She stood up, but didn't move away. "Can you wait while I pack some things?"

"You're leaving?"

"I can't stay here. I don't belong here." She paused, then added, "It's not much. The things I really cared about are at the apartment." She paused again. "If you have the time?"

He straightened. "Of course. No problem."

Her smile broke through her reserve and for an instant he saw Amelia again, then Prudence reasserted herself as she turned to face the house.

Amelia gathered her strength and mounted the steps. The door wasn't locked, which was a bit odd. Inside she found the housekeeper, Mrs. Curtis, crossing the entryway. She was a dour woman who didn't like much, including Amelia. She looked like she'd been trying to cry, but was too happy to fake it. Amelia was glad to have Luke backing her as the woman looked at her without a welcome.

"You're back." She hesitated, then said, "Mr. Knight's lawyer is in the study. He . . . came about the will." A look of secret satisfaction put a dull light in her bitter, dark eyes.

"Have I been disinherited?" Amelia said. Prudence's calm sustained her and protected her. Here in this place she'd called home, she finally understood. Amelia remembered her

319

life, but during the three critical days of her memory loss, the person who'd run out of that hospital wasn't the same person who flew out of the mountains with Luke. She'd become Amelia. It was Prudence who wasn't real. She never had been real. It had always been a façade, an attempt to please the sterile, bitter man who could never be pleased.

He may have loved her mother at one point, but he'd never been able to forgive her for betraying him with Donovan. Bitterness had been in his voice and his words as repudiated her on his death bed. It was a relief to know that she didn't have to try to please him, try to earn his love or even his respect anymore. He'd kept her around because she was useful, or rather her memory was. That was the sum of his interest in her.

She looked around her. She'd lived here for thirty-four years. And she could walk out right now and it would be as if she'd never been here. In every way that mattered, she hadn't been.

Mrs. Curtis started to say something to her, but stopped. Amelia turned the direction she was looking and saw her former father's lawyer, Henry Bannerman, a tall, stately man who looked like he should be governor, not planning bitter men's estates. He'd always been kind to her. So maybe one person would miss her. The look he gave the housekeeper sent her down the hall out of sight.

"Miss Knight, we need to talk. Your father—" His gaze traveled to Luke and he hesitated.

"—wasn't my father," Amelia finished for him. "He told me before he died."

"Legally he was," Bannerman said, disapprovingly. "He shouldn't have disinherited you. It's not right. I'll help you fight it—"

"What I'd really like you to do is help me change my name."

He looked at her, his distinguished brows arched. "What?"

"I want to change my name to Amelia. Amelia—" she smiled at him. "—Kincaid. My real father's name." She looked at Luke then and found he was smiling.

"Well, yes, we can do that, though," Bannerman stopped, his expression worried. "Are you sure?"

"Very." She patted his arm. "I'll be fine. I have some money from my mother, you know."

"And your employment," Bannerman added. "Still—"

"I'm quitting my job, too. It wasn't really my job. It was his." With these words, the rest of the weight lifted off her chest. She felt like she had back in the cabin when she didn't remember her past. She drew a deep breath and shook off the remnants of Prudence. If she was going to make a new beginning, then it should really be a new beginning. She'd start by being real.

She smiled at him, let him see the delight in her eyes.

He looked . . . bemused. He tugged at his tie, cleared his throat and said, "Well, okay. I'll do . . . whatever I can . . . for you."

She beamed at him and saw color run up under his face. "I'm going to get a few things and get out of here. I'll call your office with where I can be reached."

She turned and ran lightly up the stairs. Luke watched her until she was out of sight, then looked at the lawyer.

"Yes. Well . . ." he said.

"I know what you mean," Luke said.

Amelia walked out the front door ahead of Luke, lighter and freer with each step she took away from the Knight house. She was walking into day, she thought with an inward giggle. If she hadn't already had a surname picked out, she'd have chosen Day. Amelia Day, total opposite of Prudence Knight.

She gave a little jump to the next step and stopped. "I have a car." She looked around. "At least, I had a car?"

Luke stepped past her and stowed her one suitcase and the small box of personal items in the back seat of his car. He turned and walked back to her, the rise of the step putting her higher than him, just right to look into his eyes. If she had the courage to lift her arms, she could loop them around his neck. She should have the courage inside her somewhere. She'd learned to fly, to climb and to kick butt in self-defense class during her forays as Amelia. Not to mention the expertise with weapons she'd acquired working for John Knight. She'd taken it a bit further than Knight knew, maybe another interest she'd inherited from her real father?

"You still have a car. It's at the hospital. I have your keys in my pocket, but as an officer of the law, I couldn't let you drive it back here without a proper driver's license. I'll have someone drive it home for you later." He sounded and looked serious, except for the twinkle deep in his dark eyes.

"I see." Amelia smiled at him, watching the pulse at his neck speed up. Power—and with it courage—rose in her at the sight. Just a small pull on the throttle and she could lift off. She could. "Both my proper—and my improper—licenses got blown up by Grady. I guess I'm totally at your mercy."

"Totally?" He arched one brow.

"Totally." Amelia arched hers back. Courage was welling up inside her. Just a little more . . .

His smile took her breath away. It was tender, amused, and very sexy. It curled her toes in her very proper, Prudence shoes. It was hard to stand with curled toes, harder to think.

She took a deep breath—and her courage in her hands—

and lifted off, lifting her arms until her hands rested lightly on his shoulders. Warmth shot up through her palms and did a quick run through her body. It was a nice warm, but mixed with the cold air, she did wonder if she might start a small weather system over their heads. Even better, he didn't reject her.

He cleared his throat, but his voice was still husky when he said, "My mom . . . wanted me to invite you over for lunch. Today."

Amelia inched her hands around his neck. If she was going to fly, she might as well soar. She stepped a bit closer. A mere inch of cool air separated their bodies.

"Mom. Lunch. Sounds . . . serious?"

His hands found their way to her waist. Chills spread out from where her touched rested. She wanted to kiss him so bad her lips hurt. Flying wasn't enough. She needed orbit. His gaze caught hers and held it, upping the chill factor and the altitude.

"I am. Very." He hesitated, then said, "A lot has happened to you in the last few days. I know you've got a lot of things to sort through—"

Luke stopped. Damn, he was out of practice and had never been great with words even when he was in practice. Rosemary had made it too easy for him. She should have kicked his ass, not did the proposing for him. He'd read a few of Dani's books where her heroes always knew exactly what to say, but damned if he could pull up any of it now.

Her arms inched a little further around his neck, bringing their bodies barely together. It had been a while, but his body had no trouble remembering what to do. His arms didn't either. They slid the rest of the way around her waist, taking contact from light to firm. If only his brain could get up to speed.

Their lips were a millimeter apart when she said, "I'll admit it does feel a bit odd. Like I have two people and two memories inside me. But there's not that much to sort through . . . for me. I know what I want."

Her eyes asked him what he wanted. He sighed, relaxing just enough so that their foreheads touched. She shouldn't make it so easy for him. He didn't deserve it. Even with her help, the words didn't come easily. He wanted her so much it hurt and it scared the hell out of him. She made him vulnerable again. His body felt tight with longing and fear.

She moved until her lips were against his ear. "I can't promise you I won't ever die, Luke, but I can promise you I'll love you until I die."

He felt his insides surrender and the words he wanted to say to her quit sticking in his throat. They spilled out of him in a soft rush, not smooth or polished enough for one of Dani's books, but from his heart. From his soul. Somewhere in the mix, he asked her to marry him.

He froze. He was rushing her. "I'm sorry. It's too fast—"

Her mouth stopped his words, hot and sweet, a little inexperienced, but she was learning fast. And teaching him a few things. Their mouths touched, clung, parted, then came together again.

"I love you," he said, against her lips. "I love you."

Houston, Amelia thought, we have orbit . . .

Chapter Twenty-Four

Luke took Amelia around to the back door because only strangers used the front. He was hoping just his mom would be there. He wasn't that lucky. The entire family was gathered around the table, eating chocolate chips cookies as his mom pulled them out of the oven.

Dani was feeding pieces of cookie to Mark. She gave Luke a distracted grin. "Introducing a new food group to him." She handed him another piece, cooing, "It's the perfect food, isn't it? Oh, yes, it is."

"Pizza is the perfect food," Phoebe said, "though these cookies are a close tie."

"Can't feed a baby pizza, can we?" Dani cooed.

"Really?" Jake arched his brows. "What was that stuff Mark was gnawing on when I stopped in last week?"

Dani looked a bit sheepish. "It was just the crust."

"Hey, at least she hasn't started him on Diet Dr Pepper," Matt said.

Dani gave him a mock, shocked look. "He wouldn't sleep. Can't have that when everything I do is to get you to sleep, huh, baby."

Mark grabbed her face and gurgled, his grubby hands leaving chocolate hand prints on each side of her face.

Jake tipped his head to one side, giving her a critical look. "I finally think you look on the outside, what you are on the inside, Dani."

Dani stuck her tongue out at him. Mark did, too.

Luke hesitated, his body still partially blocking Amelia

from his family's sight. They could still get away—

Phoebe, in her usual sexy recline, paused in her cookie consumption long enough to ask, "Who's your friend, Luke?"

That brought all activity to a standstill and all eyes, except Mark's, their way.

His mom straightened, her gaze finding Luke across the kitchen, her brows arched. "Luke?"

Amelia stepped around him and smiled at everyone. "Hi. I'm Amelia."

His mom, her lips twitching, wiped her hands on the apron tied around her waist and then stepped forward, her hand out in a welcome. "I'm pleased to meet you. My son has told me so little about you."

Amelia leaned closer, and said in a loud whisper, "You know, that doesn't surprise me. He's very sweet, but a touch taciturn."

Taciturn? What did that mean?

Dani appeared at his side and whispered, "Means you don't talk enough about what really matters."

"No, it doesn't," Matt said. He lifted his son from her arms and wrapped his arm around her waist.

"Well, it should," Dani said. She smiled at Amelia. "I'm Dani."

"I read your books," Amelia said. "They're great."

Dani smiled at Luke. "I like her."

He introduced Jake and Phoebe. Phoebe gave her a languid smile of greeting.

"She's cute, but she doesn't look like she can kick my ass, let alone what's his name?"

"Ray," Jake said.

"Ray. How big was he?" Phoebe finished.

"Big," said Matt.

"Very big," said Jake at the same time.

They both measured a spot well above their heads.

Phoebe looked thoughtful. "Maybe she can kick my ass."

"Do you mind—" Luke started.

"I don't mind," Amelia said, a smile of delight transforming her face. His family stared at her, then, one by one, returned her smile, all of them looking slightly bemused.

"You're a fool if you let her get away, Luke," Dani said.

"If she can take Ray—" Phoebe agreed, her eyes dancing with laughter.

"You'll never have to worry about drunks and bores when you're out on the town," Matt said, with a shit-eating grin.

Luke looked at Amelia. Her eyes asked if he was going to tell them. Luke grinned.

"I don't know. Might be dangerous to marry a woman who can take you," Luke said. But his smile and the look in his eyes gave him away.

"I think it's already a done deal," Debra said, coming forward to hug Amelia.

"Signed, sealed and committed," Amelia said. "When you're my age, you can't afford to beat around the bush. You know what they say about girls in their thirties, marriage and terrorists."

"It's not true," Dani said, giving her a hug, too.

"No," Amelia said with a sigh, "but it feels like it's true." Amelia gave him an impish look and he smiled back.

For a minute he missed Rosemary. She'd have liked Amelia. He gave himself a little shake. If she'd been here, there'd have been no Amelia. Still, he had a feeling she approved. His brothers both gave him a discreet thumbs up. It was going to be all right. Amelia came to him, nestling into his side. No, it was going to be great. Maybe even one of Dani's freaking happy endings.